IN THE SUBURB OF POSSIBLE SUICIDE

In the Suburb of Possible Suicide

A novel
by

DAVID LAWRENCE

Adelaide Books
New York / Lisbon
2020

IN THE SUBURB OF POSSIBLE SUICIDE
A novel
By David Lawrence

Published by Adelaide Books, New York / Lisbon
adelaidebooks.org

Editor-in-Chief
Stevan V. Nikolic

For any information, please address Adelaide Books
at info@adelaidebooks.org
or write to:
Adelaide Books
244 Fifth Ave. Suite D27
New York, NY, 10001

ISBN: 978-1-951896-71-3

Printed in the United States of America

Chapter 1

My family had just moved to Great Neck Village and I was roaming around trying to get a feel for my new home. My house was a French Provincial, white brick, mini-castle on a green hill. The curvy street was leafy compared to my old sunny flat, geometrical block in suburban East Meadow. My family had gone from middle class to upper. We had arrived at wherever we had arrived.

I headed up Middle Neck Road past the boutiques, made a right on Cutter mill Road and climbed a hill that led to the train tracks. I sat on a rock watching the sun setting, dripping its red light on the tracks like one of those modern paintings with squiggly lines that my mother had taken me to see at the Museum of Modern Art. Was it Jackson Pollack? What's in a name, a label? I hated the museum. I didn't like institutions. But the art spoke to me. It told me that maybe life was worth living. Ha! I wasn't so sure of that. Anyhow, I took out a deck of cards and started playing solitaire. An ace of spades scared me. I thought it was bad luck. I ripped it up. I threw the cards out. I wasn't superstitious. Superstition played me like a flush.

A beat, greasy haired, teenager was climbing up the embankment towards the tracks. I thought he was going to start a fight with me. I clenched my fists. I had to be ready to defend myself. But he didn't even notice me. He had huge lips, which stuck to his face like a mistake. He was as ugly as Mick Jagger was beautiful. Call him an animated chunk of beatnik poetry. Yeah, that's it, he was an angry broken piece of free verse. He was…. Whew! I didn't really know what he was. But I congratulated myself on how I could see so much into someone I didn't even know. I felt clever in a not so clever sort of way. I wished I hadn't thrown out my cards.

I slipped down behind the rock I was sitting on. I was no Peeping Tom but I wasn't ready to be seen yet. I was new to Great Neck. I knew no one. I had just moved in. It was September 13th, 1963 and school started the next day. There was a different smell in the air. I didn't know whether it was from the aging season of autumn or the nervousness of moving. I was not looking forward to eleventh grade or being the new kid in town. I barely made it through tenth grade back in East Meadow. Not that I was stupid, no way. I just didn't see the importance in getting good grades. I didn't want to be controlled by the school system. I thought failing was a sign of independence.

I looked over at the Mick Jagger kid standing among weeds. He looked like he was up to no good, whatever that was. The ground rebelled against the sound of a train gassing in the distance. Chew, chew! The train was devouring the earth. It was coming down on him like a rolling stone. He rushed to the tracks and stood in the center of them like a suicidal monk, ready to burn in Vietnam, his arms spread out towards the rising red sun. On his right hand there was a dirty cast with scribbles and grass stains. He was carrying an injury with him to a new accident. Like some grand prehistoric beast the train rushed around the corner, smacking into full view. The kid looked it square in the engine and held his position. The sunlight bathed him like an injured angel. And rather than jump from the tracks in fear he held his ground.

"Kill me!" he yelled, gackling.

I held my fingers over my eyes. I didn't want to see it. Then I peeked. He ripped his sweater over his shoulders and held it out in front of him like a matador's cape. I heard the music of bullfights and the mangle of steel hooves. I thought of my favorite author in tenth grade, Ernest Hemingway. We were in Pamplona with Hemingway. And the steel bull was in the kid's face, breathing steam. Another few seconds and he would end the pain of being him and of not being him. He would die in the glory of the bullfight, trampled in steel.

"Toro! Toro!" he shouted.

And with less than a second left, when the train was about to trample him and drag him into little pieces, he broke from his trance and leaped to the side of the tracks, rolling in the grass and letting the train pass. *Ole!*

Laughing hysterically, lying on his face like an Indian scout, he looked up and watched the train rushing past. He did a little dance. It was so awkward it was beautiful like some of that modern trash my mom studied in her dance classes. The kid knew it was good to be alive. There'd be more chances to spite death. To slip out of its clutches. To annoy his own mortality.

I watched him skip down the hill. I wondered who this kid was. I stood on the tracks and pretended I was holding a cape. I felt, I could do that too. I swished my cape at an imaginary bull. I was ready to take on the world, to go to Great Neck North High School. I pulled out a sword and stabbed the bull between its shoulder blades. Where was the risk? The train was already almost in Port Washington.

Chapter 2

It was Monday morning and I was busy getting ready for my first day of school. I put on a pair of gray sharkskin pants, a black mohair sweater, a white shirt with a tab collar and black suede shoes with horseshoe taps. I didn't know how they dressed in Great Neck but in East Meadow, where I came from, this would have been a cool outfit. I wanted to look sharp for school. To show these rich kids they had nothing on me.

I went into my bathroom, looked in the mirror, rubbed some Brill Cream into my hair and combed the grease around. Then I lifted the front of my hair with my right thumb and forefinger to give myself a little pompadour. I had some friends in East Meadow but I wasn't sure how I'd fit in in Great Neck. I was uncomfortable around strangers. I pretended I hated them because I was afraid they wouldn't like me. I wiped the grease off my comb with some toilet tissue. How could anyone hate me? *Mirror, mirror on the wall / Who's the fairest of them all.* I was no dork. That face could be popular. Did I want to be popular? No. But I didn't want to be unpopular. I was no loser. Sometimes I didn't know if I was alive or dead, what was right and wrong. Boundaries slipped from me like dog piss on a driveway. I'd take myself for walks. I'd smack myself with newspapers. I wanted to hurt myself and not hurt myself.

Great Neck was a rich town. My dad had been making tons of moderate money in the insurance business and wanted to get me out of East Meadow where I had been cutting school and getting into fights. He thought the town was screwing me up. I didn't know a town could do anything but exist. Why blame architecture? I was the motivation of the town's failure. My dad wanted to make me milk toast. My dad figured putting me in a good school system would straighten me out. He had bought into the American Dream of shopping malls. Everything was for sale. Even happiness had its own boutique.

Our house was a mansion by East Meadow standards. It was on Deepdale Drive, a couple of blocks off Middle Neck Road. My house made Architectural Digest back in the thirties. Babe Ruth used to be a guest in the very room that was my bedroom. I had never seen a French Provincial home before. There was this medieval turret off the master bedroom. A steep slate roof fell from the chimney tops. There were five bathrooms and six wood burning fireplaces. My bedroom alone had two little wrought iron balconies. The tops of my windows pointed up like widows' peaks. My corner window was stained glass. The house perched on top of a hill like a traveler's overstuffed wallet. It also had the feeling of a church. The sanctity of loot. It was ornate. Like a gangster's wallet.

We drove about two miles to Great Neck North High School, which was attended by kids from Kings Point, Great Neck Estates, Kensington and Saddle Rock. The richer kids in the area. Great Neck South was attended by the kids in Lake Success and the southern parts of Kensington and Great Neck Estates. Those kids were rich but not quite as rich.

My mother drove me to school in our blue 1963 Lincoln Continental. The interior was red. It was the same car that President Kennedy was chauffeured around in. I looked something like a young President Kennedy; at least, people told me that. The back doors of the Lincoln opened in reverse. That was so cool.

We pulled up to school while the buses were arriving along with a line of other expensive cars -- Cadillacs, Jaguars and even a Rolls or two. The students tumbled out of their cars, looking like preppy, college bound members of student government. Man, did I hate student government. I could see right off that these were not my kind of kids. The boys wore khaki pants, madras shirts and penny loafers. The girls wore plaid skirts, blouses, knee-high socks and pumps. They had ponytails or flips. The boys parted their hair and wore regulars. There wasn't a pompadour amongst them. I was the only one with suede shit kickers.

I saw cliques forming, getting knocked apart and then picking up again like bowling pins on the sidewalk in front of the school. At first glance I could see that this would be a hard crowd to break. At least East Meadow was rampant with hoods. Here, everyone looked like a poster child for milk. I wasn't into that nicey, nicey All American look. I didn't wear khakis and moccasin shoes. I was foreign from these kids. I could have been freakin Bulgarian or something. They all looked like Eisenhower's nephews. They minced around with golden sticks up their asses squeezing out polite greetings to each other. I was the new outsider. The greaser in the mohair sweater. I imagined myself being stoned as some sort of Biblical punishment for being different.

"Get to know the good kids," my mother said as we stopped at the curb.

Fat chance. I looked down at my taps. These kids wouldn't like the way I dressed. I didn't like them. I didn't open the car door.

"Go, go, You'll be late," my mother said.

I got out and closed the car door behind me lightly. I didn't want to slam it. I didn't want anyone to notice me. I walked through groups of students towards the school. I heard a few snickers. Were they laughing at me? Fuck them. I'd teach them something about hate. And yet I didn't hate them. I wanted their approval.

Great Neck North Senior High was a large building; built in the twenties it looked like a fort. I wandered through the dark tiled halls looking for room 311, my homeroom class. I was nervous and kept forgetting which direction I was going in and whether the numbers were going up or down. By the time I found 311 most of the students were already in their seats. I entered shyly in my mohair sweater, kicking out chips in the tiles with my horseshoe taps. Even though my eyes were cast down, I could sense the hateful looks of other students. I bumped right into a desk, looked up and was confronted by Miss McDermott who was standing directly in front of me, banging her own knuckles with her ruler, nicking flakes of skin off her fingers. She was about fifty years old, dykish, with a rutted face. There was something about bad skin that scared me. Particularly, on a woman. All the magazines showed them as real smooth. I liked magazines.

"Young man, this isn't the Kentucky Derby," she said as I clomped past her to a seat in the back. No one wore taps on their shoes in Great Neck. They were low class. I was from the middle class slums of East Meadow.

Students giggled as I sat in the rear next to a straggly looking boy in motorcycle books with a cast on his right hand.

There were scribbles and grass stains on his cast. His hair was a mess. He wasn't laughing. It was the kid from the day before on the train tracks. It was Mick Jagger. He was part of the sunset. He didn't belong here in the world of tedium. He was a trapped jackal. He almost looked human. I felt like I could relate to him, another outcast.

"See Mr. Dibello and get those horseshoes removed at once," McDermott added. My taps were like horseshoes. Big joke! Everyone laughed.

The straggly kid next to me whispered, "Thus spoke Zarathustra."

I said, "Who's Zarathustra?"

"Nietzsche," he said.

"Is that you?" I asked.

He looked disappointed. Like I was an idiot to not know Nietzsche. I felt embarrassed. I was being outcast by the outcast. But he must have felt bad for me because he said, "No, I'm not Nietzsche. I'm Swerbuck. And I bullfight trains."

I wondered if he knew that I knew. I wanted to say it but I didn't. I was afraid he'd think I was spying on him up at the train tracks. People spied on me. I didn't spy on them. Yeah, yeah. Pump yourself up boy.

"I'm Joshua," I said. "And I'm a horse. Neigh!" We both cracked up. "I'm running in the Kentucky Derby," I added and we both laughed harder.

McDermott smacked her own hand with her ruler, sending a few scabs flying. She was standing right over me, "Do I have to give you a written invitation. Get out of here and see Dibello."

The whole class laughed as I left the room. I felt like I was naked and that they were throwing ice cubes at me. I opened and closed the door gingerly. I didn't want to call any more attention to myself.

When I got outside the classroom I realized I had no idea where Mr. Dibello was located. I thought of going back in and asking but I was afraid. Fortunately, a tall, rumpled teacher with owl eyeglasses was across the hall. I walked over to him and asked him where Mr. Dibello's room was. He stammered, "Not a d-d-dance class. You're t-t-taps are d-d-digging glitches in the f-f-floor. R-r-room one f-f-fifteen. F-f-follow me."

The shop class was a big room with high ceilings in the basement of the building. It was filled with machines and tools and six or seven tough looking guys working at benches. This was Great Neck's version of Hades. This was where they sent the poor Christian kids to study manual trades, hoping they'd learn their nice little mechanical skills so that they could earn livings and not rob the mansions that dominated these rich suburban hills of the Jewish families. Dibello appeared from behind a lathe, wearing an apron. He was a huge, ex-footballer type who looked like he had been tackled a few too many times. I could hear his body creak as he approached. I imagined him in his youth, with other players in uniforms bouncing off his powerful shoulders like moths against windowpanes. I saw him being carried on the shoulders of his fans past a goal post that was stuck on the borderline of some burned down stadium. His face had that sad, puffy look of those who had already lived their glory days and were on the backside of life disappearing like a fumbled pass.

"Give me the shoes with the cleats," Dibello said.

"How'd you know?" I asked and took off my shoes, handing them to Dibello.

"You don't get too many surprises in Great Neck," Dibello said and put a shoe in the vice, pulling the tap out with a pair of pliers. I gave him the other one and he put it in the vice.

"Why do you wear them?" Dibello asked. He pulled out the tap and handed my shoe back to me.

"Because I like to hear myself coming and going," I said. I meant because I liked to know that I was alive. Because sometimes I forgot when I looked at other people looking at me that I was something more than what they were seeing. At least I knew the noise of my own God damned feet. They grounded me.

"I like taps too," Dibello said, "but rules are rules."

I sensed that Dibello was different from the other people I had met so far in Great Neck. It's true he had to enforce the rules and take my taps from me. But he didn't respect what he was doing. It was his obligation; that was all. He was the kind of guy who wished he was still back on the football field crushing bodies instead of being some stupid den mother for wayward kids in a shop class.

I wished he could be my teacher. But no way I wanted to take shop classes and be a classmate of all the dummies. I was pissed off at the school. But I wasn't retarded. Not that I planned to take calculus or advanced courses. I'd just skate by in the disappearing middle. I put the taps in my pocket and headed back to McDermott's hell.

After homeroom I went to algebra class, chemistry and English. English was taught by my homeroom teacher again, Miss McDermott. It was like catching a double dose of acne. I don't remember who taught algebra and chemistry. I didn't consider them subjects. Because of the Cold War the government was pushing sciences. They were weapons. Science would be the end of civilization. I blamed it for everything. It was the reason we were building bomb shelters. I thought all creativity resided in the liberal arts. Not that I studied them. They were a waste of time too.

At last it was lunchtime and McDermott let us go. I made sure not to walk close to her. I was afraid one of her pimples might jump off of her and land on me.

"That's much better without the taps," she said to me as I was leaving. She thought she was being nice.

I said "Thank you" but meant "stink you." She smelled bad.

I was too self-conscious to eat in the cafeteria. It was filled with prim and preppy students who were all in boring good moods because they were about to get fed. I felt out of joint with the school population, like my hands dangling out of my sleeves were lobster claws. I decided not to eat. I felt funny about standing on line. Like someone would throw his macaroni at me.

I went outside into the schoolyard and sat down at a picnic table. After about ten minutes, students who had finished stuffing their dull faces with bland food started drifting out. Many were smoking cigarettes. It was permitted in the yard. Swerbuck came over to me.

"What do you think of Great Neck so far, new boy?" he asked me.

"I don't know."

"It's the Wasteland without the poetry," he said. "Why'd you move here?"

"My folks said the school system's better."

"What a joke! I went to school in Paris? We studied Rimbaud, Apollinaire, Verlaine and Tzara who walked around Paris with a lobster on a leash."

"Why?"

I'd never known anybody who'd gone to school in Paris. My neighbor in East Meadow moved to California. That's about the farthest I ever heard of anybody going.

"Cause he didn't have a freak in dog!"

He cracked up hysterically. I laughed a little. It was kind of funny.

"So your parents make a few bucks and thought they'd do the right thing," he said.

"I didn't even want to move here." I didn't like him copping an attitude on me.

"Not moving here would have been a good move."

Swerbuck was something different. He didn't wear madras shirts or Weejun penny loafers like the other preppy students. He seemed clever and dangerous. None of the other kids talked to him. If I became friendly with him I would never be popular. I felt a bond with him. I wanted to be one of the despised.

"What are all these chinos and penny loafers around here?" I asked.

"Part of their uniform."

"How come you're not in uniform," I asked.

"I'm an original. I'm Swerbuck. Who are you?"

"Joshua."

"I thought you were a horse in the Kentucky Derby," he said and laughed.

Swerbuck patted me on the back and said, "Welcome to Alcatraz."

"Is it that bad?"

"There's no escape. I'm the warden. I'll do my best to make you miserable."

"I already am."

"Good. It's better than being a fat happy cow," he said and yelled "moo" at the other students who scowled.

After school the bus let me off about a block from my house. As I walked down the block I saw my house sitting on top of a hill like an overgrown lap dog. The architecture of the community was well fed. The homes looked content and stuffed with themselves. As I walked up the slated path I could see the lights of the chandelier in my dining room playing through the leaded glass bay window onto the lawn.

Later at dinner we all sat around a large dining room table while May served us. My father, Hy, had convinced our day maid, May, from East Meadow, to move in with us when we came to Great Neck. She was happy to get her own room with a bathroom. It was as large as my old room. She was in her mid-thirties and built in that sturdy way of solid Caribbean women. Her delicate face didn't go too well with her sensual, rugged body. But it was kind of sexy. It was like putting the delicate face of a woman by Gaugin on top of a female wrestler. May's body was cubistic, all angles and curves. Her body rolled around itself like a bowl of fruits. I imagined her as a chunky ballerina in a Degas painting. I wanted to see her dancing in a dress made of bananas like Josephine Baker in Paris. I knew a little too much about art in a scattered way. It wasn't my fault. My mother put me in some museum classes when I was a kid. It was kind of corny.

My father looked like a dick with his crew cut. He wore his hair like that ever since World War II, which he somehow felt he was still fighting in. I purposely wore my hair greasy and long to annoy him. When May went into the kitchen to get the duckling my father went to help her. He was always helping May. My mother looked very exotic in a gypsy peasant dress and blouse like a taller version of Elizabeth Taylor. She was a ship, blowing through the house at full mast. My father sneaked around beneath her shadow, about four inches shorter than her. She was five foot nine. His favorite actor was Mickey Rooney. Dad was OK but he was a little strict for my taste. I didn't like strict. He had not outgrown the military in WWII. To me that was chicken. It was like avoiding the great ocean of the unknown. You can't capture a Tidal wave in a shot glass. I loved him and hated him.

My brother, Robert, came running down to the table late. He was wearing a tweed sports jacket with patches on the sleeves and smoking a pipe, trying to look collegiate.

"Put that out," my mother said.

"Before I smack you," my father said, while he carved the duckling.

Robert put his pipe in a ceramic ashtray and let it go out. He was two years older than me. He was six feet one inches tall with black hair. He hadn't shaved in a few days and had thick black stubble. I guess he was good looking, except for a bump in his nose. My aunt said he looked like Gregory Peck. In a few days Robert would be leaving for Curry College in Massachusetts. It was an unaccredited college with the academic standards of a day camp for lazy students. To people who didn't know him, he said he was going to Harvard.

"How'd you like school today?" Robert asked me like he was suddenly interested in my education.

"They took my taps," I said.

"What were you doing wearing taps, you idiot?"

"You used to wear them in the Meadow."

"That was the Meadow. This is Great Neck. The big leagues," Robert said. He picked up his pipe to take another puff and my father slapped his hand.

"I'll buy you new shoes," my mother said.

"His shoes are fine without the damn taps," my father said.

"Maybe he should get some of those white bucks," Robert said. I imagined Robert strolling on a yacht with a sailor's cap, smoking his pipe, wearing white bucks like he was Bing Crosby.

"No one asked your opinion," my father said, snapping at Robert.

May came in and started clearing some of the dishes. She stared at my father and smiled. I didn't think it meant anything. She was just being friendly. She must have been happy to live with us. My mother scowled. I watched May's ass swish from side to side as she left the room. Robert leered. It wasn't right to look at May like that. She was a nice person.

"Can I smoke my pipe now?" Robert asked my parents. "Dinner's finished."

"Yes," my mother said.

"This is a college bound town. You gotta fit in. You can't wear skin-tight pants, purple socks and shit kickers. You'll never make it to a good college," Robert said to me, lighting his pipe.

"You think Curry's a good college?" I asked.

"Stop fighting boys," my mother said.

"It's a boarding school for black sheep," I said.

"Baa! Baa!" Robert bleated.

"Cut the bickering, assholes," dad shouted.

"Look, we didn't spend all this money moving here for nothing. I'm buying you a new wardrobe so that you fit in," my mother said to me.

"I wanna be me," I said.

"Who's that?" Hi laughed.

"That's not you," I snapped. I got up and started leaving the room.

"Asshole," Sylvia called Hy.

"Don't worry. One day Joshua will grow up to be just like me," Robert said. I loved my brother. But I didn't want to be like him. He was a poor student. I was only playing at being a flunk out. I could do well anytime I wanted to study. I just felt that failure had more emotional fortitude.

"Set a good example," my father said. My mother sneered. She knew that I was better than that. She was instinctive. She could tell that I was just trying to hurt myself by screwing up. But she didn't know why? Neither did I.

Chapter 3

My mother took me to town to buy me some new clothes that would make me look more like the other kids. Just what I needed. Well, it might make things easier. So I went along. We went to Great Neck Department Store; a real popular store among the preppy set. I almost puked at the manikins in the window who were dressed in chinos and madras shirts, looking like lentils in a bowl of soup. But I wasn't going to put up a stink and give my mom a hard time. I wanted to make her happy. Anyhow, what difference did it make how I dressed? You can't tell a man by his clothes. Even if I was dressed like all the other apples in the barrel, I'd still do my best to be rotten. I was bruised. Not for sale.

"I'm In With The in Crowd" blared through the store's stereo system. That was the number one rock song that fall. I liked the beat. But the lyrics didn't move me. I didn't want to be "in" with any crowd. I wanted to be "out" with the "in" crowd. Or maybe I was just afraid they wouldn't accept me.

It was Saturday morning at ten o'clock and we were the first customers at Great Neck Department Store. Two salesmen were sitting near the cash register ignoring us. A fat one and a thin one, Laurel and Hardy. They must have figured I was broke. I was dressed like a hitter, wearing an old, black leather jacket and my suede shoes. My mother was wearing a designer peasant skirt and a sheepskin jacket.

"Where are the pants?" my mother asked.

"Over there," Laurel said, without looking up from his coffee and bagel.

"Where?"

"There," he said, ignoring us.

I bought everything from chino pants to alpaca sweaters. Whatever I touched my mother took. "The salesmen are rude here," she said to me.

"So why am I buying so much?" I asked.

"To teach them a lesson," she said. I didn't know what lesson she was trying to teach them. "We're rich, you know," she said.

She usually wasn't that superficial. She just wanted to show them. She didn't like their attitudes.

"Excellent taste," Hardy said, waking up to our value as we walked over to the cash register with a mountain of clothes. "We can give you installments," Laurel chimed in, suddenly friendly.

"What for?" my mother said. She reached into her pocketbook and took out a thousand dollars in cash and said, "I'll pay in cash."

Oliver Hardy and Stan Laurel licked their chops like hungry stray dogs. They were counting their commissions. Now they couldn't do enough for us.

"Would you like to open a store charge account?" Hardy asked.

"Oops. I just changed my mind," my mother said. She put the grand back into her pocketbook and told me to follow her as she walked very erectly out of the store.

"We take credit cards," Stan Laurel yelled from behind us.

"Are you coming back?" Oliver asked. "We'll hold the items for you."

"Fuck em," my mom said to me. "They showed us no respect." I had never heard her curse before. I was proud of her. I liked the way she just walked out. But I wondered why she was so upset. No one ever respected me. I didn't care. I was above other people's opinions. Or below them?

She drove me over to the Miracle Mile in Manhasset and we did our shopping at Bloomingdale's. The choice was about as dull as at Great Neck Department Store. All the cool clothes were at R & G's in Hempstead. But my mom wouldn't let me shop there anymore now that I lived in Great Neck.

We got home about two o'clock in the afternoon and pulled into the driveway, which was about a hundred and fifty yards long and was bordered by two rising stucco walls, which were topped off with blue slate. My brother Robert was waiting angrily in the garage.

"Mom, we need the car so dad can drive me to college," he shouted.

My father came down, "What took so long?" He kissed my mother on the cheek and said, "I'll call you from a hot shop."

I took my packages from the back seat of the car. The rest of my clothes would be ready next week. My father and Robert put two big duffel bags in the trunk and got into the car. Sylvia kissed Robert goodbye through the car window.

"When will you be home?" she asked.

"Not till Thanksgiving. I'm going to be studying very hard. I don't have time to be at home like Joshua. You know, I'm kind of a man now," Robert said, self-assured. I thought of his bar mitzvah and how the rabbi said he was a man then. At his reception he let out a fart and pointed at me.

I hated bar mitzvahs. That's because I couldn't sing on key. My brother and my cousin laughed at me in the front row at my bar mitzvah. When my aunt told me I sung like an angel, I lost all faith in people telling you the truth.

"I learned my independence in the air corps," Hy said, smacking Robert on the back. My father loved World War II. That's when men were men. He wanted to be a fighter pilot more than anything in the world but he flunked out of aviation school when he did a dangerous dive over his own base. He had a vision that he was attacking the enemy. The Major felt he was so gung-ho that he'd be good for morale and gave him a job as navigator. But my dad didn't have a good sense of direction. On the way over to Europe he got lost and his plane ended up in Africa.

My father lit up a cigarette. Robert packed his pipe.

"If you're gonna smoke that damn thing, keep your window open," Hy barked at my brother. They were still in the driveway.

"You forgot to shave," my mother said to Robert.

"I'm growing a beard. Intellectuals don't have time to shave their whiskers," Robert glowed. I wanted to puke. He was on his way to Curry College, carrying on like he was the captain of Harvard's debating team. He looked ridiculous with his pipe and his scruffy chin. I still liked him. He was my brother. He was mine.

"WW II was the real thing. Not some bull, faggoty Vietnam crap," my father interjected out of nowhere and threw the Lincoln into reverse. My mother and I waved to them as they pulled out. My brother was puffing up a storm with his pipe. We waved again as my father screeched onto the road backwards.

Chapter 4

I had finished two weeks of school and if I wasn't feeling more comfortable I was at least feeling less threatened. I had a permanent seat at the back of homeroom class next to Swerbuck. Larry Manson was seated to my left. He had rusty, messy hair and yellow fangs. His clothes were too tight but they weren't dirty like Swerbuck's. He had missed the first week of school because he was with his family on a sailing trip in Tahiti. He was rich. We were all rich. He was a growly, tough kind of kid who liked to curse a lot. He was always angry and sulked around like a stray mutt. His nickname was Mad Dog.

I showed up at school wearing my new chinos, a madras shirt, a navy cashmere sweater and brown penny loafers. I smelled like a new leather wallet.

"You conformed real fast," Swerbuck said. He was wearing black jeans and motorcycle boots.

"My mother bought me this crap," I said. I rolled up my cuffs to show off my red socks. To show him that I was still a hood.

"And the haircut?" Swerbuck smirked.

My mother had taken me to the local barber and made me get a regular haircut. I put some grease in it to camouflage it but it obviously didn't work. My pompadour was flat.

"I guess Joshua wants to fit in," Swerbuck said to Mad Dog.

"Fuck fitting in. I'll kill these kids," Mad Dog barked.

"Let's invite Joshua to a train party," Swerbuck said.

"You gotta be a man. You gotta go hard," Mad Dog said.

"What's a train party?" I asked.

"A surprise. Choo. Choo," Swerbuck steamed.

At that moment McDermott chugged into the class, wafting acne powders and diseased skin.

It was six o'clock the next morning before class and Swerbuck, Mad Dog and I met on Cuttermill Road. We stepped off the sidewalk and climbed the hill that led to the train tracks. The trees were thin and scraggly. A few leaves had turned color and hung like thin paper lanterns from the branches.

When we reached the top of the knoll Swerbuck said to Mad Dog, "We need some vitamins."

"The real stuff," Mad Dog barked.

I didn't know what they were talking about. Mad Dog took out three paper bags and filled them with Tester's No. 2 airplane glue.

"What's the glue for?" I asked.

"To glue your mouth shut," Swerbuck laughed. I thought of punching him the face. But he was my only real friend in town.

Mad Dog passed the bags around. "One, two, three, huff," Swerbuck said and stuck his face inside his bag and started hyperventilating. Mad Dog did the same thing. I followed, stuffing my head into my bag like a horse into a feedbag. I immediately felt numb all over. Like I was free floating inside a giant balloon, which was my cranium. I was weightless. A stretched- out yawn. It reminded me of the way I felt when I had my tonsils out and the doctor made me breathe into a basketball filled with gas and I fell asleep. Only I wasn't asleep. I was the sound of dribbling. My face was gone. Now "Dinah blow your horn" was playing in my head. I felt the ground shake like an earthquake and chips of the sky fell down on me like lava. A train burst into full view like a bull from hell. I was glued to the embankment. I couldn't move. The train kept charging. Smoke and flame flew around it.

Swerbuck jumped onto the tracks, pulled his sweater off and swirled it around him like a bullfighting cape. I unglued my feet from the embankment and started moving towards him to get him off the tracks. I moved very slowly. Like my feet were still sticking. Mad Dog grabbed me and said, "Fuck him. Let him die." The train was snorting down on Swerbuck while he was swishing his cape with one hand and playing imaginary castanets with the other. This time I thought he was going to get crushed for sure. But I couldn't afford to lose him. I didn't have anybody else in Great Neck. I threw Mad Dog to the ground and dove at Swerbuck. I hit into his side with my shoulder and we both flew across the tracks, landing on the grass, as the train heaved past us.

"Damn, you ruined my rush!" Swerbuck said, getting to his feet, wiping some leaves off his clothes.

"You were going to get killed!" I couldn't believe he was angry at me for saving his life.

What kind of asshole?

"I wasn't going to stay there," Swerbuck said.

"Yes, you were," I said. I really thought he meant business this time.

"I don't have the balls. I was faking."

"It looked real to me. Damn it!"

"What's real? Life? Death?"

"What do you mean?"

"I mean that I don't do what I say and I say what I don't do."

"Cut the riddles."

"I'm a liar."

I figured if he was honest enough to admit that he was a liar than he wasn't a liar in the larger sense of it. Liars just don't confess like that. They put things in cupboards and switch the bright colored labels. They write their feelings in disappearing ink.

"You're a crackpot."

"I feel broken. I got to glue myself together," Swerbuck said. "Mad Dog, a libation!"

Mad Dog took out three new paper bags from his pocket and filled them with glue. I took mine and held it while the other two started huffing. I had a slight headache from before. They stuck their faces into their feedbags, huffing joyously, shifting on their feet like horses. I almost expected them to lift their tails and take dumps. I could hear a numb buzzing circling over them. It was the music of their rush attaching itself to them like buzzards. I wanted to be part of their skeletal scene; I couldn't resist. I stuck my face into my bag and started huffing. I was glue. I would join Swerbuck's death-play with my diagonal misfit into Great Neck's cliquishness. I was buzzing. I was alive.

Mad Dog looked up from his glue-bag with bug red eyes, swung his head back and forth, and said, "Damn, I missed my turn with the train."

He then jumped onto the deserted tracks and, instead of mock bullfighting, unzipped his fly, pulled out his pecker and pissed onto the tracks.

"You crazy? You can get electrocuted," Swerbuck yelled, jumping back.

Mad Dog, who was still pissing, panicked and pulled his penis back into his pants, pissing down his own leg. Swerbuck cracked up hysterically laughing and Mad Dog chased him down the embankment while zippering himself up.

Chapter 5

I had been living in Great Neck about a month when I got a call from an old friend of mine, Bill Malevchek, inviting me to visit him in East Meadow. He was one of my poorer friends who lived in a Christian section of East Meadow about a mile down the road from where I lived with the other Jews. He was a tough guoy. I felt cool that he'd hang out with me even if he was only a dumb Pollock. I was feeling kind of lonely in Great Neck, so when Malevchek gave me a call I decided to take a trip out to visit him. My dad and mother dropped me off. They were visiting some old friends in North Bellmore. We pulled up to a tiny ranch house on Maple Drive. All the houses on the block were identical and were built on small rectangular plots.

"You shouldn't hang out with white trash," my dad said.

I wasn't judgmental. I liked people for no reason. It didn't matter about their upbringing. My father had only started making the big bucks a few years ago so it's not like we had any right to put our noses up in the air.

"Leave him alone," my mother shouted at Hy. I slipped out of the back seat of the Lincoln as my mother yelled, "We'll be back to pick you up in four hours."

Malevchek rushed me into his room. It was a small box of a room with a tiny desk, a cot and cardboard dresser.

"What de hell you wearing?" Malevchek asked. "Don't you got no respect for the Meadow."

I was wearing my chinos and penny loafers. My mother wouldn't let me wear my old greaser clothes. Malevchek was dressed in jeans and a T-shirt. He wore purple socks, which stuck out six inches below his hemmed pants. His pants and shirt were too tight. The only loose things on him were his brown garrison belt, which hung down the front of his pants and his pompadour which spilled down his forehead.

"Who mowed your hair?" he asked.

"It's a rule in Great Neck. You got to wear your hair this way."

"What do you mean?"

"They give you a demerit, or detention or something if you don't."

"And what kind of shoes are dem? "

"Penny loafers," I said, timidly.

"Where are your shit kickers, man?" he said, baffled. "What if you got to step on someone's head?"

"I'm doing my mother a favor. She wanted me to dress this way cause we're seeing my grandfather later and he really likes penny loafers and chinos," I said.

"Come on!" He didn't believe me.

"Also I got a broken toe from kicking this guy in the head with my shit kickers. So I have to wear comfortable shoes." I was full of lies. I had never kicked anybody in the head. But I would have liked to.

"Boss. Now we're talking. You could have never done that with these penny loafers. Your penny would have dropped out. Did you really dap him out?" He got excited.

"Really hurt him, man," I said. I threw a kick in pantomime at an imaginary head and added, "That's why I have to wear the penny loafers now. My toe's got to breathe."

"Well, still, anyway, you're dressed like a preppy," Malevchek said. The subject was closed. He had labeled my outfit shit and he didn't want to give it anymore thought. I looked at him and realized he wasn't any Beau Brummel. Maybe I didn't have to be so defensive about my new clothes. Maybe Great Neck wasn't so bad now that I took a second look at Malevchek. He was an idiot. A friend. But still an idiot.

"You got anything to eat," I said, changing the subject.

"Let's go up to Waldbaum's and get a bite." Waldbaums was a supermarket up on Merrick Avenue, a couple of miles from Malevchek's dump. It was in the middle of a strip shopping center. There were five small stores on each side of it.

"I can't eat up there."

"Why the fuck not?"

"Last year the owner of the luncheonette kicked me out for using a half bottle of ketchup on a few lousy French fries. He said I wasted more ketchup that the fries were worth." I remembered sitting in front of the luncheonette while my friends went in to eat. It was a real bummer. I bought Yodels and soda from the deli and ate in front of the luncheonette. It was all so damn unfair. Not that it mattered. Not that anything mattered. I liked Yodels too.

"Don't worry."

"Why not?"

"New owners. Besides you're with the big boss man now." He smiled, proud of himself, like he was a mafia don. It really was kind of amazing that we were friends. I guess he liked the fact that a Jew wanted to be hoody. I liked having a street friend.

Malvechek's dad dropped us off at the luncheonette in his fifty-three, lime green Chevy. He told us to walk home later and burned rubber out of there.

The luncheonette looked just like the old one I got in trouble in except I didn't recognize anyone inside. There were two counters with about seven seats at each one. Three punky kids were sitting down the end of the back counter. They looked about a year younger than us. They were real greasers, wearing bright rayon shirts and leather boots. They were joking with each other pretty loud and I could tell they might be trouble. Not that I was worried. I could handle them. Particularly, with Malevchek to cover my back.

I sat down at the first counter. I ordered French fries and a coke from a short, suspicious Puerto Rican counter man. Malevchek ordered two burgers and a shake.

I was telling Malevchek what a bunch of dorks lived in Great Neck when the fries came. They looked nice and crispy. I loved fries. I was pouring ketchup on the fries while I was telling Malevchek that I thought I could take any of the guys in Great Neck cause they weren't as tough as us in the Meadow. I was talking loud so I could impress the neighbors. I wasn't paying any attention to what I was doing because I was getting angry imagining that the guys in Great Neck thought they were as tough as me. I started shaking the bottle like I was shaking their necks. When I looked down my French fries were covered in a pool of ketchup. Crapola! Don't tell me I was going to get kicked out of the luncheonette again.

The Puerto Rican looked over, angrily. I smiled friendly-like. It didn't help. "You don't have to drown the damn fries," he said. It seems that my petty crime was spilling ketchup.

"I'm sorry," I stammered.

He shook his head. I was worried he was going to throw me out. But he just turned away and went about his business giving Malevchek his burgers and making his shake.

The three punks at the next counter laughed. They were slobs; I could see food stuck in their teeth. What did they find so funny? I gave them a dirty look but they just kept laughing. I looked away. All right, if they wanted to play hardball they were playing with fucken Babe Ruth. They'd see. After we finished eating we paid our bill. I apologized to the Puerto Rican for using too much ketchup and with a flourish tipped him a full dollar.

When we got outside I said, "Did you hear that?"

"What?" Malevchek asked.

"Those punks were laughing at me."

"Big deal. They're punks."

"Just give me a couple of minutes," I said. I stood there lighting a cigarette. Malevchek lit up too. We stood like that saying nothing when Malevchek said, "Why are we standing here?"

"You'll see why," I said.

"You know I got a lot of things to do?"

"Like what?"

"Things."

After another minute or so the three punks walked out of the luncheonette chatting like they didn't have a care in the world. They didn't notice me standing there.

I walked over to the biggest punk, who was a couple of inches shorter than me. I threw a tremendous upper cut. He stumbled back a few steps and grabbed his nose. It was bleeding all over his hands like cherry syrup on an ice cream Sundae. I gotta say, it was tastefully done. The shortest punk got all horrified and chicken-shitty, yelling, "run." All three punks took off like they had seen an alien. The big shot with the bloody nose was crying as he ran down the block. The others were pissing in their pants. You could smell the fear coming out of them.

"You didn't know who the fuck you were laughing at," I yelled after them.

Who was I? I didn't know. But I wasn't the kind of guy you could make fun of. That was for sure. I turned to Malevchek and proudly said, "They can't do that crap to me."

"What crap?"

What was Malevchek retarded? Didn't he notice anything? If you don't know when you're being insulted than you don't know anything. Then you got no class, no respect. Why'd I even come back to East Meadow to visit this prick?

"They were younger than us," Malevchek added.

"That doesn't mean they didn't deserve it," I said.

"True," he said. "You're beautiful, man."

And I knew that he knew what I did was nice. I had almost written the Polish bastard off. And now I was a little ashamed of that. I shouldn't have judged him badly. He really was my friend. Those kids were tough. I didn't do wrong. Or I did. I was chasing an image of toughness rather than a compromise with the truth.

"Wait for me a minute," Malevchek said and went into Waldbaums. I smoked another cigarette. When he came out he had something in a bag. "It's a gift," he said and handed it to me. "Take it back to Great Neck with you."

I opened the bag. I couldn't believe it. I pulled the bottle out of the bag. It was beautiful. I cracked up laughing. I was so happy that I felt like crying. My good friend, Malevchek, had bought me a bottle of Heinz 57 Varieties Ketchup.

Malevchek was my friend. The three punks in the store were my enemies. Why? That's just the way it is. Violence is like pin the tail on the donkey. Sometimes it is blind. I am hurt by the reality of my own extreme feelings.

Chapter 6

The first weekend of October Robert surprised us by coming home from college early. You'd think the snob was a professor, wearing a tweed jacket and smoking a pipe. He had grown a beard. He said his math teacher had one.

"I'm thinking of majoring in math," he said. That was surprising, considering that he had flunked intermediate algebra at East Meadow High. I don't think he did too well in geometry either.

My mother thought the beard looked good. Maybe that's because my brother had a weak chin and the hair built it up a little.

Robert wasn't too happy with his room in Great Neck. He had the small room in the back of the house. When we lived in East Meadow he had the larger room. But because he was living off at the college dorm most of the year my dad figured it made sense to give me the big room. I agreed.

I dropped into Robert's room while he was reading a strip magazine. My brother loved sluttish pictures; particularly, one's of brunnettes in black leather outfits with whips. I didn't like to look at that pervert stuff. It made me feel dirty. He quickly hid the magazine under the covers. "Hey, don't you knock on the door?" he asked.

"I thought you weren't coming home till Thanksgiving, big shot," I said.

"Yeah, well, I wanted to see how you were fitting in. It's my obligation as your older brother."

"Sure. Sure." Like Robert gave a damn about how I was fitting in. Anyhow, I felt I was fitting in pretty well. I had friends like Swerbuck and Mad Dog. I wasn't alone.

"Where's my tennis racquet," Robert asked.

"I ate it."

"Really. It's not here." He usually kept it between his desk and the bookcase.

"I borrowed it to play dad."

"Can I have my own racquet back?" Robert asked sarcastically.

I led him into my room. The difference between our rooms was almost embarrassing. Mine was a large, ornate room, with a cathedral ceiling and two balconies.

"I thought tennis wasn't for tough guys" Robert chided. He was pissed off about the size of my room. "One day you'll learn that acting tough is an anachronism."

"I only play it for dad," I said. "What's anachronism?"

"It's a word," he said. I suspected he didn't know what it meant either. I went into my closet and got his racquet.

"You at least beat dad?"

"What's the difference," I said. I handed him his racquet. My father still beat me. I hit a lot of winners but I also went for too many low percentage shots. He was more consistent. Not that I wanted to beat my dad. It would have hurt him. He loved the game. It didn't mean anything to me.

"I want my room back," Robert said, taking a couple of forehand practice swings. "I need more space for my large intellect."

"It's not your room."

"When I get back from college I'm taking it back."

"You'll be too old to live here."

"Too adult you mean," he said, put the racquet under his arm and lit the pipe that was hanging from his lip.

"I'm keeping the room."

"We'll see," he said, blew a puff of smoke, started to leave, then turned to me and said, "I read a book, *In Dreams Begin Responsibilities.*"

"So?"

"Get responsible," he said and strutted out of the room. I realized a little knowledge was a dangerous thing. Since Robert started college, he made no sense at all. His language burst from him like buckshot that sprayed out and never hit the target.

Chapter 7

I hung out with Swerbuck on weekends. My curfew was around midnight. One night I was out till about two o'clock in the morning huffing glue with Swerbuck. I knew I would catch hell if my parents realized what time it was. When I got home I sneaked in the front door quietly. On the staircase my mother leaped in front of me like an exotic bird. Masked in green wrinkle cream, she was wearing my father's blue flannel pajamas. Her hair was in rollers under a shower cap and she was shrieking like a Parrot, "Where have you been?" She sniffed around me and said, "You stink like glue."

"What glue?"

She turned on the light. "That's glue on your jacket," she yelled. There were streaks of glue across my navy pea coat.

"I'm stuck," I said. I was high and started giggling.

"I want to know what you've been up to," she shouted.

"I wish I knew," I said. I shouldn't have been so rude but her face was right in my face and I couldn't think clearly with all the glue in my brain cells and everything. I was all mixed up with anger, laughter, love and familiarity.

My mother grabbed me by the hair and dragged me up the stairs to her bedroom. It hurt but I couldn't help laughing. I liked the attention. Hy was fast asleep in the bed. She took me into her bathroom and washed my mouth out with Ivory Snow soap.

"Don't you ever do glue again. You can go blind. You can get stuck up in it," she said.

I didn't fight back. I knew I deserved it. I had done a bad thing and been rude to my mother. To punish myself more I even gargled some soap. Bubbles were coming out of my mouth when I started choking on the soap. My father overheard me and woke up. He charged out of his bed and rushed into the bathroom to help. I spit up a chunk of soap into the sink. My father was concerned and smacked me on the back, asking, "You OK.?"

"Fine," I said, clearing my throat.

"He huffed glue," my mother said. Hy looked from my mother to me, his face went blank, I could see his jawbone tighten at about the same time he smacked me across the face. It stung. It was pretty. There is something nice about high-strung emotions. They must mean something. Otherwise why are they so intense? So paternal?

"What does glue do?" Hy asked.

"It gets you high moron," my mother said.

"Don't call me moron, little lady," Hy yelled at my mother.

"I'm no little lady. I'm taller than you." She stood right next to him and towered above him. He was only five feet five inches tall and she was five nine inches. She always insulted him about his height. She acted like it was his fault. Like he had shrunk.

"You're too goddamned tall!"

"You're too goddamned short!"

The fight was on. As they argued with each other about their relative heights I sneaked out of the bathroom and headed back to my room. I threw my clothes on the chair and crept under the covers. I heard their screams coming from their end of the house. I thought of the glue I had huffed and wondered if they really made glue from dead horses. I imagined a world where horses lived forever. A world where I didn't have to swallow soap and maidens bathed naked in mountain pools like they did in some old-fashioned paintings by Botticelli or Vermicelli or whoever did that kind of stuff. I saw nymphets washing their pubic hairs in spring water with colors they stole from rainbows. Not that I knew what girls' pubic hairs looked like. I imagined they were something like ours. I hadn't really seen any yet. I would one day, I knew. I didn't have to rush it. I fell asleep.

Chapter 8

Swerbuck and I were sitting together in the school cafeteria eating gravy soaked pieces of stiff meatloaf when Swerbuck pointed out a girl who was paying for her meal on the cafeteria line.

"She's the prettiest girl in the school," Swerbuck said.

"Who?" I asked.

"The one over there," he said. "Dawn Half."

She looked like Howdy Doody's dream of Princess Summer-Fall-Winter-Spring. Her face was round like a tom-tom. And I could feel my heart beating from the first moment I saw her. The blueness of her eyes surprised me. It contrasted with her black braided hair, which rolled down her back like a car full of frightened faces on the Cyclone. There was something beatniky about her. A looseness and lack of caring about all the prim and proper posing that the other Great Neck kids were into. Not that she was grungy. It's just that she gave her beauty room to breathe. Gracefulness flew from her long, thin fingers. Swerbuck waved her over. She paid for her meal and wafted across the room, like a bubble, alighting gently at our table. The sloppy meatloaf on her tray didn't understand that it was about to have the incomparable joy of being eaten by her.

Swerbuck made the introductions.

"You new?" she asked me.

I was confused by her good looks. It was the kind of face that made you dizzy and caused you to forget your words. She was one of my first crushes.

"New?" I stammered, answering her question with a question. I felt like I was talking Russian. I was tempted to say "I'm from Minsk." I gathered myself together and articulated, "Where from you?"

"From Great Neck, silly," she said and laughed.

I felt like a jerk. I covered for myself, "I mean which part?"

"The magical part."

"Where's that?"

"Where you find me," she said. I was in love. I loved her fork. I loved her meatloaf. I loved her spoon and her jello.

Now that I knew that Dawn existed school didn't seem so bad. I could tolerate most of my classes except McDermott's. One day that bitch actually gave us an exam. She asked us, "How's homeroom like your room at home?" At first, I thought she was joking. But when I saw her stern look and the other students bending their heads down to write like they were taking their SAT's , I realized that she was for real. Naomi, a short, stringy girl with huge glasses in the front, raised her hand and said, "I never heard of getting a test in homeroom."

"There's a lot of things you never heard of young lady," McDermott said. She rapped her ruler on her own knuckles, turned red and let out an, "Ow." I had to keep from laughing. Naomi was frightened and dove into the exam.

I figured fuck it. I'd write some serious philosophical stuff to impress McDermott. I had heard enough sophisticated talk at home. My mother was always reading books and taking acting classes. I could fake it.

McDermott handed the papers back. She graded them in one day with her usual efficiency. I had written, "Homeroom is like your room at home in that it's a reversal in word order which shows an opposition between school and domestic life. However, 'homeroom' and 'room at home's' appearance in the same sentence show a coming together of reversed opposites. This is like integration down south. And I believe in Civil rights." I thought this was some of my best bullshit ever. I chuckled to myself. Then I saw that she had given me a big "*D*." Under it was written in gorgeous script, "Poor penmanship." I couldn't believe it. Here I had come up with some creative, liberal rigmarole on the stupidest subject in the world and the bitch was giving me a D. And on the basis of what? Not my ideas. Which couldn't be faulted in a rich, liberal community. But on the basis of my penmanship. I deserved an *A* for writing anything at all about such a stupid subject. I turned to Swerbuck to complain but he was looking down at his desk. McDermott had written on his paper, "*F*". Folded paper incorrectly." He had even gotten screwed worse than me.

"The woman's a genius," Swerbuck said.

"Are you crazy?"

"Music is form without content. She's a musician. She's not into meaning. She only focuses on form." He held up his pencil and started conducting an imaginary orchestra. I shook my head in disbelief as I watched him. The lunatic was in *la-la* land. Then I smelled an old lady's smell next to me. I looked up to see McDermott saying, "I know you two have a lot in common -- the lowest grades in the class. But please save your babbling for your own worthless time."

Swerbuck looked up at her, stood up from his chair and started applauding wildly like he was at the Philharmonic. "Bravo, bravo," he shouted.

McDermott grabbed him by the ear and led him out of the classroom to the Principal's, Dr. Dean's, office. She came back in a few minutes without him. Swerbuck later told me that Dr. Dean paddled him with his Board of Education. That was Dean's pet name for a thick flat piece of wood that he used to discipline students' behinds. Swerbuck said, "At first Dean paddled me softly. Like a pussy. I didn't need that pussy stuff. I wanted to respect my beating. I yelled, 'You hit like a faggot.' Then old Deany got all red in the face and paddled the crap out of me."

I thought Swerbuck was nuts. Even if I did admire his spunk. We were in the cafeteria. He took his jello off his tray, looked at me, winked, and said, "My ass hurts so much I feel like sitting on the jello." Then he did.

Later that night I showed my parents my *D* grade on the Homeroom test. I shouldn't have but I thought they'd think it was funny. After all, it was the stupidest test in the world. I was in my parents' study, a round wood-paneled, beamed room off the master bedroom. Branches leaned against the windows. I felt like I was in a tree house.

"Can you imagine giving me a *D* for penmanship?" I asked my parents.

"I can," my father said.

"Why?" my mother asked.

"Rules are rules," my father said.

"What does penmanship have to do with rules?" I asked.

"It matters," Hy said.

"He should be graded on content not penmanship," Sylvia said.

"Thank you mother."

"What was the essay on?" Hy asked.

"How's homeroom like my room at home," I said.

"That's a good subject. You have to know things like that if you want to get ahead in life," my father said.

I looked at my father like he was from outer space.

"What did you write?" he asked.

"What does it matter!" my mother shouted. "She graded him on his penmanship."

Hy got up from his chair and started to leave the room. He turned to Sylvia and said, "You don't give a damn about the truth. You stick up for him whether he's right or wrong. That makes for bad children. In the air force they punished you when you were wrong."

"He's not in the air force. He's at school," Sylvia said.

My mother thought the system was unfair and she told it like it was. My father felt the system was what kept us all from chaos. It was our job to comply with it, to be part of it. After all, McDermott was the teacher and I was only a little, stupid student.

McDermott sickened me. I felt the teachers in Great Neck were even worse than those in East Meadow. I asked my mother, "Didn't we move here because the school system's supposed to be better." My mother hugged me, "You don't always get what you buy into."

"You can do better son," my father said as he came back into the room.

I felt bad. He said "son" like he liked me. My mother threw a pillow at him.

The next day on the cafeteria line Swerbuck said, "My dad didn't take my *F* too well."

"What happened?" I asked.

"I was watching television with my brother, Brian. Dad comes in in his undies, chomping on a cigar. I told him I failed because I didn't fold my paper right. Who cares? He said, ' How could ze fail such a dumb subject in such ze dumb school like ze Great Neck High?'"

"Your father's French?" I asked.

"My father has a phony French accent. He was born in Ohio. But we lived in France for three years."

We both took plates of macaroni and salad and looked for seats. Swerbuck said, "I told my father that I was only good at the French poets. Folding paper was not one of my strengths. In the meantime my brother Brian cried, 'I want a new radio.' Dad chomped on his cigar and told Brian to shut up or he'd end up dumb like me."

Swerbuck found seats at a corner table near the garbage cans where we wouldn't be heard. Then "I yelled at my father, 'You failed in your business and your marriage.' He got really pissed and slapped me across the mouth. I laughed and said, 'Feels good.' Some blood trickled down into my mouth and I said, 'Tastes good too.' Dad yelled that my mother had failed herself and that she didn't love me. I yelled she did and started swinging wildly at my father who held my hands while laughing. I said, 'She was my mother, you fuck.' My dad smacked me again. Brian hid under the couch."

Listening to Swerbuck's story I realized I didn't have it too bad. I was thankful that my father didn't think he was French and that my mother stuck up for me and felt that the whole subject was idiotic. We both liked macaroni and scraped our plates clean. I felt bad for Swerbuck and after he wolfed down his cake I gave him my piece.

That weekend Swerbuck invited me to go shopping for a clock radio with him and his brother, Brian. When I met them in the village in front of Ben's Stereo Store on Great Neck Road, Brian was dressed up like a baby and Swerbuck was pushing him along in a carriage. He was all bundled up under the covers and had a bonnet on his head. He was sucking a pacifier.

Swerbuck steered Brian close to one of the shelves that was filled with radios. He turned to me and winked. I didn't know what he meant by that. Then Brian reached his hands out from under his baby blanket and grabbed a brown Zenith clock radio and pulled it into his carriage under the blanket. It was a funny little caper but I was scared we'd get caught. I didn't want to get embarrassed. Swerbuck bent over Brian and adjusted the covers to hide the lump of the radio. At that moment an old lady with thick glasses and a cane hobbled by. She looked into the carriage and, nearly blind, pinched him on the cheek, cooing, "What a good little girl."

"Fuck you lady!" Brian screamed. He didn't like being called a girl.

The doddering old lady fell down in shock, cane and all. The fat storeowner ran over to her to help her out, saying, "What's going on here?" In the meantime Swerbuck gunned the baby carriage out of the store, heading down the block at full tilt. I followed Swerbuck, not sure as to whether I was involved in the crime or not. I hated confrontations. I didn't want to be part of a public rucus. As we got down the block we heard the store owner yelling, "Thief!" I looked back and saw the old lady chasing after us using her cane like an oar. She had a lot more strength than you'd imagine. But, of course, she couldn't catch us. I felt sorry for her, straining herself like that. I missed my grandmother. The fat storeowner ran about twenty steps then gave up with a big sigh, bending over with his hands on his knees, looking like he had just run the marathon. As we turned the corner Brian raised himself up in his carriage and gave them the finger. In the middle of the next block, as Swerbuck and Brian were laughing their asses off and I was faking a sad smile, Swerbuck crashed his carriage into, of all people, his father, who happened to be walking around town. Old man Swerbuck grabbed both his sons by their collars.

I ran like the dickens. It wasn't my gig anyhow. I just went along cause Swerbuck invited me. I guess I was desperate for friendship. Not that Swerbuck didn't intrigue me. He was living with one foot off the edge. Occasionally, he'd balance there and pick up a book by Nietzsche or the French poets. He'd read while he was falling through space. I thought he did a lot of stupid things like bullfight trains or stealing from Ben's stereo. I wondered what would happen to Swerbuck when his father got him home. His father didn't look like the nicest guy in the world.

Chapter 9

I was wearing black clothes, dark sunglasses and holding a red rose. I thought it was the right outfit to visit the dead. I wanted grandma to know that her grandson was cool. My brother was standing next to me probably thinking some phony high-level college thoughts. He was home from college for the unveiling.

"What are you doing home before Thanksgiving?" I asked.

"I'm doing mom a favor. She wanted me to come home for grandma's unveiling," he said.

We were at Mount Hebron Cemetery in Queens. I loved my grandmother but I wondered if she cared that I was there. Like she'd know the difference. She was dead.

It was a cool, lively day. The fresh air slapped against my face like a blue memory. My brother was looking very collegiate in saddle shoes, gray slacks, a beaver coat and a school beanie. He was smoking his pipe, as usual. If they graded appearances in college he would have gotten an A.

My parents were standing at the mound. Sylvia was crying. It was her mom and she loved her. I loved her too. She was a gentle woman who used to spoil me to death. She used to let me curse in front of her. We'd laugh about that and she'd tell me, "Don't tell your mother I let you curse." I missed her but I was pissed at her for dying. She had no right to leave me

alone, unprotected. My dad was standing there erect, at attention, like he was some drill sergeant, saluting. You'd think my
grandmother died in battle rather than from cancer.

My parents had hired some rabbi to spew some mumbo
jumbo. He spoke so fast that he dribbled on his beard and
shawl. Yeah, like God would really listen to his cliches. I
half-expected Toto to pop out from behind a tombstone and
pull a curtain out from in front of him to expose what a faker
he was. I resented his saying anything about my grandmother.
He had no right. He kept bobbing up and down like he was
hanging from a rear view mirror. I couldn't understand why
people prayed to fake things when there was so much around
us to cherish. Right? Like I cherished anything. It was all a joke.
It wasn't funny. But as I long as I kept laughing I was alive and
that was something compared to being dead.

I thought of my dead grandmother and wished she were alive.
"Why do they all die?" I said, more to myself than my brother.

"Who?" he asked.

"Them," I pointed my hand around the whole cemetery.
There were hundreds of gravestones. Every hundred years
or so the whole world disappeared and started again. God
committed genocide and we thanked him. *Praise the lord for
bringing me into this earth and killing everyone I love and me.*
Are the religious so stupid that they think God is sitting up
there with a telephone waiting to answer their prayers? Yeah,
he keeps a little cloudy village for them called *heaven* and if
they follow some boring junk written in holy roller books like
the Bible and the Koran he grants them a piece of everlasting
ether. Yet the corpses roll on. There were thousands of generations of the dead. We were standing on a trillion bones.

"It was so funny the way she used to hit us. Wasn't it?" my
brother said. When grandma got angry at us for misbehaving

she'd spank us. She hit so softly it felt like a tickle. We'd pretend she was hurting us and go "ooh" and "aaah." I missed her so hard I got angry.

"She should have never left us," I said. I felt she kicked me with her absence.

"Hey, quit thinking of yourself," Robert said, like he was the knight who guarded the sacred chalice of my grandmother's memory.

My father turned around and smacked my brother, "The rabbi's praying. Keep quiet."

"He started talking," my brother said and pointed at me. If my father had a choice between smacking me or my older brother, he chose my older brother. That was protocol. Some sort of primogeniture or something.

Sylvia snapped at my father, "Leave Robert alone." She was always protecting Robert because my father was always hitting him. Once when I was twelve my father caught me selling fireworks and beat up my brother, saying he should have known better. Not that I didn't get my share of beatings. It's just my brother got more than he deserved. I felt guilty about that but, hey, I wasn't going to my father to hit me more.

The rabbi kept swirling round like a *dreidel*. I wished he'd just fall over and die. I wanted to trade him in for my grandmother. I walked up to the grave and placed a red rose on the new unveiled headstone. My father handed the rabbi a wad of bills as a tip. If he was trying to buy grandma's way into heaven, he was bribing the wrong guy. This rabbi definitely had no clout in the spiritual world. He wasn't even an orthodox rabbi. He didn't have all that paeus, talus and black robe pompous shit that the Hasids wore in Williamsburg.

Chapter 10

I got to Squire's Delicatessen early to meet Swerbuck. It was a popular deli in the middle of Great Neck Village. It was always filled with people, young, old, middle-aged, dying. It was more like a mall than a restaurant. People from all generations hung out there. Even some of the local, poor Christians came in to eat Jewish knishes and kosher pastrami.

Swerbuck told me he was bringing Dawn with him. I already had a big-time crush on her. To me she was an Indian princess riding bareback across an Arizona desert. She touched some romantic chord in me that vibrated out of control. The burnt hills hummed. She was everywhere and nowhere. I would protect her from the cavalry. I was her hero, her bow, her arrow. She lassoed a cactus. She threw me from my saddle like a bronco. What was I thinking? I hated the west. I wanted to die in Europe in a cobblestone alley. She was Swan's Way.

I had had a few girlfriends in East Meadow. I wasn't new to crushes. I started dating girls long before puberty. But Dawn wasn't like the others. She was the others. Plus seven. Seven times the sad beauty of being mortal.

I was holding a table for Swerbuck and Dawn. The waitress came over and told me that if my friends didn't get here soon I'd have to give up the table. I got nervous and I ordered meals for three people. I didn't even know if they'd like my choices. I just didn't want to give up the table. I wanted to be with Dawn. Three sodas arrived -- a black cherry, a ginger ale and a coke. I was embarrassed, sitting alone in a crowded restaurant, getting served for three. I wondered if I should drink all three sodas. Then boom, Dawn blasted into sight, her black braid flipping and flying in a blue bow. Swerbuck slouched along right behind her like a dangerous shadow. They both sat down across from me. Swerbuck started drinking the black cherry soda without even asking if it was his. Dawn motioned to the ginger ale, "Mine?" As far as I was concerned, the whole restaurant was for her. I wondered if she'd let me kiss her braid.

I wished I were the straw that went between her lips. The ice cube that she sucked on. The sandwiches came. Whew! This love thing was difficult. Did I really want to be someone else's meal? Attraction was gobbling me up.

I offered Dawn the turkey. She thanked me. I felt good that I had guessed right Swerbuck took the corn beef and said, "Your treat." I raised my shoulders like it didn't matter to me. And I grabbed the roast beef sandwich. There were French fries for all of us. I picked up a bottle of ketchup to pour on my roast beef. At Squire's prices I didn't have to worry about how much ketchup I used. I buried my sandwich in it. When Swerbuck lifted the corn beef to his mouth his cuffs receded and I could see that his wrists were bandaged. The gauze was bloody. I put my ketchup down, queasy. "What happened?" I asked.

"I tried to cut myself up like corn beef," Swerbuck said.

"Why?" I didn't want to look at the bandages. I couldn't stop staring at them.

"Because life is like the holes in rye bread," he said.

"There are no holes in rye bread," I said.

Swerbuck grabbed a piece of rye bread from the bread-basket. "That's what's missing. The holes," he said, examining the bread.

"I don't get it," I said.

Swerbuck cracked up. "There's nothing to get. It's all nonsense," he said and ripped the ketchup-red bandages from his wrists. I squeezed my eyes closed. I was afraid of seeing his gruesome cuts. But when I opened my eyes there were no cuts at all on his wrists.

"What's this about?" I said.

"Remember when my dad caught me and Brian stealing the radio," he said.

"Sure."

"He would have beaten me to a pulp. So I killed myself so he'd feel sorry for me. I pretended I sliced my wrists and bandaged them up," Swerbuck said.

"Did it work?"

"Not exactly. He beat me for trying to kill myself. He beat up Brian too."

"You're crazy," I said.

"Hey, let's make a pact," Swerbuck said. "Just in case our lives don't work out.

We'll form a Suicide Club."

Dawn hadn't said anything up till now. She was picking at her turkey. She looked up and spoke from some romantic location only known to beautiful girls, " A Suicide Club. I love it. We'll die on a deserted beach beneath a tropical sun." She stretched out like she was lying in the sand sunning herself.

"I want to die too," I said. But I didn't really mean it, fully. I didn't want to die. I liked the idea of suicide with all its drama but dying was giving in and I was a fighter. I wanted to fight death. Not make love to it. Besides I was angry with God for creating death. I didn't want to give in to it. "A toast to the Suicide Club," I said and we all clinked our soda glasses.

"In the mountains. Flying off a cliff, never landing. We'll do it on December 31,1966," Swerbuck said, picking up a butter knife and rubbing it across his throat like he was killing himself.

"Why that day?" Dawn asked.

I passed her some pickles.

"Because it splendidly doesn't matter," Swerbuck said.

Swerbuck grabbed a pickle and started sucking on it like it was a lollipop. It looked disgusting.

"I'd rather die on the beach," Dawn insisted.

"The mountains are much cleaner," Swerbuck said.

"What's the difference? We'll be dead," I said.

"I'll design clothes for the Suicide Club," Dawn said. "Headbands with red suns on them like the Japanese wear. And some robes or T-shirts."

"Give me your number. I'll call to discuss the outfits," I said. Like I gave a shit about our wardrobes? This was my chance to get into her pants. To die between her legs.

"Later," she said. Was that a rejection or a tease? I was young. Whatever girls said to me hurt.

"One for all and all for death," Swerbuck said and grabbed a handful of potato salad. "I squeeze the juice from life," he said, squeezing the potato salad. White liquid poured through his fingers. We all banged our fists on top of each other. And Dawn said, "Till death brings us together."

To celebrate Swerbuck ordered three pieces of cheesecake for the table. "The cheesecake's on me," he said.

I paid for the sandwiches, fries and sodas. He complained about how much the cheesecake cost. Dawn slipped me her number.

A couple of nights later Malevchek's father dropped him off in his green Chevy at my place. May was off and my mother didn't want to cook so we decided to go out for dinner. My mother called me into her room and said, "Would your friend want to come to North Shore Steak House with us?"

I asked Malevchek who said, "Sure." When I came back to tell my mother, my father was sitting there and said, "Malevchek's dressed like a slob."

"Leave him alone," my mother said. My dad was a snob. He was more Great Neck than Great Neck was Great Neck. He was a poseur.

"I'm not taking him out dressed like that."

"Yes, you are."

Malevchek was dressed in tight gray slacks with an orange shirt. His blond pompadour was particularly greasy and he was wearing black, suede shit kickers like the ones I wore the first day to school.

We drove up to North Shore Steak House on North Shore Road near Lake Success. There was a chilly silence in the car. My father didn't like Malevchek. In fact I wasn't sure why I was still seeing Malevchek either. We weren't that good friends before I moved. I guess I stayed in touch with Malevchek to hang onto some piece of my past that never existed. He represented East Meadow. I was attached to my past. As for Malevchek, I suppose he liked having an out-of-town friend who was rich. The fact that he was friendly with a Jew made him feel bigger than the other white trash. Even if I was an atheist Jew. I guess I was kind of exotic to him. Maybe I wasn't an atheist. Maybe I just believed that God was a shadow that had lost its body.

There were parking valets and a maitre-d at the North Shore Steak House. Most of the patrons wore jackets and ties. Except Malevchek who was wearing his Dragster's jacket over his orange shirt. He looked way out of place. My father was scrounging in his chair. He looked horrified when Malevchek forked his meat with his left hand and conveyed it directly into his mouth without transferring it to his right hand. He wouldn't have done that in the air force. He turned red when Malevchek made a slurping sound drinking his coca cola. My father was very fastidious about table manners. At home I wasn't allowed to get up from the table without asking, "May I leave the table sir?" I had to make sure to eat the salad with my salad fork and always put my spoon on the inside of my knife on the right hand side of my plate. I didn't really mind this. I felt that as much as I might be a fuck-up in school at least I had good manners.

"Do you plan to apply to college next year?" my mother asked Malevchek.

"I don't believe in it," he said, with a little piece of steak dribbling onto his lip.

My father choked on his *Duck a l'Orange* and said, "What's not to believe in?"

"Mr. Kaplan, well, it's like I believe in war. I want to fight in Vietnam."

"What for?" my mother asked.

"For America," Malevchek said.

"America has no business being there," my mother said.

"It's my duty," Malevchek said. He squeaked in his chair. I think he farted. I was impressed by his saying "my duty." I almost smelled it. Was Malevchek growing up on me? He was ready to kill for his principles. Maybe that was what I was missing in life? Some set of principles I'd be willing to die for. That was far nobler than Swerbuck's wishing to die just for the heck of it. But then again I didn't really want to kill anyone. I was a pacifist with a vicious streak.

"It's not your duty to kill farmers," my mother said.

"I have to defend our country," Malevchek said. "It's God's work."

Here's where he lost me. I hated when idiots threw the name of God around. Like they knew what God was thinking. I was an atheist but I felt like defending God from fools.

"Vietnam's Mickey Mouse. I fought in the big one, WWII," my father boasted. He loved that war. He thought anything else was a schoolyard fracas by comparison. All those corpses in Korea were nothing.

"Wow!" Malevchek said. He couldn't argue with WWII.

My father felt good now that he had mentioned WWII. He was even starting to like Malevchek because he seemed to respect WWII. But Malevchek ruined it for himself when he finished his chocolate ice cream; a poor choice for dessert compared to pie, and put his napkin on the table before everyone else had finished. That was poor manners. My father just couldn't tolerate social lapses. He sometimes quoted passages that he had memorized from Emily Post.

We were all silent in the car on the way home. Back in my room Malevchek asked me, "Is your family commie?"

"We're no commies!" I said.

I had nothing against the commies but I didn't like being called one. It was a sin in the sixties to put everyone in one income class. There should be a poor and a rich or else why was everyone working so damn hard? Equality was about having the same opportunity to fail not having the same amount of cash. Money determined social status. Business wiles were more valuable than scientific genius. America was money. My allowance depended on it.

"We'll be old enough to enlist next year. A lot of guys from East Meadow are joining. You'd make a good soldier," Malevchek said.

"The war's not too popular in Great Neck. We think we got no reason to be there."

"No reason. You want to lose this big goddamned house you live in. You want commies to put you in huts like a bunch of peasants."

"I got nothing against peasants," I said.

"You're chicken."

I hated when someone called me that. James Dean would never let anyone call him that. I didn't care if Malevchek was bigger than me. No way I'd let him disrespect me. I pushed him and stood there with my hands clenched, ready to fight. I'd kill him if I had to. I glanced around me for something to hit him with. Malevchek stared at me. He was tougher than me. He had had a lot street fights with his gang, the Dragsters. I pictured him pinning me on the floor and using my face as a punching bag. He knew he could take me out easily. But he didn't do anything. Instead I think he was impressed that I was standing up for myself. He patted me on the back and said, "Hang tough."

I liked that, "Hang tough." He made me feel good. It was nice to have one of the Dragsters as a friend. I was glad he didn't beat me up but allowed me not to seem chicken. I liked his code of honor. If I had stayed in the Meadow I might have become a gang member. Nah. I hated gangs. I was a loner. Still, I liked their principles.

Chapter 11

The next day I sat in my room thinking of Dawn, watching the sunlight dance through my Venetian blinds. I felt like fingering the light. To me sex went as far as fingering. I had never screwed. "Beachwood 45789" was playing on the radio. I sang the refrain--"Beachwood 45789, you can call me up and have a date any old time." I figured, why not call Dawn up for a date? She had given me her number. It was about time I used it.

But what if she rejected me? I played a little game to see if she'd go out with me. I spread my hand out on my coffee table. I opened a switchblade that I had bought in East Meadow and poked it carefully between each finger. At each poke I said "She'll go out with me" and then "She won't go out with me" on the next poke. I kept increasing the speed. Pretty soon I was going so quickly that I couldn't say it fast enough. I slammed the switchblade into my left thumb. Blood spurted out like an umbrella. I smiled. I didn't want to admit that it hurt. I raced into the bathroom and ran some cold water on my thumb. The blood dried up quicker than I expected. I took a closer look. A chunk of skin was missing but the cut wasn't very deep. I put some Bacitracin on it and a band-aid. I wished it were bigger so I could show it off.

I figured the cut was a good sign that she'd go out with me. I don't know why. I told myself that maybe it stood for her bleeding heart. Or I was cutting through her defenses. Anyhow, I dialed her number, breathing heavily, nervous, defensive. When someone picked up the phone I almost hung up.

"You want to go out with me?" I blurted out.

I didn't even say who I was. The voice that came back at me wasn't Dawn's. It was her father's.

"You're not my type, whoever you are. I'll get my daughter," he said.

I reddened like a tomato. My ears were little green leaves. The phone shook in my hand.

"No," Dawn said.

"Why won't you go out with me?" I had thought she liked me.

"Who said I wouldn't go out with you? Dawn said.

"You said, 'no.'"

"I said, no, my father wouldn't go out with you. It was a joke, silly.'"

I squeezed through a bubble pipe and floated into the sun. Dawn would go out with me. She liked me. She loved me. I was viciously happy. We made plans.

The following Saturday I took Dawn to the local pool hall. It was a trendy place with new, sleek Brunswick tables with blue felt. The crowd was mixed--young and old, dates, groups, even old ladies. It wasn't a hangout for hoodlums like the pool halls of the fifties. It was the beginning of a trend to upgrade pool halls and make them more family like bowling alleys. This wasn't the Meadow. It was Great Neck. Everything had class.

I volunteered to break and scattered the balls. I figured I didn't have to worry too much about Dawn sinking them. I was the man. But when she picked up the cue, I could see she knew how to play. She made a firm bridge with her left hand

and pinched her first three fingers together properly. It was as if the cue were part of her hand. She sunk eight balls in a row and missed the ninth, a bank shot, by a fraction of an inch. I had never seen a girl shoot like that.

"Where'd you learn to play?" I asked and ran five balls.

"We have a table at home," she said. She sunk the next ball and forced me to rack them up for her. She ran four and then scratched the cue ball into the corner pocket by putting too much draw on it.

The game was nip and tuck. I thought I had lost it a dozen times but kept coming back and taking the lead. Some teen-agers at the next table applauded when Dawn did a mase shot. Somehow I managed to squeak out with a victory by three balls. When she asked me for a rematch I talked her into going downstairs for pizza. I was anxious to get out of the pool hall before she made me look foolish.

The pizza parlor was a crumby little spot across the street from the pool hall. It was one of the few shops in Great Neck that wasn't sparkling new. The stained and ripped beige leather booths sat on a dirty yellow, chipped linoleum floor. We sat down in the corner. The owner, a tattooed guy with the name Enrique embroidered on his apron lifted a pie on a silver platter with a long handle, dumping it into the oven. I was complimenting Dawn about her pool game when a couple of hoods walked in and sat at the booth next to us. They were old, about twenty. They weren't little punks like the guys I had a run-in with at the luncheonette in East Meadow. They looked like the trash you see in Grade B movies. They probably had jobs. Truck drivers or something stupid.

"Give us a whole pie," the bigger one with greasy black hair shouted over to the owner. Dawn sent me up to the counter to get pizza. I was scared to go but I couldn't let her know it.

I timidly paid for my slices and brought them right back to Dawn. As I walked back to our seat I noticed the hoods had on muscle shirts. Their arms were covered with tattoos. Their hands were dirty like they had been working on a car engine. I prayed they didn't start in with me. I really didn't want to get embarrassed in front of Dawn. I didn't want to get my ass kicked. I felt like falling down on the floor crying. Enrique brought the hoods their pie. I wondered why they didn't have to go up and get it like I did. A little later I thought I heard them say, "mother fucker."

Did they mean me? If they did, what was required of me? Did I have to fight them? Did my manhood require it? If I started in with these guys I'd be a corpse. I asked Dawn if she had heard them call me motherfucker, praying they didn't.

"No," Dawn said. Thank God.

"I wish I had a mother," Dawn added.

"Everyone has a mother," I said.

"Mine had cancer. She shot herself."

"Sorry," I said. I felt like a jerk.

"Who cares!" she said. She didn't mean that. She was too pretty not to care. Only ugly girls were mean. That's why they were ugly. It was a punishment.

I thought maybe I'd tell the hoods, "Gentlemen, my mother's dead. Please refrain from mentioning her with the word, *fucker*." No, that would never work. They'd think I was faking. I looked like the kind of kid whose mother was still alive. Maybe I should tell the owner Enrique that I was a good customer and that they shouldn't pick on me. Good customer? I had only ordered a few slices. I'd never eaten here before.

"Do you mind if we finish the pizza outside? It's a nice night," I asked Dawn.

I breathed a sigh of relief when we stepped out into the cool night. I looked across the street at the light falling from the windows of the pool hall. The sky was filled with stars and I imagined God playing billiards with clusters of stardust. Then I remembered that I was an atheist and I was glad to have gotten out of the pizza parlor alive. I could prove myself against those punks in East Meadow. But these guys were out of my league. It was funny how you could be a hero in one situation and a coward in another. I decided I wouldn't go back to that pizza parlor again. It was a dump.

Dawn and I finished our meals on the sidewalk. Then I hailed a cab. "Can I give you a lift home?" I asked.

"No. Leave me in the street," she said, sarcastically. I felt like my hands were hanging out of my sleeves at an awkward angle.

When we got into the cab we sat at opposite ends of the seat. But as we rolled along lush roads past street lamps that glowed like diamond drops on pearl necklaces among the thick old trees that lined the sumptuous houses of the rich we slid closer to each other. Our hands touched. Her fingers shocked me like a joy buzzer. I vibrated. I'm not joking. By the time we reached her house, which was a ten-room log chalet that once was the guest cottage of a forty-room mansion on the Long Island Sound we were kissing. There was an Indian taste about her tongue. Like maize. I looked into her blue eyes and wanted to do a rain dance. I wanted to hop around in the dust, patting my mouth with my palm, singing, "Wa, wa, wa." Just make some dumb sound of celebration like "yes, yes, yes!" But I was too busy eating her breath.

Chapter 12

The following Saturday the doorbell rang at about eight o'clock in the morning. I stumbled downstairs in my pajamas to answer it. It was my brother Robert, standing there, suitcase in hand, looking like a long lost cousin.

"You again," I said.

"Some greeting," he mumbled as he brushed past me. "Mom and dad miss me."

His coming home so often worried me. I hoped it wasn't some kind of genetic problem, like we couldn't break away from our family. I was worried that I'd end up living home with my parents when I was an old man in my forties. I didn't plan to come home on the weekends when I was in college. Not that I wanted to go to college. But if you didn't go you were an idiot. I didn't want to go to parties and say I was only a high school graduate. No one would take me seriously. I wondered if any college would accept me.

Robert knocked on my parents' door. I heard my mother saying, "Who is it?"

"It's me. Robert. The prodigal son has returned home."

"What are you doing home again so soon?" my dad said.

That night my parents went out and my brother and I stayed home. Our maid May had a gentleman caller. Some huge black guy who was the gardener at one of the Kings Point estates. Robert and I were getting some lemonade in the kitchen when Robert shushed me and told me to follow him. He led me to the left, rear corner of the kitchen where there was a broom closet. He then opened it and moved a couple of mops away from the back wall, showing me that there was a peephole into May's room.

I was horrified. I was still a virgin. I had never even seen anyone fucking.

"Dad made this hole. I feel like Alice peeping into Wonderland," Robert said.

I didn't think Alice would do this kind of thing. And I didn't believe my father made that hole. He loved my mother. He wouldn't look at anyone else. He wasn't that kind of guy. Robert stuck his eye up against the wall and started squirming around. I stood behind him not knowing whether to run or to stay. I decided it wasn't right and I wouldn't peek. Till Robert stepped back and pushed my head next to the hole. I closed my eye for a few seconds but then couldn't resist. I saw May standing there naked dancing in front of the big black man. Her body knocked me out. I had no idea how beautiful she was with her clothes off. Her breasts fell off her body like melons from a fruit stand and her bush smelled like a sea breeze blowing into the peephole. It was salty. She danced directly over to the peephole like she knew someone was there. I wondered if she thought my father was peeking in at her and she was performing for him. She reached out and turned out the light. Robert grabbed me by the shoulder and pulled me away from the peephole. When he stuck his face to the wall he couldn't see into the room. It was dark. All he could do was hear moans.

"You hogged the whole thing," Robert said as we walked back to my room.

"I didn't even want to look. You forced me," I said. "It's wrong."

"The evolution of the species depends on procreation," Robert said, sounding like a biology professor.

"Do you do this kind of thing in college?" I asked.

"What kind of thing?"

"Peeping at girls."

"When we're not on panty raids," Robert said, picking a pair of dirty underpants up from my chair and throwing it at me.

"That's disgusting," I said.

But the whole mystery of sex fascinated me. I wondered what this need to touch each other meant. I wanted to give into it and yet I didn't want to be possessed by it. Sex would not be my master. I didn't want to want May. I wanted to be alone, answerable only to myself. I told myself I'd never lust after anyone. I thought of Dawn and I went into the bathroom and whacked off. I desired her and yet I didn't want to desire. I wanted to be neutral. To be a stone. I was afraid of emotions. But I was close to them.

Chapter 13

Our art teacher, Mr. Turko, wasn't like any of our other teachers. He actually believed that we were human beings who might have something worth expressing. He was the opposite of Miss McDermott who thought that creativity was a punctuation mark. He didn't have a spot of acne or a trace of powder on him. He was an artsy-craftsy sort of guy; his gut hung over his belt and he'd perpetually trip over his shoelaces, which were always coming untied. Yet somehow this bear of an absent-minded teacher managed to go *abracadabra* and pull our feelings out of a hat.

"This is beautiful," he said, holding up a black and white canvas of a seascape with a corpse that looked like Charlie Chaplin floating dead in the water. "Death as the unhappy clown."

It was Dawn's painting.

"When Dawn Half entered class she couldn't draw a straight line with a ruler. But art isn't about straight lines. It's about imagination," Turko said.

I imagined pockmarked Miss McDermott leaving skid marks on the imagination, crushing us with topic sentences.

I looked over at Dawn. She looked down embarrassed. Turko had seen inside her and told us where to look for her sensitive parts. She had created something beautiful and she felt fragile like a cracked eggshell.

After class Dawn and I were chatting in the yard outside the cafeteria. It was November and it was cool out so we were wearing our jackets. There were only a few people about. Dawn looked very dreamy like she was still lost in her Chaplin painting. Turko's compliments must have made her realize that she had possibilities within her that should be explored. I was frankly jealous. I felt I had possibilities within me too. But I couldn't paint. I was an artist without a medium. A saint or a fool.

"I didn't know you could paint so great," I said.

"I can't," she said.

"Then how'd you do it?"

"I don't know."

"Do you practice?"

"It just comes," she said.

Dawn didn't appreciate her gift. I did. I sneaked a kiss on her cheek. I wanted her talent.

When I went to Camp Birchwood at thirteen years old I used to take an empty garbage can to the top of a hill, get inside it and roll down the hill. The other children nicknamed me the "Garbage Can Kid." I felt like a waste. I had nothing to offer. But when I rolled down the hill in my can I got some attention. I was something. I hadn't found a can yet that would make people notice me in Great Neck.

Chapter 14

Swerbuck had a crummy two-bedroom apartment on Gate House road. Before that he lived in Kings Point. His dad was a millionaire car dealer who went bust, losing everything, including his wife. Some friend got him a job in France and he moved there with his kids. Later, he moved to his present dump in Great Neck Village. Swerbuck never forgave his dad for going bust. I had no idea whether it was his fault or Swerbuck was being unfair. It was none of my business. But I wondered.

Swerbuck's brother, Brian, was in the small room he shared with Swerbuck, reading comic books when I came over to visit. Swerbuck blasted "The House of the Rising Sun" on his stereo. "There is a house in New Orleans / They call the rising sun / And its been the ruin of many a poor boy / and Lord I know I'm one." I loved that song. So did Swerbuck. He started singing along and dancing, He was a terrible dancer. His elbows jutted out one way, his knees another way and his neck bobbed back and forth like he was a ruptured duck looking for fish. I wanted to speak to him about Dawn but he wanted to dance. He picked up a pillow from the couch, danced over to some bullfighting posters from Spain and pretended he was a matador. I put my hands up to my head like horns and charged at him. After about twenty passes I rammed him in the stomach and said, "I got you."

"I got you," he said, raising an imaginary sword and stabbing it into my shoulder. He bowed around the whole arena, then cut off my ear and threw it into the crowd.

"What do you think of Dawn?" I asked.

"You're dead," he said. "How are you talking?"

"Come on."

"I introduced you, didn't I?"

Swerbuck turned off the stereo. "So?"

"So. She's one of us."

I wasn't sure that was a recommendation. "What do you think of her painting?" I asked.

"Brilliant. Free. Like a seagull." I didn't like him calling my girl "brilliant." That was for me to say. I got jealous of his relationship with her talent.

"I kissed her," I said.

He looked like he swallowed a gold fish. He went to the stereo and put on *Dancing in the Streets* by Martha and the Vandellas.

"I need energy," he said. He picked up a can of Ronson Lighter Fluid and sprayed a stream of it into his mouth. He started dancing his jerky, wild dance holding the can of lighter fluid. "You want some," he asked, holding the can out to me.

"I run on my own fuel," I said.

"Boring," he said, slowly like he was in a tunnel trying to hear his own echo. Then he lifted the can of lighter fluid over his head and shot another stream down his mouth.

"Yum. Yum," he said. "I'm swallowing fire." I think if I had lit a match near him he would have blown up. He was always on the verge of igniting. He was like a bunch of unstable molecules. I thought of that Suicide Club crap he had talked about.

Did he want to kill himself? Maybe he just wanted to tease death? To show that he was tougher. He was exciting that way. He just didn't seem to give a damn. Or he cared too much? Part of me wanted to be like him. The other part of me wanted to get as far away from him as I could. I went home.

Chapter 15

At one o'clock in the morning the following Sunday, Swerbuck stole his father's beat-up blue Corvair. He picked Mad Dog and me up at my house. We were waiting for him in the garage. We walked to the end of my driveway and hopped into his car. None of us had licenses. We were all too young. Mad Dog sat in the middle and I sat against the door in the front seat. The car stank from Swerbuck's dad's cigars and we opened the windows to air it out. I told everyone to keep quiet because I didn't want my parents to hear us leaving. Swerbuck, like a schmuck, floored the Corvair, burning rubber, waking half the neighborhood.

"Where we going?" I asked.

"A haunted barn," Swerbuck said.

"I'm not scared of haunted anythings," Mad Dog said.

"A ghost named Crane haunts it," Swerbuck said.

"If I see him, I'll kill him dead," Mad Dog said, growling.

Mad Dog talked a good game. I didn't know him well enough yet to know if he was sincere. You needed a lot of commitment to kill someone. I wasn't sure he was like that. But he was OK in my books. He seemed to like me. I didn't have many friends.

"Who is this Crane?" I asked.

"He was murdered in the barn," Swerbuck said.

"How?" I asked.

"His brother-in-law chopped his head off with an ax for screwing his wife," Swerbuck said.

"Cool," Mad Dog said.

"Why are we going?" I asked. I didn't believe in ghosts and all that spooky fantasy stuff. I figured if you couldn't see it, taste it, touch it, it didn't exist. I mean it's hard to imagine spooks if you don't believe in a cosmic principal. All that spiritual nonsense has to hang together like a wad of nine pieces of gum. Then the devout kneel down like Moslems and pray to the gum. They get it in their hair. It doesn't make them special. It makes them sticky.

"To show we're not afraid," Mad Dog said.

The only thing I was afraid of was people. It took courage to stand up to another guy in a fight. I should have stood up to those two truckers at the pizza parlor.

Swerbuck got onto the Long Island Expressway. He wasn't the best driver. His experience was limited to stealing his dad's car late at night. He swerved from lane to lane carelessly and I was worried he'd get us into an accident. About twenty-five miles out Swerbuck got off the Expressway and hung a left under it, heading north towards Westbury. Westbury was another rich Long Island town like Great Neck. Except the inhabitants were less *nouveau riche.* There were a lot of Waspy old rich here. The homes were estates set on acres of land. Whereas in Great Neck many of the houses were on a half-acre plots and they seemed stuffed into them like Cinderella's sisters feet trying to squeeze into slippers.

We entered thinner roads that curved through bunches of thicker trees. Most of the homes were set so far back that we couldn't see them. The entrance gates were big cause there were castles behind them.

I wasn't superstitious but I felt like I was entering a ghost story. There was something wrong and spooky that I couldn't put my finger on. I felt these vibrations like sick things were going on, maybe babies being robbed from cradles. I pictured our tires running over corpses. I felt like a thumbtack was sticking in my neck.

"I'm getting bad vibes," I said.

"Don't be stupid," Swerbuck said, concentrating on the road, looking for the cut-off to the barn.

"You're gonna be in trouble you keep complaining," Mad Dog said to me. He was always threatening. I never saw him really doing anything. I was feeling that the world was out of kilter. Something was wrong. Maybe not with us but with someone we knew. I wasn't superstitious but I felt superstitious.

"Someone's sick at home," I said.

"Whose home?" Swerbuck asked.

"I don't know."

"You're sick in the head," Mad Dog barked.

Swerbuck made a sharp right turn onto a dirt road that led into a field. We drove out from under a group of trees into a long empty lot with a lot of fresh moonlight on it. Swerbuck speeded up, flooring the gas pedal and doing spins on the grass. The car skidded wildly and I hung onto the doorknob. I didn't like his reckless driving. I liked to take my own risks. He had no right to take chances for me. I thought I might hit him.

"Slow down," I shouted.

I half expected Swerbuck to speed up. He was that kind of spiteful kid. But he slammed on the brakes and skidded to a halt.

"You drive," he said.

I didn't know anything about driving. I'd never tried it before. But now I wanted to scare Swerbuck back. I got behind the wheel and took off. I didn't know how to hold the wheel straight and the car slipped all over the field. I felt a surge of power and kept turning the wheel and pumping the gas pedal. I saw the barn at the end of the field and headed towards it. I wanted to slam into it. I floored the gas pedal. Even Swerbuck got scared and started yelling. Mad Dog was ducking under the seat. Next thing I knew he was grabbing my ankle off the gas pedal and he slammed the brake with his hand. The car came to a stop. I was high. I wanted to bite him. My mouth was all scratchy. I don't know why I drove like that. I started to laugh.

"You drive like a maniac," Swerbuck said.

"I'm nuts," I said. I liked acting crazy. I liked scaring people. I didn't like him speeding so much when I was the passenger. I didn't like anyone screwing with my life. I could do that myself. I could take responsibility for my own actions. Somehow my own recklessness made me feel mature. My dad always told me to own up to things. He'd be proud of my driving. Right? He'd kill me.

We got out of the car and Swerbuck led us to the barn. He lifted the latch that secured the two huge doors and he pulled one back while Mad Dog and I opened the other. The moon drove a bunch of light into the back of the barn. Flakes of green-cheese spread across the moldy wood. There was rotting hay, an old rusty carriage and spider webs thick like erector sets. A couple of the roof beams were broken and hung down into the dirt floor. A window on the side of the barn was smashed. It looked like rocks had been thrown through it. The sound of breaking glass hung in the air.

"I'm not afraid of ghosts," Mad Dog said.

"Who cares?" I said.

I looked around for Swerbuck but he couldn't be found. Maybe he had gone back outside. Just like him to take us to some haunted place and disappear. I was on edge. An owl hooted. Mad Dog looked like he was ready to dump in his pants and said, "Really, ghosts don't scare me."

"I am the ghost of Crane. Vengeance is mine," a spooky voice said from the corner of the barn. It sounded disembodied. Like it came from the evil spirit world. I was frozen in my tracks.

"I'm not afraid," Mad Dog bluffed. He ran out of the barn.

I walked towards the voice. If it was a ghost, let it kill me now. I felt sorry for myself. I wasn't born to die in the middle of nowhere. I was meant for greater things. What? Greater. What a sad ending to a nothing life. I could have done better. There was a candle inside of me that wanted to become famous, a beacon. Would my gravestone read, "Snuffed before his prime"? Suddenly Swerbuck jumped out of the shadows laughing, "Fooled you."

"You son of a bitch," I said. We both cracked up together and smacked each other on the back. I should have known the fool would have been up to one of his tricks. We went outside to find Mad Dog. He was nowhere to be seen. We went over to the car and looked in. He was hiding under the front car seat. Swerbuck opened the door laughing and clucked, "Chick. Chick. Chick, Chick, Chick."

"I'm no chicken," Mad Dog said. "I just wanted to make sure the ghost didn't steal your car."

On the drive home Mad Dog kept insisting that he wasn't scared. He was protecting the car. He said, "I was looking for a knife that I had hidden under the car seat, just in case, so I could cut the ghost up. I wasn't afraid, you know." Then Mad Dog looked at me and said, "You look scared."

"I wasn't the one running," I said. But I was scared. Not of the ghost but I still felt that something bad was happening at home.

"You're pale."

"I keep getting these vibrations," I said. It was nothing concrete. But I just kept getting this feeling that some faceless person was dying or almost dying. There was no visual image or anything. It was like a glob of nothingness, a vanished paste.

"Vibrations mean nothing," Mad Dog said.

At around three thirty in the morning we pulled up to Mad Dog's driveway. He lived in a large gabled house on top of a hill. It was a few blocks from my house. All the other houses on the block were dark. But the lights were all lit up in his house. His parents wouldn't be having a party this late. Something was wrong. There was an ambulance in the driveway.

"My parents are dying," Mad Dog moaned.

"What's wrong with them?" I asked.

"Nothing." He leaped from the Corvair, shouting, "But if there is anything wrong, I'll kill the doctor." He raised his fist and smacked the car. Then he jumped around holding his hurt hand. He looked about as tough as Spanky in "Our Gang." He was short, scrappy, blond and ridiculous.

Swerbuck and I pulled out. We didn't have time to stick around and see what happened to Mad Dog's dad. Swerbuck had to get his dad's car home before he woke up.

"I knew something was wrong," I said. I felt weird. Like I had mental telepathy. Not that I knew there was a problem at Mad Dog's. It's just that I knew all wasn't right with the world. ESP wasn't an exact science. I wasn't a phony fortuneteller. I was just hooked in with cosmic voltage. I knew when there was a short-circuit.

"Mad Dog's parents will be alright. They'll just go to that great big kennel in the sky," Swerbuck joked. It felt good to laugh. What the fuck, why get upset over Mad Dog's parents? I didn't even like Mad Dog that much. He was OK in a boring kind of way. And his folks weren't my parents so that were nothing to me. As for Swerbuck, well, he didn't even have a mother. And his father was nasty. But I still hoped Mad Dog's father would be alright because there was something very sad and lonely about losing a parent. It made a kid incomplete. I wouldn't wish that on anyone.

After lunch Mad Dog, Swerbuck, Dawn and I were standing around in the school courtyard.

"My dad had a small heart attack. He'll make it. He's tough like me."

"How'd you know it was going to happen?" Swerbuck asked me.

"It's just something I felt," I said. "Like I was hooked in to what was going on around me."

"You're sensitive," Dawn said.

"Sensitive is for faggots," Swerbuck muttered. I wasn't even sure what faggots were. I didn't say anything back. I figured he was jealous of Dawn's being so nice to me. I felt bad for him. I was the new kid in town but he was a lonely kid.

"What if I died all of a sudden?" Dawn said. "I mean I haven't even lived. I should do something with my life."

"Like what?" Swerbuck said.

"I don't know," Dawn said.

"Death's cool. My old man wasn't afraid," Mad Dog said.

"Death's sacred," Swerbuck said. I wondered if he wanted to die or he just liked to hear himself talking.

Dawn put her hands together in prayer and said, "Like a religion."

"On the altar of death I breathe life," Swerbuck said. He sounded like he was chanting in a witches' coven.

"I'm not afraid to die. I'd die tomorrow," Mad Dog said.

"You guys are nuts," I said.

Mad Dog went inside the school. He said he had to go to the bathroom. We all followed him at a distance. He stopped at the phone booth. We overheard him crying, "Mommy, is daddy going to get well? Tell him I love him. I hope I don't have a bad heart like daddy. I want to live forever."

When he stepped out we all cracked up in his face. He said, "I knew you were here. I was just faking." Then walked away in a huff.

The rest of the week in school Mad Dog cheered up as his father started to get better. It finally came out that his father hadn't actually had a heart attack but simply a bad case of indigestion.

I didn't like school. I thought education would somehow weaken me and make me like all the other kids -- average. I wanted to either be way above average or way below. The later was the easier choice. I didn't have to work at dropping out. All I had to do was lean back and fall off the ledge.

I ran into Dawn a few times during the week and we agreed that Swerbuck and I would come out to her place for a meeting of the Suicide Club.

The next weekend Swerbuck and I took a cab to visit Dawn at her log cabin at the tip of King's Point. Her father showed us in. He was one of those beatnik rich guys. There were a lot of them in Great Neck. Their dads had built businesses for them. They were rich and irresponsible. They announced their sympathies with the working class people and denounced patriotism as a kind of provincial myopia. They could afford to play at being communists.

Her dad was musty. His wife, Dawn's mother, had died a couple of years before and he smelled like he had spent some time with her in the grave. Dawn told me her mother had cancer and when the pain got to be too much she committed suicide. She blew her head off with her husband's skeet gun. The gun hung on the living room wall like a monument. It was as if her father was trying to stay in touch with her death. He shook our hands as he looked out the window to the Long Island Sound. He was wearing an open cardigan sweater and reading a thick book. He looked smart. We went up to Dawn's large corner room that faced the sea.

"This is the first official meeting of the Suicide Club," Swerbuck said. I was a little uneasy about all this suicide route but I figured I'd go along. Dawn seemed to be into it and I was into Dawn. The Charlie Chaplin seascape that Mr. Turko had praised in his art class was framed and hanging on Dawn's wall.

"I made uniforms," Dawn said and handed out white bandanas with red suns on them. Then she handed Swerbuck a T-shirt with a beautiful drawing of him committing *hari kari*. I thought of the Japanese suicides I had seen in the movies. I could understand the shame of losing face. There was something sadly noble about suicide. The Japanese were like lost boys. They were littler than us. Swerbuck was overwhelmed by his T-shirt. He loved it.

"It's you," Dawn said.

"It's beautiful. You're a real artist," Swerbuck said.

"I don't know what I am," Dawn said.

"It's nice," I said, looking at the T-shirt.

"Art is life," Swerbuck answered and he put his T-shirt on over his sweater.

"What does that mean?" I asked. He was trying to be deep but that didn't make much sense.

"What it says," Swerbuck said.

Dawn handed me a T-shirt. It was a picture of a bird flying over a marsh. There was a sense of serenity in it. I asked her what it meant and she said, "It's your spirit rising." I liked that. She didn't have me committing *hara-kiri* like Swerbuck. Maybe she understood that I was meant to live and not to die. That I was just playing along with their little charade. Not that I was afraid to die. It just didn't make sense. We were all dying anyhow, from the moment we were born. Ask my grandmother. Oh, that's right, she can't talk with dirt in her mouth. All we had to do was wait a few years and we were blitzed. What was the rush? Ironically, killing yourself implied a mad faith in living forever. Suicide was a stupid leap of faith. It's like you wanted to escape from niggling permanence. Didn't these children know there was nothing solid? We were all dead in a finger snap.

I put my T-shirt on. Swerbuck danced around the room staring down at his with his chin against his shirt. Dawn came back from the bathroom wearing her own T-shirt--a geisha getting her head chopped off by a samurai. The geisha's face was Dawn's, with slanty eyes. She looked like she was seducing the sword.

"Why am I the only one who's not dying?" I asked. I was a little jealous.

"I'm not sure about you," she said to me.

"About what?"

"If you want to die."

"You'll see," I bluffed.

I felt left out. The three of us put our fists on top of each other and made a pact, "All for one and death for all."

On Sunday I stayed home with my family. I should have been doing my homework but I never did homework. I didn't pay much attention in class either. I don't know how I expected to pass. I don't think I ever stopped to think about whether I would or wouldn't fail. It just didn't make any difference to me. I wasn't illiterate. I had read a lot of novels. I particularly liked Thomas Mann, Hemingway, Kafka and Joseph Conrad. But I was hardly aware that I was even in school. The only time failing mattered was when I had to bring a report card home to my parents. I'd feel like a Japanese farmer watching Hiroshima turn into a mushroom.

Dawn looked so beautiful getting her head cut off on her T-shirt. It was strange. I was sure if she actually got her head cut off it would be bloody, ugly and smelly. I liked her T-shirt of my spirit rising. Maybe I'd be the bird that flew her out of herself. I'd save the fair maiden from suicide. I'd be her corny knight, her samurai. We'd leave Swerbuck in his own bag of *hara-kiri* bones.

The bell rang about eleven o'clock in the morning and a black deliveryman in a uniform brought me a cage with a rabbit in it. "Who's this from?" I asked.

"Not my job to know that," the deliveryman said.

I took the rabbit inside and there was a note taped to the cage--"For my big bunny rabbit, / Love, / Dawn."

I didn't think of myself as a big bunny rabbit. I thought of myself as the big bad wolf. I had soft, brown bedroom eyes. Maybe she mistook them for kindness? Maybe I closed them to hide my weakness? Who cared? I was touched that she'd buy me a gift and sign her note, "Starting to love you, / Dawn." I guess the girl really liked me. I stood there walking on air without walking. There was lightness to my stillness. "Starting to love you." That was honest. It was too early for love. Was she really only sixteen years old?

"Who was that at the door?" my dad grumbled as he clomped down the stairs.

"I got a rabbit," I said.

Hy looked in the cage. "What is this pellet shit?" There was already rabbit pellets of crap on the cage floor.

"It's not shit. Dawn gave it to me," I said. He was a real mood spoiler. He didn't mean bad. That's just the way he was. He loved me but he was always knocking me. Maybe it was because he was short.

"Who's going to take care of it?"

"Me."

"Then the rabbit's as good as dead," Hy said.

"We'll see," I said and picked up the cage. I started to go upstairs and my father stopped me, "That creature goes down to the basement." I took the rabbit downstairs. I was pissed that my father thought I wouldn't take care of the rabbit. I felt like throwing the rabbit's cage at his head. There was a bathroom in the basement that was never used and I put the rabbit inside it. I let the rabbit out of the cage and patted it. I stroked its little furry head. "Don't worry little rabbit. I'll take good care of you," I said.

I called Dawn and thanked her. I told her I'd cherish the rabbit.

She asked me, "What are you going to call it?"

"Little Dawn," I said.

I ran downstairs and patted the rabbit's head again.

That week whenever I ran into Dawn in school she'd ask me how Little Dawn was doing. I'd tell her the rabbit was doing great, get lost in her blue eyes and then forget about it.

The next weekend I was visiting Dawn at her house when the doorbell rang. Her dad wasn't home and she answered it. I was shocked when the deliveryman handed her a spider monkey in a cage. I wondered who could have gotten her that? Was she cheating on me? Not that we were going steady. I don't even know if we were going out. But I liked her a lot. We bought the monkey in and took it up to her room. She kissed me and said, "I love it. Where'd you get it?"

"Some place," I said. I had no idea what she was talking about. I didn't buy her that monkey.

There was a note in the cage. She reached for it and the monkey snapped at her. She pulled her hand out along with the note. Her hand was bleeding. She sucked the cut.

"It doesn't hurt," she said. And read the note, "One good turn deserves another, Kaplan."

I had no idea who signed the card, Kaplan. She kissed me again on the cheek and said, "It's so sweet of you. But the note? I thought you were poetic. Aren't you starting to love me a little too?"

"Yes, of course. I must have been in a dumb mood."

"How do I keep it from biting me again?"

"I'll call the pet shop later and find out," I said.

I figured I'd get out of there before her father came home and balled me out for giving her a killer monkey. Even though I didn't give it to her. I wondered who did as I called a cab.

"You know what I'm going to call him?" Dawn asked.

"Joshua?"

"Almost," she said. "I'm going to call him Big Joshua."

When I got home I went upstairs my parents were arguing as usual. I cut them short and told them, "Some fool bought Dawn a monkey."

"Don't call me a fool," Hy said.

"You could have told me," I said. "Why'd you do it?"

"To get her back for getting us a rabbit."

"She didn't get us a rabbit. She got me a rabbit. And you could have written a better note than , "One good turn deserves another. You make me sound like a dope."

"Well, you're not doing too well in English," Hy said.

"Well, she loves the monkey," I said to spite my father.

"Fuck the monkey. That rabbit's in our way."

'How's it in our way? It's in the basement," I said. Then I suddenly realized that I had forgotten all about it. I hadn't been down there in a week. I ran down the stairs to the bathroom. I opened the door and a stink blasted into my face. Little Dawn was lying dead on the floor. She was as stiff as a baseball bat. She had *rigor mortis.* I bent down and patted the rabbit's little head. I wanted to say I was sorry but I didn't feel I had the right to. I stank like the dead rabbit. I was a killer. I got a newspaper from the garage. I found the *New York Times Book Review Section* and started burying it in it. I stood up with my little newspaper coffin. My father came down the stairs and said, "Nice work Joshua."

I was pissed at my father for picking on me. I was angry at the rabbit corpse. I threw it down on the bathroom floor. It bounced. The newspaper came unwrapped. It looked like it was going to wake up and run away. I brushed past my father and headed towards the stairs. Next thing I knew I felt something slamming against my back. A thick chill shot down my spine. My father had thrown the dead rabbit at me.

I wanted to punch him in the face. I wanted to take the stiff rabbit and cut it up and stuff its insides down my father's throat. But I loved my damn father. And I loved that fucken rabbit. Why did he betray me and die? Who created this earth with all this death and stuff? It must have been a demon. The fools who prayed to a beneficent creator were a joke. My father's anger was like a handball bouncing against a wall, it kept coming back. I was sick of him, the dead rabbit and my life. I wanted to beat my father up. No, no, no, I couldn't do that. My father would sometimes sit and talk to me about life. He took me skiing and played tennis with me. He wanted the best for me. How could I think of hurting him?

I went outside without a jacket on. It was cold. I wandered around the neighborhood going nowhere. I imagined rabbits jumping out from behind trees. I shot them. I was Elmer Fudd. Each time I killed one I felt like crying and killed another. Bugs Bunny pointed his finger at me and said, "You're a rabbit killer." I felt ashamed. Organ music rose from the driveways. I looked around me and wondered, "What's up, doc?"

Chapter 16

We were in front of Great Neck North High School before classes. Swerbuck suggested we cut school. I hadn't done that since East Meadow but I told him OK because I kind of missed the free feeling you got when you walked down the street as all the other little suckers were marching into school. You felt like you were let loose from a chain gang. Like you were thrown across the street like a pocket full of loose change. The air tasted cleaner. The leaves in the trees were greener. You wanted to take off your clothes and run down the street, yelling, "I'm free."

"They never suspect you when you look confident," Swerbuck said as we walked away from the school. We stood up tall. We turned onto Middle Neck Road like we didn't have a care in the world. We stopped in at a luncheonette and had milkshakes and candy bars.

The owner, an old, bald guy in a white apron, asked, "Shouldn't you boys be at school?"

"We're doing an important project for the science department," Swerbuck said and winked at me.

I wished he hadn't winked at me. I was sure the old guy noticed it. Maybe he'd call the school and tell on us.

Back out on the street Swerbuck said, "See how easy it is."

"Do we really have to stay on Middle Neck Road? Wouldn't the side streets be safer," I said.

"You're missing the point. You got to flaunt it."

A block or two down a Driver's Ed car pulled over to us. I expected Swerbuck to give the teacher his story about doing a project for the science department. But instead, without any warning, he bolted, leaving me there. I looked into the car and thought I recognized the student driver. She was a cute girl with black pigtails, Ginny Gins, who sat three seats away from me in algebra class. She was sure to tell the Driver's Ed teacher who I was. I took off after Swerbuck while the teacher yelled, "Stop." Behind me I heard Ginny crashing the car into a garbage can. I hoped the teacher didn't lower her grade because of me. In the meantime Swerbuck and I made a beeline through someone's back yard and headed into the back streets of Great Neck. We crashed over shrubs and fences. When we were exhausted from crashing through strange backyards, we slowed down to a walk. Swerbuck and I smiled at each other. "Well, maybe we shouldn't flaunt it so much," he said. We walked all the way up to Lakewood Dinner on North Shore Road. We stayed off the main streets. We figured that we were as good as caught now. If Ginny didn't rat us out someone else must have recognized us.

Lakewood Diner felt good and warm. It was a haven away from the troubles we were getting into outside. We sat in a booth and ordered English muffins and cokes. Cutting school sharpened your taste buds. The little coke bubbles danced on my tongue. The English muffin stood up from the plate and said, "I'm free." We chewed in silence thinking about our troubles. Swerbuck said, "If I'm caught cutting again, I'm a dead Swerbuck. My dad is gunning for me."

"We shouldn't have walked straight down Middle Neck Road," I said.

"How else were we going to get caught," Swerbuck said.

"So you did want to get caught?"

"I don't know," he said, not sure what he was doing.

"I better call my mother," I said.

"Why?"

"So I can get her to cover for me."

"Are you crazy? Don't blow the whistle on yourself."

I headed to the phone booth while Swerbuck put a quarter in the jukebox and picked out three songs.

"Idiot," my mother said when I told her I had cut school and was at the diner. I was in for it.

"I'm sorry," I said.

"I'll pick you up in ten minutes," she said.

As I walked back to the booth, *House of the Rising Son* was playing and Swerbuck was doing a disjointed dance in his seat like Daffy Duck. I felt like hunting him with a shotgun.

"Is she going to kill you?" he asked.

"She's not even angry," I lied. "She's picking me up in ten minutes."

"What did you say?"

"I told her that I didn't feel like going to school and that no one tells me what to do."

"No!"

"Yeah, my mom respected my honesty."

"You got balls kid," he said.

"Yeah, that's right," I said, thinking of how my mom was going to kill me.

After a cup of coffee I looked out the window and saw my mother pulling into the diner. I threw two dollars on the table for my share of the bill.

"Can I come with you," Swerbuck said.

"Are you crazy?" I said and left. I got into the Lincoln very meekly. My mother had turned the engine off. The stupid act with Swerbuck was over. I was about to get a lecture. I wanted to look sorry. I tried to think of sad thoughts so that I'd get tears in my eyes. I thought of the way my grandmother used to spank me and my brother. She used to do it so softly we laughed. We loved her a lot. My eyes started to well up with tears for my grandmother who was buried over at Mt. Hebron and could never spank me again.

"I feel like killing myself. I need a shrink," I said. There was a long silence. I didn't know what to expect.

"I know its been rough for you with the move and all," my mother said. "I've been seeing a shrink myself. With your father."

WooWee. I had struck gold. Both my parents were in therapy. They were nuts. They couldn't blame me for being a delinquent.

"Who's your shrink?" I asked, with a long face.

"Dr. Rosenquest. He lives on Maple Drive. "

"Why do you see him?"

"It's not easy being married to your father."

"It's not easy being his son," I said, seeing the chance to blame my own fuck ups on my dad. She patted my head. That was beautiful.

I went to kiss my mother on the cheek. She turned away. She didn't like me kissing her. She had to save all her affection for my brother who my dad always picked on worse than me. She figured I could survive. That was all right with me. I just wanted her to cover for me about cutting school. I didn't need any kisses.

She started the engine, pulled out of the parking space and drove me home.

It was a chilly night and I was standing out on my balcony shirtless with a wet head, hoping to get a cold. If I were sick I figured my folks would forgive me for cutting school. But I was too damned healthy. I gave up and came back inside. I put on my shirt. I could hear my parents arguing in the master bedroom. I walked over and put my head against the peaked door.

"I ought to kick his skinny little ass," Hy said.

"Don't be a caveman," Sylvia said.

"If Robert was around I'd kick his ass too." I loved it. My dad was always beating up my brother for things I did. Just cause he was older.

"What does Robert have to do with this?"

"He should have set a better example for him." Robert used to cut school too.

"I'm sending Joshua to Dr. Rosenquest." Bingo! My plan was working. Let her think I'm messed up, spend a few breezy sessions with the shrink, and then I'm home free.

"He needs respect for authority," my father said.

"He needs an authority he can respect." Two points for you mom.

"The school should punish him."

"That's not for you to decide."

"We'll see." I heard my father get up and start shuffling around. I ran down the hall back to my room before I could get caught.

The next day the Principal, Dr. Hollis, called me up to his office. He had a crew cut like my father. He was six feet tall and built like a refrigerator. He wore glasses. I don't know whether Ginny Gins or my father ratted me out. Swerbuck didn't get caught. He probably forged a note from his father saying he was sick. Dr. Hollis gave me detention for a week and made me sit outside of his office, missing all my classes for three days. This was great. It was better than going to class and listening to those boring teachers mumble on about stuff I didn't care about. I also had to write, "I will not cut school," a thousand times. I guess he thought that would work its way into my unconscious like water dripping onto a rock in a cave. Some stalactite in my brain would remind me not to cut school. I wondered if he was going to use shock therapy on me. I had read in some magazine that you could teach a dog not to piss on the carpet by giving him shocks.

Hollis's secretary, an elderly woman with a face like an old bowl of pudding, whose glasses hung down from cords over her blue rayon blouse, sat there typing at a Royal typewriter. I looked at the cheap prints on the wall and wanted to paint something permanent and imitated. I wanted to be a part of history. It's just that I didn't have any talent for painting. What a bummer. I envied Dawn.

Hollis called me into his private office.

His crew cut reminded me so much of my father's I couldn't help but ask, "Were you in the air force, sir?"

"I was a chaplain in the marines," he said. I couldn't figure that. What was he doing with my father's haircut? And wasn't being a chaplain a soft, mushy job? What was a chaplain doing in the marines? Marines were supposed to be killers. He was blessing murder. And he was implicating God in the crime. "What a world?" That's what the Wicked Witch of the East said before she died. She knew what it was to have a house fall on you.

"How many times did you write, 'I will not cut school,'" he asked.

I looked down, counted the number of lines and then multiplied it times the number of pages and came up with, "Nine hundred, sir." Then I said, "Only a hundred to go."

Mr. Hollis got angry at this, saying, "Make it two thousand."

"But you said a thousand."

"So?"

"I don't understand."

"You don't have to," he said, staring at me angrily. I saw something stubborn and stupid in his eyes. How'd he get to be principal?

"That's not fair."

"Do you want to be suspended?" he threatened. I didn't want that. I didn't think a Jew was ever suspended in Great Neck. That was for the shop kids. They were all Christians. Detention was my limit.

"No," I said.

"Then get out there and keep writing," he said and showed me to the door. I went back to my seat near the decrepit secretary in the blue blouse and wrote, "I will not cut school. I will not cut school. I will not...."

My mother sent me to see Dr. Rosenquest. His office was in Saddle Rock Estates, the village right past Great Neck Estates. It was about a mile walk from my house. I passed money green lawns and big Tudor houses that fell over lots. There was something eerie about going to Rosenquest's. I'd never been to a shrink before and I was worried that he'd use a voodoo doll and shrink me. I'd scrounge up into dust.

Rosenquest lived in a Spanish house with a red tile roof. The walls looked thick, like the shrunken heads of crazies were stuck in them. I could hear the trapped shrieks of the nut cases. I walked through the screams into his office, which had its own door on the right hand front side of the house. In the waiting room I sat down on the couch near a magazine rack. After a few minutes I picked up a National Geographic and looked at the pictures of topless natives. I was afraid Rosenquest would pop out and see me looking at the pictures so I closed the magazine.

I had heard somewhere that shrinks can tell when you're lying. So I figured I'd be straightforward with him. I didn't want to make him angry. I wanted to use him to get my parents off my case about cutting. After about fifteen minutes this friendly looking fat guy with a long gray beard and a Hawaiian shirt walked into the waiting room.

"Hi, I'm Dr. Rosenquest," he said.

He looked like he wanted to laugh but was afraid to because a shrink wasn't supposed to laugh. It wasn't good for business. There wasn't supposed to be anything funny about being sick. He didn't shake my hand. I guess shrinks didn't do that either. Maybe he thought I was contagious, that he'd catch my craziness from shaking my hand. He led me into a large room with high glass ceilings, pointed to a leather couch and said, "Sit." I looked up at the roof and got worried that the birds would peek in at me and know that I was crazy. They'd tell all the other birds to drop shit on my head when I got back onto the street. I'd become a bundle of bird shit. Rosenquest sat down on a big easy chair.

"So why are you here?" he asked.

"Cause I was caught cutting school."

"So?"

"You know."

"I don't."

"Well, I have to make my parents think I'm nuts or they'll kill me." I thought I had to tell him the truth. I was proud of myself.

"So you're using me."

"That's right, I'm using you," I said.

"I don't need your business that badly," he shrugged and adjusted his shirt, which was spread out on his belly like a crumb cake.

"But I told you the truth."

"Congratulations."

"I did something else," I said. "I killed a rabbit."

"Tell it to the A.S.P.C.A."

"You got to help me."

"You're not ready. I can't take you as a patient."

"Don't kick me out." My parents will kill me.

"I don't want to take your money."

"My parents are rich."

"Go home," he said. "I'm not charging you for the session. It was a mistake."

"No," I shouted. I wanted to pull his Hawaiian shirt over his head and suffocate him. But the sun broke in through the glass ceiling and lit up his face. The light was like the light through the stained glass windows in a temple or a church. Everything went peaceful. I heard lutes playing, streams babbling and sheep baaing. Rosenquest looked like God. He had a halo that picked up some purple from the surfboard on his shirt. I heard his voice as if it was coming from a burning bush, "Come back when you are ready to talk." He was all-powerful. I got up and went to shake his hand. I wanted to touch him. He was radiant. He held his hand back and bowed to me.

I walked out into the happy suburban afternoon and thought that I wasn't finished with him yet. I hated him but I knew he could teach me about myself. There was a hint of acceptance in his rejection. I had all these mixed up angry thoughts. I was hurting inside and he could tell me how to feel better. Maybe not now. But I'd be back when I was ready. I wasn't going to be put off. I just had to suffer a little more before I could begin to heal. I didn't deserve treatment yet. I had to earn it. A couple of blocks down I walked over to a large oak tree on the lawn of an English Tudor mansion. The tree was real big and had muscles. It looked like it was doing poses. There were knots on it. I squared off with the tree and punched it. It hurt like a son of a bitch but it felt good. I held my hand and laughed, pretending that it was funny. Then I hit the tree again. Not quite so hard. I was a little afraid. Then I hit it five or six more times, harder. I was laughing and biting my lip when I looked down at my hand and saw that my knuckles were bleeding. I loved the way the blood crept down my hand. I could make myself bleed so easily. I swung my hand around my head to make it bleed more. An old black maid with silver hair was standing outside the front door yelling at me, "Don't punch Mrs. Deutsch's tree." We were all trees in a big forest. One day we'd be cut down. I ran down the block. A pigeon shit on my head. That was good luck. I wiped it off with my sleeve. It was disgusting.

I was afraid my mother would yell at me about screwing up at Rosenquest's. But she never mentioned it. I guess he spoke to her and told her to leave me alone. He was kind of all right. I think.

I didn't have much chance to be alone with Dawn, having to be at school all the time and her living all the way out in King's Point and stuff. One day we skipped our buses home and hung around school. We sneaked into an empty stairwell. I felt this magnet in her face drawing me to her. I puckered up my lips, closed my eyes and kissed her. Dawn tongue kissed me but not too deep. Her kisses were like the little button candies that came on sheets of paper at the candy store. I licked them off. And I stuck my tongue in her mouth like I was churning a big tub of butter. When we hugged I wanted to disappear inside her ear and listen to her brain. I figured if I could get in there I'd know who she was and why I wanted her so much. We heard some steps coming down the hall, got scared, straightened our clothes out and got up to leave. Mr. Dibello lumbered past us, saw me and asked, "Hey, how the shoes?"

"They'll never make it into the Kentucky Derby," I said, glad that he remembered me. He laughed and shuffled his huge shape along like he was heading towards some huddle.

"Who's that?" Dawn asked me.

"The shop teacher."

"I didn't know they taught shop here."

We walked outside. None of the other students were around. They had already gone home. I was still a little dizzy from kissing. When you stick your face into someone's and breathe in their mouth it makes you lightheaded. We stood in front of the school talking.

"I saw a psychiatrist," I said.

"What did he tell you?"

"I'm not ready for him."

"Why?"

"I don't remember."

"Were you upset?"

"I don't like being rejected."

"Maybe that's the way he felt."

"He should have seen that I was ready."

"He can't see what you're not showing."

A blond girl, Valerie, who I knew from biology class walked past on her way home and waved hello to me. I waved back. Valerie had platinum blond hair and spoke in a whisper. She imitated Marilyn Monroe. I didn't like that. I didn't like dumb blondes. I preferred smart brunettes like Audry Hepburn, the kind that walked on air.

"Who's that?" Dawn asked.

"Just a girl from science class."

"Do you flirt with her?"

"Don't be silly. She's a dummy," I said.

"You better know that I get real jealous. I get even," Dawn said, angrily. I was surprised by Dawn's anger. I had never seen it before. I didn't like anger in girls. Girls were supposed to giggle. They were sweet. Anger was ugly and for men.

"You got nothing to get even about."

"If I ever catch you with another girl I'll cut your dick off."

I broke into a falsetto voice, "And what about my balls?"

"Them too," she said, deadly serious. Then she lightened up a bit, pretended she was grabbing my dick and ran down the street with it. I chased after her laughing.

When I caught up with her I grabbed my dick back and put it where it belonged. It was about time I confessed about the rabbit. We were getting along pretty well so I figured what the heck. I held my breath like I was going under water and then I said, "I got some bad news."

"What?"

"Little Dawn died," I closed my eyes like I was going to get slapped. But nothing happened. I opened my eyes and Dawn was running down the block again. Why hadn't I taken care of the rabbit? I was a killer. I ran after her. I caught up to her and turned her around. There were tears in her eyes. I felt guilty as hell. I wanted to tell her that I was sorry. That I loved her. But she spoke first. She said, "I'm sorry."

"No. I'm sorry."

"I'm sorry."

"You didn't kill the rabbit," I said.

"I'm sorry about the monkey."

"What happened to Big Joshua?"

"It bit my father and he gave it to the zoo."

I cracked up laughing. It was beautiful. We were even-Steven. I didn't owe her anything and she didn't owe me anything.

"I promise I'll take better care of you than the rabbit," I said.

She hugged me. I held her hand as we walked down the block. We were both careless and that was fine. I liked to be loose about life. Whatever you held too tightly in your hands became your hands and then you were thumb wrestling with a mob. I liked to let things come and go.

My brother was home from college for the weekend and he met this girl, Naomi, when he was shopping in town. He asked her out and wanted me to double date with him because he didn't know the town too well. That was fine by me because he had a license and could drive me and Dawn around. We went bowling.

Naomi was a squeaky-voiced girl with thick bottle-rimmed glasses. She had brown curly hair like she was hiding toads in there. She wasn't bad looking even if she was a little dirty. She was a plain kind of pretty. If she saw a beautician and got some contact lenses she might even look good.

"I'm going to transfer to Harvard next year," my brother said when Naomi asked him where he went to school. "Where do you go?"

"C.W. Post," Naomi squeaked, proudly. It was better than Curry but nothing to brag about. As crappy as both schools were, I probably couldn't have gotten into either of them. But I wasn't trying. That was the difference. It took people like Naomi and my brother an effort to get D's. I got them like they were nothing. I just didn't care. A few times when teachers gave me higher grades I was insulted. I thought they weren't doing their jobs.

We went to Great Neck Bowling Lanes, right in the Village. It wasn't one of these super modern places but it wasn't a dump either. Robert had his own ball. It was a Don Carter autographed gyro. He pulled it out of his leather bag and polished it with a chamois cloth. Robert was playing the big shot professional bowler type and was teaching Naomi how to bowl. He stood behind Naomi, smoking his pipe, polishing his ball, yelling instructions as she walked up to the line, bent over and threw her ball right into the gutter. On her second shot she knocked over two pins and Robert applauded.

"With a little of my instruction, you'll be a bowler," he said.

Then it was my turn. I bowled a strike and Dawn and Naomi applauded. Robert gave Naomi a dirty look. Dawn, my little athlete, bowled a spare. She had wonderful hand-eye coordination. I kissed her on the cheek. And then it was Robert's turn to bowl. He picked up his Don Carter gyro. You could see he was very proud of that ball. He kept smoking his pipe while he took off down the lane, sliding sideways with perfect form up to the line and releasing a wide hook down the right hand side. The ball turned to the left at a rapid rate and knocked off the two end pins on the left side.

"The very presence of smoke can upset the trajectory of my ball," Robert said. "I should never bowl while smoking." I loved my brother but he could be such an asshole at times. He put his pipe in the ashtray at the table where we kept score, then picked up his ball again and held it under his chin staring straight ahead at the pins with a real mean look. "I'm going for the spare," he boasted. He took off down the lane like a truck with failed brakes on a hill. He slid sideways about three feet before the line and let the ball roll off his fingertips. The ball whipped down the lane towards the pocket and knocked down another five pins.

"These alleys suck. They're warped. I should bring a bevel down here and check the angle. I'm thinking of majoring in engineering," he said. The rest of the evening went on pretty much the same with Dawn scoring in the 150's, Naomi missing everything, Robert shooting in the 130's and complaining about the lanes and me shooting in the 160's which was high for me considering that I hardly played. After two games Robert insisted that we leave. He polished his Don Carter ball with a lot of love and placed it gently back in his bag. I think being beaten by Dawn and me embarrassed him. Or he was hoping to get an early shot at Naomi's boobs. My brother was pretty horny. He figured he was a big college muck-a-muck who deserved some nooky.

Robert and Naomi got into the front seat of the Lincoln. Dawn and I got into the back seat. Robert said he'd drop Dawn off first in King's Point. He was still smoking his pipe and stinking up the inside of the car.

"Can't you drop me off first?" Naomi complained. She only lived a few blocks from us.

"Come for the ride," Robert said.

"That pipe stinks," Naomi screeched.

"It's manly to smoke," Robert said. "It helps me to think."

Naomi grabbed the pipe out of his mouth and threw it out the window. Robert gave her a dirty look. He didn't stop the car to get the pipe. He smiled, "It was a cheap pipe anyway." And took another one out of his pocket and sucked on it without any tobacco. The horny old devil probably thought he was going to feel Naomi's knockers.

When we got to the end of Middle Neck Road we made a left onto Steamboat Road and drove about two miles past middle class homes to where we made a right On Kings Point Road. This was the richest section of Great Neck. The homes were spread out like neat piles of money. There was coziness about all that suburban wealth. All the houses looked safe. Dawn and I were holding hands in the back seat. We hugged and kissed as Robert drove us down almost to the end of Kings Point Road. Dawn told him to make a left on Old Pond Lane and we went down to where it ended in a *cul de sac*. Dawn's large log cabin was at the end of the block, facing the Long Island Sound. I told Robert I wanted to walk Dawn inside.

"Take your time," Robert chuckled, eyeing Naomi up and down.

"I got to go home," Naomi whined.

Dawn and I went up to her room. We climbed quietly up a flight of wooden stairs. We didn't want to disturb her father. The minute we got into her room we closed her door and started making out. I was a lizard climbing into her mouth. She lifted me out of the cave of myself then plunked me right back down inside it. Her body fell over me like a slinky. All the toys were spilling out of the chest. She let me take off her bra. I didn't really know what to do with her breasts. I started pulling on them a little and she moaned. I pulled harder and she slapped me, saying, "What are you doing?" I'm sorry I said and opened her pants and started fingering her. I didn't know anything about her vagina so I just started sloshing my finger in and out. I must have been doing great because she got hot and started moaning. She was bouncing up and down like she was in some kind of excited pain and then she grabbed onto me and swallowed a yell. I figured she must have come because she didn't let me touch her anymore. I knew something about coming because I jerked off a lot. She opened my pants and started beating me off. I felt like I was a rocket ship shooting off into outer space. Her fingers felt so soft against my steel dick. I came all over my stomach and had to go into her bathroom to wash off. Then I came back into the room and hugged her. It was time to go.

"I got to go," I said.

"Stay awhile," she purred.

"I can't. My brother's still waiting for me downstairs in the car."

"He can wait."

"He'll kill me."

There was no reason to stick around. I had already come. I wanted to get out of there.

Now I knew why men liked to fuck and flee. Not that I had fucked. But I didn't want to stay around and do a lot of huggy-wuggy stuff. It was over.

I kissed Dawn goodbye at the front door. She kept hanging onto me like there was something more she wanted, some other piece of me I hadn't given her. I couldn't figure that out. I had done what I was going to do. I had to pry her fingers loose from my neck. My brother and Naomi were asleep in the front seat of the Lincoln. Why not drive the car? This was my chance. I had always wanted to try it. I slipped into the door and gently pushed Robert further over without waking him. He squeezed into Naomi. The keys were in the dashboard. I pulled out of the driveway. I didn't know what I was doing. I had never driven on the road before. But I figured I had just fingered a girl. How much more difficult could driving be? I was a stud, a studly driver.

As we pulled out of the driveway onto the road I thought of what my father did when he drove. He'd put his hands on top of the steering wheel and jiggled them back and forth. So as we went up the road I started jerking the wheel back and forth like my father. The car swerved all over the road. That seemed wrong but I could swear that was how he did it. At the end of Dawn's block I made a right onto a larger road and sped up a little. Going faster I swerved more. Naomi and my brother were still asleep. I don't know how they didn't wake up. Next thing I knew I heard a siren behind me and saw a cop alongside of me waving me over. I pulled over to the side and the cop walked up to my window asking to see my license. I was in a panic. I could see myself spending the rest of my life in jail. What was I going to do? Then I came up with a brainstorm. I reached my hand into my brother's pocket and took out his wallet. He was still sound asleep. I found his license, pulled it out and handed it to the cop who shined a light on it. He looked at the description, six feet tall, brown hair and eyes, eighteen years old, then looked at me. I was two years younger and two inches shorter but in the dark I could pass for that. Then the cop said, "Swerving a little in your lane, huh, Robert?"

It felt funny being called Robert. I wanted to smoke a pipe. He shined the flashlight on my brother, who rolled over, "Taking your younger brother out on a date, huh, Robert?"

I played it up, "Yes, sir, it's the kid's first date."

"I'm not giving you a ticket this time," he said and handed me back my brother's license. "But stay in your lane."

"Thank you your honor. I mean, sir," I said. I was polite. It was amazing what you could get away with if you had manners. This was fun. I waited for the cop to pull past me. When I started moving again, Robert woke up and realized I was driving. "What the hell are you doing?" he asked.

"Keep quiet," I said. "There are cops watching."

I went back to shaking the wheel back and forth like my father.

"Don't do that idiot," Robert said. "Hold the wheel smooth."

"Dad shakes the wheel," I shouted.

"Only when the road knocks the wheel out of his hands, idiot."

"Oh." I felt like a jerk.

"Don't you know anything about physics?"

Naomi woke up and saw Robert practically nestled against her. She pushed him away from her and he banged into me causing me to swerve across the road.

"Can't you drive straight," Naomi screamed at me.

"I don't have a license," I said.

"Great," she screamed as we passed the cop who was now sitting on the side of Steamboat Road.

I waved to him. He honked back.

We made a left and headed back into Great Neck Village.

Chapter 17

I told Swerbuck we should invite Mad Dog to join the Suicide Club. Swerbuck was against it. Mad Dog wasn't serious enough.

"Mad Dog doesn't respect the refrigerated heaven where corpses chill," Swerbuck said.

"What do you think, corpses are martinis?" I asked. "I'll have that cadaver in a chilled glass."

"I'm not joking. Respect for death cools the bodies and keeps them from stinking," he said.

"Look. It's not like we have a popular club here. People aren't just dying to get in," I said, laughing. "We have to let Mad Dog join." I was just playing him along. I thought the whole thing was a joke. But I figured the more members the merrier. The less chance that I'd have to kill myself.

"Alright, you dog you," he said. We went over to Mad Dog's house to talk to him. He lived on Myrtle Drive, a couple of blocks from me. His parents were out and his house was all lit up like a Christmas tree. When I entered I felt like the top bulb on the Rockefeller Center tree. The brightness was all fuzzy. I felt strange, off-kilter, about to fall off a dock. We were teenage boys tossing ourselves around like coins. *Heads, I love you; tails, I kill you.*

We went up to Mad Dog's room.

"You want to be a member of our club?" I asked Mad Dog.

"What the fuck are you wearing?" Mad Dog said when we took off our jackets, displaying our suicide T-shirts. We took our head bands with the red suns on them out of our pockets and tied them around our heads.

"It's our uniform," I said.

"What's the club about?" Mad Dog asked.

"The Suicide Club. We're killing ourselves in 1966. Dawn's in with us."

"I don't kill myself. I kill other people," Mad Dog growled.

Swerbuck pointed to a faint scar, "Faith", carved on his forearm. "She was my girlfriend," he said.

I had never noticed. It was faded. I was jealous that he had done it first. I could make a better scar than that. Who the hell was this "Faith" anyhow? I took out my switchblade and started to slice "Dawn" on the back of my left forearm. The blade was a little dull and I had to slash at my arm. I rubbed till I got through the skin and made a few little slits. I waved my arm around like a helicopter to make it bleed. The blood started dripping. I poked at the blood with my finger and licked it with my tongue.

"You shouldn't do that," Swerbuck said.

"Why?"

"Cause I only carve their names after I fuck them," Swerbuck said.

"I fucked Dawn," I said, showing off, lying. Most high school boys took credit for fucking everything that wasn't tied down. It wasn't my style to lie like that. But Swerbuck ticked me off.

Swerbuck got furious. "You did not," he shouted.

"What are you getting so upset about?" I said. "She's not your girlfriend."

I had to piss and went to the bathroom. It was none of his business what I did with Dawn. He was just her friend. Maybe he had a crush on her. If he tried to put the make on her, I'd split his head open. She was mine. In the medicine chest I saw a Gillette razor blade. I took it out and unwrapped it. This was a lot sharper than that stupid switchblade. I picked it up gingerly, so as not to cut my fingers, and rubbed it lightly across my cheek. I hardly touched my cheek when it began to bleed. This was great. I didn't even have to hurt myself to draw blood. The bathroom light was like a sunny day. I liked razors a lot more than knives. I sliced my cheek some more.

I figured I'd have some fun and scare those assholes in the other room. I spread the blood around my face and came running out of the bathroom yelling, "I'm wounded."

"I'm impressed," Swerbuck said.

"Blood!" Mad Dog yelled and ran and hid under his bed.

"I still have more guts than you," Swerbuck said, deadly serious. His voice was calm like Sergeant Friday questioning thugs on a line-up. I did not expect what happened next. Swerbuck took a straight razor out of his jean's pockets, looked at it, held it up to the light, then brought it down fast and slashed his wrist. Instead of holding it in pain he switched the razor to his other wounded hand and brought it down on his good hand. He closed his eyes. I closed mine too. When I opened them I saw tears forming in his lashes and his big lips pursing like he was making love. He seemed turned on by his own pain. I stood there dumbfounded. This was going too far. I was just teasing the Gods. I didn't want to anger them. The slices on my face were like paper cuts compared to Swerbuck's gashes. "You asshole," I yelled. Mad Dog came out from under his bed, took one look at Swerbuck's bleeding wrists and fainted. There was blood, skin and white puss coming out of them. I called an ambulance.

When the ambulance arrived they put Swerbuck in the back with a paramedic. He was an Irish cop who was moon-lighting. He looked disgusted. Cops like real injuries, not self-inflicted cuts. They are paid to fight crime, not to coddle it. They like homicides, not suicides. Mad Dog and I got in the front seat with the driver.

"I got a headache," Mad Dog complained. He wasn't even hurt.

"You vant an aspirin?" the driver asked with a Yiddish ac-cent. Mad Dog nodded his head, yes, and the driver gave him two aspirins and an ice bag.

Our driver was wearing a yarmulka. He was a short guy in his sixties and had hair on his ears. His sleeves were rolled up and you could see that he had numbers branded on his forearm. He asked us, "So much there is to live for. Vhat's the matter for you kids?"

We took off down Myrtle Drive and passed my house on Deepdale. The siren was wailing. I ducked in the seat. I wanted to ask the driver if he'd turn the siren down so my parents wouldn't hear. We made a left onto Cedar Drive and then when we got to town we made a right onto Middle Neck Road and a left onto Grace Street.

"You call driving an ambulance 'so much to live for,'" Mad Dog said. That was rude of him. I wondered if Swerbuck would die.

"Youse thinks you too good to be a driver? You thinks slashing your wrists is better?" the driver asked.

Grace Avenue ran into Colonial Road, which then took us to East Shore Road where we made a right.

"Swerbuck's a pussy. If you're gonna do it, you should slash your wrists off total," Mad Dog said. Then he burped and said "I don't feel too good." The driver gave him a bag and he threw up.

"What happened to your face?" the driver asked me.

"A girl scratched me," I said.

"He scratched himself. He didn't have the balls to cut deep," Mad Dog said.

He was right. I wanted to be tough but I was just playing with hurting myself for the effect. I didn't hate myself. I loved myself. I just wanted someone else to love me too. I needed attention.

East Shore Road ran onto Community Drive. It was a wide-open road and we tore assed along. Later that year, Johnny Balanchine, a preppy, ugly kid in my class whom I didn't know too well, died in a car accident, drag racing his MGB on East Shore Road. He really wasn't the type to drag race. His car had no power. You never knew about people.

"Vhere are your cuts?" the driver asked Mad Dog.

"On other people's faces."

"Vhat is this game you are playing? My brother died in my arms in a concentration camp. They threw my mother in an oven," the driver said.

I felt like a schmuck. We were in the face of the Great Jewish God of numberless corpses. This escapee from the torture camps was the irredeemable spirit of the unfairly prosecuted dead. I imagined Jewish corpses burning in ovens shooting flames at us through their fingertips. Even Mad Dog shut up upon encountering this refugee from the Grim Reaper.

In the back of the ambulance the Irish cop was still trying to stop Swerbuck's bleeding.

"Am I going to live?" Swerbuck asked. "I don't want to die."

"You should have thought of that before you cut your wrists," the cop said. He was sick of spoiled kids hurting themselves in this rich town. He didn't know that Swerbuck was poor compared to the rest of us.

"I'm too young to die," Swerbuck cried as we made a left turn into the parking lot at North Shore Hospital.

"Shut up and lie still before I kill you myself," the cop said as he tried to bandage Swerbuck.

"It's my job to kill me, not yours." He was laughing his head off. It bounced around like a doll. His big lips blubbered. He wasn't scared at all. He was faking it. The bastard winked at me. He was OK. My faith in his wildness was restored. Attempting suicide was stupid. But, damn, it took balls.

"Fuck you, kid," the cop said and squeezed the tourniquet so tight that Swerbuck gasped.

Chapter 18

Swerbuck and I walked down the street through Great Neck Village. His wrists were swaddled with red stained bandages. He had a black eye.

"Did your father beat you up for killing yourself?" I asked.

"He's afraid to touch me. I did it to show him I had control. My face is my show. No one can hurt me but me. Anyhow, he's so worried that I'm going to knock myself off that he gave me a five-dollar raise in my allowance. As if five dollars is going to keep me from the greatest adventure," Swerbuck said.

"What adventure?"

"Going to see my mother on cloud nine. She's dead," he said.

"You're crazy," I said. "I was only playing. Why'd you try to kill yourself?"

Swerbuck stopped in front of Great Neck Department Store and looked in the window at the preppy clothes. "I hate those clothes," he said. Then we walked on and he said, "I did it because I got excited by your blood. My hands didn't belong to me. So I cut them off and sent them to my mother. But they came back to me and now I want to strangle everyone in Great Neck. I hate this town. The way they're all pissing away money because they have nothing else to do with their lives. My suicide was a dress rehearsal."

"What are you talking about?" I asked.

"I'm composing a poem."

"I'd like to write."

"It's easy. You compare this to that. Great Neck is like an outhouse with dollars for toilet paper," he said. He smiled. He was proud of himself.

"That's cool," I said. I liked that. I was feeling what he was saying. I tried, "Great Neck is like ... I don't know."

"Yes you do. Great Neck is like a woman you want to know, who everyone else thinks he knows, but no one knows. She lets you lie down with her but never make love. She is napping."

"I want to spread the legs of her mansions and fuck her," I said.

"Not bad. But she'll fuck you first."

I thought to myself that I could get the hang of this. That poems were little packages that hid secrets about how to live. Not the poems I had read in school. They were mostly boring. Or they seemed boring because we read them in school.

We walked past the pizza parlor. Swerbuck said he wanted a slice.

"Get me one too. I'll wait out here," I said. I didn't want to tell him that I was afraid I'd run into those two thugs again. Swerbuck wasn't afraid of anything. He was a moron and a genius. I envied his dumb courage.

Swerbuck asked me for a dollar fifty. I gave it to him. He was always broke.

Swerbuck went in and came back out with a slice and a coke for each of us. We walked down the street eating and drinking. We made a left at Great Neck Estates and started walking towards my house. We walked up and down hills past large, swollen houses that came out almost to the sidewalk.

"I wasn't trying to kill myself. I wanted to sharpen the razor on my vein to see if the blade could feel my pain," Swerbuck said. "Pretty good, huh?" He took a bite of the pizza.

"Do you mean it?"

"I never mean what I say or say what I mean."

He finished his pizza, took a sip of his soda and threw the can into a pile of dead leaves. Then he charged forward and did a flip onto a lawn. As he was turning over in the air I sensed he would drop from the sky and land on his head. Like some alien confused by the earth's gravity. But he landed like a cat on his feet.

"Why'd you do that?"

"Because I'm happy to be alive," he said. How? He had just tried to kill himself a few days before.

When we got to my house we went up to my room. He was going to teach me how to write poems.

"Nice room," he said. "Cool stereo." My father had bought me a new Zenith stereo. It was black with two big speakers. Swerbuck was staring around my room. He walked over to the glass doors, opened them and looked out of one of my little terraces. "I used to have a nice room, too," he said. "When I was rich."

I sat down at my desk and he sat next to the coffee table. I gave him a pen and a few sheets of paper.

"Don't let the hoods know I write poems," he said.

"Why?"

"They'll make fun of me. I don't want to have to beat up idiots. When you get their blood on your hands it's contagious. You become stupid," he said.

"I'll keep it quiet about me too," I said and started writing.

"Somewhere through life I tripped. I still limp," I wrote. I read it to Swerbuck.

"The second line is better than the first. 'I still limp' is very original," he said. "Tripping through life is a cliché."

Swerbuck read what he had written, "Life beat me up but I twisted it around and turned her fists into kisses. I fell in love with my suffering."

"You ought to be a poet," I said.

"I am. Idiot!"

"I mean in books and stuff."

"I'm not begging any publishers."

I went back to writing. I read out loud, "I lift my eyes towards something better and there's nothing better unless nothing is better."

"A little abstract but promising," Swerbuck said. "You ever read the Russian nihilists?"

"No." I didn't know who they were.

"Neither have I. But you sound like one."

"How do you know if you never read them?"

"I'm a knower."

"You know what would be better than a suicide club? A writing club," I said.

"It's the same thing. Writers love suicide. Just the other year Hemingway killed himself. And what about Hart Crane jumping off a fucken boat? That's beautiful. Rimbaud didn't kill himself but he got Verlaine so angry that he got him to shoot him. Writing when it's most beautiful is suicide. It's immense like that. So why bother with the words? Go straight to the death."

Swerbuck said this so intensely that he looked like he was praying. He wrote a few more lines, looked at his blood-stained wrist bandages and read, "I gathered my grave into a crucifix, hung it around my neck, and died an icon." He then looked at me and said, "I'm the fucken James Dean of suicide."

We wrote some more, then Swerbuck said he had to go. He went to his jacket and pulled a book out of his pocket and handed it to me.

"What's this?" I asked.

"Rimbaud's poems," he said.

"Who is he?"

"Only the greatest French poet who ever lived," Swerbuck said. "His poems make me high."

"I can't read French," I said.

"It's in translation." He picked a booger from his nose and shot it on my floor.

"Hey," I said.

"Sorry." He picked it up with his fingers and said, "Where should I put it?"

"Flush it down the toilet," I said. He went into the other room. I heard the toilet flushing. I promised myself I'd check the entire room to make sure he didn't flick it somewhere.

Swerbuck and I were standing on the sidewalk before school chatting about losers when John Denby, a squat jock came over to us.

"What you doing hanging around with that creep?" Denby asked Swerbuck.

I looked around and realized I was the only one standing right next to Swerbuck. "Creep" must have been aimed at me. Ooops! It looks like I was being tested early. Denby was challenging me. If I didn't respond I'd be marked chicken and pushed around by every punk in the school.

"Leave Joshua alone," Swerbuck said.

"I can take care of myself," I told Swerbuck.

"Stay away from Dawn," Denby said.

"What are you talking about psycho? She's my girlfriend," I said.

"She's mine."

"No way," Swerbuck shouted. But it was none of his business.

"Dawn would never even look at you," I told Denby.

"But I'm looking at her," he said.

"Fuck you."

"Let's fight for her."

"Where?" I asked. I wasn't relishing this. He looked tough and probably weighed fifty pounds more than me.

"My backyard. After school," he said, turned his back to me and pushed his way through the students who were coming to school like he was a half-back running through the line.

"Where's his backyard?" I asked Swerbuck.

"I'll show you," Swerbuck said. "I've been there before. I've seen him fight other guys."

"How'd he do?"

"He beat the shit out of them."

"Oh, great," I said.

"Just kick him in the balls. He'll fold," Swerbuck said.

"Is he all together?"

"He's mental."

"What do you mean?"

"He's been in and out of mental institutions. He's like a stalker."

"My luck. This town is filled with little mama's boys and I got to fight the one psycho nut."

"Imagine that reject thinking he could get our girl," Swerbuck said.

"Our girl?" I asked.

"You know what I mean."

"I don't."

"Forget it."

Don't tell me Swerbuck was after Dawn too? I'd have to beat his head in. Wasn't he a friend? There are no friends when it comes to love. We went to school just before the late bell rang.

Denby lived about a half-mile from school in a cheap area. He wasn't Jewish. There were no big mansions. It was like everyone lived in gatekeepers' homes, waiting for someone to drive up and drop off bags of money. Or maybe it was more like being a dog under the table. You were always hoping for scraps.

Denby was in his backyard driving wooden stakes as markers. He was making a boxing ring. After he finished he looked at us walking into his yard and said, "Three bare knuckle rounds."

"Whatever you say, asshole," I said. There was no sense in being nice or polite. I wasn't getting out of this.

"Go to that corner," he said and pointed to the right hand rear of his backyard. He then started to walk back to his corner. I followed right behind him like I was his shadow. When he turned around I kicked him in the balls. He doubled over and fell to the ground. Swerbuck jumped in the middle and gave him a ten count like he was the referee at a title bout. I jumped around with my hands up like I was Mohammed Ali. I was the champ. I was pretty. I wasn't going to get my ass kicked. Thank the glorious vacancy of the afternoon sky.

"You fouled me by the rules of Marcus of Queensbury," Denby said as he struggled to his feet.

Uh oh! Trouble in Dodge City. He looked really mad. Both insane and angry.

I didn't know who this Queensbury fellow was but I wasn't taking any chances. I kicked Denby in the balls again. He fell back down to the floor moaning in agony. This time I jumped on him, pinned his shoulders down with my knees and started punching him in the face. Blood started flowing from his nose and sticking to my fingers. I kept punching him till he cried, "I give up. I give up." There were tears in his eyes dripping into his blood. It was a beautiful sight. He deserved it for fucking around with my head. But as much as I liked chewing the juices of revenge I didn't want to get a sour stomach from my own anger. I jumped off Denby. Once again Swerbuck raised my hands in victory and yelled, "The Champ."

"I'd like to dedicate this victory to my Lord Jesus Christ," I said, imitating one of a hundred fighters I had seen on television. There was something about getting hit in the head that made you feel like you had a direct pipeline to God. I used to watch Saturday night fights with my dad. Not that I got hit in the head. But I was part of the mood of hitting and I felt a little woozy.

"Don't use my name in vain," Swerbuck said and threw Denby a tissue as we walked out of his backyard giggling.

Denby was crying on the ground. I wanted to walk back and spit on him. But that wasn't polite. My father wouldn't approve. So I didn't do it.

The next couple of days I read a bunch of Rimbaud's poems. I didn't understand them too much but I liked them. Visiting

Swerbuck that weekend I felt like I was going into some kind of Rimbaudian, French jungle. Mad Dog was over. Swerbuck's dad wasn't home. He almost never was. His brother, Brian, was down the block with his aunt. Swerbuck and Mad Dog looked like two natives who had just boiled a missionary in a pot. There was some joke between them that I couldn't pick out of the boiling bones of their camaraderie.

"Let's get high," Swerbuck said, giggling.

"Wahoo," Mad Dog chimed in, spit in his hand and rubbed down a cowlick that was standing up on the back of his head.

Swerbuck took a small plastic bag of black powder from his pocket. He opened it up and handed it to me. "Snort this," Swerbuck said.

"What is it?" I asked.

Swerbuck waved it about like a magician casting a spell and said, mysteriously, "Abu Abu from Arabia. A real rush."

I'd never heard of it. But I was game for anything. I asked, "Would Rimbaud like it?"

"He'd love it," Swerbuck said.

"Who the fuck's Rimbaud?" Mad Dog growled.

"A poet. Idiot," I said.

"I'll kick his ass," Mad Dog said.

"He's already dead," I said. "My favorite poem is 'The Drunken Boat.'"

"A boat can't get drunk," Mad Dog said.

Swerbuck went into a poetic trance and recited in a distant voice, "Comme je descendais des Fleuves impassibles, je ne sentis plus guidé par les haleurs."

I didn't know what he was saying but it sounded important. French was a rich, intelligent language. Kings used to speak it. I stuffed the bag of Abu Abu under my nose and snorted. It went into my nostrils and down the back of my throat like gunpowder. I coughed up some black grains.

"This tastes like medicine," I said.

"No," Swerbuck said.

"Yes," I insisted, coughing.

"It is medicine, you jerk," Mad Dog said, laughing like a hyena. I felt a wave of nausea and ran into the bathroom, fell onto my knees and stared into the bowl. I wanted to dive into the blue water and slip down the hole into the sewer, to swim with the alligators. I thought of rats down there and then I threw up in a big wave of buckwheat colored vomit. Chunks hung from my lips. There were no towels so I wiped my mouth with toilet paper. I pushed my hands on the bowl and stood up. I was dizzy. I didn't have my legs back. The nausea returned. I felt like I was seasick. I looked into the toilet bowl like it was the ocean. I fell down on my knees again, put my head in the bowl and threw up. I got up and went to the sink and threw some water on my forehead. I dried off with my shirtsleeve and scooped some vomit from my lip with a piece of toilet paper. I struggled back into the living room with the toilet paper still hanging from my lip. "What is this poison?" I asked.

" It's Asmidor, you dummy. It's used to stop asthma attacks," Swerbuck said, laughing. Mad Dog slapped him on the back.

"I thought it was Abu Abu. From Arabia," I said.

"I already told you I'm a liar," Swerbuck said.

"You're asthma's cured," Mad Dog said, laughing his dumb head off. I pulled the piece of toilet paper from my lip. I was all for having a little fun. But this was stupid. They shouldn't have made me sick. They were morons. Even if Swerbuck had read all of Rimbaud. I was too easy a target. I walked over to the archer. I invited destruction.

A couple of days later Swerbuck came over to my house. We were down in the basement laundry room and Swerbuck asked, "You want to get high for real?"

"I can't trust you," I said.

"This time you can."

"You fucked me up with the Abu Abu. And you even told me that you were a liar."

"I was lying."

"Just don't fuck with me this time," I said. I didn't want to seem like I wasn't hip, like I was afraid of getting high.

"No problem." And Swerbuck took a jug of Clorox Bleach off the shelf and poured some into a plastic bag.

"You doing the laundry?"

"Just snort this," he said and handed me the bag.

"Clorox? You sure?"

"It'll make you feel like a drunken boat."

How bad could it be? It cleaned clothes. Maybe it would clean my sinuses. I put my nose in the baggy and took a deep sniff. It hurt. I felt the lining of my lungs ripping, bleeding. My eyes felt like they were going to pop out. Despite the pain I was getting high.

I snorted again. Maybe I just had to get used to it. The Clorox ripped another layer off my lungs. It was a little like a glue high except it was painful. This was some strong medecine. I needed a break from it and passed the bag to Swerbuck. I didn't want to hog all of this dynamite Clorox for myself. He looked at me and laughed, saying "I'm not going to snort that poison. My lungs are already clean."

The joke was on me again. He ran from the laundry room. I chased after him as he dove into the garage slamming the door behind him. I opened it up and caught him rolling with laughter against the front of my father's Jaguar XKE. It was the same car James Bond used in the movies. It was parked next to the Lincoln. I spilled the bag of Clorox over his brown hair. "Try being a blond," I yelled.

My lungs would heal. But it would take months for his hair to go black again. He looked at me, smiled and winked, "Blonds have more fun."

Chapter 19

It was a gray day in November and it felt like it might snow. I was sitting in the back of history class next to Dawn, Swerbuck and Mad Dog. I liked history. There was something spacious about the past, like a huge closet with hidden drawers. Not that I liked the facts and the small details. I just liked that there were so many of them floating around like gnats on a tennis court. Our teacher, Mr. Albert, was fat, soft, sweaty and brainy. He wore a white rumpled suit, a blue bow tie. His shirt and belly hung out over his brown belt. He didn't bust our chops much. He didn't care about stuffing learning down our throats like a Thanksgiving turkey. This morning he was discussing Mahatma Gandhi. I loved Gandhi. I also loved Martin Luther King. I believed in non-violence. Even though I was violent myself and thought nothing of punching people in the face. One day I figured I'd outgrow that and become a spiritual leader.

Albert was rattling on that, according to Gandhi, history was a record of bad deeds. He said, "There are so many good things that happen everyday. History should record these too."

That didn't make sense to me. Who wanted to read about good deeds? History wasn't a net to catch beautiful butterflies. Goodness was, simple and plain, boring. What would history books be like if instead of the nuclear cloud at Hiroshima they described how Mrs. Gray went to the store and bought a loaf of bread and some Lipton's Tea for her sick neighbor? What would movies be like if we only recorded kindness? Imagine Goldfinger going around giving out gold coins to the poor instead of robbing Fort Knox. Or the Sioux Indians going up to a wagon train and giving the cowboys a map to go west. Headlines about murders sold newspapers. Badness was exciting. Goodness had no staying power, no *pizzazz*, no jazz. If Gandhi were an historian he'd have nothing to write about. The good events he recorded would evaporate and leave a big hole like a bagel. They wouldn't capture the imagination. Other violent, more exciting events, would pull a zipper over them.

Albert was sweating under the armpits and lecturing loudly when there was some noise on the P.A. system. It was the principal's, Dr. Hollis's voice. Damn, I hoped he wasn't calling me down to his office in front of the whole school. How many times could a guy write his name? There was some static; then I heard Hollis coughing and clearing his throat. Followed by a choking noise and what sounded like crying.

"The President of the United States has been shot in the head. In Dallas. In his car," came over the loudspeaker.

Tears spread around the room like a wet contagious virus. Girls were wailing like Arab women mourning their dead. Ostentatious tears. Gross tears.

"This can't be," Albert moaned.

"How does this fit in with Gandhi's good deeds," Swerbuck blurted out.

"It doesn't," Albert said.

"How'd Gandhi die?"

"He was assassinated too."

"The President won't die," Dawn said. A bunch of students started chanting along with her, "The President won't die."

Students closed their eyes, gritted their teeth and spoke to God. They waited for an answer to their prayers. They crossed their fingers. Then there was some more static on the P.A. system.

"He's going to be OK.," Dawn said.

Hollis' choked-up voice crackled through the speaker, "The President of the United States is dead. Everyone please go home till further notice."

Cries belted through the school like a West Side rumble. Weeping students fell on the floor like uncalled for apologies. I was annoyed. You'd think these wimps lost their fathers. That their mothers had been shot in the head. Not that some distant politician had been blown away. Did these arrogant idiots really think they were part of the first family?

"Gandhi believed in goodness," Mr. Albert cried. He tried to keep it together. He couldn't. He looked around him at the students running out of the room and yelled, "Fuck you, Gandhi." He collapsed on his desk.

Outside everyone was crying, walking around in circles, not knowing what to do or where to go. All the students loved Kennedy. He was young, good looking and wealthy. Like us. If he could die, we could too. They all cried for themselves as much as for him. Everyone had a theory about who killed him. It was the Russians. It was the Cubans. It was the CIA. Everyone tried to get closer to the dead president by pretending they knew something about his death.

I didn't know how it happened and I didn't care. It was all part of a movie to me. I saw the hot Texas sunlight catching in his damp, red hair. I imagined pieces of his head floating over the upholstery of his Lincoln and landing on the windshield where the wipers spread blood and pieces of scalp. His ghost flew up into the afternoon sky of the Lone Star State.

Kennedy's Lincoln was a convertible. It cost more than ours. But if it had a hard-top like ours, his head would still be on his shoulders.

Dawn, Swerbuck, Mad Dog and I all gathered outside the school. They crunched across the sidewalk through lumps of sadness.

"The world's over," Dawn sobbed.

Swerbuck stood there reflectively and said, "He was a great man. He should have had a chance to end his own life."

"The killer wouldn't try that on me," Mad Dog boasted.

Girls and boys were hugging each other and sobbing. I heard someone cry, "There's going to be a nuclear war." Mad Dog jumped in, "I'm not afraid of nuclear bombs."

All the crying going on sickened me. I didn't say anything. I didn't want to have to deal with mass hysteria. Saying I didn't give a damn about Kennedy was like saying I didn't believe in God. Idiots felt strongly about subjects such as these. Really, I felt Kennedy's death was none of our business. Who were we to Kennedy or Kennedy to us? It's not like he was a close friend.

"I feel like I knew him," Dawn said. But she didn't. A skinny blond girl with short curly hair hurried over and hugged Dawn. They cried all over each other like they were cousins at a funeral. They didn't even know each other. I wondered if Dawn was the right girl for me.

Everyone wanted to be a Kennedy. They thought if they cried for him they'd become part of his family. It was an orgy of crying. It was disgusting. I broke away from Dawn and the mourning crowd and walked home by myself. I was sad too. But I didn't want to share my sadness. I said to myself, "I don't give two fucks about the dead president." That wasn't true. I felt something and I didn't feel something. Whatever I felt, it didn't bear any resemblance to the messy sentimentality that

surrounded me like a Sloppy Joe. A mailman walked by me
with tears in his eyes. He loved Kennedy; he loved America. If
I were a mailman and had to earn my living carrying around
other people's stupid letters I would have shot Kennedy myself.
I would have felt this country fucked me over.

When I got to my house I walked into my winding
driveway between the white stucco walls. I was pissed off at
all the noise about Kennedy. I wanted to be the President.
I wanted the whole world to cry for me. I was jealous even
though he was dead.

The afternoon had the quiet chill of a refrigerator. Snowflakes started falling from the sky. It was the first snowfall of
the year. It was so soft, white and fluffy that it made me happy.
I walked over to the stucco wall, smiled at it and belted it
with my right hand with all my might. I punched it a lot
harder than I punched Mrs. Deutch's tree. The pain went right
through me.

Some of the skin tore off and my hand started to swell up
instantly. I punched the wall again with my swollen hand. This
time I purposely didn't hit the wall straight on. I was afraid of
breaking my hand. Even if I wanted it broken. I threw a round
house so that my pinky hit the wall first. I was chicken. I didn't
have the courage to go all the way and break the whole hand. I
wasn't Swerbuck. Blood spilled from my pinky onto the snow
that was falling onto the driveway.

"That was for you my dead President," I whispered. My
punches were a tribute to his death. Then I thought, why
should I do anything for him? He was already getting all the
attention. I could take pain too. He was no better than me. I
punched the wall again as hard as I could. This time straight on.
I let out a moan and grabbed my hand. It cracked like a little
plastic ice cube tray, popping out ice. My eyes started tearing. I

looked down at my ripped hand. I saw the President's shattered head. I bonded with him. There was blood on the wall and on the snow. I kicked the snow with my foot and painted a happy face with a smile on the wall in blood.

A couple of days later I was eating spaghetti and meatballs, with a new cast on my hand, in the high school cafeteria with Swerbuck and Mad Dog. My mother had taken me to the doctor. I had broken two fingers. She wanted me to go back to see Rosenquest but I told her I wasn't ready. Swerbuck's hand had been out of his cast over a month. I felt like we were trading places. I figured he was jealous. I had trouble twirling the fork when I tried to eat my spaghetti.

"So what happened?" Swerbuck asked.

"I broke it," I said.

"How?"

"I punched a wall."

"You're supposed to punch faces," Mad Dog raised his voice.

"Let me write on it," Swerbuck said and wrote his name.

Mad Dog wrote "Woof!"

"It's getting me out of gym," I bragged, holding up my cast.

"Gym is for pigs," Swerbuck said.

"What do you mean?" Mad Dog asked. He liked gym. Particularly, volley ball.

"The industrial military complex wants to make us strong at gym so we can kill in Vietnam," Swerbuck said. "By not going you are protesting imperialism."

"That's not why I wanted to get out of gym," I said.

"Why?" Swerbuck asked.

"Cause President Kennedy had a bad back. It hurt him to exercise," I said.

"So?" Swerbuck asked.

"My back hurts sometimes too."

"I don't get it."

"I feel close to the dead prick," I said.

"You didn't say anything when he got shot," Swerbuck said.

"I didn't realize it," I said. I was too busy being jealous about all the attention Kennedy was getting. I wondered if anyone would show up at my funeral when I died. The bastard had the whole world mourning. People were flying in from everywhere. Limousines were lining the streets. It was as if his death were honey to a million bees. And a white stallion led his corpse through Washington.

"You look a little like him," Swerbuck said. I did.

"Yeah, like his corpse," Mad Dog said, smiling. No one thought he was funny.

At two o'clock in the morning I stole my dad's Lincoln and drove out to King's Point to pick up Dawn. We parked in a long driveway off a big mansion about a mile from where Dawn lived. There were big black trees all around us. It was real private. I always felt a little afraid of the dark and I held Dawn's hand with my cast, sitting behind the wheel in case I had to make a quick getaway. When I kissed Dawn a hot, horny space opened up in my head. I wanted to turn myself inside out. To touch her with my blood vessels. Dawn struggled to pull down my pants, took my penis out and started pulling on it. I felt love for her coming out of every pore of my body. I was numb. I was orbiting earth, hard as a meteor. Then Dawn pointed at a long limo that was shining its lights at us coming down the driveway. No way I wanted to get caught with my pants down. I started the engine and as the car pulled up next to me I floored my car, brushing against some shrubs and zipping past it. I was breathing hard as we reached Kings Point Road and I made a screeching left hand turn, heading back towards Dawn's home. I was tingling. My pants were still down around my knees. Dawn and I didn't say anything till we made a left on Pond Lane and speeded to her house at the end. When we pulled into her driveway I finally I breathed a sigh of relief. Dawn said, "That was a close call."

"Too close," I said and looked down, seeing come all over my pants.

"Does driving excite you?" Dawn laughed.

I was embarrassed and asked her for a tissue. She took out her lipstick and drew a face on my penis.

I didn't get home until about four o'clock in the morning. Instead of using the electric garage opener I pulled the door up by hand. Then I drove in slowly so my father wouldn't hear the engine revving. I turned off the car and scratched my balls. I felt all crusty from not cleaning up properly. Why had I come while racing away from the limo? That was some kind of perverted thing. I was worried that it was the chase that excited me. But that was ridiculous. Dawn had been rubbing my dick. She had me so hot anything would have made me come.

I sneaked out of the garage and up two flights of stairs. First I went into Robert's room and put his license back in his wallet. I was lucky he came home a lot so that I could keep stealing his license. No one had a clue as to what I was up to. I didn't know whether my family was dumb or it was just much easier to get away with pranks than I expected. You don't hear about all the petty crimes guys get away with. Just about the screw-ups.

Chapter 20

I wasn't much into museums but I liked Van Gogh because he was crazy and cut his ear off. Hurting yourself like that shows you're sincere; that stuff matters to you; that the stakes are high. But if you hurt yourself too much you are stupid. You must enjoy the limitations of ight pain. I went with Swerbuck and Dawn to the Metropolitan Museum of Art to see the Van Gogh Exhibit. Dawn was all excited about going. She invited Swerbuck. I didn't. I knew they were just friends but sometimes Swerbuck seemed like he wanted to be more than friends. Not that I thought Dawn would dump me for him. His lips were too big and he was sloppy. His clothes were always wrinkled and dirty. No, she had better taste than that.

The Van Gogh Exhibit sprawled through many large rooms on the second floor. It was vast. I wondered how Van Gogh found so much time to paint, being crazy all his life and dying so young. His dedication excited me. If I could find something to dedicate myself to one day, I wouldn't be so angry and at loose ends all the time. We stood in front of Van Gogh's "The Sunflowers." Swerbuck said, "I want to eat the swirls of paint." He put his face up near the canvas. I pulled him back. A guard was eyeing us suspiciously.

Dawn said that the sunflowers were full of life. Swerbuck claimed they were about suicide. I said that the sunflowers were simply about sunflowers. Then Swerbuck said, "I wish I were Van Gogh. The man was a genius. He killed himself."

"Killing himself doesn't make him a genius," I said. "And you're not Van Gogh."

"We'll see," Swerbuck said.

"He had so much to live for," Dawn said.

"And so much to die for," Swerbuck said. He winked at Dawn.

"You two are sick. You belong together," I said.

Dumb thing to say. Was I trying to throw her into Swerbuck's arms? But Dawn answered, "If we were together, we'd kill each other." At least she realized they weren't a fit.

We wandered around the museum for a couple of hours. In front of "Starry Night" Swerbuck went into a trance. He looked like he was going to blast off into Van Gogh's swirling midnight sky with sparklers in his mouth. He had some secret connection with Van Gogh's work that made me jealous. I didn't like other people feeling more than me. It made me feel stupid. Like Swerbuck was drawing Dawn into Van Gogh's work along with him. I had to pull Dawn by the hand to break her away from the painting.

"Let's get out of here already," I said.

"Don't you appreciate Van Gogh?" Swerbuck said.

"I love him. But enough's enough."

"Enough is never enough," Swerbuck said.

They stopped at all the other paintings. It took me an hour to get them out of the museum. I didn't feel good till we walked down the long marble steps towards Fifth Avenue. I grabbed Dawn's hand. She kissed me on the cheek as we hopped into a cab to Penn Station. Did she mean it or was she just brushing me off with her lips?

"Let's cut school tomorrow," I said to Dawn on the telephone.

Cutting school was sexy. It turned me on. It was breaking the rules, taking chances, clutching your fate in your own hands.

"I got to ask my father," Dawn said.

"Are you crazy?"

"Hold on a minute." She left the phone. A couple of minutes later she came back. "He said I can."

"I don't understand."

"I'm an A student. He lets me do what I want."

"If you had my grades he wouldn't let you out of the door," I said.

"If your folks won't let you, how are you going to get away with it?"

"No problem. My mother's playing golf tomorrow. You and I will be at my house when the nurse calls. You can pretend you're my mother."

"Yes, son," she said, laughing.

The next morning when all the students were mulling about in front of Great Neck North at eight o'clock in the morning, Dawn and I sneaked off around the corner breathing heavily, smiling, chewing the chill morning air. I felt aroused. Like I was eating my own freedom. It tasted good like a biscuit. In the distance we heard the bell ringing, calling all the cattle back to the barn. I felt so superior, so cool as I stepped into a phone booth.

"I got bad news," I said to Dawn when I put down the phone. "We can't go back to my house."

"We can go to my house."

"No. I mean, my mother's golf date was cancelled. She's going to be home."

"The nurse will call her. You'll be dead."

"I know," I said. I must have looked like a turtle, sticking my head back into my shell.

"You better go right to school. Tell them you overslept," she said, grabbing my arm and trying to lead me back to school.

"I got a better idea," I said. I broke away from her hand and walked over to this huge tree on someone's front lawn. The cast had just come off my hand from breaking it on my driveway wall when Kennedy was shot. I didn't want to hurt it anymore so I started banging my face against the tree. I kept banging it harder and at sharper angles. It didn't really hurt. It felt kind of warm as scratches rose on my face and sap leaked into my blood.

"What are you doing?" Dawn asked and grabbed me by the hair. For a minute she reminded me of my mother, pulling my hair when I was a kid, trying to get my mouth in position to wash it out with soap.

"Bashing my face up," I said. I pulled my head away. Some of my hair came off in her hand. And I scratched my face against the tree, faster and harder.

"Why?"

"It's a cool alibi. I'll tell my mother I got into a fight and couldn't go to school," I said. Then I punched myself in the face. Right on my nose. That hurt.

"Stop it," Dawn screamed and started kissing my face all over and whispered, "You're a sick child."

I felt warm all over. Sick children got to stay in bed and drink hot coco. It was so easy to get a girl to like you. All you had to do was hurt yourself. But would my mother feel sorry for me? When I was a baby she accidentally dropped me on my head at Bear Mountain. She cried she felt so bad for me. I needed twelve stitches. Later, when I was fourteen, my brother hit me on the head with a rock. I begged my mother to punish him. She said, "Fight your own battles."

Dawn picked up a clump of leaves and tried to wipe the blood from my face. I was in love with the drama of my bruises. I wanted visible wounds. As long as they didn't hurt too much. As long as I didn't have to suffer.

Chapter 21

Charlie Yang was a local Chinese hustler. When he asked me to play cards with him, I accepted. I was flattered by his challenge. I mean he was the real thing and I was just a punk kid. He was five years older than me. I met him at Squire's Deli where he worked behind the counter. I had heard rumors that he had once hustled in Las Vegas. I felt like I was moving up into the big leagues. I was used to playing cards with local dummies like Mad Dog. I'd cheat right under his nose and he wouldn't notice it. What a sucker! I made about a hundred bucks a week off him. I should have been happy with that.

The game with Yang took place in my bedroom about four o'clock in the afternoon. I sat across from Yang on my bed. I pretended I was at a casino, wearing good slacks, a white shirt and a tie. Yang wore jeans and a sweatshirt. He cut the deck smoothly like he was slicing deli roast beef. No, better than that. He was a master musician. He played the cards like he was playing the harp. His graceful fingers shuffled notes. I could hear the music of the cards slipping across the bed.

Within an hour I was down two hundred dollars. I couldn't win a hand. Not that I thought Yang was hustling me. If he were he would have thrown me a few winning hands to keep me interested. But he didn't.

Then I drew three aces in five-card draw poker. I bet five dollars. Yang raised me ten and I raised him back ten. I drew two cards and picked up a ten and an eight. Worthless. But I still felt strong with my three aces. Particularly, when Yang only hung onto two cards and drew three more. I figured he had a pair and maybe picked up a third. Big deal. I had three aces. They'd beat any three of a kind he had. I bet ten and we raised each other back and forth three times. It was a shoo-in. I laid my three aces out on my bed. He looked at my cards, shrugged like I beat him and then smiled, saying, "Velly solly Charrey," and threw down three kings and two jacks. Full house. How could he get so lucky? I wondered if he was cheating me. He gathered in all the chips.

"How much am I down now?" I asked.

"Two hundled and seventy-five dorrars," he said.

"Let's cut the cards. High card wins. Double or nothing," I said, feeling both suicidal and lucky at the same time.

"Your poison."

I shuffled the cards and cut the deck. I pulled first. Jack. That had to be a winner. Only three cards could beat me. Maybe my luck was coming back. Yang pulled out a card and turned it over. It was an ace.

"You owe me five hundred and fifty dorrars," Yang said.

Where was I going to find that kind of money? I only had a hundred on me. I was in it deep. I hoped Yang wasn't connected with the Chinese mafia or some Tong group. He might chop my head off.

"Let me give you a hundred dollars now. I'll pay off the balance in a few weeks," I said. I figured I could win the rest back from Mad Dog. I gave him the hundred.

Yang looked around the room. His eyes fixed on a new stereo I had sitting on the coffee table.

"You give me steleo too," he said.

"No way." That was a brand new stereo. My father had bought it for me. It was worth about eight hundred dollars.

"Shouldn't gamble with money don't have," Yang said. I thought of beating him up. Then I thought of the Chinese mafia throwing me into the Hudson River in a take-out Chinese food container. And I said, "Take the fucken thing."

Yang had trouble carrying my stereo down the stairs. He was a little Chinese guy. I sure wasn't going to help him. My father ran into him at the bottom of the stairs and said, "Where you going with that, Chinaman?"

My dad was prejudiced against Orientals. They were our enemy in World War II.

He forgot for a moment that it was the Japanese not the Chinese who bombed Pearl Harbor.

"Sir, prease, your son give me steleo," Yang said. He was polite to elders. Like all the Chinese he respected age.

"Is that true?" Hy asked me.

"Yes," I said.

"Begging paldon," Yang said to my dad and tried to get out the front door. My father held the door open for him while he looked back at me angrily. When Yang was out my father asked me why I gave him the stereo. I told him I lost it in cards. He smacked me across the face, "You shouldn't gamble."

I felt a hot wave of anger and raised my hand to hit him back. I didn't. I said, "I'm sorry." I was a bit punky but I wasn't a disgusting father beater.

"You owe me eight hundred dollars for the stereo," my father said.

"Where am I going to get eight hundred dollars?" I said.

"That's your problem," my father said. He turned his back to me and went up the stairs to his room.

That night I called Swerbuck, "Set up a card game with Mad Dog."

"What for?"

"I need money." I told him I had lost my stereo to Yang and had to make enough money to buy it back. "I'll share the money with you if you help me cheat Mad Dog."

"Mad Dog's my friend," Swerbuck said.

"You won't do it?"

"Of course I will," he said. "One thing has nothing to do with the other."

I wasn't going to question his morality. After all, Mad Dog was my friend too even though I didn't like him yet I was happy to cheat him. Some people are just cheatable. It's right. There'd be a crick in the universe if you didn't cheat them. It's not my fault.

The next day Swerbuck arranged a card game at his house and invited Mad Dog. While we were playing Mad Dog was so busy talking about how tough he was that he didn't even notice me trading cards back and forth with Swerbuck right in front of his face. I dropped a king of spades on the table. Swerbuck picked it up.

"Anybody cheats here, I kill him," Mad Dog said.

"I was just picking up my card," Swerbuck said.

"You sure that wasn't his," he said, pointing at me.

"I have five," I said.

"I know. But let that be a warning."

We bet the hand up to about two hundred dollars.

I laid down my hand first. I had given Swerbuck my good cards. I had a miserable hand, a ten high. "You call that cheating," I said. "I got nothing."

"You dope. You should have dropped out," Mad Dog said, laughing at my hand.

"Beat that," Mad Dog said throwing down three kings.

Swerbuck waited a few seconds while Mad Dog started to gather the chips. "Just a minute," he said and laid out a royal flush in spades on the table.

"Fuck," Mad Dog said.

Swerbuck took in the pot.

Mad Dog was all out of chips. He checked his pockets for money. "I'm broke," he moaned.

"Tough luck," I said.

"This was a lousy night for me. I'm a good card player," Mad Dog said.

"Lousy for me too," I said. "I'm almost broke."

"You stink at cards," Mad Dog said and got up and stormed out. When Swerbuck and I were alone we cracked up laughing. We divided up his two hundred dollars.

I left Swerbuck's apartment and headed over to Yang's. I had looked him up in the phone book and he lived over a store in some cheap building on Great Neck Road. I rang the bell and he answered the door.

"Come to give me money?" he asked.

I walked in and went right over to my stereo, which was sitting right in his living room. It was too good for the cheap furniture around it.

"Hey, where you going?" he said and came up behind me.

"You embarrassed me in front of my father," I said.

I felt the room spin, my jaw tightened, I turned on my heel and punched him right in the face with no warning. He went down like a fly I had just swatted. I couldn't believe I had been scared of him. He was about as tough as wonton soup. His eye went all black and shiny. He was a joke. I was the punch line. I threw a hundred dollars at him and picked up the stereo. He got up holding his money and yelled, "Hundled dorrar not enough."

"I gave you a hundred before," I said.

"Too rittle."

"That's all you're getting," I said and walked out the door, carrying my stereo. I looked back at him and couldn't help but get a kick out of his black eye. I had never seen an oriental with a black eye before. I had my stereo back. I didn't owe my father eight hundred dollars anymore. It took me about twenty minutes before I could find an empty cab on Great Neck Road.

It felt good to be a tough guy. Even if it was pretend.

At two o'clock in the morning I turned on a flashlight and sneaked out from under my covers fully dressed. I now had a Photostat of my brother's license to use on those rare weekends when he didn't come home. Just the other night Swerbuck had said to me, "Why don't we drive into the Village."

"Great Neck Village?" I asked.

"Greenwich Village."

"You're crazy," I said. It was much too dangerous to drive all the way to the city. I hadn't even taken Driver's Ed.

Yet somehow, a few days later, I found myself doing what I said I wouldn't do. I headed down to my garage, started my car, put it in neutral and let it coast down the driveway. When I reached the street, I put it into gear and drove to Swerbuck's. Swerbuck was peeking out his second story window when he saw me pulling up. It was about twenty feet to the ground. Swerbuck stepped out onto the ledge and jumped. He crashed onto the ground in a bundle. It looked like he was hurt. But after a few seconds he jumped up, dusted himself off and ran over to the car, smiling.

"You're bats," I said as he sat down next to me.

"I'm a cat. I always land on my feet," he said.

We were off on our grand journey to Greenwich Village. This was the first time I ever drove into the city. I felt like we were on a voyage around the world. Cutting school, stealing cars, driving without a license, all these things were a big charge like sticking a wet finger in a socket. I saw bright blue sparks. I got a jolt out of being alive. In order to live you had to risk dying a little. You had to bite into the fishhook and fight against the line.

I tried to parallel park in front of Figaro Cafe in the Village. It took me about five tries, banging into the black Chevy in front of me and the Volkswagen behind. I got out feeling like Mr. New York.

"This is cool," I said to Swerbuck.

"We're cool cat beatniks," he said.

"I'm Jack Kerouac," I said.

"We're On The Road," he laughed.

When we walked into Figaro there was an intellectual hum throughout the room. I could hear the whispers of secret manifestos. The hush of revolution. A waitress showed us to a small wooden table in the middle of a throng of scattered tables. We sat on cushionless, iron chairs. I felt like I was in the throes of a bookish insurrection. I imagined a librarian floating over my head on a kite string. Swerbuck opened his huge lips, breathed deeply and then started reciting some poetry. It was thrilling. There were familiar phrases like, "I saw the best minds of my generation destroyed by madness," "starving hysterical naked," and "through the negro streets at dawn looking for an angry fix."

"Did you write that," I asked Swerbuck. That was some powerful, professional stuff.

"Bite your tongue," he said.

"No, I think it's good," I said.

"It's genius! Don't you know Ginsburg's 'Howl?'"

"Oops. Forgot."

A couple of black girls with drop-dead bodies sat down right next to us. The tables were small and they were almost in our laps. Swerbuck's mouth fell open. His lower lip hung down to his chin. He looked like a Ubangi and the girls looked like they were African natives in a Rimbaud poem. I saw them naked around a fire. I heard drums along the Congo and dreamed of crocodiles, hashish and orgies. Swerbuck, I suppose because of his years in France, had the courage to tell the waitress to bring the girls some Cappuccinos. He was being very debonair. He waved at them and they waved back, giggling. Now that the ice was broken I told them our names and they told us theirs. Cindy was a light-skinned girl who looked almost like a model. Carol was a short, stocky, dark-skinned African girl. I could see her chucking spears in the jungle and dancing on the heads of dead lions. Swerbuck felt comfortable with her because she wasn't that good looking.

"Where do you live?" I asked Cindy.

"Washington Heights," she said with an English accent. It was strange to hear a Negro speak with such a refined accent. They usually spoke with a southern drawl.

"Are you from London?"

"Bermuda."

Swerbuck was showing off, speaking to Carol in French. She didn't understand a word of it. I thought he was quoting Rimbaud.

After we finished our drinks, Swerbuck asked the waitress for a check for both tables. The girls blushed and thanked him.

"My pleasure, ladies," he bowed with a flourish. The waitress came back with the check and handed it to him. He looked at the bill and almost fell out of his seat. He tapped me on the shoulder and whispered in my ear, "It's thirty-five dollars. I can't afford that."

"You shouldn't have offered."

"I'll kill myself."

I paid the thirty-five dollars, leaving a ten-dollar tip. My father gave me forty dollars a week allowance. Most of my friends, even those who were much richer than me, got about ten dollars a week.

"It's our pleasure to take you girls out," Swerbuck said. It hadn't cost him a dime. I wanted to hit him.

We all went outside and stood next to my parents' Lincoln.

"Nice car," Cindy said.

"I have a Cadillac," Swerbuck boasted. "I just didn't feel like driving it tonight." He had a Corvair not a Cadillac. I bragged, "I also have a Jaguar."

"Why aren't you driving it?" Cindy asked.

"It's a stick-shift. I have enough trouble driving automatic," I said. That was true. I didn't even have a license.

"I bet the Lincoln is your father's and the Jaguar is your mother's," Cindy said.

"You're wrong."

"How?"

"The Lincoln is my mother's and the Jaguar is my father's," I said laughing. She laughed too. I kissed her on the cheek and said, "I have to run."

"Why do you have to leave?" she asked and slipped a piece of paper into my jacket pocket.

"Because I don't have a license and I stole my parents' car while they were sleeping," I said.

"Very funny," Cindy said.

"Well, let's just say I have to get home," I said.

Swerbuck shook Carol's hand and we got into the Lincoln and took off. We waved to the girls as we headed down the block. I almost crashed into a mailbox. On the Fifty-Ninth Street Bridge I imagined Cindy's pussy hanging up in the sky like a giant billboard. I wondered what color it was? I figured it was probably gray. I had once seen a naked black woman in a porno magazine and hers was gray. I wondered if it tasted different from a pink one. I had never tasted a pussy but I figured the pink ones were like cotton candy salted with fish smells, chum. I reached in my pocket and took out the piece of paper Cindy had stuffed in there. I glanced down and almost crashed into the divider. I straightened out and when I stopped at a traffic light on Queens Boulevard I read the note, "Cindy Hamilton -- 861-2549." I put her number back in my pocket.

"What were you looking at?" Swerbuck asked.

"Cindy's phone number."

"Big deal. I got Carol's number too."

"No, you didn't."

"Yes, I did."

"What is it?"

"I'm not telling."

"You didn't get it."

Swerbuck smacked his hand against the car door. He was upset. "So what if I didn't get it? I'm too good looking for her. My lips are too sexy."

"She liked your French poetry," I said to make him feel better.

"The bitch didn't even speak French," he said and turned away from me, looking out the side window. He caught his reflection in the window. He open and closed his mouth like a fish, admiring his lips. He asked, "Are you going to call Cindy?"

"No," I said.

"If you did, I'd tell Dawn."

I had forgotten all about Dawn. Was it right for me to even be talking to Cindy? I guess. She was a Negro. It wasn't like I was cheating with a sister white girl.

I called Cindy the next day just to see if she got home all right. She said she missed me and wanted to come right out to Great Neck. I said I was busy. She asked if she could come the weekend after next. I was worried that Dawn might catch me. And I didn't want to be seen with a Negro in my hometown. I didn't mind it in the city where no one knew me. But in the suburbs? I should have just told her no. But I didn't want her to think that I was a bigot. I insisted that she come.

I waited at the train station for her to show up on the Long Island Railroad. When she stepped out of the train she stood out. She was the only colored person. But she wasn't dark black. She was like an inkblot that had been spread thin on the paper. Like she had been rained on and all her color had been drained out. She ran up to me and kissed me hello. I felt like I was hugging my maid. I blushed. In Greenwich Village she was an African queen. Here she was a nigger. I hated that word. I could hardly even say it to myself. When I was a kid I beat up my neighbor in East Meadow for using it. But it somehow applied. I was infected with the prejudice of the community. There were flies buzzing around my rotting white soul. I sucked.

Walking through town I pointed out the local sights like a tour guide, keeping Cindy busy so she wouldn't think of hugging me in public again.

We walked past Great Neck Department Store. I said, "Everybody shops here."

"The clothes aren't very hip," Cindy said, looking in the window.

"I know." I was glad she felt that way.

"This is the most overpriced, over popular joint in town," I said as we passed Squire's Deli.

In front of the movie theater I told her I knew an usher there and could get her in for free. "Goldfinger" was playing. She had already seen it. I asked if she liked "Goldfinger."

"Bond reminds me of you," she said. I wished. Did she think all white people looked alike?

We made a left on Cedar Drive and walked into Great Neck Estates. We had to climb up and down a couple of hills. Cindy was impressed by the homes. She'd never seen anything like them. I hadn't either till I moved here. We made a right on Deepdale Drive.

"Have you ever gone out with a colored girl before?" she asked.

"Many," I said. I didn't want to tell her that she was my first.

I pointed out my house in front of us. It was French Provincial, which meant there were a lot of sloping slate roofs and turrets. It was all white brick with black gutters and window frames. It sat on top of a steep hill like a country mansion. It reminded me of the first time I saw the summit of Mt. Snow. I was riding up the chairlift through clouds and I looked up to where the clouds broke and I saw fields of snow bathed in sun above me.

"I'm impressed," Cindy said.

I was too.

We climbed up the slate walkway and rang the bell. Robert and a puff of pipe tobacco greeted us.

"What are you doing home again?" I asked.

"Mom missed me," he said. He turned to Cindy and said, "I'm Robert, his older brother. I don't live here. I go to college."

"Curry College," I said, sneering.

"I'm a great fan of Martin Luther King and the Civil Rights Movement," he said.

"I'm more into Malcolm X," Cindy said and followed me past him, up the stairs, to my room.

"Does your brother think he's flattering me because he likes Martin Luther King?" Cindy asked me.

"He's an idiot," I said. I loved him. But brothers could be embarrassing.

We both fell silent. We didn't have a whole lot to say without the ambiance of Figaro Cafe to inspire us. I sat next to her on the bed and started kissing her. Her skin was soft and sweet. I licked her ear; then we started making out, heavy. Our tongues were flashing around each other's mouths like salamanders. I figured I'd go the next step. I slipped my hand under her blouse. I figured she'd let me. But she grabbed my wrist and said, putting on a southern accent, "Just cause I'm a poor little black girl don't mean you can fuck with me."

I pulled my hand back, blushing. I felt like someone who was caught with his hand in the cookie jar. "I'm sorry," I said. "I didn't mean to take advantage."

Then she calmly unbuttoned her blouse and said, "I want you to take advantage."

I was on a springboard bouncing up and down for joy, twenty feet over an imaginary swimming pool. I tried to un-buckle her bra. She helped me. I grabbed her breasts. They were firm and round; I had to stretch my fingers to cover them; it was like palming a basketball. I was dribbling under the backboard, hoping to dunk. She reached her hand down and opened my pants. She yanked on my dick. I moaned, "Pull it harder."

She said, "I love your pink cock." She was staring at it. When she went down to kiss it my jism shot right into her eye.

"Ow," she yelled.

I rushed into the bathroom and grabbed a washcloth. I came back and handed it to her. She wiped her eye. I took off my underwear and wiped off the mess on my stomach.

I remembered a line I had heard in some movie. I said, "Was it good for you too?"

She didn't answer. Maybe she wanted to come too? I hadn't thought of that before. I thought it was slutty of a girl to want to come. Girls shouldn't have orgasms. She should be happy just to fool around.

We went into town to see James Bond. I figured I owed her something. Even if it was her second time. I bought her popcorn and bonbons. She sat there very dignified through the movie. Like she hadn't done anything wrong. She had a lot more class than Pussy Galore and the other girls in "Goldfinger." I felt bad for her that she was black. Why'd she have to be at such a disadvantage? It was like my being a Jew. But that was no problem in Great Neck.

I rushed her out of the movie when it ended so that no one would see us and walked her down to the train station. I hated myself for being embarrassed by her. There was a train to Manhattan in twenty minutes. I got her coffee and a donut in the coffee shop, then put her on the train. I couldn't look her in the eye. I had seen her breasts. We shook hands. She said, "I had a good time."

"Me too," I said.

"I'll call you."

That night I bragged to Robert while we smoked cigars on the eighteenth century couch over the Aubusson rug in front of the fireplace. I felt like I was in an all men's club, looking over at the bronze sconces and the wrought iron chandelier.

"You didn't wear a bag?" he said.

"She wanted me to put it in bareback," I lied.

"You're full of it."

"I'm telling the truth."

Robert cracked up, "I was listening outside the door."

"What did you hear?"

"Pull my dick harder."

"At least I got a hand job." I blushed and shrugged my shoulders.

The phone rang in the kitchen and Robert went in there to pick it up. I heard him giggling and chatting. After a few minutes he yelled to me, "It's Cindy."

So soon? I couldn't handle two women. Dawn was enough. And Cindy was black. There were no inter-racial couples in Great Neck. I yelled back, "Tell her I'm not home."

Robert didn't hang up. He kept talking on and on. I heard Robert giggling. I waited a few minutes more and then sneaked over to the kitchen. "Why won't you go out with me?" Robert said. He noticed me, got flustered and hung up.

"You don't have to sneak around behind my back," I said. "You can go out with her if you want."

"I don't date Negroes," he said.

"Bigot!" I was prejudiced too. But only a little. And, at least, I was ashamed of myself. It's enough to know you're wrong. Changing it is just an afterthought.

The next day Swerbuck and I went for a walk in Great Neck Estates Park on Little Neck Bay. We walked down by the water near where the boats were moored. The park had a couple of tennis courts and a swimming pool.

"I went out with Cindy yesterday," I said.

"That's funny. I went out with Carol yesterday," Swerbuck said.

"I got laid twice," I said.

"Three times," Swerbuck said. "Come on, tell the truth."

"I didn't even get laid," I said.

"I didn't even call Carol. I never got her number."

"I only felt her tits," I said.

"Really," Swerbuck said.

"Truth."

"What did they feel like?"

"Wet," I said. "I came all over myself." We both cracked up laughing. We picked up pebbles and skipped them across the bay. Girls were good to take out and talk about. But they didn't compare to a good friendship. Some of the pebbles knocked into boats that were moored there. I could have hung out with Swerbuck for the next hundred years. Then he turned to me and said, "You shouldn't cheat on Dawn."

It was his fault. He was the one who got me involved with Cindy by ordering her and Carol Cappuccinos at Figaro. He had a lot of nerve.

"You're right," I said. I decided if I cheated on Dawn again I wouldn't do it with him around. I didn't trust him. Some best friend. He was just looking for trouble.

Chapter 22

Stanley Aikens was a freckled, red-haired kid I knew from gym class. He was a lousy student like me. He wasn't as hoody as I was but he liked to hang out with hoods because no one else wanted to be seen with him. His parents were very rich and he lived in a huge English Tudor house in Kennilworth, which was an exclusive part of Great Neck where rich and famous people like Alan King lived.

One Saturday in December he invited me, Swerbuck and Mad Dog over to his house. He asked us to bring his friend Butch with us. Butch lived a few blocks from me. He was a buck-toothed, blond boy with bangs. He did great in school without even trying. I once overheard a teacher saying Butch was brilliant but lazy. I felt that way about myself too but no one had ever said I was brilliant, just lazy. And I didn't do great in school. There was a part of me that wanted to look down at myself. I don't know why I wanted to be hurt.

We all met at my house and my father drove us over to Stanley's. It was snowing pretty hard with that wet powder that you leave heel prints in. Globs of whiteness slapped across the windshield. The road was slippery and my father was skidding across it. We were all silent, scared of crashing. My father whistled old air force songs. Then he turned on opera on the radio. I hated opera. He whistled along to that too.

We pulled into a long driveway past a gate with bronze eagles on stone stanchions. The house looked like a miniature version of the Metropolitan Museum of Art. My father's breath floated out in little clouds as he told me to call when I wanted a lift home. He then skidded out of the driveway almost knocking into the gate. I imagined the bronze eagle flying off in fear of my father's driving.

We went into Stanley's house, blinded by the lights that bounced off the high ceilings of the living room, clicking our heels on the marble entrance hall. There were two suits of armor standing up in the foyer. There was a display of weapons behind glass cases. We could have been in the Middle Ages. Stanley's parents were out at some social affair. The plan was that we should all get seriously drunk. We went into a large den where there was a log fire burning beneath a huge stone chimney. There was a bar with stools around it that looked like it was part of a real Irish pub. A big stuffed swordfish hung above the bar. I planned to get drunk as a fish.

This would be a first for me. I never drank alcohol before. I took off my shoes and loosened my belt. Swerbuck suggested we start with screwdrivers.

"We don't have any orange juice," Stanley said.

"You got orange crush soda?" Swerbuck asked.

Stanley took out some cans of orange crush from a refrigerator behind the bar. He put ice cubes in tall glasses, poured three shot glasses of vodka in each and added some orange crush. "Screwdrivers," Stanley said, passing the drinks out.

Swerbuck toasted, "To Death." We all took a swig. It tasted like it shouldn't. I had never had a screwdriver before. I didn't think they were supposed to be made with soda. After a few more sips it didn't taste so bad. We each went through about three of these orange crush screwdrivers when Butch said, "Let's get a little more sophisticated. Rum and cokes?" We all yelled, "Here! Here!"

Stanley put out some new glasses and Butch poured about two ounces of rum into each one and some coca cola. Ice cubes clicked in the glasses. We each picked up a drink and Swerbuck toasted, "Here's to Cuba Libra!"

"To totalitarian agrarianism," Butch raised his glass. I raised my glass. I had no idea what he was saying.

Mad Dog drank his rum and coke and smacked his glass down on the counter and said, "I'll kill Castro."

The rum and coke sickened me worse than the orange crush and vodka. Every time I took a gulp I felt like throwing up. The room was beginning to feel like a boat in rough seas. My stomach kept falling down a hatch. We wandered out into the backyard to get some fresh air. I forgot to put on my shoes and the cold snow startled my socks. I tried to catch snow-flakes on my tongue. They tasted like rum.

Butch started dancing through the snow, singing through his buckteeth, "I have a mind of snow."

"I'm shooting Cubans," Mad Dog yelled. He pointed his finger and pretended his hand was a gun. "Rat-a-tat-tat-tat!"

Swerbuck held his side and keeled over. "You got me," he said and fell to the ground.

We were all so drunk we didn't realize that we were shivering, coatless, in the white rush of snow. Like little kids, we were having stupid fun when the back door opened and Stanley's parents barged in, all dressed up, standing like grim photographs in the crime scene light that poured out onto the snow. Stanley's father was wearing a tux and his freckles and red hair stuck out like a fire truck. His mother wore a black evening dress. I froze, not from cold, but from fear. The party was over. Stanley's father walked over to Stanley who was laughing, drunk in the snow, and picked him up by the scruff of his neck, dragging him into the house. He slapped him across the freckles. Stanley threw up. Mr. Aikens yelled at the rest of us, "Go home."

We stumbled back into the den and brushed off as best we could. I called my father and asked him to pick us up. I told the guys he was on his way.

"Your father can't drive to save his life," Mad Dog said.

Swerbuck called a cab.

"I'm going with Swerbuck," Mad Dog said.

"And me. That's a triumvirate," Butch said.

When the cab came Swerbuck, Mad Dog and Butch got in while I fell to the ground in a pool of vomit. I think I fell asleep there. I woke up freezing as my father slid into the driveway. He got out of the car, took one look at me and kicked me in the ass. He shoved me into the back seat of the car.

"If you were in the air force, we would have court-martialed you," he said. He pulled out from Stanley's house. I heard a crunch as we skidded into the stanchion again.

"Yes, Captain," I said, and threw up on the floor in the back of the Lincoln.

When we got home, I was fast asleep. My father shook me awake and made me clean up the back seat of the car. He then followed me upstairs and shouted, "Next time you'll know better." He closed the door behind me and went into my brother's room. I heard a slapping sound. He was beating up Robert. Robert yelled, "Why?"

"Because you should have taught your brother," my father yelled.

"What?"

"To drink like a man."

That was so unfair. My brother had nothing to do with it. But I wasn't going to say anything and get my ass kicked more. I heard him coming back towards my room and hid under the bed crying. I felt closed in, trapped. I threw up again. My father came into my room. He couldn't get at me under the bed.

"Coward," my father said. "Come out." He tried to move the bed around. I stayed under it and moved around with it. When he saw he couldn't get his hands on me, he went back into Robert's room and beat him up some more.

"I didn't do anything. Hit Joshua, not me," Robert yelled.

"Don't tell me who to hit," Hy screamed and smacked Robert again. Then he left Robert's room and headed back to me again. Sylvia ran into the room just in the knick of time, yelling "What are you doing?"

As scared as I was of my father, he was more frightened of my mother. She was five inches taller them him and ruled him like a queen. She was better looking and he was always worried she'd leave him. They loved each other when they weren't fighting. We all loved each other. We were a loving family. We were just always at odds.

"They were bad," my father said.

"I didn't do anything," Robert yelled.

"You're an idiot," Sylvia shouted and slapped Hy across the face. I gagged under the bed.

"You're setting a bad example for the kids," Hy moaned. "You shouldn't hit me." Hy went back to his room.

"Drop dead," my mother shouted.

She went into my brother's room and comforted him, "Your father's a jerk." She kissed him. I got jealous. I crawled out from under my bed. I went into the bathroom and took a shower. I couldn't tell that I was crying with the hot water dripping down my face.

Chapter 23

My family always went to Mt. Snow for Christmas. I decided to ask my parents if I could invite Dawn. I went up to their study. My father said, "No way. You're not married."

"Don't be so prudish. This is the sixties," my mother said.

My parents kicked me out of the room and discussed it further. I don't know what my mother said to my father but about five minutes later they invited me back in and told me it was OK to invite Dawn.

Dawn had no trouble getting permission from her father. He was very progressive; he was almost a communist.

My brother decided to join us. "I'm doing you a favor," he said. All my friends wanted me to visit them but I figured I'd give you and mom and dad a break."

Mt. Snow was anything but rustic. It was the Coney Island of Vermont. Rock and roll blasted through the snowflakes and ice-skaters bounced around a rectangular rink like bumper cars. There were nine double chairlifts crisscrossing over the slopes like cars on a Ferris wheel. My family and I spent every Christmas there since I was five years old. There was an outdoor heated swimming pool in front of the lodge, surrounded by snow banks and picnic benches. Smoke rose from the pool; skiers clomped by in their boots like the noisemakers they give out as party favors.

I had been skiing since I was five years old. I was damned good for a city boy. I had even been to summer ski racing camp just a few years ago. But I was so crazy about Dawn, with the snowflakes falling around her like a white fur hat, that I didn't mind spending my time on the beginner slopes with her. This was unusual for me. I usually only thought about getting as many runs in as I could on the expert slopes.

On the chairlift I put my arm around her. I kissed snow from her little, runny nose and said, "You're my snowflake girl."

"I hope I don't melt," she said. "I want to be yours forever."

"Then why'd you join the Suicide Club?"

"Why'd you?"

"I may drop out," I said.

"Look, it was Swerbuck's idea anyhow. He's in love with death."

"Are you in love with him?" I said. I didn't know where that came from. I never really thought too seriously about her liking Swerbuck before. I had some suspicions at the Museum but they were only suspicions. I didn't take them seriously.

"Drop dead," Dawn said and turned away from me.

"I just don't want to lose you," I said. I kissed her. We stared into each other's eyes. I thought I saw something familiar there. I thought I saw myself.

Our feet slammed onto the ramp and tangled beneath us. We fell down into the snow laughing, getting all mixed up in each other. The attendant pushed the emergency stop button and the lift came to a halt. Dawn was squiggling helplessly on her back like a turtle on its shell. The attendant straightened her skis out and helped her get to her feet. I pressed my poles to the side and pushed myself up. When we were safely off to the side the attendant walked back to his hut and started the lift again. I felt ridiculous. I had never fallen off a chairlift before. I was an expert. I was in love.

We always stayed at the Andiron's Ski Lodge when we went to Mt. Snow. It was a series of five buildings all spread out like a small Indian Village. That night we dined by candlelight in the large dining room in the administration building. There was a moose head over the fireplace. A pair of snowshoes and antique wooden skis were hung on a stone wall.

"Does Dawn's father know that she's sharing a room with you?" my father asked me. Dawn looked down at her fruit cup. I glared at my father.

"Shut up," my mother said, kicking him under the table.

I felt like hitting him with a grape.

"Dad. It's a new generation. They don't have the same values we did," my brother said, puffing on his pipe, acting like a professor. I wanted to kiss him for sticking up for me. Even if he was ridiculously pompous.

"My father let's me do what I feel's best," Dawn interrupted. "I'm a woman."

"Is my son a man?" Hy asked.

"Drop dead," I said.

My father got out of his chair, raising his hand to smack me. I ducked as my mother slapped him and pulled him back down into his seat.

"Let's go Dawn," I said and took her by the hand.

"Thank you for the meal Mr. and Mrs. Kaplan," Dawn said, politely.

"Joshua owes me an apology for being fresh," my father said to my mother. I didn't feel I owed him anything. "I'm sorry," I said and walked out with Dawn before the main course came. My mother yelled at my father, "You idiot. They didn't even eat yet."

Dawn and I went outside to the building that contained our unit. We walked through snowdrifts on an open-air walkway. The snow came down in pails of yellow underneath the lights.

"My dad's an asshole," I said.

"If you think that, why'd you apologize?" Dawn asked.

"Why'd you thank him for dinner?"

I took my key out and opened the door to our room. I lifted Dawn up and carried her across the threshold. I had never spent the night with her before. I'd never spent the night with any girl. She smelled warm like a fur blanket.

I laid her down on the bed and kissed her. I said, "My father should show me some respect."

"You should respect yourself," Dawn said and pushed me away from her. She went to her suitcase and took out a suicide club banana. She wrapped it around her forehead.

"What's that for?"

"I want to die in your arms," Dawn said. She then jumped back onto the bed next to me and we started kissing. We tore each other's clothes off. We threw socks, pants and underwear up in the air and watched them fall to the floor like snow. I touched her between her legs. It was all wet. I hoped she didn't pee in her pants. I was hard as a rock. I took out a bag I had stolen from my brother. I couldn't rip the wrapper open. I did it with my teeth. I pulled the bag out and tried to roll it over my dick. It kept sticking to my skin. I wasn't lubricated. Dawn grabbed the base of my dick and pulled the bag down over it. My penis had a sad face, trapped inside. It was like a fish you buy in a pet store in a plastic bag.

"Where'd you learn to do that," I asked.

I wondered how much experience she had. I pushed into her pelvic bone a few times before I found her vagina. Then I heard a sloshing noise. I felt like I was inside a wet underground cave. My parents had taken me to Howe Caverns when I was twelve. I hoped there weren't stalactites in there. She moaned like she had sat on a stake. I ground my teeth, breathing hard. I plunged in and out, pulling my stomach in so that my dick pushed out. I was an airplane flying through clouds. No visibility. Then lightening hit me. My dick vibrated like a crash landing. I tingled like an electric fire. I came. I'd never felt anything so good. A flock of birds took off from an African tree.

I was no longer a virgin. I didn't have to lie about it anymore. Dawn took off her suicide club bandana and scooped up some blood from her vagina with it. She showed me her red triumph. She was a woman. I was a man.

I wanted to thank her for being Dawn.

Someone was banging on our door.

"Who is it?" I shouted.

"Your father."

What the hell was he doing here? I didn't want him catching us. Dawn hid in the bathroom. I pulled my pants on over my sticky condom. I hoped he wasn't going to pick on me again. I opened the door and there he was, looking all embarrassed, apologetic, standing in the snow, holding Dawn's and my dinners in his palms like a waiter.

"You forgot these," he said.

I wanted to tell him I loved him. I did and I didn't.

We spent seven days at Mt. Snow. By the end of the week Dawn was an advanced novice and I was able to take her to the top of the mountain and lead her down some of the intermediate slopes. We sometimes skied with my brother and father. My mother stayed inside the lodge and read Proust's *Remembrance of Things Past*. My father no longer made any wise cracks about my sharing a room with Dawn. I guess my mother had really balled him out. I spent every night with

Dawn. The beauty of the wintry mountains and the way her body sprung against me like a mountain cat exhilarated me. She tasted of winter, pine trees, maple syrup and snow. Her naked skin confused me. I didn't want to know who was inside it. I wanted to invent her. I wanted her to be me. I was happy. I wanted to live forever.

A week after we got back from Mt. Snow Dawn came over to my house and gave me a painting she had done celebrating our trip. We were wandering through a blizzard in our ski parkers, wearing snowshoes. It was as cold as a scene out of Doctor Zhivago. Snow, mist and light were confused with each other like a manic episode. I heard Russian music, rising from the brushstrokes. I leaned the picture up against the headboard on my bed. It was steamy with life like a hearty peasant's soup. It was nothing like Dawn's usual morose dark paintings.

She told me the painting was a present for the good time she had in Vermont.

"I love it," I said.

"It scares me."

"Why?"

"It's not me. It's too light."

"So why'd you paint it?"

"It just came out that way."

"It's inspired," I said.

"My mother died when I was fourteen."

"You told me."

"My father is very close to me."

"How come he let you go away with me?"

"He trusts me."

I wondered what he trusted. She screwed me every night. "I love the picture."

"Really?"

"You made me look better than I do in real life."

"You'll grow to look as good as the picture."

"How?"

"Life imitates art."

"I prefer life," I said, moved the painting off the bed and kissed her. She started undressing. Right in my parents home. I was scared. Dawn wasn't. She was very modern. She took off my clothes. I wasn't hard. She blew me. I didn't come in her mouth. I put on a bag and we screwed. I had to put my hand over her mouth she was moaning so much. After about fifteen minutes I came. She came too. I think. I didn't care. It would have been soft of me to worry about her orgasm. I was no pussy.

"We're supposed to be friends," Swerbuck said when Dawn and I met him at Squire's for a bite to eat. It was crowded with people coming out of the cold in heavy coats. Swerbuck was angry that we hadn't invited him to go to Mt. Snow with us.

"It has nothing to do with our friendship," I said.

He hung his head down, hurt. "I would have invited you guys," he said and sulked throughout the meal. He stuffed himself with pastrami, French fries, a knish, Cole slaw, potato salad and a Dr. Brown's black cherry soda. When the bill came, he said he forgot his wallet and stuck me with it. I didn't mind. I was rich and he was broke. I would have been insulted if he offered to pay. I didn't want to be trading places with him.

He ordered a milkshake to go. We stepped outside into the cold night and John Denby came out of nowhere, walked up to me, stared me straight in the face, pointed two fingers at me and said, "You got two strikes against you."

"Fuck off," I said.

"Stay away from Dawn," he said.

"Who are you?" Dawn asked.

"You're sick," I said to Denby.

"I'll show you who's sick," Denby said, slapped himself across the face twice and took off his parka to fight. As he got it half way down his back, Swerbuck jumped in front of me, threw his milkshake in Denby's face and kicked him in the balls. Denby collapsed to the ground in pain and yelled at me again, "You fouled me by the rules of the Marquise of Queensbury." I hadn't touched him. He was furious, foaming at the mouth. I could see why he'd been in and out of institutions. He started licking the sidewalk.

"That's three strikes against you," he screamed.

"Swerbuck kicked you. Not me."

"Thanks a lot," Swerbuck said.

"You think he doesn't know," I yelled at Swerbuck.

"Then why you telling him?" he said.

"I blame you," Denby shouted at me.

"Fuck you," I said. I turned to Swerbuck and said, "I could have taken care of Denby myself, you know."

"This was a Christmas present for you," Swerbuck said, then turned around and kicked him in the kneecap. Denby shrieked in pain. Some adults who were coming out of Squire's yelled at Swerbuck, "Cut it out." They asked Denby if he was all right. As we walked away Denby yelled, "You're dead Joshua."

Rock and roll music blasted through the gymnasium. I rocked to *Street Fighting Man*. I saw myself as a hood, knife-fighting in the South Bronx. I grooved to *My Boyfriend's Back*. I was sure it was written about me. When *You Belong to Me* came on, I danced slowly, cheek-to-cheek, with Dawn and became lost in the perfume that rose from her neck and circled her long black braid. I almost cried listening to the lyrics, "See the pyramids across the Nile / Watch the sunrise from a tropic isle, / Just remember all the while, you belong to me."

I never attended any of the dances at East Meadow. I wasn't a bad dancer but I didn't have a girlfriend and most of the dances ended up in rumbles. I didn't want to rumble. It was too much like war. I was a loner. If I was going to fight it was for personal reasons. But Great Neck dances were not about fighting. This was a polite, well-groomed affair. We had to wear jackets and ties. The girls floated around like balloons in giant dresses, swirling through yards of fabric. Or they were cotton candy rising up into their own pink sugar. I had grown a couple of inches in the last few months and my sports jacket didn't fit me. My hands looked stupid hanging out of my sleeves. Dawn was dressed in a navy blue shoulderless, ruffled dress. She was beaming in her conception of her own beauty like a beacon in a fog at sea. I didn't like the way she looked. Girls shouldn't dress up. They were so much prettier in jeans and T-shirts.

Mad Dog was dancing with a great looking blond; a cheerleader, Nancy Guern. I couldn't imagine how he got her to go out with him. He was all dressed up. He had bathed and got a neat haircut. He almost looked collegiate. I overheard him boasting to her, "My dad's rich. He's a big dentist."

"Do you plan to be a dentist like your dad?" Nancy asked.

"I'm going to go into his practice. I believe in teeth." He smiled.

"I never realized what a sweet guy you were," Nancy said and batted her eyelashes at him.

"I do what I can," he said and gave her a sincere look.

Swerbuck was sitting alone on a chair near a table set out with plates of cookies. No one was talking to him. I felt bad for him. It was terrible to go to a dance without a date. Asking someone to dance was scary. When you're in your teens getting rejected can last a lifetime.

"He looks lonely," Dawn said.

"He shouldn't have come without a date," I said.

The stereo was blasting *I Can't Get No Satisfaction* by the Stones. Everyone got onto the dance floor and started dancing. Dawn had this great way of dancing off beat to the music. I let her lead. I tried to follow her.

Swerbuck got caught up in the song and started dancing in his seat. The chair was shaking. It looked like it might break.

"I don't need a partner," he yelled, jumping up, knocking his chair over and dancing all by himself. I had seen him dance before in his apartment. He turned into a broken triangle, all angles, knocking against himself in wild geometric moves. He was coming apart at the seams; pieces of him were splintering off.

A crowd formed around him, laughing at his weird dancing.

"Look at the drunken chicken," a hood from shop class said.

"His legs don't belong to his body," a varsity football player said. He mimicked him, jerking his limbs around like gum-balls falling out of a machine.

Swerbuck didn't pay any attention. He was lost in the music. Pretty soon almost everyone was mimicking him, making fun of him. I wanted to sneak out and crawl into a hole for him. But he just kept dancing faster and harder. I hoped he'd dance so fast that he'd spin off into outer space away from the creeps who were laughing at him.

Dawn kept looking over at him.

"He needs help," she said. I thought she meant that he needed to see a shrink. But she broke away from me and went over to Swerbuck. She started dancing with him. She imitated his spasmodic steps. When she did them they looked normal, even cool. She choreographed his awkwardness, turning it into gracefulness.

"We're doing the latest French dance," she yelled to the crowd, making everyone feel stupid that they didn't know the steps.

"It's the Rimbaud," Swerbuck yelled.

Everybody started imitating them, doing the "Rimbaud." A chant went up, "We're doing the Rimbaud." A red head from algebra class tripped on the floor trying to jerk her leg like him. Her boyfriend picked her up.

"This dance is tough," he said.

She started dancing again.

Swerbuck became the Fred Astaire of the gymnasium. He had invented a new dance, "the Rimbaud."

"You're beautiful," Swerbuck said to Dawn.

"You are too," Dawn said.

I felt awkward dancing next to them by myself. I was the odd man out.

Swerbuck looked around him at everyone doing the "Rimbaud" and said to Dawn, "I'm a pretty good dancer."

Dawn didn't say anything. She just kept dancing.

Chapter 24

The recreation room in my basement wasn't used much. It was sparse. There was a television set, some barbells, a few chairs and a couple of benches.

Swerbuck took a rolled joint out of his pocket, lit it, inhaled deeply and then passed it on to me. I imitated him, inhaling deeply. This was my first time. The smoke hurt my lungs; it tasted like rubber and it burned going down. I watched the rolling paper glowing bright red, squiggling like a lost idea. I held the smoke in my lungs like I was filling a basketball with air. Then when I couldn't hold it in anymore I spit the smoke out, coughing. Swerbuck applauded, "That's holding it down deep."

"You high?" Mad Dog asked.

"I don't feel anything," I said and passed the joint to him. He rifled five or six inhales and passed the joint back to Swerbuck.

Swerbuck inhaled fiercely, gargling the smoke in his mouth, swallowing it into his lungs and then spitting it back into the room, saying "I'm in a straight jacket in a rubber room. My mouth is cotton and my lips are candy. I'm the amazing, psychedelic Swerbuck."

He passed the joint to me. This time my lungs really burned when I inhaled. But I held the smoke down to show I wasn't chicken. I blew it out and passed the joint to Mad Dog.

He looked proud about the way he took short blasts. Like he was an expert or something. He glanced around the room three times, made a crazy look with his eyes and then grabbed Swerbuck by the neck, saying "I'm a thriller killer." Swerbuck smiled at first but Mad Dog wouldn't let go. He was strangling him. Swerbuck ripped Mad Dog's hands from him, "You want to die?"

Mad Dog stepped back scared, looked down at his own sneakers, and passed Swerbuck the joint.

Swerbuck sucked the whole joint in with his big lips. He rolled another one.

"Life is just a distortion of death," Swerbuck said, passing the joint to me. I took a deep drag, held it down and passed the joint back.

"I like pot," I said, and giggled.

"It's as good as suicide," Swerbuck said, taking two big drags and passing it back to me.

"Huh?" I dropped some of the ash off into an ashtray and took another toke.

"It puts you in touch with the numbness," Swerbuck said. "You know who understood numbness? Hemingway. He killed himself."

"He killed lions and tigers and bears," Mad Dog laughed. He chanted, "Lions and tigers and bears" like he was the Cowardly Lion from Oz.

I finished the joint.

Swerbuck grabbed a dirty towel from the weight lifting bench and used it as a cape, swirling it around the room. I pretended I was a bull and charged at him. As I came at him he stepped to the side and let me pass. He was real smooth.

Mad Dog sat down on the floor and fell asleep.

"Bullfighters are beautiful. If I were a woman I'd fuck one," he said.

"That's disgusting."

"I want to fight a whole locomotive," he said.

"You're going to kill yourself one day."

"Bull," Swerbuck said, giggling. Then he added, "No train's gonna get me. It's too messy. I'd rather let the horns of a bull lift me into the kingdom of heaven." He lit a fat joint and passed it to me.

I pretended I was a bull again and charged at Swerbuck with the joint hanging out of my mouth. This time he didn't get out of the way and I gored him. He fell to the floor. The joint fell out of my mouth onto him. He smiled as it burned through his shirt. He didn't care. He picked it off his shirt and put it between his lips while he was still lying down. He put out the sparks on his shirt with his fingertips. It must have hurt but he pretended it didn't.

Swerbuck jumped back to his feet and said, "I changed my mind. I don't want to die fighting a bull."

"Then how?" I said, taking the joint from Swerbuck and inhaling.

"I think I want to die in the mountains where the air is clean. I can fly," he said.

"I'm dying with the bulls," I said. But I had no intention of dying. I was never down with that suicide stuff. I liked to hurt myself to get some attention. That was about it. When you were dead attention didn't do you any good. You had to be a schmuck or not thinking too clearly to kill yourself. I wanted to feel hurt. You can't hurt when you're unconscious.

"I'm the bullfighter," Swerbuck said.

"Make up your mind."

"I'll die in the mountains."

Swerbuck took the roach, stuffed it in his mouth, and swallowed it. I thought that was the funniest thing, eating the ashes and all.

I started getting hungry. My stomach was aching. Like it was turned inside out with a giant hole in it.

"Anyone want munchies," I asked.

"Yes," Swerbuck said.

"Don't forget me," Mad Dog said, waking up on the floor.

"I'm the amazing munchie," Swerbuck said, blowing out smoke.

I could hardly climb the stairs to the kitchen. I had the giggles. When I got there I didn't remember where anything was. I looked all over for potato chips, pretzels, ring dings, candies. After what seemed like an hour all I found was coca cola and donuts. They looked so good I felt like a man in the desert who found an oasis of soda pop. I opened two large bottles of coke and a box of donuts. I forgot that I was supposed to bring them downstairs and I drank and ate them all. I had sixteen donuts. They were delicious. The coca cola was a bubbling waterfall in my mouth. I choked a few times in my haste. When I finished my snack I went back downstairs, empty-handed.

"Where are our munchies?" Swerbuck said.

"I couldn't find any snacks," I said.

"What's that sugar powder on your lip?" Swerbuck pointed. I licked it off.

"I'm gonna kill you," Mad Dog said. His voice came from a long way off. I felt like I had disappeared into a garbage can and was rolling down a hill like I had done at Camp Birchwood when I was twelve. I wanted to be the Garbage Can Kid again. So what if I had eaten all the snacks. I didn't mean anything by it. I was high. The pot was like a wet suit I was wearing. I jumped down into the past. The past that never was. And found it as beautiful as moonlight on a Catskill Lake. And realized that I could make grass grow on gravel if I believed. There were lilies in the imagination just short of madness. I picked butterflies from a joint.

Chapter 25

It was nine thirty at night and my mother had just come back from a meeting with Miss McDermott at parent teacher night at the high school. She took me into her study and said,

"Your teacher is an idiot. She told me that you're not going anywhere in life unless you improve your penmanship. I asked her, 'Have you read any of his essays?' 'I can't read his penmanship,' she said. I spent a fortune moving us here for the education system and all she cares about is your penmanship. I tried to make her understand, 'It's the contents that count.' But she said, 'Not in my class.'"

"I told you McDermott's an idiot," I said. "What can I do?"

"I hate to say it. Write neater."

"Mother, you just said its contents that counts."

"Not in her class." My mother shrugged her shoulders, as if to say, what can I do?

I felt betrayed. My mother was a turncoat. She said one thing and did another. Even if I was a fuck up, I was pure. I was a diamond.

My father was listening outside the door and came in. "Damn straight it's not the contents that counts. You better get used to the real world son. It's no cake walk."

"Who asked your dumb opinion?" my mother barked at him.

"My dumb opinion? I'm the one with a college educa-tion," my father reminded her. He had a B.A. from Columbia University in business. He always held this up to my mother who only had a high school diploma. She had been studying to be an actress. When World War II came along she married my dad who left her pregnant while he went overseas to fight the war. He didn't get to see my brother until he was one year old. He always resented Robert's being born while he was overseas.

"Your degree is just a piece of paper," my mother said.

"A piece of paper you wish you had," my father said.

They were always fighting. I think they loved each other like boxers who pummel each other for fifteen rounds and then hug and kiss at the end. I hated their fighting and sneaked out of the room to get away from them. As I left I heard my mother say, "I read more books than you." My mother read all day. She was writing a novel. I was proud of that. And my father shouted, "Oh, yeah. You never read Chaucer."

My father had a regular doubles game over at the Great Neck Tennis Courts. One Sunday none of the other guys could make it and my father asked me to join him. I hadn't played in sev-eral months. In the warm up I sprayed the balls all over the place. My father called me to the net and said, "It's rude to hit wildly in the warm up."

I got really angry and couldn't concentrate. I served first. It took me seven tries to get a first serve in. He slammed it back down the line for a winner. The next serve I angled wide to his backhand side and the best he could do was lob the ball down the center of the court. It fell short and I ran up to it to put it away with an overhead. I bashed the ball with everything I had. It went right into the bottom of the net.

"Take a little pace off the ball," my father shouted.

Fuck him. Fuck him. Fuck him. I hit a tremendous serve straight down the centerline on the deuce court.

"Ace," I gloated. The bastard didn't even say nice shot. He had no manners. He really pissed me off. I double faulted.

It was my father's serve. We switched sides of the court. He had the softest serve known to man. It was like a woman's. And that was the first serve. The second barely made it over the net. I think he purposely hit his softest serves to me so that I'd get angry and hit long. I should have played the percentages and hit them in the center of the court. Instead I got so excited that I sprayed them all over the place. He was like a tennis judo master who was using my own strength against me. I was so inconsistent we hardly had a rally. We played for an hour and I lost 6-0, 6-2. I sucked. We shook hands at the net and trying to be a gentleman I said, "I'm sorry I didn't play better."

"What do you expect? You don't practice," he said.

"I'm busy in school," I said.

"From your grades you don't practice too much there either," he said.

We were still standing at the net when some other people came onto the court. My father patted me on the back as we walked off, saying, "I know what you're feeling. I was young once too. But your feelings don't matter. The world's going to measure you by how you perform. You have to do things according to Hoyle. You have all the cards in your hands."

His simple-minded lecture made me feel like he cared. I forgave him his old-fashioned views and know-it-all attitude. I looked at his squat build, his sandy thinning hair and his wrinkled forehead. There was something historic about him. Like

World War II. Like the Statue of the Unknown Soldier. He had survived. You could have put his face on the hundred-dollar bill. Or Mount Rushmore.

Dawn, Swerbuck and I met at Squire's Deli to celebrate our third quarter report cards. March still bashed its horns around the street corners. Dirty snow littered the curbs.

It was a little chilly in the restaurant. The heat was down. We didn't take off our coats. We all had matzo ball soup to keep us warm.

"What you guys get in English?" Swerbuck asked.

"A," Dawn said.

"D," I chimed in, embarrassed.

"Beat you both," Swerbuck said. "I got an F."

"You know more about poetry than the damn teacher," I said.

"Do you think she could really understand me?" Swerbuck said. "She's an idiot."

"I don't think you could understand you," I said.

"I am the king of unknowableness," Swerbuck said, smiling. He stood up and bowed as we applauded. "Let's make up a poem. I'll do the first line."

We all agreed.

"The house disappeared into its own attic," Swerbuck said. "Dawn's turn."

Dawn struggled. She couldn't think of anything. Then she said, "I didn't like what I saw upstairs."

"Great," Swerbuck said.

I felt tense. I didn't want to seem stupid to Dawn. I struggled to come up with something clever. Then I let go, "I danced with the unhappiness of the roof beams."

Swerbuck applauded me. "McDermott doesn't know squat. We're poetic geniuses," he said.

"What are we going to do about our grades?" I asked Swerbuck.

"I'm going to show them to my father," Dawn said.

"I mean Swerbuck and me."

"Do what we always do. Threaten suicide," Swerbuck said.

"Not again," I said.

"It always works."

He was right. When my mother caught me cutting school and I told her I felt suicidal she sent me to Rosenquest. Swerbuck got a raise in his allowance after he pretended he slit his wrists when his dad caught him stealing the radio in the baby carriage with Brian.

"We'll write suicide notes," I said.

"I'm in," Swerbuck said.

"Even if I got bad grades I wouldn't do that," Dawn said. Her father didn't believe in the school system. He didn't really care about her report cards. She wasn't in a military family like mine or a fucked-up, family like Swerbuck's.

"We're a team," Swerbuck said.

"All for one and one for all," Dawn said.

We put our fists out on top of each other.

"All for one and *death* for all," Swerbuck said. I didn't know if he thought it was cool to talk about death or if he was in love with it. Maybe he wanted to die so that he'd see his mother in heaven. Or to get away from his father. Or just because he had some sort of death gene. Was suicide inherited? Who knows why people did or didn't do the things they did. Explanations were a lot of crap. Things just happened. Reasons were copouts, for fools. Swerbuck and Dawn giggled.

Mad Dog showed up at Squire's. He was all bundled up in a heavy parka with a ski hat. He looked like a cute leprechaun. But he had the swagger of a street kid from *Our Gang*.

Dawn tapped her fingers on the table for a few minutes. She hated the way Mad Dog was always trying to act tough. She didn't like being around him.

"Got to go," she said, stood up and put on a pink parka with fur trim on the hood. I told her I'd pay for her check. She gave me a kiss on the cheek and put on red mittens.

Mad Dog ordered some hot borscht. He lapped it like a puppy, sticking his head in the bowl, slurping and licking the red beats and sour cream. He chewed his potato knish with his mouth open. His manners stank. When we were ready to go I offered to pay for Swerbuck's check. Swerbuck told me he could pay for himself. He looked through his wallet. He had one dollar.

"If you insist," he said. I paid for him. I knew he was broke and I wanted to help him out. Mad Dog paid for himself. He was rich.

We walked out onto Middle Neck Road, made a left turn and passed the overpriced, charming, boutiques down to Allenwood Road. We made a left and headed down to Great Neck Park. It was about three acres of land laid out between stores and modest houses, a block away from the train station. There were a few benches and a little playground. It was empty because it was cold and late.

When we stepped inside the park, Mad Dog reached into the pockets of his ski parka and said, "Look what I got." He took three bottles of Robitussin cough syrup out of his pockets.

"I don't have a cough," I said as he handed me one.

"You idiot. The codeine gets you high."

East Meadow hadn't prepared me for life. No one there knew about drugs and the variety of way of getting high. I was unsophisticated about so many things. I felt like a jerk.

We sat on the cold green park benches under some tall trees. The playground was on the other side. The trees were old and much bigger than the trees in East Meadow where the whole community had been bulldozed and all the trees were planted in the last ten years. We opened our bottles and started drinking the cough syrup. It had a rich, thick sweet taste that was sickening. I felt like a dead mouse was caught in my stomach lining. I had to force myself to get it all down.

"If you drink Robitussin before you get a cough you'll never get sick," Swerbuck said. He finished his bottle and threw it into the garbage can.

"Basket," he said.

He started climbing a big tree. He stood up on a low branch and faked a couple of coughs. "Hey, the Robitussin doesn't work," he shouted down, laughing.

"I hate the taste of Robitussin. Can't we just get codeine pills?" I said.

"Do I look like a pharmacist?" Mad Dog said and took another swig of the Robitussin.

Swerbuck kept shimmying higher up the tree. Every time he reached a branch he'd swing from it and yell, "Me, Tarzan."

I didn't want to see him splattered on the ground. I'd get in deep trouble just for being there if he died.

"Climb down," I yelled.

"I'm gonna jump," Swerbuck said, and burped. I could almost see a bubble of Robitussin floating out of his lips.

Mad Dog covered his eyes.

"Don't be a schmuck," I shouted.

Swerbuck kept climbing higher. He reached the top of the tree. He must have been eighty feet above the ground. I could hardly look up there without getting dizzy. He was swinging back and forth on a branch like he didn't have a care in the world. He looked like he was swinging from moonbeams. He was the acrobat of lunar light. Then he stopped swinging and wedged his foot in the cradle of a branch.

"My foot's stuck," he yelled. "Help me out."

"You want to act like an asshole, help yourself," I yelled. But I didn't want to see him fall and get squashed like an inkblot.

Mad Dog took his hands off his eyes and yelled, "Help!"

He covered his eyes again.

"Call the Fire Department," Swerbuck yelled.

"Wait here," I said to Mad Dog and walked out of the park to a phone booth on Station Road. I found a dime and put it in. The connection wasn't very good. The fireman on the line said, "You have a cat in a tree?"

"A boy," I said.

"What's he doing up there?"

"Ask him," I said. I was frustrated by Swerbuck's foolishness and the trouble he was getting us into.

I walked back to the park. In a few minutes I heard sirens blaring; two huge fire trucks and an ambulance pulled up at the park. A pack of about ten firemen rushed over to Mad Dog and me. It was like a scene from the Keystone cops, with firemen running all over the place. I was high on Robitussin and the firemen seemed plastic toys. They asked me where the boy was stuck. I pointed to the tree. They shined a light on him. He was shaking. It looked like he was freezing up there. A big Irishman in a black rain slicker spoke into a megaphone, "You alright son?"

"My leg's real bad," Swerbuck said. He sounded like he was in pain.

"Hold tight," the Irishman said. He went back to the fire truck and then drove it right over the curb up into the park. That was the coolest thing I'd ever seen. I'd never seen a fire truck riding around a park before. They raised one of the ladders all the way up and a young skinny fireman in a black rain slicker climbed up with a rope and a hoist. He had to separate two big branches to get Swerbuck's foot free. Then he threw the rope over a branch, put Swerbuck in the hoist and lowered Swerbuck to the ground. He was so efficient. It was beautiful.

I was worried about Swerbuck. I hoped his ankle wasn't broken. I wouldn't be able to hang out with him as much if he couldn't walk. Swerbuck hobbled over to Mad Dog and me and put his arms over our shoulders like someone who had been shot in the leg.

"We can take you to the hospital son," the Irishman said.

A paramedic from the ambulance said, "Get in. I'll drive you over."

"I'll be alright. My dad's a doctor," Swerbuck lied.

"Stay away from trees," another fireman said.

"You guys saved my life. I love you all," Swerbuck said.

"Nice kid," I heard one of the fireman saying to another. The skinny one who climbed the tree said, "I don't think it's broken." A short fireman slapped the big Irishman on the back and said, "You run a good unit."

They were all feeling pretty good about themselves, congratulating each other, when Swerbuck took a few steps away from us, turned around, laughed and yelled, "fuck you all" as he took off down the block.

I should have known the bastard was faking. What a joker! Mad Dog and I took off full speed after him. We were running for our lives. But after about a hundred yards we realized that the firemen weren't chasing us. That was strange. We slowed down. We couldn't figure it out.

"Those fat bastards are too slow to chase us," Swerbuck said.

"They probably don't think we're worth chasing; it was such a stupid stunt," I said.

"We're like lumber jacks, the way we climb trees," Mad Dog said.

"You didn't climb anything," Swerbuck said.

I looked back and saw the big Irishman talking on the walkie-talkie.

"I think they're calling ahead to cut us off," I said.

"Don't be ridiculous," Swerbuck said.

At the next corner two tough looking Irish cops in a police car rode right up onto the sidewalk. They swung their doors open and walked over to us. All the firemen and cops in Great Neck were Irish. They were huge with pug noses. They shined their lights on us and made us put our hands up in the air while they frisked us. They put us in handcuffs and threw us in the back seat of one of the cars. I hoped they weren't driving us back to the firemen to get a beating. But they drove us home instead, telling us that we were a disgrace to Great Neck. That we belonged in Levittown with the white trash. With them.

"Please don't tell my parents," Mad Dog cried.

"Shut up, punk," the fat cop said.

"I'm sorry sir," Mad Dog said. He was scared of cops. Firemen too. Almost everyone.

They dropped me off first. Swerbuck waved to me, smiling, as I got out of the car. Mad Dog was crying into his gloves. A young cop with a crew cut walked me up the slate path to the front door. It was one o'clock in the morning. My father came down to the door in his pajamas.

"Your son's a menace," the cop said.

"What did he do?" Hy asked.

"I'll let him tell you."

"I was in the air force," my father said.

"That's nice."

"We wore uniforms too. I flew a lot of missions over Italy."

"You should watch your son better."

As I walked in the door Hy smacked me across the face.

"What's that for?" I asked. Wanting to hit him back.

"What's that not for?"

"Don't you want to know what happened?"

"It happened."

"But what!"

"Your flunking report card. And now this! I'm not interested in your lies."

"One of these days!" I said, threatening. Damn. Somehow he must have gotten his hands on my report card before I had a chance to write a suicide note.

"One of these days, what?" my father said. His hands were clenched in fists. He had done some boxing in the air force. He bunked with Jerry LaStarza. He thought that made him a fighter. Even if LaStarza never so much as threw a punch at him. He looked like he was getting ready to hit me again.

I slinked up to my bedroom. I was scared to slam my door. I did it anyhow.

Later that night I wrote the suicide note I had planned to write for my bad grades. Now I had another reason to write it. This cop fiasco. The note would get me out of trouble. Suicide came in handy. It made life easier. My mother would be worried about me. I wrote on a brown paper bag like Abraham Lincoln did when he penned the Gettysburg address, "Nothing's working right for me. I keep failing. I should be dead." I kept it under my pillow. In the morning, after my father had left I put it on the floor outside my mother's bedroom.

A few hours later she knocked on my door and called me down for breakfast. As we sat there eating croissants and orange juice she showed me my suicide note.

"You better go back to see Dr. Rosenquest."

"I don't know if I'm ready," I said. "I'm sorry about acting so bad."

"If you keep pushing your father he's going to send you to military school."

"I'll think about Rosenquest," I told her.

I wasn't much of a skate boarder. I didn't even consider it a sport. It was more of a game. Skiing was a sport. I didn't mind wiping out on snow. But crashing on cement was stupid. You could really get hurt. Swerbuck, on the other hand, was a wild man on the skateboard.

Spinny Hill was the steepest hill in Great Neck. A lot of the better skateboarders in town went there to test their skills. There were shiny spots where knees were skinned on the pavement and dark spots where blood was spilled. The hill was so steep that cars usually chose to go around it. Swerbuck, Dawn and I met there with our skateboards.

Dawn was afraid of skateboarding. She would go about ten feet before jumping off her board. Her startled blue eyes looked larger when she rode on her skateboard with the wind in her face.

Swerbuck pushed off down the hill first. He went full-blast like he didn't care about crashing. About three quarters of the way down the hill he smashed like a bowl of squashed fruits. He rolled over three times, his skateboard landing on his stomach like a rotten banana. He really looked like he was hurt. Dawn and I skateboarded down to him. He was in a heap next to the curb.

"You alright?" Dawn asked.

"No. I'm alive," Swerbuck said.

"That's stupid," I said.

He got up and asked, "Did you write your suicide notes?'

"My mother wants to send me back to the shrink," I said.

Dawn said, "I told you I didn't need one."

"My dad said if I want to kill myself I'd be doing him a favor," Swerbuck laughed.

"You poor boy," Dawn said.

"We'll kill ourselves just to spite them," Swerbuck said.

"How are you going to spite your father? He wants you to kill yourself," I said.

"So we'll do it because life is meaningless," Swerbuck said.

I wanted to tell Swerbuck that he was an asshole. That life was meaningful.

"Do you really mean all this suicidal stuff?" I asked.

"No."

"I didn't think so."

"But the clock's ticking," Swerbuck said.

"What for?" I asked.

"1966. Our suicides."

I remembered that we had all made a pact to kill ourselves on December 31st, 1966.

"Fuck that," I said.

Swerbuck picked up his skateboard and started running up the hill yelling, "First one up the hill is President of the Suicide Club." Dawn started running up after Swerbuck. I was in no rush. I didn't want to be President of the Suicide

Club. Watching them run up ahead of me I felt like they had more in common with each other than with me. Swerbuck had taken a big lead and he started running backwards up the hill motioning to Dawn to follow him. She was laughing as she struggled to catch him. They looked like they liked each other a little too much. I was beginning to get pissed off. But I wasn't going to run up after them. I didn't want to be President of that stupid Suicide Club. I wondered if Swerbuck was just playing with me, like he did with the Abu Abu, the Clorox Bleach and the firemen.

Dawn got on her skateboard and headed down the hill very timidly. She jumped off after about ten feet and fell down. Landing on her rump, she looked like a little girl. I couldn't help but love her. She was as pretty as an Indian Princess in an animated Disney film. I ran over to her and helped her up while Swerbuck flew by us like an ambulance rushing to its own accident. By some miracle Swerbuck made it all the way to the bottom of the hill. He just missed crashing into a truck at the bottom that was barreling down East Shore Road.

The week in school passed like it wasn't there. It was amazing how fast the scotch tape of days could peel itself from the paper of memory. I felt no obligation to learn anything. I didn't know what class I was in. It could have been science, music or math. It wasn't like I was trying to fail. It was as if failure was my shadow and it was happening behind my back while I wasn't looking. It meant nothing to me.

On weekends I screwed around. Like the time I went up on Swerbuck's roof. It was on top of his six-story apartment building. Swerbuck danced around holding a towel, swirling it like a cape, capturing moonlight in the terry cloth. He handed me a half-empty bottle of scotch.

"Nectar of the Gods," he said.

I took a gulp and gagged. I had never tasted anything so awful. He grabbed the bottle back and chug-a-lugged the rest of it.

Swerbuck jumped up onto the two-foot wide, three-foot high wall that surrounded the roof.

"Follow me," he said.

I jumped up right behind him. I felt dizzy and was afraid to look down. We were eight stories up. I wasn't too good at heights. Swerbuck turned around and said, "You gotta pretend you're walking on the ground."

I remembered when I went horseback riding in the mountains at Lake Louise. The trail guide said that you were supposed to lean out over the cliff to push your horse in closer to the mountain. I shifted my weight out over the roof. I was scared hanging over the building but I wanted to push my feet to the inside. I didn't want to lose my footing. My knees were shaking. Swerbuck jumped from the ledge onto a ten-foot long two-inch wide wrought iron fence, which was in the middle of the wall. He walked across it like a tightrope walker in the circus. I pictured him with clown make-up on and an umbrella over his head with a crowd of giggling children applauding him.

"What are you trying to prove," I yelled at him.

"I'm immortal," he said and jumped up and down on the fence, did a *plie* and leaped down onto the rooftop.

I didn't want to be shown up. I tried to step onto the wrought iron fence. I was worried I would fall to the left down six stories onto the concrete. I was shaking back and forth.

"Hang onto me," Swerbuck said and held my hand. A strong breeze hit me and I wobbled more. I looked down at the ground and the world started spinning. I saw myself splattered on the cement below. My foot slipped over the fence and I panicked as I started falling off the roof. I saw my life ending on the sidewalk. A startled scream stuck in my throat like a dead bird. Swerbuck yanked me back onto the roof. We both fell to the floor. He was laughing. I felt like I had died.

"You almost made it," Swerbuck said.

"Made what?"

"The first suicide," Swerbuck laughed. He patted me on the back like that was something to be proud of.

The night after the rooftop fiasco I saw Dawn. I felt so much safer with her than I did with Swerbuck. We went into my bedroom to mess around. My parents were home. They didn't care. I was the only one of my friends who could close the door to his bedroom when he had a girl over the house. Why? That's not something I wanted to ask my parents. I didn't want to screw up a good thing.

I had stolen a scumbag from my father's drawer. I was embarrassed to buy them in a drug store. I didn't want the druggist staring at my crotch.

Dawn loved the Beatles and we played their album on my stereo. I was glad that I had taken the stereo back from Billy Yang. We were naked under the covers and Dawn sang in my ear "This Boy" while we were humping. It was so warm and sweaty under the covers that I felt like a thermometer whose glass bubble was bursting. I wanted to see if I could come real slowly. I thought of things I hated like baseball, school, and fraternities to keep from coming fast. It didn't work. My dick had a will of its own. After a few minutes I came. Right when I was thinking of Mickey Mantle.

"Don't tell me you came already," she said.

"I'm sorry. I'll finish you off with my finger," I said, pulled out, and started to finger her.

She grabbed my hand and said, "I don't need charity."

"I want to," I said and put my finger back up her. I then stuck my other fingers in, one at a time. I was amazed at how much she could stretch. I got my whole fist in there. That's where babies came from, I thought. I could see how they could fit. I started mumbling silly things to her, pretending I was a rapist, "I'm going to hurt you with my big dick." Then for some reason I started getting angry and said, "You little bitch." This excited her.

"I'm going to fuck you till you scream," I said. "And Swerbuck's going to fuck you."

I don't know why I said that. It was stupid. At that moment Dawn came in a burst of groans and moistness. She was glowing with sweat and happiness. I felt like she had cheated on me.

"Why'd you say Swerbuck's gonna fuck me?" Dawn asked.

"Did it excite you?" I asked, angry. I was jealous. "I was just being stupid."

"He's just a friend."

"Swerbuck's a prick. I was up on his roof and he made me walk across this little ledge six stories up," I said.

"That's exciting."

"Exciting? I could have died," I said. "If Swerbuck didn't grab my hand, I wouldn't be here now."

"You owe Swerbuck your life then."

"I almost owe him my death."

Dawn kissed me. I turned away sulking. She didn't seem to care that Swerbuck almost cost me my life up on his roof. Maybe they both wanted to see me dead. So they could run off with each other. No. They were just friends.

The last day of school fell on top of us like a burning log in a burst of summer green. McDermott was swaddled in veils of acne. She sat on her desk with her legs crossed and said, "I hope you all have a good summer and remember that discipline is law. Rules are rules."

The students had tears in their eyes from choking on her discipline all year. McDermott let out a sneeze. She pulled a handkerchief with a monogram of Minnie Mouse from her boxy pocketbook and blew her nose. I wondered if she had a niece who had given her the handkerchief. She certainly didn't have a child. She was too homely.

"I hope you all take away something from this class," McDermott said.

"What I want to take away from this class is myself," Swerbuck said.

McDermott picked up an eraser and threw it at him. The bell rang and we ran out of the room.

We lay in the backyard sunbathing on lounge chairs. Summer vacation had started and my brother was home from college. I showed my brother my report card. I had dropped it in the bathtub, rubbed out all the wet grades and wrote in new ones. I figured it was easier than writing a suicide note.

"It's a mess," Robert said.

"On purpose."

"Why?"

"I told mom my report card fell in a puddle. Then I changed my grades."

"She believed that?"

"Didn't she believe you when you did it?" I asked. I had once peeked into his room in East Meadow and saw him spilling a glass of water onto his report card and writing in new grades with a fountain pen.

"I never did anything like that," Robert said, offended. He handed me back my report, "*A* in trigonometry. Give me a break."

I put on some *Ban de Soleil* sun tan lotion. It was orange and very French. I lay back on my lounge chair. The heat felt good on my body. The sun said hello. I wished I were at the beach. I wanted to see girls in bikinis. Now that the school year was over I felt like it was a wonderful to be alive.

I had never had a summer job and I didn't plan to have one this summer either. I was going to hang out, mostly with my friend Swerbuck. A week or two after school ended we were at Squire's Delicatessen. Swerbuck had a bottle of vodka under the table in a brown bag. We both ordered orange juice and French fries. We drank half of the juice and Swerbuck filled the glasses up with vodka. He then toasted me.

"To Tropicana Orange Juice," he said. Then he took a handful of French fries and chewed them with his mouth wide open. I looked the other way.

"What did your dad say about your report card?" I asked him.

"The old bugger doesn't even know I got it yet. I may just show it to him to upset him," Swerbuck said.

"I forged my whole report card—straight A's. My parents think I'm a genius," I said.

"You are," he said. He then pulled some pills from his pocket and said, "Take these. They're good for you." He handed me two of them.

I was suspicious. I remembered getting sick with both Asmidor and Clorox. "What are they?"

"Ginseng," he said.

"I don't trust you."

"I'll show you I'm telling the truth," he said and took three of the pills and swallowed them.

I swallowed them.

When we walked out of Squire's about an hour later I didn't know whether I was walking forward, backwards or upside down. I was out of balance. Off kilter. I couldn't tell whether the walls of the buildings were sidewalks or the sidewalks were walls. I once felt that way skiing in an alpine storm in Utah when the light was so flat that I couldn't tell whether I was skiing downhill or up. Swerbuck put his hand in front of me and stopped me at a red light as a car shot by. "What does a red light mean?" I asked.

"It means go," he said. And I started walking across the street again. He had to drag me back before another car hit me.

"You got to watch out for cars," he said.

"What's a car?" I asked. It sounded familiar.

"Something that runs you over."

When we got back to Swerbuck's apartment, I said, "Gotta go pee pee."

"You better stay here tonight," Swerbuck said.

"Why?"

"You're stoned."

"I am not a stone. I am a rock."

He said he was calling my parents. I didn't know I had parents. I went to the bathroom and stood over the toilet bowl trying to figure out what to do. I heard Swerbuck speaking in the other room, "Don't worry Mrs. Kaplan. Yeah. He's fine. He felt tired and went to bed early."

I wondered who he was talking to and what he was talking about. I pissed in my pants. I looked in the mirror and yelled out to Swerbuck, "It's wet in here. Can I have some more Ginseng."

"It's not Ginseng. It's mescaline," Swerbuck said as he entered the bathroom. "You need to freshen up," he said and pushed me into the tub, fully clothed.

"Is mescaline a vitamin?" I asked.

"I don't see why you're so damned high. I had more than you did," he said. He turned on the shower.

I stood there under the spout crying. I felt ashamed of myself for being so high. I should be punished. "Am I bad?" I asked.

The water fell down on me like little parachutes over Germany. I didn't know if the water was hot but a lot of steam was rising up like anti-aircraft fire. I made up a poem. I said it out loud. Not for Swerbuck but just talking to the shower. I said, "My memories are dying. The showerhead has many holes in it. I am hot with meaning."

Next thing I knew Swerbuck stuck his hand in the shower, yelled 'ow,' and turned off the hot water.

"I am disappearing down the drain of bad intentions," I said.

Swerbuck turned the water on again. This time I think it was cold. I couldn't tell. I was disconnected from my body. I took off my clothes and sat on the side of the tub. I thought of Dawn. I wanted to touch her like I touched the water, to finger the print of her wave, to gargle with her voice. Swerbuck left me in the shower a few more minutes and helped me put on a big, blue bathrobe. He led me out into his room and gave me a bed.

"Go to sleep," he said.

The minute I closed my eyes I was lost in cartoon land. I saw comic faces disappearing and reappearing. I was a stick figure. Little pieces of me kept falling off. Pretty soon there was nothing left. I was gone. I thought I had died. I couldn't find myself. I was in a panic. I pinched myself and woke up. I was still alive. I let out a deep sigh of relief and fell back asleep.

During the night I heard a door slamming and Swerbuck's father shouting, "Ze can't just invites ze friends to sleeps here." Then I heard a smack.

"I can do whatever I want. I'm the amazing Swerbuck."

I heard another slap.

Swerbuck's younger brother Brian cried, "Why do I have to sleep on the couch?"

The next morning Swerbuck walked me back to my place. He had a black eye.

"Did your father do that?" I asked.

"Don't worry about it."

"I'm sorry."

"Hey, I'm the one who should be sorry. I slipped you the mescaline."

He was right. He owed me. When we got up to my room Swerbuck said,

"Hit me in the face."

"Why? You already have a black eye."

"I want some girl to feel sorry for me."

"With that ugly face? Don't worry. Any girl will feel sorry for you."

He pushed out his lips and said, "I got beautiful lips."

"Ubangi lips," I said.

"Come on, hit me. I fucked you over with that mescaline."

"I liked the mescaline," I lied. I didn't want him to know how he had scared me. How my body wasn't my own. How I had lost myself.

"Chicken."

"Say it again," I dared him.

"Cluck. Cluck. Chicken." He closed his eyes, readying himself for the punch.

James Dean would never take that insult. I turned like I was walking away from him, cocked my right hand and then sprang back and belted him in his good eye. Swerbuck fell back a few steps. He opened his eyes. They were tearing.

"Hey, not so hard," Swerbuck moaned.

"Make up your mind," I said.

"Hit me harder! You're a chicken!" he shouted.

This time I belted him so hard that he fell to the ground. When he got up you could see that he was going to have two black eyes. I helped him to his feet.

"Put some cold water on it so it doesn't swell."

"I want it to swell."

I sneaked Swerbuck out the garage door. I didn't want my mother to see his black eyes. When we got outside he hugged me and said, "You have no idea how much you helped me."

I was glad when Swerbuck left. I could think about Dawn. I opened my desk drawer and pulled out a razor. I laid it out like a sacrament on my papers. I went over to the door and made sure it was locked. I didn't want anyone interrupting me. I then opened my armoire and took out my suicide costume -- the T-shirt and bandanna Dawn had made for me. I put them on and sat down at my desk again. I picked up the razor blade and tried to carve Dawn's name into my arm. I was afraid to dig the blade in deeply. I was playing. I was not serious about hurting myself. I scratched the surface. It didn't bleed. I kept scratching it in the same place. After about thirty scratches a little blood rose to the surface. It was a slow way to carve initials but I was afraid to dig the razor in deeper. I felt like I was opening and closing around her. Like she was written in me like Allah was written in a Moslem. I didn't want to go nuts like Swerbuck and slice my wrists. I didn't need that all that melodrama. I smeared some of the blood from my arm onto my face. I went in the bathroom and looked in the mirror. I was an Apache Indian scalping myself. The blood looked cool. I went back into my room and tried to write a poem in blood. It was too messy.

Chapter 26

I don't know why Dawn decided to throw a party. I never understood why anyone threw a party. I thought people went to parties to find dates so that they could leave the party. Dawn didn't need a date. She had me.

Dawn's father was out of town.

About one hundred and fifty kids showed up. It was an open house. The *cul de sac* was covered with teenagers burning rubber and parking on the grass. A Rolling Stones album was blasting through the house. The music disappeared across the waves of the Long Island Sound.

Dawn and Swerbuck were chatting with each other in the corner of the living room. I went over to say hello. They were busy talking about Van Gogh's paintings. They hardly paid attention to me. I asked Dawn where the drinks were and she pointed to the bar.

I walked over to the bar. Mad Dog came up to me and said, "I'm not afraid of anyone. Cause what the fuck? You only die once."

"Why you telling me this?"

"I don't know," he said, biting the air.

I grabbed a glass of scotch. Down the hatch. I almost retched. Scotch tasted like vomit. But I wanted to develop a taste for it. It was a man's drink.

I looked across the room and saw Dawn and Swerbuck still talking. I hated Van Gogh. It was his fault. It was at his exhibition that I first sensed there was some connection between them. Swerbuck was probably telling her how her paintings reminded him of Van Gogh's. Dawn was probably thinking how deep Swerbuck was. She probably thought he could teach her things. Probably, probably, probably. I didn't like probably. It ruined other possibilities.

I kept refilling my glass. Swerbuck lit up a joint and passed it to Dawn. They passed the joint back and forth. I wondered if she tasted salvia from his fat lips on the joint.

In the mean time I was getting drunk from all the Scotch. Mad Dog pointed to Dawn and Swerbuck. "It looks like they're getting pretty chummy," he said.

I wanted to go over and break up their little chat. But first I'd show Dawn that I could flirt too. I saw this cute blond walking by. It was Valerie from biology class. I used to joke around with her in the back of class. It was a toss up for who was a worse student. We both got F's. I guess that was because there wasn't an F-. I went over to her and asked her to dance.

"Biology was fun, wasn't it?" she said.

She flunked biology and still thought that it was fun. She was my kind of girl. Or Swerbuck's? That creep, never. I put my hand on her hip and we started to dance. We moved in and out of the chairs, couches and tables. We were the only ones dancing.

Dawn was glaring over at us dancing. Swerbuck was standing next to her talking into her ear. He was pointing at me.

Valerie told me that she was even thinking of becoming a biologist. That is, after she passed the make-up course in summer school.

"What do you want to be when you grow up?" she asked.

"Nothing," I said. I grabbed the scotch bottle off the bar and started gulping it down. During "Earth Angel" I stepped on her foot. I didn't apologize.

"You're very rude," she said, rubbing her foot.

"I'm sorry."

She left me standing there dancing by myself. The scotch was taking effect. The room started swirling and I went into the bathroom. Sweat was dripping off my forehead and my stomach felt like it would fall out of my belt. I dropped to my knees and started throwing up into the toilet bowl. I saw a giant seagull the color of scotch in the porcelain. It flew back into my mouth and opened its wings. I couldn't breathe and I passed out.

From a long way off I heard knocking on the door. Then a female voice yelling, "I have to piss." It sounded like Valerie. I heard a loud crash and someone broke through the door. I looked up and it was Swerbuck. He slapped my face, waking me, and dragged me out while Valerie jumped onto the toilet.

I found myself lying on a bed in one of the rooms on the ground floor. Swerbuck and Dawn threw three sets of covers over me to keep me warm even though it was summer. I was convulsing and shivering.

Dawn asked Swerbuck, "Will he be alright?"

"What do you care? He was cheating with Valerie."

"They were just dancing," Dawn said.

"You didn't see them in the bathroom," Swerbuck said. I never thought he'd be a Judas. Or a liar.

I wanted to say I was just throwing up in the bathroom. But I couldn't talk. My tongue was swollen in my mouth. I threw up again in the sheets.

"Yuk," Swerbuck said, grabbing Dawn's hand and leading her out of the room. They slammed the door on me. I wanted to get up and follow them but I couldn't move. I don't know how long I lay there.

I was drunk and I was hallucinating. I was in a movie theater. Big titles came up across the screen, *The Swerbuck and Dawn Show.* "Somewhere over the Rainbow" started playing and the film began. I saw Swerbuck and Dawn on a sweltering, technicolor day in July. They were both wearing their Suicide Club outfits and were besides the train tracks off Cutter Mill Road. Swerbuck stepped on some dog do and wiped it off with his finger on his pants. He took a yellow tube of Tester's No. 2 Airplane Glue out of his pocket and squeezed some into a brown paper bag. The bag got wet and drippy in the heat. They each huffed some.

"Joshua cheated on you," Swerbuck said.

She stuck her head in the bag of glue and said, "I'm falling through a hole in the earth. I'm Alice in Wonderland. I'll get Joshua back for cheating on me."

I yelled at the screen, "I'm innocent." The actors couldn't hear me.

Swerbuck licked some glue from Dawn's nose and dragged her onto the tracks. She yelled, "We're going to die!"

"Good," he said.

The train came around the bend. Dawn bit his hand to try to get him to let go. She got blood on her teeth and Swerbuck laughed hysterically.

"You're sick," Dawn yelled. "Let me go."

The train was coming down on them. I heard Harry James playing "The Flight of the Bumble Bee." I wanted to save Dawn but I couldn't move. I was pinned down by a scotch colored eagle. Swerbuck wouldn't let Dawn go. Just when train was about to annihilate them, Swerbuck threw them onto the ground along side the tracks. The ground shook as the train blasted by. And Dawn lay in the grass laughing and crying.

Swerbuck tried to kiss her. She grabbed his big lips and pushed them away.

"No kissing," she said. "That's for Joshua."

Well, at least that was something. Maybe she still liked me.

He got angry and said, "You blew me the other night but you can't kiss me now?"

Liar. Pants on fire. She'd never do that. The whore.

"That was out of anger," Dawn said. She did. The bitch.

"You should be angry. Joshua cheated on you," Swerbuck said.

Why did he keep saying I cheated on her? All I did was dance with Valerie.

"Tell Joshua that you fucked me," Dawn said, ripped off her skirt and let Swerbuck fuck her right on the embankment where the train had just passed by.

This almost killed me. I wanted to pull the movie screen down. I wanted to throw popcorn at it. I didn't have any.

"Till death do us part," Swerbuck said.

A song came on, "Happy Trails to You." The movie ended. Dawn stepped out of the screen and spoke directly to me, "I felt like I was on some great adventure with Swerbuck. I still loved you. But that was different. That was human love. Swerbuck was other worldly."

She stepped back into the screen and it went dark.

I was freezing under the covers in ninety-degree weather. I imagined I was skiing naked at Mount Snow. I was under the lift line and people riding the chair lift were laughing at me. I crashed into a huge snowdrift and got covered in powder. It took my breath out of me. I felt like Icy Fingers, the doctor who examined us in grammar school, had me by the balls. I thrashed around in my blankets. I wanted to get away from Icy Fingers.

Mad Dog woke me up and pulled me out of the bed. I wiped the snow off of my shoulders. What snow? It was summer. He led me out to a taxi. It was ninety degrees out. I was freezing. I was having convulsions. As I stepped outside still wrapped in Dawn's blankets I looked back and saw Dawn and Swerbuck dancing in her second floor window. I got really pissed and yelled, "I don't need you. Any of you." Then I mumbled, "I hope you kill each other."

I had a killer headache and didn't leave my house for two days. I didn't know whether I had seen Swerbuck and Dawn cheating, imagined it or predicted it.

When I finally went out into the summer sunlight I was wearing dark sunglasses. My eyes were still sensitive to the light. But the warm air felt good. It was nice not to be drunk. I just wanted to go for a walk and reintroduce myself to the living. I strolled down Deepdale Drive, breathing deeply the flowers, leaves and smell of success. The houses looked so secure. Like nothing could go wrong in them.

When I got to town I stopped at Squire's and got lemonade at the counter. It went down a little rough. I ordered an English muffin to put something solid in my stomach. And then I got a soothing vanilla ice cream. My nausea was beginning to clear up. My headache came and went in little spurts. I went back outside to enjoy the clear blue day. There were women everywhere, shopping in the boutiques. A thin redhead in clothes so tight she squeaked, holding a poodle on a leash was pointing to her Aston Martin and telling a store clerk to put her new antique coffee table in the trunk. A fat kid yelled at his mother that he didn't like the clothes at Great Neck Department Store. When I reached Cutter Mill Road I turned to the right. About three hundred yards ahead of me I saw Swerbuck and Dawn. They were holding hands and climbing up the embankment that led to the train tracks. My nightmare had come true. I wasn't hallucinating in a drunken coma. I was looking into a crystal ball.

I thought of sneaking up behind them and following them. I could catch them making love right next to the tracks. The way I had foreseen it. But I wasn't a peeping Tom. I wasn't that low. Also I didn't want to see it. I was afraid I would go blind.

When I next went out with Dawn I made up my mind that I wouldn't tell her that I had seen her with Swerbuck. We had dinner at Squire's and shot some pool. Later we took a cab back to her house. In the backseat I told Dawn that I was sorry that I got drunk at her party the other night. She didn't say anything. When we got to her house I asked if I could come in.

"No," she said. "I'm really tired and want to go to bed."

"I won't stay long," I said.

I told the cab driver to wait. I whispered that I might be a long time but that I have plenty of money. He winked at me.

Up in her room Dawn put on a nightgown and prepared for bed as if I wasn't there. She walked around yawning, ignoring me. She was cold, a snow woman. She lay down on her bed and pulled the covers up to her chin. She then turned on her side. I wanted to tell her that I felt like I was losing her but I lost the words instead. I said, "I'd like to talk."

"Talk," she said.

I didn't know where to begin. If I told her that I was afraid of losing her, she'd think I was a wimp. I looked around the room and saw that she had done a lot of new paintings. They were mostly charcoals with bizarre scenes out of horror movies.

There were headless bodies and dragons eating little children. A monster was popping out of a hatched egg. It looked a little like Swerbuck. It had big lips and a serpent's tongue.

"I don't like these paintings," I said. I was sure she was leaving me for Swerbuck. It was in her art.

"Yeah, yeah," she said and dug her face into her pillow to try to shut me out. I sensed she really wanted me to go. But I wasn't going. I wasn't leaving the playing field open for Swerbuck. He would have stayed. He would have fought for his woman. My woman.

"Your paintings scare me," I said.

She squeezed her eyelids tight and readjusted her face on the pillow.

"You seem headed towards death," I added.

"Very profound," she yawned and rolled away from me.

"Look, I think you're letting our relationship slip away. There's something between us and I feel lost in your black hair. So don't let your blue eyes fade," I said. I was upset and getting confused. "You know what I mean. That love is strange and has no reason. And we have love. Or had it. And I don't think you're going to find it so soon with anyone else," I said. I felt like crying. "Swerbuck doesn't know anything about love. All he wants to do is kill himself. He'll bring you with him because he doesn't care about you. It's like he's on a skateboard on Mt. Everest. And he wants to take you along with him. I just think you should think about it. You and I could be riding that train that he wants to throw you in front of. We could be skiing. Didn't you like it at Mt. Snow. I really like you, love you! There, I've said it. I love you."

Tears were in my eyes. I looked over at Dawn, waiting for a response, expecting her to say she loved me too. She'd have to be an ice sculpture on the North Pole not to melt at my entreaties.

But she was snoring, fast asleep. She hadn't heard a word I said. I couldn't believe it. I walked close to her. I wanted to bite her nose right off her face. I was frightened by my own anger. I straightened the blankets out around her and kissed her cheek. As I turned off her light I felt ashamed of myself for kissing her. I loved her. I hated her. I walked downstairs and went out to the cab. The driver turned to me. I had only been a half hour.

"Didn't get any action, did ya?" he said, smiling.

His voice shocked me. I was thinking of Dawn sleeping in bed while I was rattling on like a fool about how much I loved her. As we drove down the block I wanted to look back and see if Dawn was looking out at me from the window. But I didn't.

"I got plenty," I said. "I'm a fast worker."

"In and out," he said, laughing. "That's how I like it."

When he dropped me off I tipped him an extra couple of bucks.

A few days later Swerbuck came over my house. We wrote poems together. He looked down at his and read, "She was my friend. I liked her like popcorn at the movies."

"Not bad, huh?" he said.

Then he finished, "I wanted to eat mine with butter."

"What are you trying to say?" I asked.

"That women are scrumptious."

Did he mean that he wanted to eat Dawn like buttered popcorn? He should have told me that he was in love with her. I might have forgiven him. No, I was lying. If he told me he wanted to eat Dawn, I would have bashed his head open.

It was my turn to read what I was writing. "I ate the hook so that I could get a taste of the sinker. I didn't expect the ocean to turn against me. The waves were riding surf boards out to sea."

"That's dishonest," Swerbuck said. "You never ate the hook."

"You're dishonest too," I said, trying to get him to admit his betrayal.

He looked at me sadly.

"I want to tell you something," he said.

I braced myself. If he told me he was fucking my girl I'd have to hit him. It was a matter of honor. It was one of those life situations I felt I was too young to handle.

"I want to tell you," he said.

"Yeah?"

He walked over to my window, opened it, stepped out onto the balcony.

"I want to tell you that I can fly," he said.

Then he jumped out into the twilight. He just disappeared from the balcony like he was a bat. I ran over to the window. I thought he'd be badly hurt. It was about a twenty-foot drop. I looked down and Swerbuck was rolling around down on the lawn. He brushed some grass clippings from himself and stood up, laughing. I wanted to kill him but I couldn't help laughing too. We both smiled at each other like we were best friends. He beat his chest like Tarzan.

The front door opened and my mother ran out screaming, "Kill yourself on your own property."

Swerbuck bowed to my mother. "I can fly." Then he ran down the street jumping up and down, yelling, "I'm Superman."

That night I couldn't fall asleep. I was sure Swerbuck was having an affair with my girl. I didn't want to lose Dawn. It was important to me that some girl liked me. I felt out of place in Great Neck. The pillow under my head felt lumpy. I kept moving it around. I buried my face into the sheet. Dawn made me feel like I was worthwhile. If I lost Dawn to Swerbuck, who would I have left? I'd no longer even be able to be friendly with Swerbuck. I'd be alone. I'd be an outcast in an angry town. I was sweating under the sheets. When it was morning I was still trying to fall asleep. My legs had pins and needles. I got up and walked around to get my circulation back. When it was time to get up to go to school I made up my mind not to obsess about Dawn. If she didn't want me, she could leave. Let her have Swerbuck. I didn't need either one of them. I just wasn't going to think about it anymore.

Squire's Deli was pretty empty when I met Swerbuck a few days later for a snack about four o'clock in the afternoon. We sat in a corner booth near the kitchen. Swerbuck didn't want anyone near us. He was looking down-in-the-mouth, like he was feeling something other than his usual ecstatic self. Like he was up against something he didn't want to have to deal with.

"I got to tell you something," he said.

"What?"

I expected he was going to tell me he was seeing Dawn.

"I'm Superman," he said, laughing. I laughed too, thinking of him flying out of my window, my mother screaming at him.

"Come on. What do you really want to tell me?"

"I got this hot tip from Myra Kaye, the daughter of the owner of Yonkers Raceway," he said. "I go to the track a lot. I know when a tip's good."

Myra was in our biology class. She was a short, cute girl with long black hair who looked something like Cher. She was one of the few girls who was friendly with Swerbuck. He used to sing "I Got You Babe" to her while he chased her down the hall, trying to pinch her butt. She was a good student. For some strange reason she liked him.

"What's the horse's name?"

"Tiger Blue," he said. "In the eighth race. She's a shoo-in."

"How much you betting?"

"I'm broke. But you bet for both of us. I'll take twenty per cent of your winnings for giving you the tip," he said.

"Did Dawn tell you to come down here to give me this tip?"

"No."

"You got nothing to say about Dawn?"

"No."

Swerbuck looked around him like he was seeing if the place was bugged. He started to say something then held back. He looked down at the table. Then he said very timidly, "Isn't this tip on Tiger Blue reason enough to call you down to Squire's?"

"I'll tell you after the race," I said.

The tip promised to be golden. I wanted to bet a lot of money but I was broke. I figured I'd raise some money. I'd sell something. I thought of what I had that was valuable. My stereo? No. My dad would go nuts again. What about my printing press? My uncle had given it to me as a gift a few years earlier. I had done one job with the press for him where I made a thousand smeared business cards and charged him twenty-five dollars. He never hired me again. I wasn't very neat.

I had a neighbor, Ben Stein, who was a year younger than me who had pimples and wore glasses. He was an intellectual nerd. I figured he might like a printing press. He could feel like Guttenberg or something. Ben came over my house to see it and I told him I'd sell it to him for three hundred dollars.

"I don't have that much money," Ben said.

"It's worth seven hundred dollars."

"It's used."

"Two or three times."

"I can only afford two hundred and fifty dollars," Ben said.

"Sold," I said. I knew it was worth more but I was desperate for that money to bet on Tiger Blue. I was going to make a fortune on that horse. Ben went home, got the money and came back with a little red wagon. He put the press and the type in it, gave me the money, and wheeled his new equipment home. He looked like a lonely boy in his short pants and sneakers wheeling my press out of my garage. I felt so cool compared to him. But I also felt that in the long run he might do better than me in life. He was the kind of kid who would study all the time, get into a great college and find a good job. The dipshits inherit the earth. They study harder and get all the top positions. While the glamorous, dangerous kids like Swerbuck end up dead. I imagined Swerbuck as a dead pig with an apple in his mouth. I wondered where I'd end up. I had a little bit of Ben in me. Some of Dawn and a lot of Swerbuck.

Swerbuck stole his father's car out of the garage and drove me to Yonkers raceway. My pockets were filled with Ben's money. Swerbuck's brother Brian wanted to come along. Swerbuck told him he was too young. He had to pay off Brian five dollars so that he wouldn't tell his father that he was going to the track. It was my five dollars.

Swerbuck sped the whole way to Yonkers. He honked his horn at a cute mother and daughter, opened his window and yelled out, "I'm French." I turned red and ducked down in my seat. I thought it was rude to flirt with a mother in front of her daughter or vice versa. That's family. It's sacred. After we parked at Yonkers I was worried that they'd ask for proof of age at the gate. I had my brother's license but Swerbuck had nothing. I held my breath as we approached the gate. We paid two dollars each to get in. The three hundred pound guard didn't even ask us for I.D.

"Why do you think they didn't ask us for proof?" I asked.

"All they care about is collecting our money."

I took out a roll of bills and showed it to Swerbuck.

"Where'd you get all that!" he asked.

I didn't want to tell him I had to sell my printing press to Ben Stein. "I stole it from my parents."

Swerbuck was impressed.

I went up to the window and bet the whole two hundred and fifty dollars on Tiger Blue in the Eighth. I bought chances at win, place and show.

"You idiot. You should have bought all win tickets. It pays more money. Besides, you have to show confidence in your horse," Swerbuck said.

"Better safe than sorry," I said.

"I hope you didn't jinx the horse by not betting all the way," Swerbuck said.

We went right up to the fence to watch the race. Everyone was chatting with each other. There was real camaraderie like we were members of the same club. I felt very adult.

"This is cool. I've never been to a race before," Swerbuck said.

"I thought you were a regular," I said.

"Well, I am sort of. I don't actually come here. I give the money to my uncle who bets for me."

"Where do you get the money?"

"Ahm, my uncle gives it to me to bet for me." Swerbuck tried to change the subject and looked at the board.

"You're ridiculous," I said.

"The odds are holding at twenty to one. We're going to be rich. We can buy a yacht. Or at least a Sailfish," he said. "Don't forget my twenty per cent."

The race started and the horses came trotting out of their gates. Tiger Blue was huge. She looked like a heroic horse from the Ben Hur movie. Her muscles had a shimmering life of their own. Her jockey cleverly held her back and she opened in last place. At the quarter she had moved up to seventh place. She'd have to pick it up pretty soon.

"She's a slow starter," Swerbuck said.

"How do you know?"

"I got a feel for these things."

At the half Tiger Blue had moved up to fourth place. Swerbuck was jumping up and down next to me. "She's gonna win, she's gonna win!" he shouted.

At three quarters Tiger Blue was in second place and building speed.

"You're a genius kid," I shouted at Swerbuck.

I was counting my money. I'd walk out of here with five thousand dollars. I'd buy Dawn some jewelry with the money I earned off Swerbuck's tip. Poetic justice. Maybe I could patch things up with her. I'd take her to dinner. Tell her I loved her. Then at the last second three other horses pushed their way up through the pack and trotted past Tiger Blue. I couldn't believe it. They tore past her like she was in slow motion.

"Fix! Fix!" Swerbuck yelled. "Tiger Blue should have won."

An old gambler in blue seersucker pants and a yellow jacket yelled at Swerbuck, "Your horse is a nag."

"The driver pulled back on the reins," Swerbuck shouted. "I know the owner's daughter, Myra Kaye. Her old man's mafia. A cheat."

I tried to "shush" Swerbuck but it was too late. A cop came over to us and asked us for I.D.

"You didn't ask for I.D. when I came in," Swerbuck said.

"Mr. Kaye wouldn't take kindly towards your calling him a cheat," the cop said.

"He stole my money," Swerbuck said.

"My money," I whispered.

The cop grabbed Swerbuck by the collar and pushed him towards the gate. I followed. When we got out of range Swerbuck gave him the finger and ran. He couldn't resist having the last word. Even if it was a finger. I ran after him. The cop didn't care about beating us up. We weren't important. He was just happy to see us go. He didn't want us badmouthing his boss.

When we were out in the parking lot Swerbuck said, "I'm pissed at the cop. And you. You should have bought all the damned tickets to win."

"Are you crazy? Our nag came in seventh."

"We lost either way. We should have gone out with a bang not a whimper."

"Where'd you get this stupid tip? Not from Myra Kaye!"

"I did too."

"She should have known better."

"I already spent the winnings."

"Some 'shoo-in' horse."

I ran up to Swerbuck and kicked him in the ass. I did it a little harder than I should have. Swerbuck fired an angry look at me like he was ready to start swinging. He bit off a smile like it was the tip of a cigar. We ran to the car.

Swerbuck drove so fast you'd think he wanted to catch up with my lost money. He floored his Corvair on the service road of the highway.

"I needed that damn money," Swerbuck said.

"That was my fucken money," I repeated.

The road was winding and pretty empty. We approached a parked Cadillac where a man in a suit was tinkering under his car. Swerbuck pulled the Corvair over to the side of the road about a hundred yards past the Cadillac. He got out and told me to follow him.

"What for?" I asked.

"Just follow and be quiet."

We slinked behind some trees on the side of the road and worked our way back towards the man who was fixing his

Cadillac. He was on his knees with his head sticking under the car and his ass up in the air. Swerbuck jumped out from the trees, ran over to the man and grabbed his wallet, which was sticking up out of his back pocket. The man felt him grabbing his wallet and jerked his head up, banging it into the car.

"Thief," the man screamed. His face was dirty and blood was dripping down from where he smashed his head.

"Quiet," I said. But the man kept screaming "Thief!" And pointing at us. I had no choice but to punch him in the face to silence him. He fell down and banged his head against the car again. I started kicking him again and again in a panic. Swerbuck grabbed me, yelling, "He's out cold." I looked confused.

"Let's get the fuck out of here," Swerbuck said. "You didn't have to kick him so much." Then Swerbuck kicked the man. And we ran back to the Corvair and tore ass out of there.

In the car Swerbuck said to me, "You crazy? You might have killed him."

"You kicked him last," I said.

"You want to go to jail for life? They don't have the death penalty for minors. We'd rot," Swerbuck said. He then flipped through the wallet he had stolen.

"Two hundred dollars. Not bad," he said.

He threw the wallet out the window and handed me a hundred dollars. I stuffed the hundred into my pocket. I couldn't believe it. I had sold my printing press and almost killed a guy just to get one hundred dollars.

"Next time we'll roll a richer guy," Swerbuck said, optimistically.

"I'm beginning to hate you and myself," I said.

"Hey, I got you some money. Don't be a sore loser."

"Loser's the word."

"Cry baby."

"This shit's stupid."

"It's all preparation for dying in 1966."

"What about living in1964?" I said.

"Tiger Blue could have won that race," Swerbuck said. "She's a tiger. And blue's my favorite color."

Abe Siskin was a boy who was one grade behind me in school. He was a nice Great Neck preppy kid. He came from a rich family and was the kind of student who would end up a pros-ecutor, a judge or the head of his father's law firm. He was the kind of boy I hated. And so when I heard he was having a party in Kings Point I decided to crash. Along with Swerbuck and Mad Dog.

It was one of the last parties of the summer. Servants sailed across the manicured lawns carrying silver trays. There was a wooden dance floor laid down just for the party. Statues and fountains mingled with the guests. Champagne glasses floated in the air, held up by their own bubbles.

When we walked up to the entrance to the yard, wearing T-shirts and cut-off jeans, we looked like trouble.

Abe Siskind saw us coming up the driveway and went to meet us. He was wearing glasses with coke bottle lenses. He had on stupid Bermuda shorts and saddle shoes with black socks. He was about five feet four inches tall, one hundred and eighty pounds and had a scruffy beard under his chin that went down to his neck.

"Do you have invitations?" Abe asked, knowing full-well that we didn't.

"This looks like an open house to me," Swerbuck said.

"I'm sorry. It isn't," Abe said.

I turned my back to go. But Mad Dog was ready to fight. Abe was about the right size for him. He walked over to him and slugged him right in the glasses. The glasses broke and scratched Abe's nose. The punch didn't even have enough force to knock Abe down. Abe took the punch with calm dignity. He was a gentleman. He just stared at Mad Dog as if he were disappointed in him, as if he were some alien creature. Then he picked up his glasses and walked back into the party. Mad Dog turned to us and said, "Ha. I taught that fucker not to mess with me."

I felt like knocking Mad Dog out. It wasn't right what he did to Abe. But as stupid as what he did was, I still liked the little bastard. He was a potato, lumpy and earthy. Abe was a kiwi. Too exotic, too well mannered. I don't know what it was that I liked about Mad Dog. Maybe it was the way he smiled when he threatened to kill someone. Or the glint in his eye when he said he wasn't afraid of anything. Or the cowlick in the back of his rusty hair.

"Next time I'll kill you," Mad Dog yelled. But Abe was already back in his party.

Chapter 27

The Fall term started out a lot better than last year. I no longer had McDermott as my homeroom teacher. I had this new teacher in the school, Mr. Gordon for both homeroom and English. He was a great guy who believed that literature could teach us about life. He wasn't hung up on grammar, spelling and penmanship. He wanted us to grow as human beings. We discussed modern poets and he encouraged us to write our own works. He was beautiful.

I also took chemistry and intermediate algebra. I hated both of them. I thought science was for idiots. I felt they should give Einstein the electric chair for his contribution to the greatest killing machine of all time, the atomic bomb. Swerbuck didn't have to worry about committing suicide. The scientists were going to blow up the world for him.

My other classes were history and French. Both of these involved a lot of memorizing. Considering that I never opened my books my chances of passing weren't too grand.

All in all this promised to be a great year despite most of my courses. I was now a big shot senior who knew his way around.

A couple of weekends after the new term started we took the Long Island Railroad over to the World's Fair at Flushing Meadow Park. It was the big deal of the summer. It didn't mean much to me. I hated tourist attractions and crowds. And I didn't give a damn about the products of dumb countries, such as Canadian tractors and Chinese gongs. Still, it was better than hanging around Squire's deli. One thing I did like were the waffles at the Belgium Pavilion. And the restaurant on top of the space needle was pretty cool. Not that I ever went there. No way I'd wait on a two-hour line to ride up some stupid outdoor elevator.

There was a bratty kid sitting next to us on the Long Island Railroad with his mother. He looked a little like Swerbuck's brother with brown hair and pudgy cheeks.

"I want some gum," he said to his mother.

"You can't chew it with braces," his mother said.

"Come on, mom, please."

Swerbuck handed the kid a piece of bubble gum. It was nice of him.

The kid was all excited. "Thank you."

His mother grabbed it away and handed it back to Swerbuck. "He can't have it." She whispered to her son, "It might be poisoned."

I thought of the day before when Swerbuck almost killed his brother, Brian. He and I were at the playground in Great Neck Park. Brian was on the swings and Swerbuck came over and started pushing him back and forth. At first Brian started giggling and going, "Wee-wee." I thought it was sweet to see brothers having so much fun. But Swerbuck kept pushing harder and Brian kept flying further out with his feet pushing up towards the sky until it looked like he was going to go over the top.

"Slow down," I said.

"Sure." He didn't. He kept pushing Brian faster and faster. I was worried he was going to fly off into outer space and orbit the earth like a sputnik. He started making this loud-pitched scream that came from his throat and I couldn't tell whether it was a shriek out of fear or a cheer because he was having so much fun.

"Don't push so hard," I said. "He's only a kid."

"Fuck kids," Swerbuck said and pushed harder.

"You're going to hurt him."

"I should."

"Why?"

"He invented our parents. He should die."

"What does that mean?" Did he even know? His brother could have fallen off the swing and broken his neck. But I was drawn to the way Swerbuck went over the line. I felt like a paper glider that got caught in the air currents he created. Even if he was a jerk at times, he was a force to be reckoned with. He was a tornado.

"I mean nothing. I always mean nothing," he said. He pushed harder. Brian started screaming as the swing rose above the top, stalled in mid-air, then dropped down again. Swerbuck pulled the swing back to the end of the chain and pushed Brian forward with one huge heave-ho that sent him flying over the top like a dive-bomber at a carnival.

As he went upside down I covered my eyes. I didn't want to see Brian all smashed up. I peeled my fingers away from my eyes one by one. When I finally looked, there was Brian still swinging, having the time of his life, laughing.

"That's dangerous," I said, shaking my head.

"That's why we're friends. We're both dangerous," Swerbuck said.

"I wouldn't hurt a fly," I said.

I had become bored with all his always playing around about suicide. But I admired his love of life. You had to find life very beautiful to take a chance on losing it. There was a ballet in suicide. A formal, ritualistic dance with death that was romantic. It somehow affirmed life.

Just then Brian got off the swing and started running out of the park. Swerbuck ran after him. I saw a garbage truck speeding down the block. I yelled out for them to watch out. The truck was barreling down on them. Just before Brian stepped out onto the street Swerbuck caught him by the collar and pulled him back. He just missed getting squashed by the speeding garbage truck. The driver blasted his horn.

He smacked Brian, "You idiot. You almost got killed." He then took him by the hand, looked both ways before crossing and walked him out of the park.

Skinny and straggly, Swerbuck looked like Jesus crossing the street. Except he was Jewish and had big lips. He had one hand on Brian's shoulders and the other arm held straight out into the air like a cross. He had saved his brother's life. He had risked his brother's life. He walked down the street like he was walking on water.

The train pulled into the stop at Flushing Meadow Park. The mother walked out ahead of her son. Swerbuck slipped the kid the piece of gum. They both giggled.

When we stepped out of the train it was like we had walked out onto an elaborate Lionel train board. There were little buildings scattered all over, exhibitions from Belgium, the Netherlands, France, Brazil, Germany, Spain and Japan. It would have been exciting if I cared about anything but my own broken heart. Not that it was broken from Dawn or anything. I was just born with it broken. The busy lights and the crowds mingling reminded me of how alone I was. I smiled at nothing. It was good to know about pain. At the Mexican Pavilion we stopped in to get some beers. I don't know why they called it the Mexican Pavilion. There was nothing Mexican about it except a few waiters with stupid sombreros and horsehair blankets stuck on the walls like tapestries.

"I never had beer before," I said.

"It puts hair on your chest," Mad Dog said.

The waiter asked us for ID's. We all showed him phony ones. When he went to get the beers, Swerbuck showed us his ID and said, "It's my father's drivers license. Do I look like I'm forty-two years old?"

I paid for Swerbuck's beer. Mad Dog and Swerbuck drank their beers in one huge gulp straight from the bottle. I sipped mine. I didn't like the taste. It was almost as bad as Scotch. After a few bottles the bar began to become lopsided and the yellow lights were flickering green. I was getting kind of numb. I burped. It tasted like beer. I felt a little fuzzy like a sock turned inside out.

"This is strong stuff," I said.

"It's twice as strong as American beer," Mad Dog said and guzzled another one.

I went into the bathroom of the Mexican Pavilion and threw up.

When I came out I had a coke. Coke always settled my stomach.

We stepped outside to get some fresh air and I noticed Buffy Angelo. He was a shop student at Great Neck North High, a real grease ball. He had long brown oily hair that curled over his shirt collar. He was wearing a torn sweater, grease stained gray slacks and boots that were several sizes too large for him. His sloppy yellow teeth oozed tartar onto his lips. He was drinking something in a brown bag. Swerbuck stopped Buffy, "You bother her again, you're dead."

Mad Dog added, "I'll kill you too." I didn't know what Swerbuck was talking about. I'm sure Mad Dog didn't either.

"What the fuck you talking about?" Buffy asked Swerbuck. Then looked at Mad Dog.

"You were bothering her at the cafeteria," Swerbuck said.

Swerbuck pushed Buffy. Buffy got pissed and took a punch at Swerbuck. Swerbuck ducked and Buffy missed. I jumped on Buffy, knocking him to the ground. Mad Dog ran over from behind Swerbuck and kicked Buffy in the face. A police whistle blew.

"I lent her money for her lunch, that's all," Buffy said, lying on the floor, touching a big bruise on his face.

I saw the cops running from about a hundred yards away. We took off and ran past the Spanish Pavilion and made a right into an alley. We stopped at the end of it to catch our breath. The cops didn't follow us.

"Why'd you kick him in the face," I said to Mad Dog.

"Why'd you push him down?"

"I don't know."

"Me either."

"Swerbuck, what's your problem with Buffy?" I asked.

Swerbuck looked like he wasn't going to answer. He started to speak. Then stopped. After a few more seconds he blurted out, "Buffy was flirting with Dawn at the cafeteria. Don't you notice anything, Joshua?"

"I trust Dawn," I said. I didn't. "Buffy said he was just lending her money."

"Fuck Buffy," Swerbuck said. "Dawn likes me." It was all coming together. Ever since the Van Gogh show I had sensed there was something going on between them. I tried not to see it. I couldn't turn away any longer. That was alright. They couldn't hurt me. No one could hurt me. You couldn't hurt what was already damaged.

"Big deal, she's your friend," I said, trying to downplay it.

"She's more than that."

"Dawn and I are like one," he said and held up two fingers signifying that they were joined. He then rolled up his left sleeve showing pink scars on the back of his forearm. Block letters stood up about a quarter of an inch above his arm -- DAWN. I remembered that Swerbuck had once told me that he only carved the names of girls he had fucked into his arm.

"You fucked her?" I screamed.

Swerbuck grinned. I imagined pubic hairs coming out of his mouth and Dawn humping away under him like a frothing coyote. I heard her moaning, "Make me come. Joshua never did."

I lost it. I threw him to the ground, sticking my fingers in his mouth, trying to peel his huge lips from his face like an orange rind. I picked up a rock and held it above his head like an imitation rock. I hesitated. I was furious but I didn't want to kill him. Then the rock took over. It had a momentum of its own. I whacked him on the head. I didn't do it full force. Just enough to make little holes in his head. Like the little slices I made in my arm with the razor blades. I held back. I didn't try to kill him. But little pieces of scalp kept chipping off his head. Clumps of hair attached to white skin with blood on it. Time slowed down. I was underwater. I pounded him in slow motion. Swerbuck covered his head with his hands. The rock came down on his fingers. They got mangled and started bleeding.

"Help! Help!" I heard Mad dog yelling. I looked over at him. His face was pale white with fear and he was pointing at us. He looked like he had stared into a death mask. But Swerbuck wasn't dead. He was just a little red and messy. I wondered why Mad Dog was making such a big deal about nothing. I had work to do. I was numb. I went back to hitting his head when five cops ran over to us with guns drawn. You'd think they were busting a murderer or something. Mad Dog and I raised our hands over our heads. I dropped my blood stained rock. I felt like someone who was interrupted dancing. Swerbuck was unconscious on the ground.

"What the fuck is going on here?" a young red-headed cop asked.

"I'm innocent. He did it," Mad Dog cried.

I was still feeling kind of high and sick from the Mexican beer and the exhilaration of beating Swerbuck's head in. I felt almost like I could pass out. I looked at Swerbuck who was asleep on the ground. I wondered if he was dead. If I had killed him that would be pretty cool. But spending the rest of my life in jail would suck.

An older cop with a gray mustache asked me, "Who are you?"

I wasn't sure. Swerbuck didn't look too good lying there. It struck me as kind of funny that I had stolen his chance to commit suicide. He thought death was such a big deal. But it was nothing. A body lying on the ground like a sack of potatoes.

I thought of my dead rabbit. I loved that rabbit. I killed it. I threw up.

"I'm a bad boy," I said.

"You bet your ass you are," the cop said.

"Leave him alone," Swerbuck said. He was rolling on the ground, holding his head. There was blood all over his hands and his shirt. He sat up and then slowly got to his feet.

"He's my friend."

I felt like hugging him. It would have been such a pain in the ass if he had died.

"With friends like you he don't need enemies," the young red-headed cop said.

"I tried to stop Joshua," Mad Dog said to Swerbuck.

The cops searched us for weapons and asked us a bunch of stupid questions about where we lived and what we were doing here. What did he think we were doing at the World's Fair? We wanted to see the freaken exhibits.

"If you're gonna fight you should fight fair," a fat cop told me. "You shouldn't hit him with a rock."

He was right.

"I'm sorry," I said. "I'm sorry I'm me."

I was. I didn't feel right about bashing Swerbuck's head open and causing so much trouble for the cops.

They escorted us to the entrance to the Fair. As we were leaving the young red-headed cop yelled, "You better not come back." We just kept walking.

"Who'd want to come back to this dump anyway?" Swerbuck said.

I felt the same way. I didn't care about the World's Fair. I didn't understand what all the excitement was about. The only exciting thing that happened at the Fair was my splitting Swerbuck's head open. And I felt bad about that. It wasn't a nice thing to do. And what for? Over Dawn. Who was Dawn? A long black braid and some blue eyes. I didn't even really know her. I never even liked her that much.

We walked into the railroad station.

"I got a headache from that stupid beer," I said. I gagged on the train platform. Nothing came out.

"Don't talk to me about headaches," Swerbuck said, ripping a piece of his undershirt and holding it up to his head. The blood soaked through it.

"Maybe you need stitches," I said, concerned.

"You worry about your head, I'll worry about mine."

If Swerbuck had had the rock instead of me, I would have certainly needed stitches. I just put little holes in his head. He would have killed me. He wasn't the kind of guy for half way measures.

When we got back to Great Neck Estates we split up from Mad Dog. I took Swerbuck home with me. I filled my bathtub with water. Swerbuck jumped into the bathtub fully dressed in his blood stained clothes.

"You really wanted to kill me," he said. "I'm going to make you the President of the Homicide Club."

"What did you mean when you said Dawn likes you?" I asked.

"I think we've had enough of that for one night," he said and dunked his head under the water.

"You didn't fuck her did you?" He dunked his head under the water again. I felt this urge to grab his head and hold it under till he was dead. He came bobbing up again.

"Ask her. Not me," he said.

He got out of the tub and took off his clothes. He was standing there naked. I gave him a bathrobe. He put it on and asked if I could get him an ice bag for his headache. I went downstairs and got one and came back up. He sat on my bed in my room with the ice bag on his head. If Swerbuck wasn't going to answer my questions I knew what I had to do. I phoned Dawn.

"How long you been seeing Swerbuck?" I asked.

"What about the girl you fucked?" she said.

"What are you talking about?"

"Swerbuck said you were fucking that blond at my party. That Valerie."

I turned to Swerbuck. "You prick. Why'd you tell Dawn I was fucking Valerie?"

"I told you to watch out for me. I'm a liar," he said, smiling. I had split his head open but he had stolen my girl.

"You two deserve each other," I said to Dawn, slamming down the phone.

"Now I don't feel bad about cracking your head open," I said to Swerbuck who was fiddling with his head.

"Yeah and you're the guy who says he wouldn't hurt a fly," Swerbuck said.

"I guess I'm a liar too," I said. I hardly felt a thing while I was smashing his head open. Time was suspended. So was conscience. I was operating in a bubble. That scared me.

"Friends?" Swerbuck asked and laughed.

"Friends," I said.

"We even about Dawn now that you busted my head?"

"I guess," I said.

"Schmuck," he said and leaned over on my bed and hugged me. The movement hurt his head. "Ow," he said. "You bastard."

Chapter 28

"You want to see guys shoot up?" Swerbuck asked me. We were at Squire's with Mad Dog. I practically lived there. My parents had gotten me a charge account and I was racking up about one hundred dollars a month in bills. Swerbuck had forgiven me for splitting his head open. Maybe he felt the blood washed away the guilt he felt about taking away Dawn. I forgave him for stealing Dawn. As best I could. We were kids. Everything meant a lot at the same time it meant nothing.

"I don't want to be in the same room with that junk," I said. I was afraid of heroin. I had this fear that I might use it myself. Heroin addicts were like the walking dead. Shooting heroin was the kind of thing Swerbuck would do. I played with disaster at a distance. I liked to look at tragedy through binoculars. I didn't want to be part of the train wreck. I cut my arms. Swerbuck slashed his wrists. That was like injecting yourself with heroin. It was a dead end. I wasn't in love with death. I flirted with it.

"Let's do it," Mad Dog said.

A few hours later I found myself at a heroin shooting gallery on the upper west side. I had never seen anyone shoot heroin before. I didn't mind getting a little high but becoming an addict was a leap into permanent failure.

Four locks were opened before a short, stocky Puerto Rican let us in. We entered a small one-room studio where an albino and two Negroes were sitting around, stoned out of their minds. One of the Negroes was a skinny, old guy, about forty, with purple hair, wearing ripped pants and an undershirt. The other was a young, queer guy, with dyed blond hair. The shades were drawn and the lights were real low. I guess the drugs made their eyes sensitive to light. It smelled like they hadn't been out of there in days. There was hardly any furniture. The price of their heroin habits could probably have furnished a small palace. The albino was sitting on a dirty old pillow shooting up. Mad Dog winced when he looked at the needle. Then he told me, "I used to mainline. I kicked the habit."

"Let me see your tracks," I said.

"They're all healed."

Swerbuck went over to the Puerto Rican, who wasn't shooting up, and asked how much for four-nickel bags of grass?

"Twenty dollars. Thez de the best Acapulco gold," he said.

Dog and I kicked in seven bucks each.

"Put in eight each," Swerbuck said. "I turned you on to this place."

"No way," Mad Dog said. I put in nine dollars, Mad Dog seven and Swerbuck four.

The Rican said he had to go out and cop the grass. He'd be back in ten minutes.

"Make it fast, if you know what's good for you," Mad Dog said.

The Rican sneered. Swerbuck lit his last joint. The Rican smelled it and said, "You smoking sheet, man. That's cuts with oregano. Not like me quality drugs."

Then he left to meet his connection.

The Negro with the purple hair shot up some heroin. As soon as he pressed the plunger into his vein he started having a bad reaction. Hives were breaking out all over his arm. The dyed blond Negro queer said, "Don't worry, sweetie. I've had hives before."

"The hives are good luck," the albino said. But they were festering all over his arms and didn't look like good luck to me. I was worried the guy would die in front of us. He was sweating a lot at the same time that he had the chills. I wanted to get out of there. I hoped the Puerto Rican would get back soon with our pot.

There was a rattling at the door and the Puerto Rican came crashing in, slamming the door shut behind him, blurting out, "We got fucked. The connextion steals my twenty and runs. I can't catch hims no way. We get robbed."

I knew the Rican was lying. If he were some punk in Great Neck I would have kicked his ass. But I was out of my element here. I was in the big time among the smack addicts and the hustlers. If I made a move on these guys they'd probably take out a gun and blow my head off. I figured I'd better get my ass out of this stupid place. I never should have listened to Swerbuck. This dump wasn't for me. I was a sucker. A suburban white boy. I didn't belong in a heroin shooting den.

Mad Dog raised his fist at the stocky Puerto Rican and yelled, "If you don't want none of this, you better give us our money back."

Now we were in for it.

The queer blond, Negro guy took out a gun. I started inching towards the door. He pointed it at Dog, lisping, "Time for de widdle boys to go back to windergarten."

"Don't shoot," Mad Dog cried and ran past me to the door. He couldn't undo the locks. The old Negro with the purple hair, hives and all came over and opened the locks for him.

We all beat it. I could hear those creeps laughing at us as we flew down three flights of stairs and ran out into the street. We raced down a couple of blocks and then around several corners till we reached a subway stop on 96th Street.

We were out of breath. Mad Dog shook his fist at the buildings and said, "I kill people for shit like that."

"They shouldn't have laughed at us," I said.

"Let's go back and get them," Mad Dog said.

"Let's do it," I said. I was testing him. No way I was going back to face a gun.

"You mean it."

"Yeah."

"I wish I had time. I got to get home," Mad Dog said, changing his mind.

Swerbuck was sweating. He wasn't feeling too good. Maybe it was a reaction to his own oregano joint, which he smoked at the shooting gallery. He was getting paranoid. He pointed to an old lady with shopping bags and told Mad Dog, "That bitch is an undercover agent."

"You want me to beat her up?" Mad Dog said.

"Don't you touch that old lady," I snapped at Mad Dog. This whole evening had been a waste. I pissed away money and almost got shot. These guys were too stupidly dangerous to hang around with. What was I doing with them? I had rejected everyone at school for them just because I was afraid I'd be rejected. I never gave the preppies a chance. I wouldn't now either.

"Can I have my four dollars back?" Swerbuck said.

"Drop dead," I said. "I lost nine."

"The cops are onto us," Swerbuck said.

"I ain't afraid of no cops," Mad Dog said as he ducked down the stairs into the subway.

"I'm a cop," I said, "Boo!"

Mad Dog ran from me.

"I'm so broke," Swerbuck cried and ran after him.

Later that night when I got home I didn't feel like going to sleep. I took a few Dexedrine pills that I had stolen from my mother's bathroom. She used them for a diet, even though she was thin. I wanted to escape from the earlier part of the evening. I locked myself in my bathroom and took two of them.

My bathroom was the size of a small bedroom. In the front of it there were two sinks, a tub and a toilet bowl. In the back there were double door sliding closets with floor to ceiling mirrors. I looked into the mirror. Not bad. I wasn't gorgeous like Bobby Finer who lived around the corner and was a male model. But I had a kind of a dark romantic look. I mean just cause I lost Dawn didn't mean I couldn't find another girl. I was a nice guy. I was polite to girls. I could see a lot of girls going out with me. Why should I want to kill myself? I didn't. That was Swerbuck's idea. I started talking to the mirror. I'm not sure what I was saying but my mouth was moving quickly. Words were tumbling out of me like handfuls of dice thrown across a green felt craps table. I said nonsensical things like, "I'm not small. I'm larger than shrinkage. My veins are blue balloons. I have fallen into the valley of adolescence but one day I'll be a mountain. Not a mean mountain. But a good father to my children. I'll call them Joshua. All of them."

I must have stood in front of the mirror for five hours talking to myself. I was becoming more and more wide-awake. I was sweating from the exertion of talking so rapidly. My hands were shaking. When morning fell onto the bathroom floor I was still talking away into the mirror, "Die? Not me. Suicide is stupid. Fill my life like sandwich bags with dramatic moments. I'm drama. I'm a whole fucken musical. I'm a lunch box. I want to live."

Later I heard knocking on the bathroom door. I looked at my watch. It was two o'clock in the afternoon. I had been in the bathroom about twelve hours. I heard Robert's voice, he must have come home from college again, "Hey, you're not the only one who has to go to the bathroom around here." I was curled up on the floor with my head resting on a couple of my old mohair sweaters that I was talking into. I had taken them out of the closet. I was shivering.

"I'll be right out," I said. My mouth creaked. It was all dried out from talking to myself. It was caked with blood. I didn't remember a word I had said. I went into my room.

The autumn leaves were falling off the trees and my dad woke me at about four o'clock in the afternoon to rake them from the steep slope that rose up to our French Provincial castle. I was exhausted from staying up the whole night talking to myself. I had a chip on my shoulder. It got chilly towards dusk and I really didn't enjoy raking the crumbling brown leaves. They flew around in the wind like small ducks. Every time I collected a pile of them, the wind would blow them, twisting and quacking, back into the sky. Then they'd dive back down like they were looking for fish on different parts of the lawn. As my mind started drifting my piles of leaves kept getting smaller and smaller. Till I was almost working in reverse, spreading the leaves back out across the hill.

"What are you doing out here? Goofing off," my father said as he walked over to me.

"Why don't you leave me alone?" I said, half listening to him, trying to catch a flying leaf between two fingers.

"You can't do anything right," Hy said. Then he raised his fist like he was going to hit me. I picked up the rake and waved it at him, "Go ahead, I'll kill you."

My father looked scared. I was calling his bluff. I had taken enough. I wasn't going to be his whipping boy anymore. He put his fist down like he was lowering a flag to half-mast. He said, "I'm telling your mother you have to see a shrink." Then he turned on his heel, military fashion, and marched back into the house.

I felt terrible. I had never threatened my father with a rake before. I had humbled him, the soldier. I wanted him to be the strong one. I put my rake over my pile of disappearing autumn leaves to keep them from floating down our steep lawn.

At first I was embarrassed to go back to Rosenquest. He had kicked me out and here I was at his door like a beggar. But after a few minutes I felt right at home. I meant business this time; I really wanted to straighten out my life.

"I threatened to hit my father with a rake," I said. "I shouldn't have done that."

"That's right."

"But I still feel good," I said.

"About what?"

"About standing up for myself," I said.

"Uh huh."

"I showed him I wasn't his play toy."

"Don't let your father define you," Rosenquest said.

"What do you mean?"

"Don't be your father's false image of you."

"You mean be myself?"

"Uh huh, " he continued. "You are who you are. You are not who he wants to see you as."

"When he walked back into the house, he looked so alone," I said.

"That's not your problem. You have to be a friend to your-self," he said.

"But I don't want to hurt him."

"Then don't pick up weapons. Use your mind."

"I get angry."

"Love him."

That was the answer. Love. Forgiveness. Not anger.

I thought Rosenquest was great. I wasn't the same person he threw out a year ago. I could see goodness. I no longer wanted to laugh at it. I could be redeemed through it. I was inching towards enlightenment.

He cut the session after forty-five minutes, "Ill see you same time next week."

I stopped in the bathroom on my way out. As I was standing there pissing, I noticed a picture on the wall of a train going through the Alps. Under it was a caption, "Life is a journey not a destination."

I imagined myself on a train that went on forever. I passed mountains, chalets, children, cows. It stopped at every station and let people on and off. While following the train in my imagination, I accidentally missed the bowl and pissed on the floor. I took a piece of toilet paper, wiped it up and flushed it.

Every day I looked forward to Mr. Gordon's English class. I discovered that education could be fun. That it wasn't some-thing to be avoided like castor oil or McDermott's class. One day in December he picked a test booklet off of his desk and said, "This is the best class essay on E.E. Cummings."

I sat there and hoped it was mine. We had been asked to write about one of my favorite poems, "the Cambridge ladies who live in furnished souls." I loved the lines, 'the Cambridge ladies do not care, above Cambridge if sometimes in its box of sky lavender and cornerless, the moon rattles like a fragment of angry candy." That said it all for me. I saw the heavens as a candy shop and imagined God as a giant caramel nougat.

"The essay was written by Mr. Swerbuck," Gordon said.

We were all shocked that it was Swerbuck's. I had hoped that it was mine. The class thought Gordon was joking and started to laugh.

Swerbuck whispered to me, "I'm ashamed."

"Why?" I asked.

"Because it's an honor to fail in a dumb school like this."

Gordon called Swerbuck up to get his paper. I knew Swerbuck had it in him to get A's but it was against his principles.

Swerbuck stood up from his chair, made a sweeping bow like one of the Three Musketeers, and glided up to Gordon to get his paper. Gordon shook his hand. Swerbuck went back to his seat pretending it was all a big joke. But his eyes welled up with tears of pride.

After class I had lunch in the cafeteria with Swerbuck and Dawn. We were all good old buddies again. Except Dawn was now Swerbuck's girl. I didn't have to worry about her cheating on me anymore. She wasn't mine. We ate hot dogs with sauerkraut and beans.

"I'm impressed that you did so well on your essay," Dawn said. She kissed him on the cheek. I tried not to be jealous. She didn't deserve me.

"I shouldn't have even written it," he said.

"Why?" I asked. It was just like him to be spiteful like that.

"Because Cummings is a fake."

"What do you mean?" Dawn asked.

"He wrote poems."

"So."

"Anyone can write poems. I want to be a poem," Swerbuck said, glowing.

"I'm a painting," Dawn said and pretended she was making brush strokes on her face.

"There's a harsh beauty in a bag of bones," Swerbuck said.

"What does that mean?" I asked.

"It is what it is."

Dawn finished her hot dog and started eating his while he was talking.

"That's mine," he said.

"When I eat, I eat for you too," she said. And took some of the sauerkraut that had spilled off his hot dog.

I wanted to puke. I was glad to be rid of Dawn. At least I got to eat my own hot dog. I took a big bite of it covered with sauerkraut and really enjoyed the taste. Then I ate some beans.

A couple of days later I was over at Swerbuck's. He was busy chopping up a rock of coke on a mirror with a razor blade. He was surgical and precise about it. He liked the ritual.

I was standing in front of the bullfight posters imitating a matador. The Rolling Stones was blasting on the stereo.

Swerbuck rolled up a dollar bill and took a snort. "I am inhaling God," he said. Then he looked at himself in the coke mirror and said, "Nice lips." He pushed the mirror over to me like I should take a hit.

"No thanks," I said.

"Are you crazy? This is Christ's flaky wafer," he said.

"I don't want any," I said.

"This coke will take you places."

"Life is a journey not a destination," I said. "It's all about the process of growing up." I should have been footnoting Rosenquest about the journey quote.

"Too bad," Swerbuck said.

"Too bad, what?"

"Too bad you're growing up. That's a dead end too."

If life is a journey and I keep traveling I'll never die. I'd be eternally *en route*.

Swerbuck took another hit of coke. It made his nose run. He gobbled down the mucous, looked up at me and said, "Fuck, that's good." Then Swerbuck took out a huge roll of twenties.

"How'd you get that?" I asked. "Dealing?"

"No way," he said. "Playing Batman."

"What do you mean?"

"I answered this ad from these two perverts who live in a mansion out at King's Point. This old white-haired man paid me five hundred dollars to have sex with him and his wife. She was all dressed up like Cat woman. I played the Penguin and the old man was Batman."

"That's disgusting," I said.

"No, that's business," Swerbuck said. "I used to be rich. Now I'm poor. You wouldn't know about necessity."

"I'd rather die."

"You will anyhow," Swerbuck said. "Batman told me to do his wife. She went berserk cause I got that French style."

"You are crazy," I said.

"For five hundred bucks I figure I can do anything. The pervs were loving it. And he gave me five hundred bananas for that. It didn't mean anything. Nothing means anything."

"You're sick," I said. "I thought I was like you. I'm not."

"Sick? They're the sick ones. It's the easiest money I ever made. And you're more like me than you think."

"When you make love to them, you become them," I said.

"I'm not them. I'm Swerbuck," he said. "I'm even better than that. I'm Swerbuck with five hundred dollars." He walked over to his window, opened it and waved his bankroll around.

"I'd rather be Joshua broke," I said.

"That's because you're not broke," Swerbuck said. He then took his bankroll and threw it up into the wind. The bills floated on the air like green leaves. I ran to the window, reached out and managed to catch three twenties. The rest of the money floated down the block.

"Are you crazy?" I said.

"That's just to show you rich people I don't need your money," he said. I was holding his sixty dollars. He grabbed it out of my hand. I thought he was going to throw it out the window again.

"I'm glad you caught these. I'll buy you lunch," he said.

He didn't.

My senior year was going about as badly as my junior year except for English where I was pulling B's. Mr. Gordon inspired me and made me feel like working. But the other teachers made studying about as appetizing as swallowing someone else's chewed peach pit. After each quarter I still had to wash my grades off of my report card with water and write in new ones to keep from getting balled out by my parents.

One day in February something happened to me that changed my life. It was a small thing, really just a little comment from another student, Jimmy Fogell. Yet somehow it had a big impact on me. It was like a little rock falling, knocking into a bigger rock and then starting an avalanche. It's always the small crap that blows you over. I had an aunt who died in a car crash because she spilled some coffee on her lap and lost control of the car. I mean, coffee. It's supposed to wake you up. Not put you down.

Jimmy Fogell was one of those high school champion-type kids who was on the football, baseball and track teams. He was a good-looking, all-American guy with blond hair and blue eyes. He walked around the school halls in his khaki chinos, wearing a blue and gold sweater with varsity letters. He would have made my father proud. Not only was he a great athlete, he was a straight A student and the President of our class. Disgusting.

One day we were standing on line together to go into the cafeteria and he turned around to me. He had never spoken to me before. At first, I thought he was speaking to someone else but when I looked at him I knew he was addressing me because he looked like a judge talking to a defendant. He said, "You're not as stupid as people think." Then there was a resounding silence and a moment when all motion stopped. When he picked up his plate of meat loaf and potatoes, the noise of the cafeteria rushed back in.

I put my food on my tray and followed him. What did he mean? Was he telling me I was stupid or that other people were stupid to think I was stupid? Was it a compliment or an insult? It was as if an oracle had spoken and predicted the rest of my life. I caught up to him at the cash register and asked, "Do you mean that people think I'm stupid?"

"What do you think? The way you act? Geez," he said.

I was too stunned to say anything else. I found a seat by myself and ate. I couldn't believe the secret he had told me. That people thought I was stupid. I had no idea. Here I was feeling superior to everyone and I didn't have a clue that they thought I was a dope. Was I sleep walking? How could I not have noticed the impression I was making?

I decided that I'd show those pricks that I was smarter than all of them put together. I'd be the new Joshua. I'd show them that I was an army of brain cells going through basic training to become a brain. My drill sergeant would be study. I would dedicate myself to books as a means to an end, proving I was smarter than everyone. I'd become a straight A student. I had never thought that was something worth doing before. Now it was the only way to prove I was no dummy. I wanted to thank Fogell for opening my eyes. But he was eating there with some of his football friends and I was afraid to go over to him. There were little milk containers all over the table and dishes of apple pie. Just because he talked to me didn't mean that the other jocks would. We lived in two different worlds. His was a world of acceptance, approval and love. Cheerleaders followed him around. I lived on the other side of the goal post somewhere between out of bounds and the parking lot. I was an alien. I'd have to prove myself before we could speak again.

I couldn't wait to see Dr. Rosenquest that week and tell him about Fogell. I was falling off my chair with excitement. Rosenquest was as calm as usual. I guess he was used to seeing patients get fired up with inspiration then burn like ash into a heap of indifference.

"When Fogell told me that I'm not as stupid as people think, it was a revelation," I said.

"Don't get too grandiose."

"I didn't know people thought I was stupid."

"Don't tell me what you thought. Tell me what you *felt* when Fogell said, 'You're not as stupid as people think.'"

"Angry. Like I'd read a million books just to show them I'm not stupid!"

"Joshua, you don't need to prove anything. Read books because you want to learn."

"I'm not a dope you know. I'm going to study."

"You can study for the wrong reasons too."

"I'll show them."

"Why?"

"I'm hurt." I felt like crying but I didn't. "I feel betrayed."

"By whom?"

"Them."

"And?"

I looked down and said softly, "Myself." I had wasted four years in high school learning nothing just to show everyone I didn't give a damn. I had let myself down. Wasting all my intelligence on a dare to myself. It was sad. I thought I was clever but I was a fool. I lived in a glowing whirlpool of negatives, drowning in my own shining disenchantment. Now was the time to prove how smart I really was. I couldn't do anything about the past. It was a corpse surrounded by the flies of disinterest. I could never recapture it. It was incontinent. It had shit all over itself. But from this day forward I wouldn't waste anytime rebelling against the school system. I would be as good as I was bad. I would dedicate myself to the front side of the moon. I would be a scholar. A monk.

Our yearbooks came out about a month before graduation. I remember sitting around the courtyard during lunch break signing them. They had purple covers with gold lettering -- *Class of 65.* It had been a month since Fogell woke me up and I had really started studying. My term grades hadn't turned around yet. I needed a lot more time for that. There were too many gaps in my knowledge that had to be filled in. But my test grades had gone up from D's to C's and B's. I was seeing less of my friends because I was staying in studying. Not that I had many friends. Swerbuck was pretty involved with Dawn now; and Mad Dog, well I could never tolerate him much, anyway.

Ginny, the girl in pigtails, who had been in the driver's ed car the day Swerbuck and I cut school, asked me if she could sign my yearbook. This shocked me. She'd never really noticed me much before except to rat me out. I handed her my yearbook. She took it over to a picnic table. Swerbuck came over to me without a book.

"Don't you have anything for me to sign?" I asked.

"My dad wouldn't give me the twenty-five dollars to buy a yearbook," he said. "Can I sign yours?"

"After Ginny," I said. I felt bad for Swerbuck. His French, asshole father could have bought his son a God damned yearbook. If I had the money I would have bought it for him myself. No I wouldn't. He stole my girl.

Ginny returned my yearbook to me and Swerbuck grabbed it from me before I had a chance to read what Ginny wrote. He sat down at the picnic table and took his time writing. When he came back to me he said, "You don't deserve such a good friend as myself."

I walked away from the others to read my yearbook. I opened to Ginny's picture first -- "Dear Joshua, You're deeper than anybody knows. Love, Ginny."

How'd she know that? It seemed this was the year for surprises. I felt like Moses picking up the tablets. At each corner there was a revelation. I thought she thought of me as a loser like everybody else. I had believed what Fogell said about everyone thinking I was stupid. But she sensed something deeper in me. Like Fogell. It seemed that a number of select people had looked at me and noticed something wonderful; something I hadn't seen, some light beneath all the pretentious stink of darkness. I don't know why I had never asked Ginny out? I should have dated Ginny not Dawn. Ginny would have never left me for Swerbuck. She would see him as too twisted, a jungle tree choking itself off at its own entangled roots.

I then turned to Swerbuck's picture. His lips were sticking out of the page like they'd swallow me. I thought I saw them moving as I read the inscription, "We were too much alike to see how different we were. / I treasure what we had and I leave it to you. / Best, /Swerbuck."

Swerbuck was part of the fabric of my life. He had been there through the ups and downs. He had introduced me to my girlfriend, Dawn, and then he had taken her away. He was me without any self-restraint. While I was walking near the edge, he was madly going over it. When I made little scratches on my arm with a razor blade, he cut out chunks of skin. He was everything I wanted to be, all that I was afraid of becoming and part of what I considered idiotic. Now he was quickly becoming everything I had outgrown. He was that stupid kid who thought he was a genius. Or he was that genius who acted like a jerk. Fogell would have never seen talent in Swerbuck. He wasn't deep enough to see Swerbuck's mad genius. I wasn't as deep as Swerbuck either. It occurred to me that maybe I had smashed Swerbuck's head open with the rock because I was jealous of his brain. Because I wanted to take a piece of it out of his skull and feel it in my fingers and try to know what genius was. Then I'd throw it in the garbage because I didn't want his intelligence sitting there, taunting me. I couldn't approach his level of pure negativity. It was out there shining like an undiscovered star, a hole in the sky, a flashlight in a serial killer's cave.

I walked back to the other kids. I hardly noticed them. I was lost in thought. No one asked me to sign their yearbooks. I guess I wasn't that popular. Everybody seemed to like me but no one wanted to take me home. At least not in their yearbooks.

I was busy studying for finals. Something I had never done before. I figured I better get some good grades to make up for my abysmal record. The four colleges I had applied to--B.U., Hofstra, Miami U. and Syracuse had already rejected me. It didn't look like anybody was going to take me. Who could blame them? My record stank no matter what my good intentions were. If I didn't get into a college, I could be drafted into the Vietnam War. I was already hearing reports of friends of friends who had their legs blown off over there. There was nothing uglier to me than an amputated leg. I got dizzy thinking about it. Maybe some good grades on my finals would get me into some last minute school. I really wanted both my legs. I wanted to walk.

I was sitting in my room reading Joseph Conrad's, "Heart of Darkness," when my dad walked in. Surprised, he asked, "Studying?"

"I got my finals coming up," I said.

"It never bothered you before," he said. He was goading me. He wanted to fuck up my head so that I'd fail. I wasn't going to fall for that. I simply said what Fogell had taught me, "I never realized people thought I was stupid."

"You must have been asleep," he said, smirking.

"Thanks dad," I said, ignoring his taunt. Regularly, I would have told him off. But I looked at him and felt sorry for him. He needed to keep me where I was, to keep his world orderly. He had already labeled me. He didn't want to have to put a new tag on his luggage like I was some new country to which he was traveling.

But I wasn't going to be his flunkey anymore. I wouldn't be his disgrace, his blemish, the mole on his cheek. He wouldn't be able to blame my mother for me. To use me as a subject to fight about.

He slammed my door going out, upset that I didn't argue with him.

And I felt like my father's heart was the "Heart of Darkness." It was the opposite of Swerbuck's heart, which was on the surface where anyone could see it. My father's was deeper. His was the cruelty that lurked beneath everyday good manners. He was the patriot who sat in an airplane dropping bombs on Italy in WWII. I realized that neither Swerbuck nor my father were role models for me. I'd make my role model Tinkerbell. If you really really believed in fairies Tinkerbell would live and your life would be blessed. You would be surrounded by light. I'd carry sunshine in little sandwich bags. Then open them up and eat bright toast.

I was surprised I had gotten so much out of Joseph Conrad. Just by my father interrupting me. It was amazing how life and art got mixed up with each other like carrots and celery in a blender.

It was Saturday before finals and Swerbuck and Dawn invited me to meet them at Squire's Deli for lunch. I figured I could take a couple of hours off from studying. I was in a daze from all the work I had done and Squire's seemed almost unfamiliar to me. I was lost somewhere in Joseph Conrad's dead mind, not far from my chemistry workbook. Swerbuck and Dawn were friendly and chatty but I felt there was a long distance between us.

I had brought a book of Robert Frost's poems with me. Swerbuck noticed the cover and said, "He's corny. Why don't you read Ezra Pound?"

"Because that isn't our assignment," I said.

"Are you interested in knowledge or grades?" he asked.

"Both."

"Two roads diverged in a wood, and I--I took the one less traveled by, And that has made all the difference," he quoted.

Swerbuck didn't like Frost but he knew him. He knew all the poets. He was damn literate for a flunk-out, degenerate mess. I said," Be careful your road doesn't end at a cliff."

"I'm not afraid. I can fly," he said. And he lifted his arms like they were wings. His eyes were so intense that I felt he really believed he could fly. I almost expected him to take off from the table and fly around the restaurant.

There was a moment of silence and Dawn said, "I'm glad we could all stay friends."

I nodded my head with approval. My ego was no longer involved. I felt people grew and sometimes they grew in different ways and if their way wasn't your way then that's the way it went. And I thought that sitting here wasn't really what I should be doing now with finals coming up on Monday and I said, "I got to split. I got a lot of reading to do."

"What are you trying to prove," Swerbuck said. "Stay awhile."

"I'm trying to prove that I'm not stupid."

"Who cares?"

"Fogell"

"What?"

"I do."

"Don't you give a damn about the Suicide Club?" Swerbuck asked.

"That's dead for me. I'm out. I want to live."

"I knew over a year ago when your mother bought you those khaki pants and you got that regular haircut that you'd become like all the rest of them," he said. "You had so much promise. Even if you didn't know who Nietzsche was."

"Look. I'm really learning things I never knew before. From books," I said.

"I've read a million books. They've never done anything for me," Swerbuck said.

"You have to learn from life," Dawn said.

"From death," Swerbuck said.

"They're the same thing," Dawn said. What did she mean by that? It was ridiculous. To me life and death were opposites. They didn't come full circle and join. They were antagonists. They crashed into each other like two trucks in a head-on collision. You could hear the fenders squash, then fall away from each other. At night in the junkyard you can hear the metal moan. Along the road life goes on in its singular breathiness and gives voice to the intimations in the shoulder sluices. Death finds itself in accidents and wooden boxes.

I didn't want to discuss death, "You can get in touch with yourself by reading."

"I'm what they're going to be writing about," Swerbuck said.

Dawn rolled up her sleeve. Swerbuck's name was carved in her arm. It was frightening, she had completely fallen under his sway. She was his zombie. It pissed me off to see the scar.

"So you fucked him. That's your business," I said. But it hurt. I wanted my name to be carved in her arm. I wanted to belt him but I rejected the Joshua who beat him with a rock at the World's Fair. That was no longer me.

We all went outside and smoked a joint. I had to conquer my anger. I wanted to forget my pain. Fuck it, I'd done enough studying for a while. I'd get back to it. We followed Swerbuck back to his house. As usual his dad and Brian weren't home. Sometimes I wondered if he really had a family. Swerbuck broke out some scotch and we had another joint. The joint made me high and I started giggling. I hated scotch. I only had a jigger. We all went into Swerbuck's fathers room and got comfortable on his king sized bed. Dawn took off her clothes in front of both of us. I was amazed that Swerbuck wasn't furious about his girlfriend getting undressed in front of me. Then Swerbuck started getting undressed and so'd I. We both started feeling Dawn up and she was getting hot as hell. It was like Swerbuck and I were sharing one of those Kitchen Sink ice cream dishes at Jahn's Ice Cream Parlor. There was more than we could ever eat. I was expecting to get struck down dead at any moment for what we were doing. It went against all my private feelings of intimacy. But I was high and sad and up for anything. Dawn turned towards me and kissed me on the lips. I looked into her blue eyes. I think she was asking me for help. To let me know that she wanted me to take her back from Swerbuck. In the middle of all this bliss I felt a hand on my leg that wasn't Dawn's. I looked down and it was Swerbuck's. I didn't know what to do. I felt this longing for Dawn. I certainly didn't want Swerbuck. And I just wasn't into all that Batman perversion that Swerbuck was into. Camaraderie and all, aside. I took Swerbuck's hand off my leg and threw it back at him. I was upset that he could think of me that way. It cheapened our friendship, the closeness I felt towards him in having split his head open and the curiosity I had about how he stole my girlfriend. In all this resounding silence, the doorbell rang. We jumped into our clothes and ran out of Swerbuck's dad's room. We didn't even have time to make the bed.

It was Mr. Swerbuck and Brian at the door. Before Swerbuck could introduce us, his dad slapped him across the face and yelled, "I didn't say you could have friends over!"

I walked out with Dawn, saying, "Thanks for having us over Mr. Swerbuck."

"Fuck you, kid," he said.

As we were walking away from Swerbuck's apartment we saw Swerbuck opening his window. He yelled out to us, "My dad's a pig! Oink! Oink!"

We laughed. Swerbuck always had the spirit to fight back. Then we saw Papa Swerbuck come up behind him and smack him across the face again.

He yelled, "What were you doing in my bed?"

"Playing Goldilocks and the three bears."

His father hit him again and Swerbuck laughed. His father drew the blinds.

Dawn and I walked down the block and I said, "I can't believe you're going out with him."

"I didn't see you keeping your pants on," she said.

"Fuck you."

"I saw the way you looked at me. You still want me," she said.

"And if I do?"

"It's too late," she said. She kissed me on the lips and ran off down the block.

"Wait up," I yelled.

She turned and said, "I'm a million light years away from you. I could never wait up long enough." And she took off running again.

I should have chased her. I should have grabbed her by her black braid and shook some sense into her. I should have told her that Swerbuck can only lead to no good. But it wasn't my place. I was the jilted lover. I would only seem jealous. I had no say over her future. I could not stop the sadness of what was inevitable.

I walked home. I wanted to enter the pure, monastic world of books. To sit at my desk in a priest's robes. What was

I doing hanging out with these freaks, getting high and naked? And what was Swerbuck doing putting his hand on my leg? I imagined myself, naked, stepping in between the jacket of a huge volume and closing the flaps over myself so that I became the contents of the book. I looked at the table of contents. Dawn and Swerbuck weren't there.

"Press harder. No pain, no gain," my brother said. We were in the basement of the house weightlifting. It was a couple of days before graduation. I had already received my grades. They were a major improvement. I got all C's and B's for the semester. I was heading for F's before I started studying. I must have aced most of my finals. It was the fastest turn around in school history. I don't know how the teachers didn't accuse me of cheating.

I strained hard on my eighth repetition of bench presses at one hundred and fifty pounds. My brother helped bring the barbell up to the stanchions where I released it.

"Not bad for a beginner," Robert said. I had started lifting when I was studying for finals to try to relax my mind from all the strain. I decided I wanted to perfect both my body and my mind. I wanted to be pure and clean, unlike Swerbuck and Dawn. I wanted to be a Spartan warrior, not some Dionysian clown. "Put on two twenty-fives on each side," Robert said.

"That's two hundred pounds big boy," I said.

"I can handle it. I was on the weightlifting team at Curry College," he said. I had never heard of a weightlifting team before but I figured I'd see what he could bench press before I ridiculed him. I put the two plates on the barbell.

Robert lay back slowly on the bench, making sure his spine was flat.

"Give me a little boost," he said, putting his hands on the bar. I lifted the bar up and released it to him. He started bringing it down slowly, like he had complete control, like it was easy. Then when the bar was about half way down it crashed onto his chest. "Ow. Get it off me," he screamed. I cracked up laughing as I tugged the bar back onto the stanchions.

"What's so funny?" he said as he got up.

"I thought you were superman," I said.

"You going to blame me for having a cramp," he said.

"Well, if you have a cramp I guess you can't lift." I decided not to make fun of him. I'd give him some slack.

"That's right. You're smarter than I thought," he said.

The football field was filling up with parents in suits and ties and dresses. The parking lot and streets around the school were crowded with luxury cars. A sign hung over the goal post, "Class of 65." The bleachers started to fill up and the cloudless sky was celebrating graduation day with drum rolls of sunshine. Our hearts were beating with anticipation of the rest of our lives. Our sorrow for what was passing was caught in our eyes. I looked out from the gymnasium where I was waiting with the other students and saw my parents climbing the bleachers. My mother towered over my father. They actually looked proud to be here. They wandered around in the delusion that I was a real student. Not some fledgling.

We wandered out double file and stood in front of the Principal, Dr. Hollis, who was standing behind a podium telling our parents how grown up we all were and how we were going to take on the responsibilities of the world now that we had been educated at Great Neck North High. Applause all around. Then all the students sang the school song. It was some corny theme that I forgot the day after we sang it. I didn't actually sing it anyway. I mouthed it. I was tone deaf. Then Dr. Hollis called us up one at a time and gave us our diplomas. I felt like such a fake going up there. I didn't deserve to graduate. But I'd show them in the future.

When Dr. Hollis shook my hand he said, "Didn't think you'd make it, did you?"

I smiled. What else could I do? He was right. I was thankful I was getting out. I could start over again somewhere else with a clean slate. I could get good grades, approval. I could shuck this feeling of uselessness that covered me like leaves over kernals of corn.

After the ceremony all the parents went up to the Principal and told him how much they loved him. Dawn, Swerbuck and I walked into the back of the football field to chat for a few minutes. In our ceremonial gowns I couldn't believe that we were the same weirdos that almost did a threesome in Swerbuck's father's bed. The sun aimed its spotlight on us and we were center stage in our own drama. I stepped in some dog shit and wiped it off my heel with a twig.

"Where you guys going for the summer?" I asked.

"I'm off to Europe," Swerbuck said.

"I'm going to paint. Maybe I'll go to art school," Dawn said. She looked at Swerbuck who seemed disappointed. "Or go to Europe with Swerbuck," she said. Swerbuck smiled.

"I'm going to go to summer school at Adelphi. If I do well maybe I can matriculate," I said and asked Swerbuck, "How you going to get out of Vietnam if you don't go to college?"

"I'm fighting my own war. I'll be dead before they draft me."

"Are you still thinking of committing suicide?"

"Ask me no questions, I'll tell you no lies."

I couldn't help but admire his courage. He would have the balls to kill himself. He had drama. And he had my girl, Dawn. Well, he could have whatever he wanted. I had my books. Or I would have my books. Studying would protect me from Swerbuck like a cross discourages a vampire. And if that seemed dull or not so cool then what the heck. I wasn't ready to die. I'd rather be a prig than a corpse. We all wandered back towards our families. As I walked past the Principal I noticed he was speaking to Mr. Swerbuck who was saying, "My son, he studies Apollinaire in France."

I didn't see Dawn's father.

My mother kissed me. My brother said, "If you follow in my footsteps, you'll be a scholar too."

Back at our house my father said, "Well, I can't exactly say you graduated with honors."

"I'll get my honors in college," I told my father.

"That's the attitude," my mom said. "Who cares about high school anyhow?"

May came walking out of the kitchen into our dining room with a graduation cake with candles on top. I blew them out and everyone applauded. My mother cut the cake and served it. There was a little candy student on top in a graduation cap and robe.

Robert was feeling left out and he hit us with some big news, "I'm transferring to Miami U."

I knew he had applied. I was thrilled for him. Even though it wasn't a great school, it was a lot better than Curry. "You got in?"

"Just heard today," he said.

"How you going to drive home every weekend?" I said, laughing.

He threw his napkin at me.

I liked the cake. It had chocolate, vanilla and strawberry ice cream inside. I felt good about graduating. It was better than flunking out.

"Let's go to the movies to celebrate," my mother said.

"I don't know, mom," I said.

"Why not?" Sylvia said. "Don't be a spoil sport."

"I have to study."

"What study?" Robert said. "You just graduated."

"It's like a muscle. Like weightlifting. I don't want my new habits to get soft," I said.

"You're not even in college yet," Hy said.

"Summer school starts soon and I got some books they're going to be using at Adelphi in my anthropology course. I want to get a head start." Then I got up from the table. Robert went, "Boo." I could tell that he was worried that I was going to be a better student than him. I already had the better room.

Chapter 29

I had taken driver's ed the last semester of high school and after failing the driving test twice I finally got my license. It was amazing that I failed the test, considering that I had been driving illegally, using my brother's license, for two years. I guess the examiners just didn't want to pass a spoiled ass kid who was driving his parents' Lincoln. Anyhow my folks let me drive the Lincoln illegally to Adelphi University for summer school.

It was a beautiful campus in Garden City, Long Island and when I arrived there I felt like I was in a cloud at the top of Mt. Snow and students were rolling through snowflakes carrying books. I was in education heaven, a million miles from the prison of Great Neck North High School. I don't know where I got this idea that school would save me. It wasn't just that it would get me out of Vietnam. But that it would put me in touch with myself and save me from shrinking and rotting like an acorn in a bunch of dead leaves. Could it have been just because Fogell had called me stupid? Was that the trigger that got me studying a hundred hours a week? Maybe. I felt like knowledge would keep me from falling into a junkyard of scrap thoughts. When I pulled into the parking lot in my huge Lincoln I felt light as cotton candy. The world was pink and

fluffy. I had come home from a disastrous detour into negativity. Failure peeled from my forehead like a band-aid. And I
entered an unblemished safe zone like soldiers stepping across
the border into Belgium during World War II. I picked up my
books and got out of the car. I wanted to kiss my books. They
were little icons. I was in love with the black ink on the pages.
Reading was no longer a curse. It was a stairway to heaven.

Professor Norbund, my anthropology professor, was a
bouncy egghead, in his early thirties, filled with irrepressible
energy and a manic love for everything primitive. He'd dance
around the front of the class holding up artifacts from his
travels in Africa. I had never seen a man so consumed with
his studies before. It was like we didn't exist and were listening
in to him talking to himself, making faces, wiggling his ears,
growling. A dribble of saliva would bounce around his chin
when he got particularly excited and his lips would go purple.
The first day of class he let us go early and told us, "Go edu-
cate yourselves." The next day we didn't know what to expect
when he turned on a phonograph and started playing some
vaudeville strip music. Some of us started to giggle. Then Professor Norbund started dancing around like he was going to
do a strip tease. I couldn't believe it. He threw off his tie and
shook his hips around and around. Then he took off his shoes
and shirt. There was a hole in his right sock and his big toe
stuck through. A fat girl next to me said, "This is disgusting,"
and walked out. Norbund ignored her and took off his belt.
The record skipped and then started repeating itself. Norbund
went back to the phonograph, cleaned the needle and started
the record over. A football player type raised his hand. When
Norbund didn't call on him he blurted out, "What are you
doing, sir?"

"I'm stripping," Norbund replied.

"Why?" a good-looking cheerleader type asked.

"To shake you up," he said. Then he sang, "Shake, rattle and roll," and gyrated his hips again. "To teach you the unexpected. Maybe they teach like this in a whorehouse in Borneo. I'm crazy here but I'm normal in Borneo. I've been to Borneo. Have you? Or maybe not. But that's what this course is all about. Comparisons. Cultures. Comparative culture. Moral relativism. Get it. Got it. Make it yours like an igloo cools a toe or a fire heats a coal," Norbund said and continued dancing around the room.

A couple of other students walked out. I was intrigued. Here was a professor who took chances. He was an educated version of Swerbuck. But instead of death he had chosen life. He stopped dancing, turned off the phonograph and got dressed again. He looked exhausted like a man who had just achieved orgasm and wanted to take a nap. He was pale, academic and meek. Looking at him you'd never know that he was the philosopher of Borneo whorehouses and the striptease academician. He made me uncomfortable but there was something I admired about him.

Surely, education at Great Neck North had never been like this. I felt like a racehorse. I wanted to run out of the starting gate, blast through academia and shoot the broken legged horses of my past.

Summer school lasted six weeks and I got A's in both anthropology and psychology.

I was still seeing my psychiatrist, Dr. Rosenquest. He respected the work I was doing. But as usual he was a realist. He reminded me that if I didn't get into a college full-time I'd end up in Vietnam. I spoke to my parents who made an appointment with Mr. Tibalt, a high-paid, private guidance counselor. I went with my mother to see Mr. Tibalt in a rundown office in

Hempstead. He was a big, bald, sloppy looking guy who had some scabs on his scalp and dermatitis on his hands.

"He's an A student at Adelphi," my mother said.

Tibalt looked at a folder and said, "Two A's don't mean anything. They'll never let him matriculate with his high school grades."

"He has to go to college," my mother said.

"I have some connections at Emporia College in Kansas. Joshua can go there and then transfer out after his freshman year," Tibalt said.

"I never heard of Emporia," I said.

"You got to go somewhere. Or you'll end up in Vietnam," Tibalt said.

No way I wanted to go to Vietnam. I'd sooner kill Tibalt than shoot some Vietnamese farmer. I hated war. I wasn't afraid to kill but I wanted to kill who and when I wanted. I didn't want to kill when the army told me to. Killing was emotional, personal. And I wanted to die on my own terms. There was nothing more sacred than one's own death. I couldn't let the military dictate that to me.

"Where in Kansas?" I asked.

"Kansas, Kansas," Tibalt said. "The Wizard of Oz was filmed there."

I loved the Wizard of Oz. I wished the straw man would use his new brain to come up with a solution for me. But I didn't want to go to Kansas. I didn't want to be at some fourth rate college. I remembered how I made fun of my brother for going to Curry College. Was Emporia any better? I wasn't a flunkey any more. I got two A's at Adelphi. I should be given a chance at a real college. I'd be embarrassed to tell anyone I was at Emporia. What a disgrace. My past was catching up to me and dragging me into its own failed shadow. I could taste the darkness around my lips.

"I'm not going," I said to Tibalt. He scratched a scab off his baldhead and looked at me disappointed. There was sadness in his eyes like he was visualizing me being shot by a sniper in Vietnam.

"We'll see."

The bus drove through dust balls on the flat plains of Kansas. Everything was blown in the wind. The indifferent fields were popping up in irrelevant places. It didn't matter to the fields that corn was sticking out of them. The birds hung from the still air like targets at an arcade. My education was becoming a form of draft dodging. I kept looking at my watch and I felt that the road was being measured in hours scalped from my life, that Emporia would amputate a year of my existence, that I would be a stump. Looking out at the wheat-colored fields I felt like I'd almost rather have gone to Vietnam. But I didn't want to kill gooks. I liked their cooking.

When I arrived at Emporia I felt like I was pulling into a Hollywood Set. There was something prefabricated about the campus. Like it had been set up to fool the draft board but that there wasn't really any school there. A few small buildings and antique cars were scattered around a wheat field. The students all wore jeans and T-shirts. Some wore overalls like farmers. None wore Great Neck collegiate clothes. These kids weren't preppy. They weren't preparing for the Ivy League Colleges. They looked to me like big, strapping mongoloids. These kids were not part of the hippy generation. They were dumb, large hicks who looked like they were living somewhere back in the fifties with the characters from "Father Knows Best" and "Leave it to Beaver."

I carried my duffel bag up to a sign that said, "Freshman Orientation." I followed a bunch of red-necks into the auditorium. I was one of the puniest guys there. I think the whole school consisted of football players. This was my punishment for being a wiseass; I'd have to spend the next year with a bunch of fucken lumberjacks. Maybe I was being punished for that time I split Swerbuck's head open with a rock. Swerbuck? Now I knew why he wanted to commit suicide. Maybe he had been to Kansas. We all chose seats in the auditorium. Nametags were passed around which we were supposed to fill out and put on our chests. A large blond football player sat down next to me. He was so broad he looked like he was wearing shoulder pads beneath his T-shirt. He could have been a locomotive pulling twenty freight cars of timber. "Hi. I'm Wosheffsky," he said. "Where you hale from?"

What was that "hale from" crap?

"I'm from New York," I said.

"Never been there. I'm from Hayes. Hayes, Kansas. About three hundred good miles the other side of, whatever? I've never been this far from home. Mom says it's good to travel. Broadens you," he said. "Who are you?"

"Joshua."

Wosheffsky seemed like a nice guy. Dumb as a Polish sausage but nice. He had a friendly open attitude for a brontosaurus. But still I had promised myself I wouldn't hang out with dumb people. I was in training to be a scholar. I had to make up for years of not studying. If I paled around with idiots, I'd become a degenerate again. I had to protect myself against regression, against being myself. I didn't want to be swimming around in the bottom of the toilet bowl with yesterday's crap.

"Why'd you choose Emporia?" I asked.

"They don't got no college in Hayes. Besides, Emporia has a good football team. I sure can tackle a bag of bones," he said. "Why you come all the way here?"

I could see from that big farmer's grin that he knew I was a flunkey. I was here because no one else would take me and I was too scared to go fight in Vietnam.

"I may not be staying," I said. I was afraid if I stayed here I'd become Polish. I'd end up a pig farmer. I told Wosheffsky to hold my place. I had to make a phone call. I made a beeline to the phone booth and called my parents. My dad answered the phone.

"I feel like killing myself," I said.

"Who is this?"

"Your son."

"Robert?"

"No. Joshua. I mean it dad. I want to kill myself."

My father said, "Everyone feels that way when they first go to college. You just got to stick with it."

"I hate these hicks. I'm not cut out to be one of them."

"Who said you're a hick?"

"I'll turn into one if I stay here. I want to go to a good school."

"You got to earn that. You call yourself a liberal but you're a snob. You won't even give good, old-fashioned Americans from Kansas a chance."

"They hate me. I'm a Jew."

My father hung up the phone on me. I banged my head against the phone booth. It hurt. I did it again. I felt Swerbuck pulling me into a bloody whirlpool of his own hurting. This wasn't right. I didn't want to go back into all that self-destructive bull.

I went back into the auditorium and sat down next to Wosheffsky. He had a big smile. He was glad to see his new buddy. I guess he visualized me visiting his house and tending the pigs with him; maybe helping Auntie May make a blueberry pie. My head hurt from where I hit the phone booth. I felt a large bump with my fingers. There was no sense in doing that. If I wanted to communicate through the phone to my father I should have used my voice not my head.

A pimply college senior in overalls led Wosheffsky and me to our dorm. We were both assigned to Dorm 3, the largest dorm in the college. It was a huge room in a basement where there were about twenty cots and no dividers. Eight concrete columns held up the ceiling. Next to each bed there was a metal locker and a small wooden desk. I wondered how behemoths like Wosheffsky got their legs under these desks. Some students were already in their beds napping. Others were wandering in. Many of them were locals and knew each other. All of them were over six feet tall with fat, wide faces. They were like Mr. Potato Heads before the eyes, nose and lips were put in. They were mostly ears and hair. Put them in trench coats and they'd make perfect, indistinguishable FBI agents. I figured I was going to have a lot of trouble fitting in. I was a Jew in a land of pigs. That wasn't kosher.

I went into a bathroom stall, said to myself I could stick it out, and broke down and cried. The tears came over me in a torrent. I couldn't help myself. I was petrified that someone would hear me and call me a crybaby. I had made a wreck of my life and I didn't fit in here, there or anywhere. "You're a piece of shit," I said out loud to myself. "You're so busy telling everyone else that they stink that you forgot to stick your nose up your own ass. You're going to have a lot of wiping to do before you clean up your act." I heard someone walking into the bathroom, then opening the stall next to me. I shut up.

Later that afternoon I went with Wosheffsky back to the auditorium for an orientation lecture by Dean Hamilton. I tried to stay optimistic. Maybe Dean Hamilton had been kicked out of Harvard for smoking marijuana and was now teaching here; perhaps, the college was filled with troubled geniuses. No such luck. Dean Hamilton droned on about the proud athletic tradition of Emporia. He then said he expected the school to get accredited within a few years. I didn't even realize it wasn't accredited. This was as bad as Curry College. I pictured my brother laughing at me. The lucky bastard was down in the sunshine at Miami U. Dean Hamilton complained, "Elysian College, in the neighboring town, just got accreditation last year and they don't even have a football team. In fact, it's a God damned girl's college. Is that fair? Next year will be our year. We're due."

I phased out after a few minutes. Dean Hamilton looked like Hitler up there shouting at the youth corps.

"I'm the first guy in the family to go to college," Wosheffsky whispered to me. "Most of them didn't even graduate from high school."

How was I going to spend a year in this place? I felt like I was going to die. That the air would poison me.

"Why don't you go out for football?" Wosheffsky asked me.

"Because I'm too small and I stink," I said.

"I'll teach you," he said. That was very sweet of the big lug.

"I'm only five foot ten and one hundred and forty pounds," I said.

"Maybe you could be a cheerleader," he said.

I hated male cheerleaders. I remembered them in their saddle shoes and cheerleading sweaters in Great Neck. Why the fuck would I cheer for the football players? If anything, I'd want to see them dead for stealing away everyone's attention from me. What was I doing here anyway? I belonged in fucken Harvard. Jimmy Fogell knew I wasn't average. Ginny thought I was deep. I got A's at Adelphi. Let my people go from these freaken wheat fields.

I figured I'd rather be a failure anywhere than a success here. This was a no win situation. I wanted to crawl up into a ball and have someone kick me into the distant corner of a field.

"What you gonna do?" Wosheffsky asked.

"Kill myself," I said.

"Wow. I never saw anyone kill himself before," Wosheffsky said. His mouth dropped open in amazement.

"Watch me," I said.

A teacher who was standing in the aisle like one of Hitler's storm troopers threw an eraser that hit me on the shoulder. His finger was pressed against his mouth, "Sssh!" I sat erect and looked up at the stage. I could swear Dean Hamilton was doing the goose step. I felt like helping him kill the Jews. Me first. The next morning I planned to kill myself but first I needed a motorcycle.

An ironic sun hung overhead in a blue sky as I walked down a road through an ocean of wheat fields on my way to Morgan's Motrocyles. A salesman, Jethro, who looked like a Hell's Angel, introduced himself.

"I'm Joshua," I answered.

"We got almost the same name," he said. "We're practically family."

Like I needed the sale's pitch to kill myself.

"Want to see some Harley's?" he asked.

"I only got five hundred dollars," I said.

"You sound cheap. You a Jew from New York?" he asked. He didn't say it like an insult. He actually asked out of curiosity. I don't know why we had reps as cheap. I never knew a Jew who was cheap. Every Jew I knew in Great Neck was *nouveau riche* and spent big time.

"Are you a hick from Kansas?" I asked.

"Originally from New Jersey," he said. "Let me show you something in your price range."

I should have walked out but I didn't know where else to go to get a motorcycle and I wanted to get this suicide over with. He showed me an old, beat-up Dukati, "This was my nephew's prize possession. It runs like a top. I'll give it to you for five hundred bucks."

It hurt me like hell to give this bigot money. But politics had no place in suicide.

I drove the Dukati out of the bike shop. It was a flimsy little bike but it had a lot of zip. I took it out for a spin for about an hour before I drove it back to the campus. It was fun to ride it through the flat wheat fields of Kansas. I almost wanted to crash it just to feel myself fly over the handlebars. To see if I was indestructible.

Later that night I was in my dorm reading "Hamlet." I couldn't get away from Wosheffsky. He was curious about me; he'd never seen a New York Jew before. And he was in awe of my upcoming suicide. He was like a disciple. I was getting worried that he might want to commit suicide with me. He tapped me on my shoulder, almost knocking me out of bed with his giant paw.

"What you going to do?" Wosheffsky asked.

"About what?"

"The suicide."

"I don't know yet."

"Can I watch?" I shook my head, no. "I never saw one. Except our neighbor, Samuel Hemmings. He hung himself. But I didn't actually see it because my mother wouldn't let me in his barn. Though I heard about it," he said.

"Listen, it's all an act. I'm just trying to get out of here."

"What do you mean?" Wosheffsky asked. He looked disappointed and confused. He couldn't figure why I'd want to get out of here. He was having the time of his life. His whole family was proud of him. He was a college boy.

"I'm going to fake it," I said. He looked mystified. "I'm going to get my bike up to about five miles per hour. Then I'll head for the curb on the side of the road and jump off. I'll run over and lie down on top of it until an ambulance comes. The ambulance will be my proof. I'll tell my mom about it and she'll send me a plane ticket out of here."

"I'm glad," Wosheffsky said.

"About what?"

"That you're not killing yourself. I mean, you're a nice guy."

He wasn't such a bad guy himself. It's just that he was Midwestern and large. Kind of like a friendly boxer who's always slobbering around with loose jowls.

"Thanks Wosheffsky," I said.

"You're crazy, you know."

"I'm living in a crazy world. I have to do crazy things to get sane results," I said.

"Huh?"

I figured it was time to place a call home and set my plan in motion. I went to a phone booth and called my parents. I tried to think dark, deadly thoughts to get into the mood. I pictured my grandmother when she was sick in the hospital before she died. Unfortunately, Hy answered the phone again.

"You got to let me come home," I said.

"You just got there."

"I'm afraid of what I'll do to myself," I said. I thought I was a clever bullshitter. But part of me really was afraid. Kansas was like a rich, seven-layer cake of boredom. I didn't think I could eat another slice. I might really kill myself. Wouldn't that make Swerbuck happy?

"Quit using emotional blackmail on me," Hy said.

Where'd my dad learn the term "emotional blackmail?" Must be from my mother.

"I'll kill myself," I said.

I heard my mother in the background asking, "What's going on Hy?"

"He's saying he wants to come home."

"Is he alright?" my mother asked.

"Yes, he's just a little homesick," Hy said. "He's pretending he's going to kill himself."

"You idiot. Let me have the phone," my mother said. I heard them scuffling for the phone and the line went dead. Hy must have hung up on me.

The next day I cut classes and took my Dukati out. I drove it over to a quiet place on the road where there was a fairly large curb. I was going to fly over the curb, land and then jump off and let the bike crash on the grass just before the woods. Then I'd go over and lie down on it like I had tried to kill myself. I revved the bike up on the street. I felt a little guilty that I was just pretending and had no intention of hurting myself. I didn't like to feel like a faker. So I figured I'd make it more realistic and instead of going five miles an hour I'd go fifteen. I took off and headed for the curb. Just before I hit it I pulled back on the handlebars, doing a wheelie and bounced onto the grass. The only problem was that I bounced too hard and the whole bike flipped over. My cuff was stuck in the chain and I couldn't break free from the bike, which landed on top of me. My leg got twisted and snapped like a twig. I wasn't wearing a helmet and my forehead banged against the handlebars. I was in a pool of blood when the ambulance showed up and woke me with its screaming siren and pulsing red light.

After that things moved fast. I got eight stitches in my head at the hospital. The doctors put a steel pin in my leg and a cast up to my thigh. I called my mother. I could hear her screaming at my father that it was his fault. They released me back to the school two days later. Dean Hamilton picked me up at the hospital in an immaculately polished 1965 Chevy. He must have been very proud of that car from the way he took care of it.

"Are you going to finish out the year?" he asked. He looked nervous.

"I'm going home."

"There's no sense in suing the school. It's not Emporia's fault," he insisted.

"I never thought it was," I said. He breathed a sigh of relief.

"I figured you being from New York and your father a lawyer and...."

"My father's not a lawyer."

"Good."

Wosheffsky skipped football practice to help me pack. You could see that his muscles underneath his shirt were anxious to hit someone. But he was fascinated by my injuries. He was jealous. He rarely got hurt that much in football.

"I thought you were going to fake it," he said.

"I did. I just fucked it up," I said. "I got my leg caught. The damn bike flipped on me."

"Sure. Maybe you were trying to kill yourself. You can't fool me. You sure go all the way when you want," he said.

I let out a groan. My leg hurt me. "This time I think I went a little too far," I said.

Wosheffsky picked up my duffel bag and escorted me to the bus. I was on crutches. He put my bag in the compartment under the bus.

I turned to him. This was goodbye. I'd certainly never see him again. I said, "Knock em dead football player." I was going to miss the dimwit. I couldn't figure out how he managed to maneuver all that brawn and still keep his balance. It was like his strength was moving in different directions, trying to get out.

"Next time try to kill yourself. You might get lucky and miss," Wosheffsky said, guffawing.

I hugged him lightly but he grabbed me like a grizzly bear and almost squeezed all the breath out of my aching body. I could have gotten killed just saying goodbye to him.

After I managed to tumble into my seat and lean my crutches against the window I waved to Woshoffsky. He waved back and ran after the bus. I think the big dope had tears in his eyes. I was hoping he wouldn't reach out his big paw and stop the bus from leaving. But in another minute he was gone and I was on my way to the airport. I had no plans. I didn't know how I'd get out of the draft. I was worried about what I'd tell my parents. I was like a blind man playing with a jigsaw puzzle. But I figured if I just gave it time I'd stumble my way into figuring out where all the pieces fit. My thumbs would develop second sight.

When I saw my parents at La Guardia airport I decided I'd play the apologetic, humble game. I had tears in my eyes when I told my mother in the car going home that, "I'm sorry I tried to kill myself. I didn't mean to hurt anyone."

Sylvia yelled at my father, who was driving, "It's your fault you Neanderthal. You should have told him to come home when he said he was depressed." She slapped him, almost causing an accident.

"I thought he was blackmailing us."

"You idiot," Sylvia said and hit him again. "Does that broken leg look like blackmail?"

"I was wrong."

"I'll say. You better call that Dean friend of yours and get him into L.I.U.," Sylvia said.

"I don't know if...."

"You want him to end up in Vietnam and get killed. I swear Hy, if that happens I'll kill you myself." Then she hit him over the head with a magazine.

"I'll do it. I'll do it."

"Thanks dad," I said. He gave me a dirty look in the rear view mirror.

Chapter 30

A couple of days later I called Dawn and we met at Squire's Deli. She took one look at the cast on my leg and the bandages on my head and said, "So you tried to graduate from the Suicide Club ahead of us."

I felt ridiculous. I was the one who didn't believe in suicide and here I had almost killed myself. I looked at Dawn and felt horny for her. I imagined her as an Indian princess lying in a skinny leather thong on a grassy slope along side of a waterfall. A flute was playing, lambs were dancing, everything was pastoral. The day was clear and vivid to me like when I was tripping on mescaline. Only I wasn't high. I was in love again like when I first met her. Then, suddenly, the setting was messed up. Dawn metamorphosed into a two-headed dragon. One head was hers and the others was Swerbuck. They traded fiery kisses.

"I didn't try to graduate from the Suicide Club. I faked suicide so I could get out of Emporia," I said.

"You fake pretty good."

"Yeah. It almost looks real," I said, laughing and pointing at my cast. She laughed too. I guess the whole thing was kind of funny in a painful way.

"What you going to do about Vietnam?" she asked, serious again.

"I'm going to go over there and kill gooks," I said.

She threw a package of salt at me. The waitress came over. "I'm only kidding," I said and we ordered a couple of roast beef sandwiches, French fries and sodas. I started plucking out pickles from a little metal pickle dish that was on the table.

"So what you gonna do?" she asked.

"My dad knows the Dean at L.I.U. For five hundred bucks contribution to his temple, he said I could go there," I said. "Where's your boyfriend?"

"Barcelona. I may go over there and take a few courses. Paint. Learn Spanish."

The thought of fat lips Swerbuck having Dawn over there made me sick. But I didn't want to think about it. What I needed was books. I was becoming afraid of people. If I could just spend my days turning pages, I wouldn't have to deal with people. The fools would respect me when all I was doing was hiding out from life's bandit emotions. There were always more things to learn, more life to consume, more vitamins to suck from this earth.

"Do you really like Swerbuck?" I asked.

"He fills a gap."

I wondered if she meant her cunt. "What gap?"

"Some need. I don't know. You can't explain everything, Joshua."

"If you try you can."

"Listen. He doesn't hold back. He's himself."

I felt this sudden stupid urge to go to bed with her again. Maybe just to wreck her relationship with that sicko. I said, "You want to sleep together for old times sakes?"

"What's that about?"

"I don't know." I didn't.

"I thought we were friends."

"We are but he's the wrong guy. He'll destroy both of you."

"You're someone to talk. Evil Knevel."

"I didn't try to kill myself. It was an accident," I said, feeling like a jerk. I thought of how it felt when I crashed my motorcycle with the world turning upside down over me. I liked it. It was like walking down a dark street in a red light district and coming upon this beautiful blond hooker. I'd flirt with her but I'd refuse to fuck her because I didn't want to get a venereal disease. Death was like that. I could flirt with it but I wouldn't want to fuck it and die. I mean, assuming death was a woman and all that.

The sandwiches, soda and fries came. If I wanted to kill myself there'd be no sense in eating. I held my French fry up and said, "By this fry I choose life."

"What are you talking about?" Dawn asked.

"Could you pass the ketchup," I said. And I started to demolish my food. All this talk had made me hungry.

Dr. Rosenquest was a little shocked to see me walking in with a bandaged head and crutches.

"So why'd you try to kill yourself?" he asked.

I was disappointed in him. He shouldn't have assumed that I tried to kill myself. I said, "It was an accident."

"No such thing," he said.

"I hated Emporia," I said.

"Did you think you deserved to be in Harvard?"

"I got A's at Adelphi."

"You have to prove you can get more than two of them."

I got really angry. "I will and if I don't..." I shouted. But I cut off the sentence before I could finish it.

"You'll what?" he said very calmly.

"I was going to say "I'd kill myself," I said.

"Is that what you really want?"

We discussed suicide for about twenty minutes. He and I both knew that I had no desire to die. I was just thrashing around to make a statement; I was a model looking to pose for a photographer. I wanted to affirm that I was someone by threatening to annihilate myself. He told me to close my eyes and imagine myself dead. I couldn't. I saw myself as the Goodyear Blimp, flying over Yankee Stadium, getting a lot of attention. It was pulling a banner with my name on it, "Joshua." Everyone was shouting, "Joshua, Joshua." I realized I didn't want to be a failure. I wanted to be a star.

"I want to succeed," I said.

"But for what reason do you want to succeed?"

"I don't know."

"Is it because you're afraid of failing?"

"Maybe."

"Well?"

"I'm afraid I'll fall apart and become a bum and kill myself," I said.

"Why would you do that?"

"Because if I can't succeed I don't deserve to live."

"Who told you that?"

"Nobody."

"You can succeed by just standing still."

"How?"

"Love yourself for who you are."

"I don't even like me for who I am."

"When you learn to like yourself, everything else will fall into place."

"How do I do that?"

Rosenquest looked at his watch and said, "Time's up." It annoyed me that I was just one little chunk of his time. That I wasn't the most important thing in his world. After all, we were discussing my life. As we walked out, I said, "I want to be a star."

"Let's discuss it next time," he said.

I passed a midget in the waiting room. I guess she had her share of problems too.

The Vietnam War was in high gear. Every day they'd list the names of the dead in the newspapers. Young men my age were being shipped home in coffins. The students across the country protested. They marched on Washington. They sang anti-war songs. But still the war went on and the politicians dribbled out platitudes about saving the free world by killing peasants in rice paddies halfway across the planet.

I was called to Fort Dix for a physical. I had gotten into L.I.U. so I had a student deferral from the draft at the moment but they wanted to check me out to see if I'd be worth drafting after I graduated. My cast had just come off and I was able to limp around. As far as I was concerned, there was no way they were getting me. I wasn't about to kill anybody because I was told to do it by some redneck lieutenant. I wanted to put a bullet in the forehead of every officer. I wanted to kill my own side. Not that I was violent. I wanted to kill all violent people, like soldiers, and particularly the ones in authority.

I figured I could get myself a 1-Y deferment. I'd let them think I was neurotic and needed some psychotherapy. I didn't want to make them think I was too crazy or I'd get a 4-F, which was for real nuts, and would ruin my record when I was looking for a job later.

They assigned us to several rooms and put us through some intelligence tests that were designed for blue-collar workers. Their focus was on spatial relationships and tools. I lived in outer space and didn't know a saw from a wrench. I didn't do well. Then they sent us into a large hall and told us to take off our clothes, all except our underwear and our shoes. This was embarrassing as hell. I ended up standing there in knee high motorcycle boots, wearing baby blue bikini underwear.

We stood on a line to get blood tests. I was chilly standing there when someone pinched my ass. I turned around ready to kill and I saw this dumb, giggling face. It was Mad Dog, laughing his head off at me. Dressed in boxer shorts and Weejun loafers with black socks. It had been a long time. We shook hands and patted each other on the backs.

"You look like a queer biker," Mad Dog laughed.

"Hey, I didn't know I'd be walking around in my underwear," I said.

"It'll be great to kill gooks together," Mad Dog said. He was the toughest talking coward I ever met.

The line was moving along towards the doctor who gave the vaccination. A lot of guys looked nervous. Like they were afraid of needles. The only needle I was afraid of was a heroin needle. Something you couldn't come back from. Like Vietnam. I always needed an out. I didn't like permanent mistakes, just little errors.

"How'd you do on the IQ test?" Mad Dog asked.

"Not well," I said. I couldn't believe I hadn't done well on their stupid intelligence test. Particularly, when I was running straight A's in college.

"I scored in the ninety-ninth percentile," Mad Dog boasted.

"That's great." Proof positive that the tests didn't mean a thing.

"What was your score?"

"Sixty-seventh percentile." What did they expect? I wasn't a mechanic. I couldn't identify different types of screwdriver heads and drill bits. What did that have to do with intelligence?

"You dummy," Mad Dog cackled. "They're going to put you in the motor pool. You'll never get to kill gooks."

"I'd rather kill you," I said, imagining putting a bullet hole right between his eyes and watching his smile freeze in mid-air, then fall.

A huge black guy in the front of the line fainted as the doctor put the needle up to his arm. A Puerto Rican behind us had an epileptic fit. He fell to the floor writhing. Then another small white guy had an epileptic attack too. A couple of male nurses had their hands full attending to them. I figured they were both faking.

"Faggots can't take a shot," Mad Dog snarled. "Let me go ahead of you. I got guts." He walked up to the doctor and said, "Give it to me hard." The doctor inserted the needle and Mad Dog fainted in a dead heap on the ground, the needle sticking out of his arm.

When I got to meet with the army psychiatrist, I saw my chance. I wanted to let him know how I felt about this stupid war. I sat across from him in a little cubicle made out of white curtains. He was a middle-aged man with gray hair cut in a flat top. Psychiatrists were supposed to have long hair and beards. There was virtually no soundproofing in the curtains and I was worried someone walking by might overhear me. But fuck it; I had to do what I had to do.

"Have you ever done drugs?" the psychiatrist asked.

"Pot, mescaline and glue," I whispered.

"Acid?"

"Twice," I lied. I had never done it. I was afraid of hallu-cinations. Mescaline had freaked me out and I'd get visions on something as mild as pot. No way I was messing with acid.

"Any gay experiences?"

"Yeah. A *ménage a trois*."

"How's that?"

"Me and a girl and another guy," I said. I thought of Dawn and Swerbuck. But it wasn't really a ménage. I didn't even let Swerbuck touch my leg and I sure didn't touch his. Still I'd rather pretend I was a fag than get my dick blown off in Vietnam. I had this gangrene of fear eating me up inside.

My mother had a cartoon framed in her bathroom wall of a naked woman in the park imitating a statue with the caption, "Public opinion doesn't bother me." It did but her goal was to not let it bother her. I didn't care what the shrink thought of me. I didn't care about public opinion. I was invisible to their slurs. I had erased myself. I was a smudge on a page of societal clichés. If I had a gun and no one were looking I'd shoot a bullet through one of the shrink's ears and out the other. I'd knock out his earwax. If I could get away with it. If my con-science wouldn't bother me too much.

"You make me sick," the psychiatrist said. That was a shock.

"You're really open minded," I said.

"In the army an open mind is a bullet in the brain."

I saw a bullet in his brain. It turned into a rose that opened in slow motion. I wanted to smell his hair. Death has many petals. I wanted to touch the rose.

Chapter 31

In November Dawn wanted me to go to Manhattan to attend some anti-Vietnam peace march. I really didn't feel like it because I had already received a 4-F for mental problems. I was only trying for 1-Y. My record was ruined by the 4-F. I'd probably have trouble getting a job. I'd deal with that when I had to. I guess the shrink thought I was nuttier than I was. But at least I wouldn't be drafted. Even if there were a third World War, they wouldn't take me. They'd probably send senior citizens to fight ahead of me.

While we were on the Long Island Railroad heading into the city to attend the march, I said, "They're never going to draft me. I don't care about Vietnam anymore."

"That's selfish. What about the dying soldiers?"

"They don't care about me," I said.

"That's disgusting."

It was. Even if I felt that way. I figured I better change my tune. I didn't want to turn Dawn off completely. I was starting to like her again.

She reached into her pocketbook and took out some slides of her paintings. She handed them to me and passed me a magnifying glass. "Look at these," she said.

They were bizarre charcoals of the horror of war. It was as if screams were trapped in the slides. Sadness was mangled in crushed chiaroscuro. Gray brains fell out of helmet flaps; eyes dropped from heads like eggs. Feet were twisted in their sockets and running in the opposite direction from their bodies. A hand was looking for its wrist.

"These are my anti-Vietnam charcoals. What do you think?" Dawn asked.

I was stunned. I thought I had gone into the belly of death and been ground up in its intestines. I was shit in a bed-pan. I was in pieces. I said, "I think you should be drawing not marching."

I went through the slides. One horror after the next. Everything was a sleuth of movement. I came to the last slide like a detective looking at a clue. It was a charcoal portrait of me with a large cross on top of me. But it wasn't a Christian cross; it was an X. "What's this?" I asked.

"You."

"You're having trouble crossing me out of your life, aren't you." I meant it kind of flippantly but she looked over at me and said, "Yes."

I suddenly felt sadness for our past and all we were missing. This was the girl I once looked at as an Indian princess bouncing through fields of maize with her black braid following her like a secret. I had bathed in her blue eyes and drowned. I said, "We belong together. Swerbuck's wrong for you"

Big mistake. She jerked her neck like she was breaking free from the closeness we were both feeling. She wasn't ready to leave Swerbuck. She said, "Maybe you and I belong together in some other life."

She threw her slides in her bag. I guessed she preferred Swerbuck because he was so fucked up she could mother him. For some reason Dawn needed Swerbuck. He inspired her. They both were bloody, wet and warm like slit wrists. There was death like the flavor of a lifesaver in her loving.

When we got to the city we took a cab up to the fifties and joined the parade going down Sixth Avenue. There were no cars. I felt like I was at the Macy's Day Thanksgiving Parade.

"I like being with you," I said.

"Is that a proposition?" Dawn flirted.

"Depends on if you want me propositioning you."

"You know we're only friends now," she said. I was disappointed but relieved. Dawn was a little too wild and unconstructed for me to handle. I wanted to cut off the edges of my life with a paper splicer. To live in a flotilla of right angles.

"Did you hear about Denby?" Dawn asked.

"No." I hadn't thought of that nut since that fight in his backyard.

"Don't you read the papers?"

"Nope. I only read books." I didn't care what was going on in the world. Why waste my time with the newspapers, which were saturated with the flotsam and jetsam of daily irrelevances?

"He hacked his sister to death with an ax in a cabin in Maine."

That sick fuck. It figured. I should have killed him when I had him down in his backyard.

The crowd started singing, "Give Peace a Chance." Who gave Denby's sister a chance? All these bleeding heart liberals. What did they know of death? What did I know of death? Dawn started singing along. I was worried about singing off key. I was vain, even at a protest.

"I'm glad you're not going to Vietnam," Dawn said and kissed me on the cheek.

I blushed. "I told the shrink at the army physical that I was crazy and queer."

She wiggled and held her wrist limp, "You're such a sweetie."

"Cut it. You know queers are foreign to me," I said. "But I'd rather fake it than to get killed or come back an amputee."

"Sing along."

"I don't like to sing."

"You're against the war, aren't you?"

"I don't sing well." Then I started singing out of spite. I was way off key.

The marchers moved down to Bryant Park on Forty-Second Street. A crowd had gathered at the podium in the park. Peter, Paul and Mary were singing anti-war songs. The protesters were dressed like shit and looked dirty. They were voices without bodies, echoes escaping from acid mouths. There was no substance to them. They were ghosts compared to the flesh and blood reality of the Green Berets who they didn't recognize as human. Even if they were right about this war they were wrong. Not in their arguments but in their demeanor. We walked closer to the podium. I guess I felt that songs and protests couldn't really do much to stop wars. Whereas Dawn's pictures could change our consciousness and make wars unacceptable. They were real. Not this phony, back-slapping protest crap.

"I'm gonna split," I said.

"What's the problem?"

"I can't use people getting blown up in Nam as an excuse for a folk song party," I said. I really wanted to get away from her. I had no business loving her anymore. It wasn't right. I had taken out a piece of Swerbuck's head. I shouldn't now try to steal his girl. Even if he did steal her from me.

"This isn't a folk song party. It's about solidarity. And standing up against a rotten war," Dawn said.

I whispered in her ear, "It's ducking out of fighting and letting other people die for you." Then I kissed her on the cheek and walked away.

I passed a group of amputee veterans on wheel chairs who were protesting the war. I couldn't look at them. Amputations frightened me. They made me dizzy. The veterans burst out with "Give Peace a Chance." I thought I heard Malevchek's voice. I was afraid to look back. When I was almost out of range I turned around and glanced over my shoulder. I saw a blond guy with no legs in a wheel chair. It was Malevchek. I had to get out of there. There was no way I could face him. He was in my memory as a tough, scrappy kid. He was stupid. Now his body was dumb. I couldn't face his missing limbs. I kept walking. I hated this fucken war. It had turned him into a stump. He had taken the legs out of my years in East Meadow.

Chapter 32

Everyday I took the Long Island Railroad to Brooklyn from Great Neck. Long Island University was thought of as mediocre but the professors went out of their way to be difficult to prove that they were better than their reputation. I took an exam in Political Science where the highest grade in a class of a hundred students was fifty-five. It was mine. In English I beat everyone with a sixty-two. I studied my ass off, twelve hours a day. Everywhere I went I had my nose buried in a book. I used to read while I was walking down the street, on the subway, in cabs, during meals, on the toilet and in the bath. I had to justify my existence. I measured myself in the number of hours I spent studying. I had gone from a thug to a scholar. If I studied less than eight hours any day I was worthless. I'd punish myself by adding on an additional two hours to my study schedule the next day. When I rode the Long Island Railroad home at night I'd look out the window and wonder if the people in the houses were reading? If they weren't I felt they were wasting their lives. Sometimes after crashing all night for an exam I would fall asleep on the train going to school. I'd get so angry at myself for wasting time that I'd bite a piece off of my hand. I'd get hair and flesh in my teeth.

I once dropped a squib of toothpaste on "Dr. Faustus" because I was trying to read while brushing my teeth. Another time I was so tired that I purposely fell asleep with an open book over my face in the hope that I could learn by osmosis. With all my obsessive studying, despite the huge gaps in my knowledge, I managed to knock out perfect report cards, 4.0 each semester. It validated that I really was a worthwhile human being and not some dog poop on a city curb. I showed my parents my final report card for the year. We were in their study. My father jumped out of his chair and hugged me, "I knew we could do it."

"What do you mean 'we?'" my mother asked.

"It's just a word," Hy said, sullenly.

"You're great, son," my mother said. She kissed me on the cheek.

"You think the Dean will take me off probation?" I asked my father. When the Dean accepted me at L.I.U. he had to put me on probation because of my crappy high school grades.

"I think he'll put you on the Dean's list," Hy said.

"He already did!"

"That's wonderful," my mother said.

"Wowee! A chip off the old block," Hy said.

"Block head," my mother said. She thought my father was a fool. He wasn't. He just acted silly sometimes.

"You're just jealous that I have a brilliant son," Hy said. "And I must say, it reflects well on me."

That night we all went to North Shore Steak House to celebrate my report card. Robert was home from Miami University for the summer vacation.

"What do you think of your younger brother?" Hy asked.

"He's getting up there with me." Robert was pissed. I made him look bad.

"And what was your index, Professor?" I asked.

"They don't give grades in Miami. We feel it discourages true education," Robert said.

"You're full of it."

"So you staying at L.I.U. next year?"

"I already got accepted to Hunter College."

"I hear it's mostly girls," Robert said, winking.

"I'm there for the education," I said, priggishly. I really wasn't looking for girls. As much as I didn't want to admit it, I hadn't gotten over Dawn.

My mother tapped her tablespoon on her glass three times, "Hear Ye, Hear Ye, your father has an announcement to make."

"That's right," Hy said. He reached into his pocket and took out an envelope. "In honor of your excellent grades, Joshua, we got you both plane tickets." He took the tickets out of the envelope and handed one to each of us.

"Tell them where they're going," my mother scolded Hy.

"To Europe," Hy said.

I looked at my ticket to London and was thrilled. My father told me it was an open-ended ticket and we could travel all around Europe on it. We both shook my father's hand and thanked him. I hugged my mother. My brother kissed her. I wondered what Robert did to earn a plane ticket. I was the one with the 4.0 index. He didn't deserve to join me but what the hell, it would be good to have some company with me. This studying was really paying off. I was getting a free trip to Europe. Not to mention I was keeping out of Vietnam. Death couldn't touch me while I was riding this high. The written word was immortal. And the Suicide Club was for losers. I no longer wanted to be an outcast. I had studied in anthropology that African natives who were ostracized from their tribes committed suicide. I pictured Swerbuck in a loincloth causing the other natives to hate him and then killing himself because he had no friends. He'd scare off Dawn eventually. Then maybe she'd come back to me.

My father looked at me, tears welling up in his eyes, and said, "Son, I hope I wasn't too tough on you growing up. I just wanted you to do right."

"You weren't tough enough, dad," I said.

"You should have beat his head in," Robert said, taking a big puff of his pipe, blowing a smug smoke ring, smiling.

He was right. He should have beaten my head in for being an idiot. I didn't feel idiots had a right to live. I hated my former self. I looked at the clock and realized I could get three hours of studying in tonight. It didn't matter that the semester was already over.

The waiter brought in a graduation cake. It was a big strawberry short cake with "Happy Graduation" on it in blue frosting. My family sang, "Happy graduation to you."

"I didn't graduate," I said.

My father looked embarrassed. "You graduated from your freshman year," he said.

"I told you to order a cheese cake to celebrate Dean's List," my mother said.

I landed in London smelling of youth, filled with eagerness, facing a foreign bonanza of European shops and curios. I was hungry for culture. Robert and I stayed in a Bed & Breakfast near Paddington in London. It was a five-story walk-up with one bathroom on each floor. We shared a room with two beds. I was amazed that London was such a short city. Most of the buildings were like brownstones in Greenwich Village. They had a cozy, lived in feeling.

Petrol fumes exfoliated like dead flowers from the small putt-putt cars. The cabs had running boards. I felt like I was in a twenties gangster film stepping up onto them. There were parks and trees and houses and lives that circled around like miniature railway trains on a train board.

I wasn't much into doing touristy things. But my brother was into seeing all the sights. He bought a guidebook and went from Big Ben to Buckingham Palace. I wanted to just blend into the city. I went to restaurants and movies. I spent a lot of time wandering around Hyde Park. I followed businessmen carrying newspapers and pretended I was on my way to work. I stopped in pubs and ate fish and chips. I couldn't drink their beer ever since I had thrown up at the Mexican Pavilion a couple of years ago. I drank coca cola. I wandered around like I really lived there rather than checking out tourist sights and trying to cram everything into a week. As a result I saw almost nothing. Still I felt like a Londoner. My brother probably did the right thing but no way was I going to admit to myself that I was some asshole tourist. I was practically under the delusion that I was born there. I was tails and a top hat. I was old London.

Our second day in London Robert wanted to go to Wimpy's for lunch. He thought it was cute. Wimpy's was London's version of White Castle. We sat outdoors and ordered some burgers and milkshakes. The burgers tasted like cardboard laced with gasoline and the milkshakes were lumpy. Robert said, "The food sucks."

"Why'd you insist on coming here?"

He took out his pipe and lit it. "To see the effect American culture has had on Europe. It's a synergistic phenomenon. You must remember that dad sent us here to experience Europe's transitions," Robert said, pompously, swishing some smoke around in his mouth and shooting it out in a sequence of small smoke rings.

"Dad sent us here because I got straight A's," I said.

"Keep studying. Next year it's Japan," Robert said smiling, pulling his pipe from his lip.

I was taking a sip of my milk shake and burst out laughing, spitting some milk onto Robert's cheeseburger.

"You idiot," he shouted and threw his burger at me.

I threw mine at him and blew some milkshake at him through my straw. At this moment a Liverpoolan waiter came over and yelled, "Get out, you bloody Americans." I threw ten pounds on the table.

"Thank you very much sir. Come again," he said.

I think we were the first customers ever to get kicked out of a Wimpy's.

After lunch I tried to talk Robert into going to Carnaby Street to look at some of the clothing shops. He didn't want to go. He wasn't into mod fashions and Beatles clothes. He liked to dress like a Professor. His taste in music went to an earlier generation, that of Fabian and Del Shannon. He decided to visit the Opera House so that he could say he had been there. I don't think he had ever been to an actual opera in his life.

The area around Carnaby Street was filled with clothing shops for the seventeen to thirty set. In the windows were all the latest English styles. Victorian collars, bell bottom pants, men's high heel shoes in bright colors, crushed velvet jackets--styles that had only just begun to creep into America, mostly in the magazines. I was afraid to go into the stores. I felt a little hickish. Also I was worried that they'd make fun of my American accent. I finally found a large store that looked something like Great Neck Department Store and screwed my courage up. I went in and was immediately accosted by this mod young salesman with brown shaggy hair and crooked teeth. I asked him to show me some pants and he said, "Bell-bottoms are the rage." He picked out some in rich woolen patterns. I tried on a pair of brown tweed bell-bottoms. I came out of the dressing room and the salesman said, "Absolutely fab."

He seemed kind of gay but I wasn't sure. The English are very sophisticated in a feminine sort of way.

"You really think its fab, mate?" I said, putting on a half-ass English accent.

"You look like an American Beatle." I was surprised that he noticed I was American with my accent. All the girls were madly in love with the Beatles. That made me jealous.

I thickened my accent, "Blimey, ya sure they're not too bell, bloke?"

"They're mod, they're you," he said.

"The fabric is regal as the queen," I said,

"I sold Paul McCartney the same pair last week," he said, as he started measuring me. I didn't believe him about selling McCartney the same pair. But then the salesman said, "You look like McCartney." That was a compliment. Still, I was getting uncomfortable about the compliments and figured he was setting me up for more sales. So I decided to split before I got suckered in. I said I'd take the bellbottoms and left a fifty pound deposit even though the pants were only forty pounds.

"They'll be ready tomorrow," the salesman said.

"See you then, sport," I said. But I had no intention of coming back. No one was wearing bellbottoms in the U.S. I didn't want to be the only asshole.

I went back to the hotel and met Robert. We went for a walk in Hyde Park, which was a couple of blocks from our hotel. We wandered around the green lawns under powerful trees, passing a lovely lake with swans and paddleboats. At the perimeter of the park we could see English buildings surrounding us with their musty facades, juggling tradition, ritual and bricks. I was still upset about my morning outing at Carnaby Street. I told my brother about it. I told him I didn't want to wear bellbottoms. And that I had overpaid for them.

My brother said, "If you don't want to wear them, why'd you buy them."

"I felt pressured," I said.

"You got to learn to do what you want, not what others want."

Robert tried to light his pipe with his English wooden matchsticks. But it was hard to light his pipe in the breeze. He must have gone through a dozen matchsticks before he got it going. I hardly think it was worth it. I had bought my own rolling paper and tobacco and rolled my own cigarettes. I took one out and lit it. It was a lot easier to light than a pipe. The tobacco tasted sweet like the smell of exhaust that the cars sprayed around the streets of London.

"They can keep the deposit. I don't want the damned pants," I said.

"Are you crazy? Get your money back," my brother said.

"They altered them. I can't." I was timid about going into stores. I was scared about exchanging things or canceling orders. I thought of salesmen as bull dogs in a pen barking at me. I wasn't afraid to bust someone's head open in a fight but I was intimidated about speaking up for myself.

"Don't let them take advantage of you. We're not the colonies anymore. You're an American."

"Don't worry, I'll get my money back," I said. I didn't plan to. I didn't want to be put in an embarrassing situation. I told myself that loss was a part of life. And the loss of a pair of bellbottoms was no big deal. Let my brother worry about that.

I had more important fish to fry. I had to find a life for myself. I had to read my way into existence. I wanted to become as solid as a paragraph with a topic sentence.

Robert, puffing his pipe, looked out onto the lake through his sunglasses and said, "You should try my sunglasses. They change reality."

He took off his sunglasses and handed them to me. I tried them on and handed them back, "They don't change reality. They only change your view of it." I really wished I hadn't bought those stupid bellbottoms.

"Your view of reality is reality," Robert said.

"According to your view," I answered.

"But what if my view is your view?"

I didn't want to answer that. I could play Philosophy 101 just as well as he could. But I chose not to.

Two cute girls in skirts and short sleeve blouses came past speaking French. Robert turned around, watching them wiggle away from us. He tripped over a bench.

"Fuck. Ow," he said, rubbing his shin. "I can't wait to get to Paris and see the nudes. I hear the Louvre is like a peep show."

I had this terrible image of my brother puffing away on his pipe while beating off in front of one of the statues. I'd die.

After a week of some great English theater and a lot of spicy biriani in Indian Restaurants we left on the hydroplane for France. I was wearing my new brown tweed bellbottoms. I had actually gotten up the courage to pick them up in the morning before the store got crowded. I didn't ask for my ten pounds change. I had no intention of wearing them back in the States but I figured they'd be all right for Europe. They were even kind of cool over here. Robert said on the hydro-plane, "When we get there, the French girls might think you're a rock star in your bell bottoms. They'll get naked for you."

"You think they're going to get naked because of my pants?"

"You never know. We're in a foreign country."

"I think there's something foreign in your head."

The water was rough and the hydroplane didn't skim over the waves the way it was supposed to. I was never too good in boats. It knocked about and the walls felt like they were closing in on me in the small compartment. The room started to spin and I got nauseous. I staggered into the bathroom where I threw up. When we landed in France I was weakened, dizzy and dehydrated.

"You're not much of a seasoned traveler," Robert said.

"Like you're Ferdinand Magellan," I said.

I was glad to be in France, a country known for its culture, celebrated for its artists. I wiped some chips of vomit off the corner of my mouth. On the train to Paris I became hungry again and ate a sausage with mustard. For some reason I always craved stinky food after I threw up. I liked the look of the trees from the train windows as we sped through the countryside. They really looked French. Like they had accents.

The Hotel Suez was a squat little hotel for cheap Spanish, German and English tourists on the Blvd. St. Michel in Paris. We were the only Americans there. The concierge was a seedy old woman in a dirty, dress. She had grease stains on her torn pocket. Robert and I were standing along side of her in our sports jackets and ties, looking like members of the New York Athletic Club. We were hungry and didn't know any of the restaurants in the district yet. Robert asked the concierge in a thick, broken French accent, "*Pardone. Where et le restaurant, s'il vous fat?*"

The concierge grimaced. She was outraged by his mispronunciations. She put her finger to her mouth and shushed my brother. "Go across the street to *L'Acropole.*"

Robert was impressed by her English and wanted to compliment her, "*Parldez vous, English, mucho.*"

"I only speak French," she said and walked away.

As we walked out Robert said to me, "She shouldn't be so embarrassed about her English. How else is she going to learn if she doesn't practice?"

We walked into a large, paneled restaurant. There were long tables and wooden chairs with arched backs. The place was filled with students from the Sorbonne, which was around the corner. We were the only ones in jackets and ties. I felt out of place. Like someone who had crashed a party and gotten caught. No one came to seat us so we sat ourselves down at the end of a long table. At the other end a beautiful brunette and a blond were dining. They were so pretty that I was afraid to look at them. There was something stunning about French women with their slight waists and long necks. I noticed my brother staring at them. I hoped he wouldn't say anything stupid to them in his pigeon French. The waiter came over and my brother stuttered, "*Uh. Ah. Uh. S'il.*" The French words wouldn't come out. They didn't want to be warped. But after a few more, "*uh, uh, uh's,*" he said, "*Gerkin, s'il vous fat....*" I felt like disappearing under the table and banging my head up against it until I was unconscious.

"What do you want?" the waiter asked in English.

"I want to speak French," Robert insisted.

"Go to Berlitz," the waiter said, threw the menus down and walked off.

Robert looked over at the two beautiful girls next to us and said, "*Bonsort, comment tallez-vous.*"

"We're from Omaha," the brunette said.

What a relief! "Why don't the French don't like us?" I asked.

Two good-looking Frenchmen in silk shirts, ascots and jeans showed up and sat down with the girls. They each kissed them on the cheeks.

"They seem to like me," the blond said.

Then the four of them started speaking fluent French together. I felt like the asshole of the western world.

The waiter came back to us and my brother ordered "*two entrecokes and haricotz vertes.*" The waiter shook his head, stuck his fingers in his ears and ran off to the kitchen. When we were finished my brother asked for the check, "*L'addition.*" I believe he got that much right. I paid and my brother insisted on shaking the waiter's hand goodnight. The stunned waiter looked horrified when my brother said, "*Merki bocups, gerkin.*"

A few days later my brother and I visited the American Express office. It was near the Opera. I hated the opera. Listening to fat people singing in foreign languages was like listening to a rabbi sing in Hebrew. It reminded me of the embarrassment I faced at my own bar mitzvah when I sang off key. We were right across the street from Maxim's. The American Express Office was a neat glass building. It didn't fit in with the other older, surrounding buildings. Being inside, I felt like I was no longer under the constant scrutiny and criticism of the prissy French. They were like a bunch of catty, gossiping women. I noticed a bullfighting poster of Barcelona on the wall. I thought of my old friend Swerbuck and the way he dodged trains.

"I used to dream of being a bullfighter," I said to my brother.

"Bullshit," Robert said.

"I did. Or was that just Swerbuck?" I said.

"That nut. Is he dead yet?"

"Why don't we grab a student flight to Barcelona?" I suggested. I was excited.

"Cause I want to go to Amsterdam," Robert said. "Go yourself."

"Myself?" I was scared.

"Chicken," my brother said.

"You want to repeat that," I said, getting angry.

"Chicken."

A year ago I would have punched my brother for that. James Dean would die rather than be called chicken. In fact he did die trying to show off how fast he could drive a car. But I didn't much care about being a chicken anymore. Still, I was no chicken. I brushed past my brother as I walked over to the counter and bought myself an airplane ticket to Barcelona.

When I got off the plane at the airport in Barcelona, carrying my backpack, I felt like a bandito in *The Treasure of Sierra Madre*. I imagined castanets hanging from graceful hands above the long swishing green and gold dresses of Spanish ladies. Matadors wrapped themselves in their red capes as bulls brushed by like locomotives. I held the afternoon sun in my hands and drank from it like a gourd. The mules carried goatskin bags while peasants kicked their legs against their flanks. I was in Spain. Well, not exactly. I was in the airport. But it didn't matter. Spain was in me. I was Spain. I imagined Swerbuck jumping out from behind a baggage cart, yelling, "You didn't think you'd get here ahead of me, did you?"

After muddling through a long line at customs, I got outside and hailed a taxi. It was an old American Chevy. The driver, a short man with thinning black, curly hair, a vest and short sleeves, said, "Jes. You like tour the city?"

I asked the driver, "how much?"

"Five dollars American."

"Sold," I said. It was cheap. A lot better deal than I would have gotten in France where the snotty drivers acted like they were doing you a favor to take your money.

"Okey dokey," the driver said and put his foot to the ground and burned rubber. While whipping in and out of the narrow streets filled with motorbikes he told me stories about the city. He was familiar with every building we passed. I listened more to the music of his voice than what he was saying. I didn't really care when a building was constructed or who was the greatest singer who ever visited the opera house. I disliked facts. Not that I distrusted them; I just thought they were irrelevant. They were trampolines to keep one from falling totally into an experience. I wanted to immerse myself in Spain, to get lost in its music like a shoe moving across a crowded dance floor. We made a sharp corner and he pointed up ahead, "That's the bullfighting stadium."

"I once had a friend who thought a train was a bull." I thought of Swerbuck and the way he used to hold his sweater out in front of the onrushing train in Great Neck. I missed him. He was larger than life; strange and foreign like Barcelona. I wanted to get out and walk around the stadium. The closest I had been to an actual bullfight was the posters in Swerbuck's apartment.

"Did he fight the train?"

"Yes."

"Your friend, he crazy?"

"Yes."

"Is he dead?" the Spaniard chuckled.

"Not yet," I said. I wondered. It wouldn't surprise me if he were dead.

We pulled over to the curb and I got out. The stadium was quiet with all the hushed snorts of the bulls who had died there.

I looked up at the seats that surrounded the arena. Long rows of empty seats where people came to watch death. I imagined them filled with bloodthirsty fans. I looked down in the dust of the arena itself and a young man and a girl were play-acting as if they were having a bullfight. The man was using a shirt as a cape and the girl was charging at it like a bull. He bent to the side like a matador, graceful, elongated, arched. Then he leaped out of the way. I took a few steps closer. It couldn't be? No way. But it was! I ran forward yelling, "Swerbuck! Dawn!"

"Joshua!" they started. We all grabbed each other, kissing and hugging. Dawn was crying. I was laughing. Swerbuck was puzzled, frowning. I hoped he still didn't hold it against me that I split his head open at the World's Fair. I still resented his stealing Dawn.

"How you bums doing?" I asked.

"We missed you," Dawn said.

"I missed you too," I said to Dawn.

"I didn't miss you," Swerbuck said.

"I can't believe it. What are you doing here?" Dawn asked.

"I got straight A's. My dad gave me a present," I said, proudly.

"Shame on you," Swerbuck said and fell to the floor in mock pain. "You're an insult to our failing record at Great Neck North."

"Did you really get A's?" Dawn said. "That's great."

"So what you doing with your lives?" I asked.

"Living," Swerbuck said.

"I mean for a living," I said.

"Dying," Swerbuck answered.

"Come on. How you living here?"

"My uncle. He hires me as a courier to fly things around the world for him. We got a small place in town," Swerbuck said.

"I'm painting," Dawn said.

"I'm glad," I said. "Can I see your work?" I remembered the slide she showed me of myself at the Vietnam protest. The one where I was crossed out. I wondered if she had done any other paintings of me. I wanted to know if I was in her mind like she was still in mine.

Swerbuck looked pissed. The prick had stolen my girl and now he looked annoyed that she was even talking to me. I should have killed him at the World's Fair. No, no, no! I didn't even want to think like that. And I certainly didn't want to kill him here. I wouldn't do well in a Spanish jail. I was a student. I was no longer a street thug.

"We live at Seventeen Plaza de Barcelona," Dawn said. She wrote down her number for me.

We all walked out of the stadium together, the dust of the bullring covering our feet. I was excited that I had run into them again. I was in touch with a precious part of my fucked-up past. I knew I'd never again feel emotions as strongly as I did those teenage years in Great Neck when I smashed my fist against the driveway wall, sliced my face with a razor blade or drank scotch till I was unconscious. I had no wish to repeat those days. But I didn't want to forget them either. Swerbuck walked up to a beat-up, filthy motorcycle that was parked on the sidewalk.

"You want to try it?" he asked.

"I have no luck with motorcycles," I said. I thought of the crash in Emporia Kansas when I broke my leg and smashed up my face.

"You have to know how to ride," he said, boasting.

"Visit us for dinner," Dawn said and kissed me on the cheek. I wondered if she was flirting. There was some real warmth in that kiss.

"Yes, do," Swerbuck said, imitating a fag, and kissed me on the cheek with his big lips. I wiped my cheek.

They got on the bike. Swerbuck looked over his shoulder at me and said, "Five months."

"For what," I asked.

"Suicide day," he said. I remembered that when we formed the Suicide Club a couple of years ago at Squire's Deli we agreed that we'd all kill ourselves on December 31, 1966. It was August now. Dawn frowned at him as he kick started the bike. The engine shrieked. He had taken off the muffler. Swerbuck tore off with Dawn on the back and did a wheelie as I shouted, "That club's dead." He couldn't have heard me. I walked over to my cab and got in.

"Friend drives crazy, jes?" the driver said. "He has deads wish."

All of a sudden the sky opened up and it started to rain. It was a sun shower. The driver put on the windshield wipers and sang, "The rain in Spain, she stay mainly on the plain."

"I think she's got it," I sang.

That night I got a call from my brother, Robert, in my hotel.

"I thought you wanted to be alone," I said.

"I am alone. I was just calling to say hello.'

"Hello."

"I got laid."

"Where? How? So fast?"

"I'm quite a lover. I know how to seduce them."

"Tell me."

"Well, there's this section in Amsterdam they call window shopping. And the girls line up in the window and you pick them. So I found this nice Caribbean woman who looked like our maid, May. Cause I was kind of home sick. And would you believe it, I asked her to dress up in a maid's outfit."

"Are you bragging that you seduced a hooker?"

"She could have picked any man. She liked me. I think it was my pipe. I looked intellectual."

"That's sick."

"Dad used to fuck May all the time."

"He did not," I said. No way I wanted to think of my father fucking May. I only wanted to think of him fucking my mother. Actually, I didn't even want to think of him fucking her. Once when I was thirteen years old in East Meadow I walked into my father's room and caught him having sex with my mother. I started crying. I thought they were hurting each other.

"I really saw him fucking May," Robert said.

"Fuck you," I said and hung up. My father was not a cheat.

A couple of days later I went to Swerbuck and Dawn's apartment. It was a small place in the back of a complex with a view onto a dump. It was cluttered with paints, paintings and bullfighting posters. Garbage littered the floor. A low coffee table sat tilted on three legs. The light bulbs on the lamps burned into my eyes because they didn't have lampshades. The kitchen was right in the living room. And the cushions from the couch were spread out on the floor. It was like the furniture itself was imitating abstract expressionistic art. Spider webs sweated in the humidity. The originals of Dawn's charcoal slides were everywhere. Macabre scenes in shades of gray. And colorful, wild acrylics bubbled forth in wide swatches of repressed sadness.

I looked around for my picture. But it wasn't there. I felt left out, rejected. I wanted her to be proud of me. Well, I supposed, I didn't belong there anyway. I was no longer her boyfriend. I was no longer part of Swerbuck's madness. I was some guy hiding in his books imagining himself some scholar in cheap clothes.

"You're work's great," I said to Dawn.

"Swerbuck doesn't think so. I tell him he's at the root of my painting. But he doesn't care," Dawn said.

"Your paintings are too optimistic," Swerbuck said.

"They're dark," I said. No way I saw any optimism there.

"It's not the painting. It's the act of painting. Too positive," Swerbuck said.

"Maybe I feel positive," Dawn said, flinching like she was afraid Swerbuck would smack her with the back of his hand.

"How can you feel positive when people are killing each other in Vietnam," Swerbuck said.

"At least I paint them," she said.

"What are you doing about Vietnam?" I said to Swerbuck.

"I am Vietnam," he said.

"No you're not."

"I am the world." He spread his hands around an invisible globe.

"You're nothing," I said.

"Then the world won't miss me when I'm gone."

Swerbuck lit up a joint. He took a giant tote, almost swallowing it with his big lips and then passed it to Dawn. Dawn took a *petite* drag and then passed it to me. I turned it down and passed it back to Swerbuck.

"You're too old for that Suicide Club game. But if you're going to do it, do it and quit bullshitting about it," I said.

"I'm not ready yet. I got another five months."

"Can we quit talking about death," Dawn said. She seemed turned off by Swerbuck's obsession. Maybe there was hope for me yet.

"I'd like to quit talking forever," Swerbuck said and went to kiss Dawn on her cheek. Dawn turned away before his big lips caught her.

"Let's go for a walk," Dawn said.

"Fine," I said.

"I want to stay and smoke another joint," Swerbuck said. I was glad he was staying. As Dawn and I started to walk out Swerbuck said, "I still owe you a beating."

"The World's Fair's been torn down. Forget about the past," I said and headed out with Dawn. I hoped he didn't start a fight with me again.

Dawn led me to an outdoor cafe about five blocks from where she lived. There were neat little tables lined up like little Spanish soldiers. Leafy trees hung over the terrace. The red wine flowed from carafes like rain on gutter pipes. The waiter brought us over a large carafe that held about a quart. Sitting there, I felt like I had my ankles wedged into the dirt of Spain. I heard the hooves of dead bulls running. Dawn and I reminisced and she told me a lot about her history with Swerbuck. She told me how she fell in love with him when he took her to the train tracks and they sniffed glue and he held her on the tracks till the train almost ran them both over. It was such a rush. She talked about how he visited her a year ago and had two black eyes. He told her he got them defending some girl against her bully boyfriend. Now I knew why Swerbuck had me punch him in the eye.

"He said you cheated on me with some Valerie something. That's why I blew him."

"You blew him?" I wanted to die. "He lied. I never cheated on you." But it was too late. You can't call back a blowjob.

"You hear from Mad Dog?" she asked, changing the subject.

"I saw him was at the draft board. He fainted cold when the Doctor tried to give him a vaccination," I said.

"He flunked out of school," Dawn said.

"The way he bragged I thought he was getting straight 'A's.'"

"When he flunked out they called him back to the draft board. He told the army he was a crazed killer, figuring it would get him out of Nam. But it backfired. They sent him straight over there. First mission he starts running from the Cong, takes a bullet in the ass and gets shipped home. My dad ran into him in the supermarket. He's working the cash register. He wears his purple heart on his apron."

"I don't care about Mad Dog. He was always a jerk. Is Swerbuck still writing?"

"No."

"He's probably jealous of your paintings," I said.

"I know."

"Why don't you get away from him? All he wants to do is destroy you and your work the way he's destroyed his own."

"I can't."

"Why not?"

"He needs me. He's got nothing. I'm his lost mother. I'm Wendy. He's Peter Pan."

"And what do you get out of it?"

"Something."

"You don't need his craziness."

"He's the chaos I paint from. My pallet."

"What ever happened to that painting you did of me? Where you "x'ed" me out," I asked.

"Swerbuck slashed it up with a knife."

"Fuck him."

"He was getting you back for the beating you gave him."

"What a jerk!" I said. I suddenly felt very close to Dawn. That somehow she'd figure in my future. I felt she was going to be my wife. It was an intuition, like that time I felt someone was going to get sick and Mad Dog's father had a heart attack. "Maybe you and I will have a child some day."

"I don't think so," she said. "Have some more wine." She poured herself and me some from the large carafe of red.

"I'm intuitive about these things," I said. I pictured living with Dawn in Great Neck and bringing up a little son. He'd look like a combination of Dawn and me. He'd be a Jewish Indian with bright blue eyes. We'd let him grow his hair long; he'd comb it neatly in a ponytail. We'd encourage him to be a good student and to fit in with the other kids. I'd also want him to be a genius who could paint like Picasso and write like Hemingway. And a great athlete. My son would be the all American boy that I wasn't. He'd be Jimmy Fogell with a brain and a romantic quality.

"This time you're not too intuitive," Dawn said.

"What do you mean?"

"I'm already pregnant." She staggered me. My dream house was caught in a tornado; it swirled up into the air like Dorothy's house in Kansas but instead of dropping on the witch in the rainbow colored Land of Oz it fell down on my head. My intuition that we'd have a child was wrong. Like most intuitions.

"Congratulations," I lied.

"I haven't told Swerbuck yet."

"Why not?"

"He'd want to kill it."

"He'd want you to get an abortion?"

"Either that or he'd kill it after it was born. Life frightens Swerbuck."

"You can't stay with him," I said.

She shook her head and shut her eyes like she was gathering up her resolve, then said, "I'm going to leave him." Then she looked scared that she had said that and added, "But not yet."

"When?"

"When I'm dead."

"And the baby?"

"You mean my art?"

"The baby? The pregnancy?"

Tears came to her eyes, "It's a mistake."

"How?" She couldn't be this cold. Mothers were supposed to love the life in their wombs. My mother was cold to me sometimes, sometimes she favored my brother, but I knew she never regretted having me.

"I don't give a damn about life." She poured the balance of the carafe into our glasses.

"Yes you do. You have life inside of you."

Dawn smiled. The wine must have been affecting me because it looked like an evil spirit was leaking out of her blue eyes and her hairline. The beautiful Indian princess was transforming in front of me. Swerbuck had used his evil magic on her to turn her against her own child.

"I don't know what to do," Dawn said, crying. She picked up the whole carafe of wine and guzzled it.

I did my best to hold her up and keep her from falling as I escorted her home. Her hand felt like a serpent. She was poisonous. We walked past shops and houses under a jungle of stars. Lights blinked at us like damaged retinas. The moon was a goatskin wine bag.

Swerbuck answered the door. He was stoned. He looked at Dawn and then said to me, "Trying to get my girl drunk so you can fuck her."

"You're the one who fucks other people's girlfriends," I said and left. As I went I heard them both giggling as they fell to the floor.

I stayed in Barcelona another few days hoping to hook up with Dawn again. Every time I called her apartment Swerbuck answered the phone and laughed as he said she wasn't there. Then on the morning I planned to leave there was a knock on my door. I opened it and there was Dawn, wearing jeans and a plain white T-shirt. Her black braid was draped over her shoulder. The suicide bandanna with the red sun on it was tied around her forehead. She looked down at her feet, shyly, and said, "The other night after you left I told Swerbuck that I was pregnant."

"What did he say?"

He said, " I don't want the baby biting my dick off."

I told him, "'You really do need help.' He got off the bed and wandered over to the bureau and took out his works. I didn't tell you but he's been shooting heroin off and on," Dawn said.

I remembered when Swerbuck took us to the shooting gallery on the upper west side and we got ripped off. I thought of the black guy getting the hives and looking like he was going to die. I knew Swerbuck was sick but I didn't think he'd stoop so low as to shoot heroin. I thanked God that I had broken away from his influence.

"He offered me a shot of heroin," she said. "Fuck off. No way I'm putting that poison into my baby."

"'What's the difference? The baby has no future,' Swerbuck said. I told him, 'That baby's innocent.' Swerbuck sprayed the needle into the air and said, 'I'm getting the whole world high!' And he smoked a joint as a chaser. Then he started dancing around saying, 'I'm the anti-Christ.' I said, 'You're the devil.' And he said, 'Want to fuck the devil?' And he jumped on me and we started fucking and I got to tell you, as pissed as I was at him, it felt good."

"I don't need to hear that," I said.

"I thought you'd want to hear the truth."

"When did I ever?" I said.

Dawn walked me downstairs to get my cab to the airport. I kissed her on the cheek. I couldn't stand the thought of kissing her lips after Swerbuck's huge lips had been there. I could smell his germs. I had lost my girlfriend to a disease. I couldn't wait to get back to America.

I went through customs in about half an hour and found my seat on the 747 Pan Am jet. I got stuck in the last row, center aisle, sandwiched between two fat German ladies on one side of me and two German men on the other side. I tried to lose myself in my writing. I tucked my elbows in between the armrests and wrote, "A dead squirrel falls from a tree. The power mower rips her fur into leaves. In the cemetery you can chew the silence forever and never get fat. I want to eat all of experience and compete with low flying planes for a bird's eye view of Shea Stadium. I want to fuck a seagull."

What the fuck was I writing? It made no sense. It was all images. I saw the world in bursts of flavor and symbols. Life was a sucking candy. I wanted to lick out all its color. I wanted to live with one foot over the edge like the time I almost fell off Swerbuck's roof. In Spain I realized I was still closer to Dawn and Swerbuck than I wanted to admit. And that frightened me. I was afraid of my own creativity. When I got back home I'd take up Latin. I'd learn a dead language. Something no one spoke anymore. Its grammar would lock me into life. Its uselessness would give me purpose. There was nothing practical in it. Nothing I could get out of it. It was pure.

Half way across the Atlantic after lunch I started writing another poem. The fat German lady next to me spilled her fudge Sunday on it. She mumbled some German apologies and tried to wipe it off with her napkin. It smudged further. I ripped the page out, crumbled it, put it in my mouth and chewed, mumbling, "Delicious." She laughed, pointed at me to her fat friend and said, "American." The two German males on the other side of me looked over and laughed too. I pictured them walking through the Bavarian Alps, eating bratwurst. Germans were always eating. I think Hitler wanted to eat the world. I wondered if I'd ever see Dawn and Swerbuck again.

Chapter 33

I studied around the clock and pulled almost all A's on my papers and exams at Hunter College. But when it came to my finals after the first semester I was worried that I didn't do well. Even though I got straight A's at L.I.U. I was insecure.

Hunter College was on Park Avenue between Sixty-Seventh and Sixty-Eighth Street in Manhattan. I transferred there after my freshman year. The building looked like a co-op for multimillionaires. It probably was the most expensive location for a college in the world. It was incredible. There was no tuition because Hunter was part of the City System. An amazing benefit was that ninety per cent of the class was female. The first class to accept males was in 1965. The halls were awash with good-looking girls. I started attending Hunter in September, 1966.

It actually didn't matter where I was. I really didn't pay much attention to my surroundings. I spent all my time reading. Any moment I wasn't studying was a waste of breath. I discovered that there was no sense in socializing. I could never find a better friend than Aristotle, or Mann or Freud. Books were my social circle. Everything I could want was in them. I wanted to come down with an illness so that I wouldn't be able to go outside; I could spend all my time in bed reading.

The first semester I was worried about my poetry final. The thought of living through my winter recess without knowing how I had done on the exam was too much for me. I had to speak to my teacher, Professor Borner, about my exam. I decided to see him to find out how badly I had done. I checked out his office hours and dropped in on him, saying "I'm sorry Professor Borner. I'm a little insecure and neurotic maybe. I don't mean to be. But I think I flunked and I don't want to, I mean, I can't wait till they, you, mail me my grade."

Professor Borner looked surprised. He reached into his drawer and pulled out a test booklet. He slowly opened it up. It was mine. He scratched his hair, shook his head, looked at me and said, "You don't know your own work too well. You got an *A*."

"I love you, Professor Borner," I shouted, jumping out of my seat, shaking his hand. My Christmas vacation was saved.

"Don't love me. Love yourself. You did it," Borner said.

"Yes. Yes," I said. I was so confused and excited that I kissed my own hand. Then I kissed his. I dashed out of his office. I almost forgot to say goodbye. I turned, "You're the greatest teacher in the world." He shrugged his shoulders, put his head down and smiled.

I skipped down the halls. I played the walls like they were bongos. I tap danced, laughing, giggling and whistling to myself. I was Gene Kelly in *American in Paris*. A cute blond appeared around the corner, walking in my direction. She was adorable, about five feet six inches tall, slim, gray-blue eyes, wearing a little yellow and brown, mini skirt. I usually wasn't too bold about going over to girls I didn't know. But I was delirious. I said, "I'm Joshua Kaplan. I just got an *A* in English."

I felt like a jerk.

"I'm Nicole Mayer. I'm impressed," she said, smiling.

"Really?" I said, excited. "Let me buy you a cup of coffee."

"Big spender."

"No, I mean, you're the first girl I saw after my grade. The *A* you know. You're my good luck charm."

"I'm magic," she said. "But I don't have time for coffee."

Dawn had also said she was magic when I first met her. I felt like there was something going on here. Like Nicole might become my new girl. I looked up and down at her. She was beautiful in a light and lively, floaty way. She was the froth on cola. She was smoke that would slip through my fingers if I grabbed her. She was a row of a thousand doors that all had to be opened.

"If I can't buy you coffee can I get your number," I said.

"It's not for sale."

"For free," I said. I was worried. If she escaped she might disappear for good.

"A-MEAN-60."

"What's that?"

"An anagram. Don't call unless you get straight *A*'s," she said. "I only go out with smart men."

"I'll study for our date," I said. Was she joking or did she mean it? I'd prove to her that I was brilliant. I was going to get straight *A*'s. That's what I was all about. I was an *A*-machine. I wasn't sinking back down that cesspool of flunk-outs with Swerbuck again. I'd be class valedictorian. I'd pop brain cells like flashbulbs. I'd find my excitement in being a drone laboring among library shelves. That was what was cool. I'd be the hipster of the encyclopedia. The nerd of academia. I'd rock and roll among dusty volumes.

I told Nicole that I was leaving for Mt. Snow with my family but I'd call her the minute I got back.

I led my father and brother over to the lip of the Jaws of Death. This was the steepest slope at Mt. Snow. I hadn't been back to Mt. Snow in a couple of years. This Christmas it was buried in early snowfalls. The whiteness lay on the ground like bricks while new flakes swirled above us like troops of dancers kicking in white boots. My mom was back in the lodge. She was never a big fan of skiing.

The Jaws of Death was on the north face. That's where all the expert slopes were. Mt. Snow wasn't as difficult an area as Stowe or Mad River Glen. In fact it was known as a gentle, intermediate area. Except the north face, where the trails were narrow and steep.

The Jaws of Death wound down the mountain like a python. After my father had side slipped half way down the first steep drop he yelled, "You're gonna get me killed on this slope."

"This is a challenge. You always told me to push myself to my limit," I said.

"That's for you. Not me," he said, laughing.

"Go for it."

"I can't. I'm hung over from last night," he said.

"Aren't you the guy who told me to drink in moderation," I said. I felt like I was becoming my father's father. I remembered the hard time he gave me a couple of years ago when I got drunk at Stanley's party in King's Point and I ran around without shoes through the snow.

"I must have been drunk," he said.

"Would you two stop talking and start skiing," Robert said. He pushed off and yelled, "Follow me." We watched as he picked up speed heading straight down the fall line. He hit a bump and flew up in the air, landing on the tails of his skis.

Then he hit another bump and his skis flew up over his head; he looked like he was being launched to the moon. He landed about twenty feet below the bump on his head in a pile of deep powder with his arms, legs, poles and skis spread out around him. My father and I rushed down to him worried that he was hurt. He looked up at us; his face covered in snow, and said, "These damned bindings are loose. Else I would have never fallen." We saw he was all right and we cracked up laughing.

I then pushed straight off down the slope and yelled to Robert, "Follow me."

He yelled, "Fuck you." And threw a snowball at me.

After skiing The Jaws of Death we spent the rest of the morning cruising intermediate slopes. We met mom for lunch in the cafeteria and my father agreed to spend the afternoon driving her into the town of Dover to go antique shopping. Robert looked exhausted and said he wanted to go back to his room and do some studying. Also he had left his pipe there and could use a good bowl of tobacco. I went off to the bar to get myself a hot toddy. I didn't plan to hang around. I didn't like crowds. I just thought I'd grab a drink and go back out to the north face and bash some moguls. I loved Vermont. It took you over. It was like memory was obliterated in a cloud of snow. The past was yesterday's blizzard. So you can imagine what a shock it was when I saw Mad Dog walking into the bar, wearing a purple ski outfit. He had blond snow bunnies hanging onto each of his elbows.

"Joshua, you old draft dodger you," he greeted me with a hearty handshake.

"Took a bullet, I heard," I said. "In a very sensitive spot." I smiled.

He reached into his pocket and took out a purple velvet jewelry box. He opened it and put it in my face. "You know what that is?" he said.

"What?"

"The purple heart. I'm a hero." He snapped the case closed and put it back in his pocket.

I had never seen one before. It was impressive. Even if he was shot in the ass while running away.

"I was shot in the thigh," he lied. "Almost severed the bone. I'm lucky I'm alive." He then introduced me to his two blonds -- Veronica and Stacy. They had that vacant, joyous look of snow bunnies, like they had just popped out of Easter eggs at a bachelor party. Their faces were air-brushed like the pictures in Playboy Magazine. They were much too good-looking for Mad Dog. I would have expected to see them on the arm of some Hugh Heffner, playboy type. Not classless Mad Dog.

"Where you going to school these days?" he asked.

"Hunter," I said. I was proud of this. Last time I had seen him I was still at L.I.U.

"Larry's at Columbia pre-dental," Veronica said. "The night division," she cooed, playing up to Mad Dog. I didn't think of him as Larry. To me he was always Mad Dog.

"During the day he runs a supermarket chain," Stacy chimed in. Dawn had told me he ran a cash register.

"In my free time, I'm taking karate at Tiger Schulman's. I'm hoping to get my black belt soon. If my war wound doesn't interfere," Mad Dog added. The girls swooned and patted him on the back. I had had about all I could take.

"I'm going out to ski," I said.

"I used to be a ski racer. But since my injury I've had to quit," he said.

"I hope you feel better."

"Hey, how's that nut Swerbuck?"

"Alive," I said. I no longer liked Swerbuck enough to chat about him.

"He wouldn't be if he stole <u>my</u> girl," he said. Two years ago I would have punched Mad Dog for putting me down like that. But I wasn't interested in Dawn any longer. I wanted Nicole.

I turned away without saying goodbye. The past never measures up to your illusion of it. Mad Dog was better off forgotten. I spent the afternoon skiing by myself. The snow came down like amnesia. The land was blotted out in whiteness.

We returned to Great Neck on January 3rd. I felt solid as a rock. I lay down on my bed with my hands under my head and got this feeling that life was good; that depression was a waste of time; that fighting yourself ends up in a broken mirror. I was an athlete; I was a scholar.

I went downstairs to the mailbox. I put my folks' mail and a week's worth of newspapers in their room and went back to my room with my letters. There were my results from Hunter and a letter from Swerbuck. I was more interested in my grades. I opened the envelope carefully, worried that bad grades would fly out and attach themselves to my forehead like sticky red darning needles. I still didn't have any confidence after all those years of doing poorly in school. I closed my eyes, held the report card up and took a deep breath -- straight A's. I breathed a sigh of relief and kissed the report card. I'd done it. I'd done it before at Adelphi, then L.I.U. and now Hunter. It was no joke. I really was a good student. I loved my grades. I loved myself. I rushed to the phone. I hadn't called Nicole all vacation. I remembered her number--A-MEAN-60. I was a little scared that she wouldn't remember me or that she wouldn't want to speak to me. But I was armed with my good grades. I wanted to share them with her. I dialed. A girl answered the phone. It sounded like her.

"Nicole?"

"Yes," she said hesitantly, not knowing who I was.

"It's Joshua."

"You must have gotten straight *A's*," she said.

"How'd you know?"

"That was the deal. No *A's*, no date," she said.

"But you didn't see my report card."

"I work at the Registrar's Office. I peeked."

We both cracked up laughing. "You cheat," I said. "How's Saturday night for dinner?"

"I have to check my calendar," she said and put me on hold for a couple of minutes. When she came back she said, "You're a lucky man. I'm going to cancel my date with the U.S. Ambassador."

"Good deal. I'm his boss, the President," I said. "I'll pick you up at 6:00."

"I'll meet you at *La Crepe* at 55th and 3rd at 7:30."

"Since you're making all the arrangements, are you treating?" I asked.

"I'm treat enough."

"We'll see."

She hung up. It was a little abrupt. But I didn't think she meant anything by it. I liked her independence. She was going to be a tough one to handle. There was no way she'd be involved in any self-pitying suicide escape. She was all about living. I hoped I was strong enough for her. That I could keep my grades going and that I wouldn't fall back into my old masochistic crap. I had to stomp out my old sadness with combat boots. To step on the shadow of my attraction to weakness. And to avoid the wild side of disappearance.

"Joshua, did you see this?" my father asked, walking into my room. He handed me *The Great Neck Village Gazette*. In the lower right hand column there was a small article, "Dawn Half and Swerbuck killed in motorcycle accident in Spain."

I almost fell onto the bed. I felt like I had been punched in the gut.

"Wasn't she your girlfriend in high school? The one that got you the rabbit?" my father asked.

My mother came into the room and said, "Swerbuck was that crazy kid who jumped out your window. I knew he'd come to no good."

"Could I have some privacy folks?" I begged.

They shuffled out of my room. My mother closed the door behind them. I looked at the article. It was a few lousy lines telling you nothing except that they fell off a mountain in the Pyrenees on their motorcycle. I could have written a whole book about them. I loved them. I hated them. The newspapers buried them in three lines of ink. The article was a shallow grave. The next page was a full-page ad for an auto repair shop in town.

I didn't believe men should cry. I cried like a baby. I thought I had gotten over Dawn. I opened the letter from Swerbuck. I wondered if he had written to me about his death.

December 31, 1966

Dear Joshua,

"*Jadis, si je me souviens bien, ma vie etait un festin ou s'ouvraient tous les coeurs, ou tous les vins coulaient.*" Rimbaud's "*Une Saison En Enfer.*" Thingschange Joshua. By the time you open this Dawn and I will no longer be with you.

You probably wonder if I know that Dawn's pregnant? It's an incentive. I was serious about our club, as you can see. But you weren't. You lost your love of death. And if you don't love death you can't love life. I was starting to lose Dawn. She was growing up. So you see I had to stop her. To keep her from becoming mediocre. Before she gave birth. Follow us.

Your friend,

Swerbuck

I wanted to know more about how they died. I called Swerbuck's house and his father answered. I reminded him who I was and asked him what happened to his son. He told me, "It's Dawn's fault. She unbalance ze motorcycle. He was great rider. And genius. He knew all of Rimbaud's poems."

I knew that there was no way that Dawn caused Swerbuck to crash. He did it on his own, intentionally. He took Dawn with him. She would have wanted to stay alive for her baby.

"I loved your son," I told his father.

"Faggot," his father said and hung up on me.

I thought of Swerbuck and Dawn in motorcycle jackets with red sun bandannas riding through the mountains. I figured Swerbuck suddenly pushed the throttle up and aimed straight for the ledge. Dawn yelled "no" as Swerbuck yelled "yes." In her confusion she probably grabbed onto him tighter as they flew over the ledge and arced out into the air one thousand feet above the rocks. But instead of falling I imagined them rising up into a halo of sunset like a giant bird. They flew into permanence. They couldn't die. They were part of the inalienable confusion of youth.

I remembered when Swerbuck jumped off of my balcony. I wanted to know him better now that he was dead. Now that he could no longer take anything from me like my innocence or my girl. I put on my suicide T-shirt and my bandanna, opened the glass doors to my balcony and stepped out. I wanted to do something to be closer to my crazy dead friend. I stepped over the rail in my window. I was nervous about heights. I remembered when I almost fell off Swerbuck's roof. I closed my eyes and held my nose like I was going into a swimming pool. I jumped. I landed hard on the lawn and sprained my left ankle. I got up and shook it off. I said to the moon, "That one's for you Swerbuck. And you too, Dawn." I limped back to the front door and went back up to my room.

I found out from Dawn's father that she was being flown home for burial. I waited at Kennedy Airport under a rainy black sky for Dawn's arrival. Her coffin was wheeled out of the cargo hold into a special area in the baggage section. I went over to a worker who was handling it and asked if I could open it and take a look.

"Are you crazy," he said.

I took a hundred dollars out of my wallet and slipped it into his hand.

"Make it fast," he said, sliding the bill into his shirt pocket.

The mortician must have done a lot of work because her face looked unmarked. It was all made up like she was going to a prom. She looked so alive that I almost thought she was faking her death. I thought she winked at me. I hadn't kissed her in a long time. I couldn't resist. I kissed her lips for the last time. They tasted like chalky rubber. Her face smelled.

Dawn's family buried her in Mt. Hebron cemetery in Queens. That was the same place my grandmother was buried. It was raining that day and the ceremony took place under umbrellas. I stood way in the back where I couldn't be noticed. I didn't want to share my grief with anyone. After a while the rain stopped and a rainbow came out. It was like a peacock dancing over the moist ground. I waited for the family to leave. When they were gone I put on my suicide club bandanna and slowly walked over to Dawn's grave. I had a red rose under my coat. Like the one I had at my grandma's burial. I took it out, held it up into the moist rainbow and placed it on her grave.

After the funeral I went home. I was feeling sorry for my dead friends. I was also feeling bad that I wouldn't see them again and that I didn't have the courage to do something as stupid as they did. In my room I was looking at a painting Dawn drew of me a couple of years ago at Mt. Snow. It was all snow, mist and light. I heard Russian music again looking at it. It was a scene out of the vast whiteness of Dr. Zhivago. Dawn had once said, "Until death do us part." I guess she knew back then that I wouldn't be going on that journey with her. I thought I might read for a while to get my mind off my problems. I took Rimbaud's poems off the shelf. No, that wasn't going to help me. I needed life, a person. I dialed Nicole's number. It was the wrong number. The voice of a gruff man answering, scared me. I tried again. Nicole picked up. She said, "Joshua," before I had a chance to say anything. We were surfers. We had caught the same wave.

"How'd you know it's me?" I asked.

"I'm magic."

And I thought of the magic of my youth passing. And I thought of the miracle that was Dawn and the sadness that was Swerbuck. And I thought of Nicole. And I thought of how I was opening the magic curtains of a new and wonderful girl. Of how she was behind the drapes like the Wizard of Oz in the Emerald City. A green light surrounded us. It was the birth of our futures.

About the Author

David Lawrence produced, starred in and wrote the documentary "Boxer Rebellion" that played at the Sundance Film Festival in 1993 and the Vienna Film Festival in 1994.

Lawrence's book "The King of White Collar Boxing was a finalist for the Bakeless Non-fiction Prize (Breadloaf). It was published by Rain Mountain Press. His poetry "Lane Changes" was published by Four Way Books.

Mr. Lawrence has currently signed a movie option for "The King of White Collar Boxing" with a popular television and screenwriter. His new book of poems, "Living Among Madison Avenue" is being published by Future Cycle Press.

Lawrence has published a thousand articles in historical periodicals, such as "Daily Caller" and "American Thinker." He has also published letters in "USA Today," "The NY Post" and "The Daily News."

Lawrence has published more than nine hundred poems in North American Review, Midwest Poetry Review, Chicago Tribune, California Quarterly, William and Mary Review, Confrontation, ACM, Folio, Laurel Review,, Poet Lore, Mudfish, Hawai'i Review, People Magazine, New Laurel Review, Coe Review, Green Hills Literary Lantern, New Delta Review, Minnesota Review, etc.

Lawrence is also a model, former business mogul, professional boxer, rapper (three rap albums), lyricist (Sam Wayman's "Magic Man" album), jailbird, former professor and stand-up comic. He is a member of SAG and has acted in commercials and independent films. He has a Ph.D. in literature from CUNY and was Phi Beta Kappa. He studied acting at good theater schools.

He has been interviewed on CBS, ABC, MSG, BBC, etc. There have been documentary television shows about him on MSNBC and BBC. There were feature articles about him in New York Magazine, Men's Journal, People Magazine, Time Out, etc.